# AN AUGUST HARVEST

## BEN MARNEY

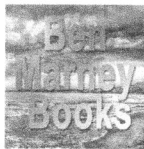

AN AUGUST HARVEST

By

Ben Marney

# DEDICATION

*For Rex...my only dog*

*And*

*For my wife Dana*

# SPECIAL THANKS

*A special thanks to my sister-in-laws and brilliant editors,*
*Susan Jordan and Druscilla Hutton*

*Apparently, you two actually listened in English class.*

*Thanks for correcting all my dumb mistakes*
*and making me look a lot smarter than I am.*

# AUTHOR'S NOTE

This is my fourth novel, but it's very different from my other three. This time, I didn't want to write about a psychopathic serial killer. Don't get me wrong, I love writing those kinds of books, but on this book, I wanted to try something else, something less violent. I did my best, but at times this book gets violent as well. I just can't help myself.

If you're a dog lover like me, I think you're going to love Charley. He's based on the only dog I ever owned. He was also an Irish Setter named, Rex. Well, actually his full name was, Sir Rex Maxwell Vanguard the 3rd. He was a very special dog and I still miss him to this day…

# DEFINITION

## AU-GUST

Something marked by majestic dignity or grandeur.
Something monumental, exalted or very special.

# 1

## VALENTINE'S DAY

It was February 14th…Valentine's Day…exactly one year later. Before I did it, I wanted to see that old building again. So one last time, Charley and I slowly drove around it.

When I was in high school, at least once a week, I would park across the street from that old pile of bricks, sit on the hood of my beat up car and sketch it for hours. It didn't look much better back then, but I loved the architecture and…well…that building had been a big part of my life. It was built in 1849 and was the oldest prison in Texas. Its official name, when referred to as part of the Texas Department of Criminal Justice, was "The Huntsville Unit", but everyone around here called it "The Walls".

No, I wasn't an inmate; my father was the connection. He worked there for thirty-five years…he was the warden.

I'm not sure how he did it, but somehow my father didn't bring his work home with him. The man I knew was a soft-spoken, gentle person, who was hard to anger. He'd never laid a hand on me my entire childhood. He let my mother enforce any discipline I may have needed. Dad was a kind, tenderhearted, very supportive father. As a result, I was one of the lucky kids and had a wonderful childhood.

Dad died a few years ago. He made it to eighty-five. Mom only lasted another year. I think she died from loneliness and a broken heart.

After one last cruise through town and a slow idle around Huntsville's old historic town square, I headed to the interstate, driving south on I-45.

I knew my fate, but I wasn't sure what was going to happen to my dog, Charley. At least I thought he was a dog. He looked like a dog and barked like a dog, but trust me, he was not your typical K9. You'll probably think this is crazy and maybe it is, but I was pretty sure Charley was psychic and...I swear on my mother's grave...he understood English.

I tried to leave him at home that morning, but he knew something was up and wouldn't let me leave without him. The only thing I could think to do was to take him with me and tie him up to the boat's steering wheel later. I prayed that the Coast Guard would find him before he starved to death.

I knew what I was about to do was a sin, but I couldn't take the guilt and pain another day. No, I didn't have a family I was leaving behind. I used to…but I killed them.

All my friends kept telling me that it wasn't my fault, it was just an accident, but I knew better. I froze like a stone. I just sat there and didn't do a goddamn thing to prevent it!

My wife's name was Rita Marie Walters. We met in the third grade. She had bright red hair, freckles and the bluest eyes I had ever seen. She didn't like me much back then, but I eventually won her over. She finally let me put my arm around her at the Saturday afternoon matinee movie when I was 10, and let me kiss her for the first time when I was 12. I know it's a cliché, but we soon became the definition of "high school sweethearts." She was my only girl, my one and only, my true love.

After high school, she stayed in Huntsville and went to Sam Houston State University. I went to Texas A&M, located in Bryan, about an hour and a half drive away. For those four years, I drove that 130 mile round trip about a million times. And every time I drove away, back to A&M, my heart ached until I saw her again.

After I received my degree in architecture and she received her degree in English, we got married. Two years later, we had a little girl. We named her Audrey after Rita's grandmother.

Everybody told me that I needed to move to Houston, because it was exploding, growing like crazy and there was a lot of work for architects. Rita and I talked about it and I even interviewed with a few of the big Houston firms, but I just couldn't imagine living in that big city and raising our daughter there. I guess I was just a small town guy.

In Huntsville, we knew everyone and everyone knew us. In those days, you could drive from one side of town to the other in a few minutes and you'd probably see ten people you knew on the way. Rita and I had gone to the same church there our entire lives; I'd had my hair cut there at the same barber shop since I was two years old; we had great friends there; there was a good elementary school; a good high school and there was Sam Houston State University. Huntsville, Texas was a very special place.

We loved everyone there and they loved us. So, against everyone's advice, I decided to open my architecture office in an old historic building in Huntsville's town square.

I can still remember my father beaming with pride and my mother and Rita crying the day I hung the *"GRANT NASH ARCHITECTURE"* sign on the door.

I had only been open a few months when my life long best friend, Marshall Taylor and his father walked into my office.

"We're looking for a new architect," he said, grinning. "You know where we could find one in this hick town?"

Marshall's father, a very successful attorney and the richest man in town, had decided to use some of his land to develop a new upscaled subdivision and Marshall had talked him into using me as the architect and to oversee the construction. That one project launched my career.

Marshall and I had met in kindergarten and had been best friends ever since. Growing up we did everything together. We went to Vacation Bible School together, played Little League together. In high school, we played together on the offensive line of the football team, rode the bench together playing on the baseball team and usually came in last running side by side on the track team. Neither one of us were great athletes, but we loved sports and doing anything else you could imagine two best friends would do.

To my parents, Marshall was like their other son, and I'm pretty sure his parents felt the same way about me.

He stood next to me as my best man when Rita and I said our wedding vows, and paced with me in the waiting room when Audrey was born. And he had his arm around my shoulder and cried with me at both of my parents' funerals. When his parents died, I had mine around him. We were much more than just friends.

He was without question the smarter one between us. In fact, he was the valedictorian of our graduating high school class.

I began drawing and sketching pictures when I was about four years old. I always knew that somehow my artistic ability would be part of what I did when I grew up, but never considered architecture until Marshall suggested it to me.

He wasn't artistic at all, but discovered his love for science in high school. On his summer break between his sophomore and junior year, he landed a job at our local hospital. I'm not exactly sure what he did there that summer, but whatever it was, it convinced him that his future was to become a doctor. Specifically, a doctor of internal medicine. From that summer on, his goal and obsession was to become a world-renowned doctor. A goal I'm very proud to say he accomplished. Today, Marshall is recognized as one of the best gastroenterologists in the world.

He was still in medical school the day he brought his father into my new office.

Through all those years we'd spent together, I hoped I had, but I wasn't sure that I had, truly expressed to him how much I loved him like a brother, and how much what he did for me that day he brought his father into my office had affected my life.

Marshall's father's subdivision was a very successful development. It sold out quickly, and two of the houses I designed made it into the pages of "*Architectural Digest*." After that, my phone began to ring and my little architecture business took off like a rocket. Soon, I was spending more time in places like Dallas, Houston or Austin than I was in Huntsville.

At first, I drove my car back and forth, but as my business grew, the time I was spending in my car became counterproductive. To solve this problem, I learned how to fly and bought my first private plane. It was an old Cessna 150. It only had two seats, one usually packed full of blueprints and spec manuals, but that old plane got me to my projects in half the time it took me to drive there. Over the next five years, I logged thousands of hours flying that old plane back and forth to my projects and back home to Huntsville.

I landed a huge project in El Paso. It was without a doubt the biggest and most profitable project of my career. However, El Paso was 750 miles away from Huntsville, a 1,500 mile round trip flight. I calculated that flying my Cessna 150 with its cruising speed of 122 mph, would take at least 6 hours each way. So I began to look for a faster plane.

I found a partnership deal on a Baron G58. It had twin engines, six seats and a cruising speed of 200 knots or 230 mph.

It was ridiculously expensive, but it would cut my round-trip flights to El Paso down to about seven hours. The only problem was I had never flown a twin-engine plane before. So after a few months of training and getting certified to fly twin engines, I bought into the partnership and began flying that plane.

～

MY FATHER USED to tell me, "Save your money, son and count your blessings each day, because life isn't fair and can turn on a dime."

I never paid much attention to that. I just filed it away as one more of Dad's pessimistic philosophies of life. I had always assumed he felt that way because he was born during the Great Depression and learned it from my grandfather, who like so many others in those days, lost everything he'd worked for his whole life overnight. But now...I understand exactly what he was talking about. I learned graphically how very fragile life can be. I was living the American dream and in a blink of an eye...my perfect life...shattered into small pieces.

I realize now I should've seen it coming. There were signals and warnings that I chose to ignore. All I could think about was my career, completing this new project in El Paso and all the money I was going to make when it was finished. Never once did I even consider the risk I was taking to get it done.

Why would I ignore them? Well...it was because of *whom* the warnings were coming from.

I have no doubts that you will think this is completely crazy and I wouldn't blame you if you did...because the warnings were coming from my dog, Charley.

I mentioned earlier that I thought Charley was psychic. And yes, I know that sounds a little nuts, too. Trust me, I was just like you, but now there's no doubt in my mind it was true.

$\sim$

I FOUND CHARLEY, or rather Charley found me, at the mall. I wasn't there shopping for a dog that day. In fact, buying a dog had never crossed my mind. Growing up, my parents had a few different dogs, but they were those little yapping things and honestly, I never really liked them much. Rita grew up with cats, so the thought of us getting a dog was never discussed.

I was walking out of Barnes and Noble, flipping through the pages of a new book I'd just bought, when I heard the commotion. It was coming from the next store over–it was the pet shop.

I heard someone yelling, "Don't get near him, he bites!"

Curious to what was going on, I stopped in the doorway and looked inside. I couldn't believe what I was seeing. There was a crowd surrounding two people, a man and a woman, holding long poles with loops on the ends. They were trying to slip the loops over a dog's head, but the dog wasn't having it, growling and snapping at the loops. Did I say dog? I meant to say puppy. The ferocious animal that everyone in the store seemed to be so afraid of…was a puppy maybe a foot long and a foot tall.

It looked like something out of a Saturday morning cartoon. I couldn't help but laugh out loud. When I did, everyone in the store turned to see who was laughing. When the puppy saw me standing in the doorway, he took off running and jumped up at me. Not knowing what to do, I grabbed him up into my arms.

Everyone in the store gasped and screamed, thinking this ferocious beast was attacking me, but instead of biting me, he started whining and licking my face.

I put him down on the floor, but when I did, he started jumping up and down on his hind legs, reaching his tiny front paws up at me, howling for me to pick him back up. When I did, he wrapped his front legs around my neck and made a high-pitched whining, almost a crying sound as he licked my face.

The store manager ran up to me. His face was flushed and he was out of breath. "Be careful with that dog. I've called for animal control. They're on their way. He seems to like you, so if you could just hold on to him until they get here, I'd really appreciate it. You're the first person he's ever let touch him."

"Seriously? You called animal control for this little guy?" I asked. "What are they going to do with him?"

"Well, sir, I'm convinced there's something wrong with that dog. He's crazy. They'll probably put him down."

When he said that, the puppy laid his head on my shoulder, whined in my ear and got very still. Then he lifted his head and looked me in the eyes.

"Are you really a crazy dog?" I asked him, staring back into his brown eyes. He lifted his upper lip, exposing his teeth and gave me a small growl. Then he licked my face and…I swear this is true…he gave me a smile and started wagging his tail. That was all it took.

"Call Animal Control back and tell them not to come." I said. "I'll take him."

"Are you sure?" the manager asked. "That dog has been a real problem since he arrived in this country."

"What are you talking about?"

"That dog is a full blood Irish Setter. His parents were both champion show dogs. He arrived a few weeks ago from Ireland and has been a pain in the ass since he got here. He hates everyone, snapping and biting at anyone who gets near him. Well, everyone except you."

"What's his name?"

"Sir Charles Radcliffe the Third," he said without emotion.

"Sir Charles? Are you kidding?"

"No, sir. That's what it says on his papers."

I looked down at the puppy. "Sir Charles? Do you want me to call you Sir Charles?"

He lifted his lip again and snarled.

"Ok then, how about I call you Charley." His tail started wagging and he gave me that silly smile again and licked my face.

Rita was a bit stunned and frowned at me when I brought him home, but Audrey screamed with delight. I *was* worried and not sure how he would react to Rita and Audrey.

I know this sounds stupid, but on the ride home, I had a long talk with him, telling him about Rita and Audrey and I warned him that if he wasn't nice to them, he couldn't stay. When I put him down on the floor he immediately ran up to them, smiling and wagging his tail.

Although he never actually bit anyone, he came close a few times and he made it very clear that he didn't like any of my friends and did not like to be petted. He scared the postman and the UPS guy so bad they refused delivery to my house, so I had to get a P.O. box to get my mail and drive to the UPS office to get my packages.

The only two friends Charley accepted were Marshall and Mike O'Bannon.

When he first met Marshall, he snarled and growled at him, his usual greeting, but when I told him that Marshall was my best friend and that we had grown up together, he instantly stopped growling and ran up to him, smiling, wagging his tail.

Marshall's mouth flew open and stared at me with wide eyes, "I thought you were kidding."

"I tried to tell you, " I said grinning, "He understands everything I say."

Marshall squatted down and looked him in the eyes. "Grant tells me you don't like the postman."

Charley lifted his lip and growled.

"What about the UPS guy? What's wrong with him?"

Charley snorted and barked.

"Ok, one more question. What about Mike O'Bannon? We grew up with him, too."

Charley lifted his lip, exposing his teeth. "Woof, woof."

"Come on, Charley. He's really a good guy. Will you give him a chance?"

Charley lowered his lip and thought for a second. "Arrr, arrr, arrr." Then he smiled and wagged his tail.

"Why did you ask about O'Bannon?" I asked.

Marshall grinned. "He's in the car. He was afraid to come in."

From that day on, Marshall, Mike O'Bannon and Charley have been buddies.

So now do you believe me? Even a world-renowned doctor, the smartest man I know, believes Charley understands English and is possibly psychic.

So what were the warnings and signals Charley was giving me? And if I believe what I'm telling you, why would I ignore them?

Well, like you are thinking now, Charley's actions and reactions, although amazing and cute, were impossible. How could a dog understand English and predict the future?

~

THE DAY I bought my first plane, I took Charley up for a quick flight. He absolutely loved it. From the minute he got in the plane, he showed no signs of fear. During the flight, he constantly stared out the windshield, barking and wagging his tail.

He loved flying so much I often took him with me on my trips. When I couldn't take him and tried to explain why, he would turn his back on me and pout. When I would get back from my trip, he wouldn't be at the front door barking like usual. Instead he would avoid me for a few days, giving me the cold shoulder. Rita and Audrey thought it was hilarious. So to avoid his scorn, I tried to take him with me as often as possible.

But this all changed when I bought my new plane. It actually started when I first showed Rita the brochure with pictures of it. I held it up for Charley to see and he immediately lifted his lip and growled. When I explained why I was buying it, he continued to snarl and growl at the pictures.

A few days later, I took him with me to the airport to see the new plane in person.

In the past, all I had to say was, "You want to go flying?" and he would instantly start spinning around in circles, grab his leash and run to the car. But on that day, he didn't move. I had to drag him to the car. When we got to the airport he refused to get out, so I drug him out of the seat and led him to the plane.

All I'd had to do before was open the passenger door and he would jump in the seat, but not in this plane. No matter what I said, he would not move. And for the first time since I'd owned him, he snapped and bit my hand when I reached toward him to pick him up. With blood trickling down my fingers, I drove him back home.

That was eighteen months ago. Charley hasn't flown with me again. And when I had to go on a trip, he did everything he could to prevent me from leaving, including blocking the front door. When I would finally get past him and leave, Rita told me that while I was gone, he wouldn't eat and constantly paced the house, checking and re-checking the front door until I got back.

It seems so obvious to me now. I should have realized why he was acting so strange, but I just couldn't or wouldn't see it.

≈

IT WAS FEBRUARY 14TH, Valentine's Day, and I had a big day planned for my girls. I had hidden the two heart-shaped boxes of chocolates in the closet, and had made the florist promise me twice that the two arrangements of long stem roses would be delivered at 9:00 a.m. sharp.

My plan was to drive them to Galveston, take them to brunch at a fancy restaurant and spend the rest of the day cruising the Gulf of Mexico on our boat, but those plans changed when the phone rang at 7:30 a.m.

It was the foreman of one of my projects in Austin. There had been an accident and one of the construction workers had been hurt. A section of the steel support beams had collapsed. The building inspector was there on-site, questioning my design.

I could hear the tension in the foreman's voice. "Grant, I think you need to get over here and fast."

I had already told Rita and Audrey what I had planned for the day, so when I woke them up and and told them why I had to fly to Austin, they were both very disappointed.

"Why don't we go with you?" Rita asked, smiling at Audrey. "After you take care of your business, we can go out for dinner there in Austin."

Audrey's blue eyes sparkled up at me. "Could we go, Daddy?"

"I don't see why not?" I said, pulling the two boxes of chocolates from the closet. "At least this way, I'll get to spend all day with my two favorite girls." I handed them the candy. "Will you be my Valentines?"

When the three of us walked down the stairs, Charley started barking. He was standing in front of the door to the garage, trying to prevent us from leaving.

"Sorry, Charley, I have no choice this time. Move!"

He didn't move and started barking louder.

"What's wrong with him?" Rita asked. "I've never seen him bark like this before."

"I have no idea, but we're not getting through there. Go out the front door, I'll keep him busy here."

Rita was right; I'd never seen him bark so hard and loud. He was barking, almost screaming and whining at the same time. When I closed the front door, he went completely ballistic, jumping up on the windows, sounding more like someone screaming than barking. He was still jumping up and down in the window, when I backed out of the drive and drove away.

When we got to the airport, I checked on the weather and got an all clear all the way to Austin. There wasn't a cloud in the crystal clear blue sky, a perfect day for flying. I had the tanks filled with fuel and did my walk around check. Then we all climbed in and headed to the runway.

When we reached the end of the runway and were lined up for take off, I did everything on my normal final pre-flight checklist, except one thing.

On every other take off I had done in that plane, before I hit the throttles, I had repeated these words out loud.

*"If an engine fails before V1: Close both throttles and use the brakes to stop on the remaining runway.*

*"If an engine fails after V1: Take off and deal with the problem as per the 'engine-out' procedure."*

Repeating those words out loud were supposed to give me an instant review of what to do if something happened, but this time, I was too shy or embarrassed to say it out loud in front of Rita and Audrey.

We had just reached speed and lifted off the runway, about 50 feet off the ground, when the right engine suddenly coughed and stopped. I had trained for this many times in the simulator, but never in real life. I tried to think of what to do, but I had panicked and my mind was blank.

The plane twisted hard right. I think I hit the pedals and pulled the wheel hard left, but I'm really not sure. I remember looking up through the windshield and seeing the ground–we were inverted, upside down. The last clear memory I have was staring into Rita's terrified blue eyes. Then everything went black.

## 2

## GRAND THEFT

Marshall's image gradually appeared when I opened my eyes. He was standing over me. I was groggy, confused and disoriented. "What's going on?" I whispered, "Where am I?"

"You're in the hospital," he said. "Stop talking and be still."

I tried to sit up, but when I moved, a pain shot down my side like a bolt of electricity. "Why am I here? What happened?" Marshall looked away.

"Marshall!" I tried to yell, but my voice was gravelly and weak. "Tell me what happened, talk to me."

Biting his lower lip, he stared down at me. His eyes were swollen and red. Then he pulled a chair up beside the bed, sat down and took a deep breath. "You don't remember?"

"Remember what?"

His eyes darted from side to side as he searched for words. "Do you remember flying your plane?"

The second he said the word *plane* it all came back. "OH GOD, WE CRASHED!" I yelled.

"Yes," he said softly.

"Rita, Audrey! Are they OK?"

He lowered his head, "I'm so sorry Grant, but...no, they're not."

"Oh no!" My voice cracked. "Are they dead? Please tell me, Marshall... are they dead?"

He took my hand and squeezed it. Tears were rolling down his face. "Little Audrey..." he choked and wiped his eyes, "She...she's gone. I'm so sorry."

It felt like a hot poker had seared my heart. I tried to speak, but couldn't catch my breath. I began to hyperventilate, bawling, coughing and gasping for air at the same time. The only words I could get out were, "My poor baby."

Marshall bent over my bed, wrapped his arms around me and we cried for a long time.

I really didn't want to know, but I whispered, "What about Rita?"

He leaned back, wiped his eyes and slowly shook his head. "She's still alive, but...she has suffered severe head trauma. We're not seeing any brain waves. It's killing me to have to tell you this, but I'm afraid she's gone, too."

I wish I could describe it, but there are no accurate words to explain the pain that was racing through me at that moment, so I'm not gonna try. But that pain...that throbbing, searing pain...has never gone away.

Inexplicably, I wasn't hurt at all; just a few minor cuts and bruises. My beloved Rita and my baby girl were gone, and I didn't even break a damn bone.

An hour later, Marshall put me in a wheelchair and took me to see Rita. I wish now that he hadn't, because when I think of her, instead of seeing her smiling face, her bright red hair and her beautiful blue eyes...all I see is a lifeless lump of a body, with tubes and wires every-where. I tried, but I couldn't find her beautiful face. Her head was so swollen and disfigured she was completely unrecognizable. And that's the image I couldn't stop seeing.

My injuries were so superficial I was released from the hospital two days later. Following hospital procedure, the nurse put me in a wheelchair and pushed me out the front door, where Marshall was waiting. Walking with a slight limp, I followed him back inside and rode up the elevator with him to Rita's floor.

In a small office there, with Marshall sitting next to me, I listened carefully to her medical team explain her injuries and grim prognosis.

"Mr. Nash," the doctor began, "did Rita have a signed DNR?"

I glanced over at Marshall, not understanding the question. "Has Rita ever signed a do not resuscitate document?"

I shook my head no.

"Have you and Rita ever discussed it?" he asked. "Do you know what she thought about it?"

I shook my head again. "We never talked about it."

"Mr. Nash, in that case," the doctor said sliding a document in front of me, "we're going to need your permission."

I raised my head and looked at Marshall. "No! I can't do it. She's still alive. Maybe she'll wake up...how do they know for sure?"

Marshall put his arm around my shoulder. "Grant, do you trust me? Do you believe I'm a good doctor?"

"Yes, of course."

"I've known Rita almost as long as you have...and you know that I love her, too." He looked directly into my eyes. "Grant, Rita has no brain activity. You have to trust me on this. She's never going to wake up." He took my hand and squeezed it. "You know in your heart what she would want you to do."

That afternoon, at 3:30 p.m., February the 17th, I leaned over her bed and kissed my beloved Rita for the last time.

∽

I COULDN'T WATCH them unplug her . I didn't want to watch her die, so I left and waited in the lobby until Marshall came down and told me that it was all over.

After that, he drove me home and gave me a strong sedative to help me get through the night. As you might expect, Charley already knew and quietly snuggled with me on the bed until I fell asleep.

I don't remember much about the next few days, because I slept through most of them, thanks to the strong sedatives. When I did wake up, all I did was relive the crash moment by moment, my mind flashing with images of me just sitting there, frozen like a stone, watching the ground getting closer and closer through the windshield. Then I would see Rita's frightened blue eyes.

"God, why take them and not me? How could you let this happen?"

After a few hours of screaming at God and wallowing in my sorrow, I would take another pill and fall back to sleep.

Every time I opened my eyes, Charley was lying there next to me. He never left my side. I didn't realize it at the time, but neither did Marshall. He was there taking care of Charley and looking after me.

Marshall had also made all the arrangements for the burials. The morning of their funerals, he pulled me out of the bed and threw me in the shower. Then he helped me put on a suit, tied my tie and walked me to the waiting limousine in my driveway that drove us to the church.

I have no memories of the funeral, only a few flashes. I know I was there physically, but can't remember a single word the preacher said, or anyone else that may have talked to me that day.

Marshall told me all my friends were there and I appreciated them coming, but for whatever reason, that day has been erased from my memory banks.

~

I DECIDED to do it on Valentine's Day, exactly one year after the crash. To be honest with you, I don't remember much of that year, because for most of it...I was drunk. I could remember a few embarrassing flashes, but the rest of it was a complete blur.

I guess that was a good thing, because everybody told me I'd made a complete ass of myself since the funeral. Maybe if I had been a stronger man, I could have pulled myself up out of the ashes of my life, moved on and survived it, but I was too weak. Instead, I gave up and crawled inside of a bottle to numb my pain and hide from the horrible reality of my shattered life.

In those twelve months, I had lost my business, my partners and all of my friends. I wanted to call Marshall to tell him goodbye, but he was so disgusted with me we hadn't talked in months and I knew he wouldn't answer my calls. Even Charley wouldn't look at me.

When I got to the marina, I knew what I was doing could have been considered grand theft. I didn't own the boat any longer; the bank had repossessed it a few months earlier. But I didn't pay the payments because I was broke. I had the money. I hadn't paid the payments because that boat had too many memories of Rita and Audrey connected to it…memories I just couldn't think about.

The truth is I had more money in my bank account than I'd ever had…six million dollars to be exact. Five hundred thousand from Rita's life insurance policy and five and a half million from the *Beachcraft* corporation, as their way of saying, "We're sorry for building an engine that stopped running for no apparent reason." Yeah, so far all of the experts couldn't explain why that engine had stalled.

That five-and a half-million dollar settlement check was the reason Marshall and I hadn't talked in months. He wanted me to sue their pants off and take them for a lot more, fifty or a hundred million, but I couldn't do that. I would have had to relive the crash over and over during a trial. And because the experts couldn't find a reason the engine had stopped, the lawyers representing the insurance companies had actually accused me of crashing the plane on purpose to collect the insurance money. I was infuriated and couldn't believe it when my lawyer told me, but they were prepared for a war and I knew I wouldn't have survived a trial like that, so rather than fight them, I settled. I tried to explain why I did it to Marshall, but he didn't want to hear another one of my excuses.

The last words he had said to me were, "I used to admire you, but that was before I realized you were such a coward. I know why you didn't want that trial…you couldn't stay sober that long! I'm really sorry about Rita and Audrey. It was a real tragedy, but I'm sick of watching you use that tragedy as an excuse. I loved Rita and Audrey and I'm embarrassed of what you're doing to their memories. You're pathetic! It's time, past time, for you to accept what's happened and move on with your life. I'm not saying to forget them; we'll never, ever forget them, but Grant, they are dead and you are alive! If you ever crawl out of that bottle and decide to become a man again, give me a call. Until then, I don't want to talk to you."

~

AT THE MARINA, I punched in the gate code and walked down the dock to the slip. Fortunately, the bank hadn't changed the keys and she fired right up. The security guard just waved at me as I backed her out of the slip and headed for the Gulf. On my way through the channel, the day we found that boat flashed in my mind...

We were at the Houston boat show when Rita saw her, and it was love at first sight. Of course, it didn't make much sense for us to own a boat that size. We lived in Huntsville, 130 miles from Galveston and the Gulf of Mexico. But she had dreamed of owning a boat like this her entire life. My architecture business was booming, we could afford the payments, so I gave in and bought her.

It was the first time I'd been at the helm that Rita and Audrey weren't laying up on the forward deck. My girls were true sun worshipers. They were lousy deckhands: never helping me untie her from the slip or wash her off after one of our cruises, but they were great sunbathers. I was smiling just thinking about that. It had to have been the first time I'd smiled in months.

It's interesting how the mind works. You would think I would have been sad that night; distraught, maybe even crying knowing what I was about to do, but I had none of those emotions flowing through me. All of my sadness went away the second I had made up my mind what I was going to do.

The hum of the boat's engine seemed especially calming as I made my way through the channel markers. I hadn't planned on going very far, so when I could just make out the glowing lights from Galveston, I killed the engine.

I took the deck line and tied Charley's leash to the steering wheel and put his water and food bowls beside him. When I set the bowls down, he growled and turned his back to me

"Come on, buddy, look at me. I know you're mad, but please let me say goodbye. You know I have to do this. I can't live with it any longer. Please Charley, look at me."

He turned around and stared up. "I know you tried to warn me about that plane, but I didn't listen to you."

"Arr, arr, arr," he growled and put his paw on my knee.

"I know you don't want me to do this, but I can't live with this guilt anymore. Don't look at me that way. I KILLED THEM, CHARLEY!" I screamed. "Don't you understand...I FROZE! I could have done something! I just sat there and let it happen. I killed them, Charley...I killed them."

"Woof, arrr, arrr, woof." He pulled back on the leash and bit at the deck line securing it to the wheel.

"I know you hate being tied up like this, but I'm afraid you'll try to jump in after me. I can't let you die too. Don't worry we're only a few miles out. I'm gonna call the Coast Guard and tell them where you are. I left a letter to Marshall on the table. He'll take good care of you."

He was looking up at me with the saddest eyes I'd ever seen. "Wooo, wooo, woooooooooo," he whined.

"I know, buddy...I'm so sorry. May God forgive me…"

I reached for the hand mic on the radio and pushed the button. "Mayday, Mayday! Man overboard! I repeat, man overboard!"

When someone answered, I gave him the latitude and longitude of our location. Then I bent down and kissed his nose. "I love you, Charley."

I took a few deep breaths, stood up, walked to the back swim platform and jumped into the water.

~

IT WAS February and the water was freezing, something I had counted on. The article I read on the Internet had said the colder the water, the sooner hypothermia would set in, paralyzing my body and hopefully making me fall unconscious before I drowned.

I didn't try to swim; that would generate body heat and delay the hypothermia, so I just leaned back, looking up at the stars, floating still, not moving in the freezing water.

I had wondered if what I had heard was true, that right before you die, your entire life would flash before your eyes. I waited for it quietly, but that never happened.

Something *did* flash in my mind, but it wasn't a montage of pictures of my life. It was the image of Rita's face. But I didn't see her beautiful smile. She was angry, glaring at me.

Then I heard her voice. "Grant, what are you doing? Don't do this! This is not your time! You have much more to do. Swim, honey, swim now!"

I blinked my eyes and the vision of her face was gone, but her words repeated in my head. "This is not your time! You have much more to do. Swim, honey, swim now!"

I tried to swim, but my arms wouldn't move; hypothermia was setting in. I heard her voice again. "Swim, honey, swim now!"

With all my might, I tried to move my arms, but my body was frozen and I began to sink under the water.

Frantically, I kicked my legs hard and that brought me back to the surface, coughing and gagging, spitting up water. Again, I tried to swim, but couldn't move my arms. I began slipping back under the water. I tried to kick my legs again, but this time, they wouldn't move. I felt sleepy and numb.

As I sank further and further, I opened my eyes, stinging from the salt water, hoping to see Rita's face one last time. But all I could see...was darkness.

# 3

## SHARKS

I felt something brush my legs. Then I felt a sharp pain in my right shoulder that brought me back to full consciousness. I opened my eyes, but couldn't see anything. The image of a shark flashed through my mind. "Please, God, not this way!"

The shark had me by my shoulder, pulling me up. When we broke the surface of the water, I could hear Charley barking, as I gasped for air.

The shark was under me; I could feel him pushing on my back. When I finally got my breath, I realized what was happening. Charley was only a few feet away from me, swimming and barking like crazy, and the shark wasn't a shark. It was a porpoise. There were three of them circling me, and they had pulled and pushed me back up to the surface.

Charley swam up to me, bit down on my wrist and started pulling me back toward the boat.

Suddenly, the sky lit up and we were illuminated in a bright light and I heard voices.

"We've got you, sir. Just relax." It was the Coast Guard.

The diver slipped a life ring around my neck and the next thing I knew, I was lying on the deck of their boat, wrapped in warm blankets. Charley was standing over me, whining loudly and licking my face.

They took us below to the galley and gave me hot coffee.

"That's some dog you've got there." I looked up to see an officer standing in the doorway. It was the captain.

I nodded and petted Charley's head. "Yes, sir, he is."

He sat down next to me. "I'm Captain Adams. My medic tells me that you're gonna be okay." He reached out his hand and shook mine, then tried to pet Charley, but pulled back when he growled.

"Sorry, Captain, but he doesn't like to be touched by strangers." I looked down at him, "Come on, Charley, he saved us. Be nice to him. I think you need to go thank him."

Charley walked over to the captain, wagged his tail and licked his hand.

The captain started laughing. "You are very welcome, Charley."

The galley crewmen brought the captain a cup of coffee. He took a sip and looked at me. "Do you feel up to answering a few questions? I need some answers for my report."

I shrugged. "Sure."

He flipped the pages of his yellow pad. "We ran the numbers on the boat. It's registered to Grant and Rita Nash. Are you Grant Nash?"

"Yes, that's me."

"Can you tell me what happened? How did you and Charley wind up in the water?"

I wasn't sure what to tell him. If I told him I had jumped, trying to kill myself, I was sure they would take me back to shore and lock me up in a psychiatric ward for evaluation. "I can't remember," I lied. "I just slipped and fell in. Charley must have jumped in after me."

Charley raised his head and growled.

The captain put down his pen and petted his head. "I don't think he believes you, and neither do I. Mr. Nash, we found the note on the table, the one you left for Dr. Taylor. I know you didn't fall in. You jumped."

"Please don't put that in your report. I'm not crazy. It's... just that..."

"I know all about it, Mr. Nash."

I raised my head. "How could you know?"

"I just hung up with Dr. Taylor. He'll be waiting for us at the dock." He took a sip of his coffee and grinned. "It's a very, very small world we live in. Dr. Taylor saved my son, so I owed him. I'm not going to mention anything about how you wound up in the water in my report, but I do think you need to get some help. Honestly, I'm not sure how you survived, the water temperature is 48 degrees and it's shark infested, but somehow you did."

He lifted his eyes and wrinkled his brow. "Mr. Nash, you've been given a second chance at life. In my opinion, it's a miracle that you are alive and sitting here. Don't throw that away."

I reached down and petted Charley's head. "Don't worry, Captain, trust me, I won't.

I took a sip of my coffee and looked over the table at him. "Can I ask you a question?"

"Absolutely," he said. "What do you want to know?"

"You've dealt with people who have experienced hypothermia before, right?"

"Yes, a few times."

"Did any of them hallucinate?"

"No," he said, shaking his head, "I've never heard of that before. Why, did you?"

"I'm not sure. You tell me. Were there porpoises swimming close when you found me?"

"Yes, there were three or four dolphins around you."

"I think one of them pulled me up to the surface. I know it sounds crazy, but I think he saved me from drowning. Is that possible? Or was I just dreaming?"

He grinned, shaking his head. " They weren't porpoises, they were dolphins. There are no porpoises in the Gulf of Mexico. And no, I don't think you were dreaming or hallucinating. I have no doubt that could have happened. In fact, they probably also saved you from being attacked by sharks, because these waters are full of them."

My degree is in marine science, and I have done some research on dolphins. Since man built the first boat, there have been thousands of verifiable reports about dolphins saving humans from drowning and shark attacks. It happens all the time. Apparently, dolphins are the only animal, besides humans and dogs, that show true altruism. They probably heard Charley barking and came running. Like I said, you are a very lucky man."

~

TOWING my boat behind the Coast Guard cutter, we slowly made our way back to the pier. Marshall was standing at the end of the gangway as Charley and I walked down it. When Charley saw him, he took off running, jumping up and down, barking and wagging his tail.

When I made eye contact with Marshall, I opened my mouth to say something, but he held up his hand, "Not one word, Grant! I don't want to talk to you right now, you selfish bastard! Just get in the car and don't say a Goddamn thing until we get to your house."

There was a woman sitting in the front passenger seat, so Charley and I got in the back. "Hello, I'm Brenda," she said, "Marshall's friend."

"Don't talk to that asshole!" Marshall snapped, putting on his seat belt and cranking the car, "and don't try to pet the dog. He doesn't like it."

No one said a single word for the next two hours as we drove the interstate back to Huntsville. Quietly, I stared out the window, counting the stars and petting Charley's head, who was snoozing on my lap.

Once we got inside my house, I fed Charley and put the coffee on. Brenda and Marshall poured themselves a cup and we settled on the stools around the island in the kitchen.

Marshall sighed, ran his hand through his hair, punched his phone and held it up for me to see. "You called me yesterday three times, but I didn't call you back." He locked eyes with me. "Were you calling to tell me goodbye?"

I looked away, nodding my head.

He wiped his eyes. "Grant, when they called and told me what you tried to do, I lost it. I was so angry at you. I couldn't believe you could have been so selfish to even consider something like this. And then when I saw you walking down that gangway, I wanted to slug you."

"But for the last few hours driving here, I've been going over and over this in my head. I'm not sure why I haven't realized this before, but it finally hit me why I was so angry. Grant, I'm not mad at you...I'm furious at myself. Furious for being so stupid, furious for being so full of myself, and my own expectations of how I thought you should be acting. I'm furious for not being a real friend. A real friend would have returned your calls."

He wiped his eyes again with his sleeve. "If you had died out there...I...I would have never been able to forgive myself."

I shrugged. "I didn't expect you to answer..."

"Please, Grant don't talk," he said, interrupting me, holding up his hand. "Let me finish."

He slid off the stool and started pacing the kitchen. "I can't imagine living through what you have this past year. No one should ever have to live through something like that, but unfortunately, you did. And where was I? I'm supposed to be your best friend. Hell, it's a lot more than that! We grew up together, we're like brothers, but where was I when you needed me? I deserted you."

He sat back down on the bar stool facing me. "I haven't been much of a friend, have I?"

"Marshall, I don't blame you for anything you've done, because no matter what you did, it wouldn't have made any difference. It wasn't your fault. I chased you away. Hell, I chased everyone who ever cared about me away. I just couldn't face all of this sober. When I was drunk, I felt numb and it didn't seem to hurt as much...so that's what I did. I know you tried to save me, but I didn't want to be saved."

Marshall reached across the island and grabbed my hand. "Do you understand what would have happened to me and everyone else that loved you, if you had died tonight? Grant, you're my brother...the only brother I've ever had, and I hope you know how much I love you. Please promise me, you'll never do anything like this again. Promise me."

We were both crying like a couple of babies with tears dripping off our cheeks. I let go of his hand and wiped my face with a napkin.

Marshall wiped his face as well and stared at me. "Grant, have you lost your faith in God?"

I stood up, walked to the coffee pot and poured another cup. Nodding my head slowly, I said, "Yes, I guess I did."

"What about now?" Brenda asked.

I looked at her and smiled. "Since the crash, in my rare sober moments, I would pray for some kind of answers, but I got nothing. My life just seemed to continue on that downward spiral. As far as I knew, I had been a good man, a good husband and a good father. I kept asking him what I had done to receive His wrath and why He took away everything and everyone I loved...but He never answered. After a few months, I quit praying and sort of drifted away. I was too angry and lost to believe in Him anymore. I felt like He had either abandoned me for no reason, or that He didn't really exist. Either way, I didn't want any part of Him."

"But you feel different now?" Marshal asked.

"Yeah," I said, nodding.

"What changed? Did He finally answer you?" Brenda asked.

I shrugged my shoulders. "I think so. This is going to sound strange, but I saw Rita tonight...when I was out there in that water."

Marshall raised his eyebrows and smiled. "You saw Rita? She gave you God's answer?"

I shook my head. "No, it wasn't like that. When I was floating there in that freezing water, her face appeared out of nowhere. But she wasn't smiling."

"Was she pissed at what you were trying to do?" he said with a chuckle

"Oh yes, she was extremely pissed. She told me to swim, that it wasn't my time. She said that I had a lot more to do." I looked him in the eyes. "Marshall, how would she know that?"

He nodded and shrugged. "Do you think he told her?"

"What else could it be? A few minutes later, the dolphins showed up and saved me. What do you think?"

He grinned. "According to the captain, it's a miracle you survived. I don't know of anyone else that can do this sort of thing...you know... miracles. So yes, I think His hands are all over this."

I lifted my head and stared into his eyes. "I don't know exactly what Rita meant by me having *more to do*, but trust me, with God's help, hopefully I'm going to find out."

~

THAT AFTERNOON, I loaded Charley into my old truck and drove to Huntsville State Park. It was his favorite place in the world. He loved chasing after the birds and squirrels living there in the woods.

After a long hike, I pulled two bottles of water and a bowl out of my backpack. I filled the bowl and sat down next to Charley by the lakeshore.

When his water bowl was empty, he plopped down and rested his head on my legs.

"Charley, I haven't had the chance to thank you for saving my life," I said, rubbing his head.

He lifted his eyes, "Arrrrr, arrrrr," he growled.

"I know. It was a stupid thing to do."

"Arrrr, arrrr, arrrrrrrrrr!" He held out his last word extra long.

"Was that last one a cuss word?" I asked, smiling at him.

He lifted his eyes and stared up at me. "Woof!"

I started laughing. "That's okay. I deserved that."

He raised up, licked my hand and started wagging his tail. "Woof, woof, woof."

"I hope this means that you've forgiven me. I promise I'll never do that again."

His tail started wagging faster, then he jumped in my lap and licked my face.

We sat there quietly for almost an hour, watching the water rippling on the lake. As I sat there, Rita's words kept running through my mind, "You have much more to do." I wondered what she was talking about.

We walked back to my truck and I slowly drove back to my house with the windows down, so Charley could hang his head out the window biting and barking at the wind blowing in his face. He loved doing that. It was the only time he acted like a real dog.

When I pulled up in my driveway and looked at my front door, I suddenly realized what I needed to do.

Like me, Charley was staring at the front door, wishing Audrey and Rita would come running out to greet us.

He turned his head, looked up at me and made a small, sad high-pitched whine. "Yeah, I know, buddy, I miss them, too."

Charley was normally anxious to get out of the car, barking and whining until I opened his door, but that day he didn't make a sound. He sat there quietly beside me staring at the front door.

After a few minutes, I looked over at him. "Charley, there are too many memories in this house. I think we need to get out of here - sell everything but this old truck and just take off, just you and me. What do you think about that? Do you want to go find a new life for us somewhere else?"

"Woof, arrrr, woof!" he said, wagging his tail and giving me that silly smile.

# 4

# THE ROAD LESS TRAVELED

The next day, I got up early, and with Charley by my side with every step I took, we started going through drawers and closets.

Through out that morning, everything I touched triggered a memory of my amazing life with Rita and Audrey. I fought it off as long as I could, but I finally broke down, hugging Charley in my arms as I wept.

When I got off the floor, I realized that I would never be able to do it myself. Not only was it too emotional, there was just no way I could decide between what was expendable or what was a priceless keepsake I couldn't live without. But I knew in my heart, if I was going to survive and have any chance at finding a new life, it had to be done. That afternoon, I called Marshall and asked him to do it for me. He contacted a realtor to list the house and a company that specialized in estate sales to empty it out.

I was able to get rid of the cars. I called another high school buddy of mine, who worked at a Ford dealership and he gave me a good price for our two SUVs. The only vehicle I kept was my old truck.

I say old because it was. A 1954 Ford F-100 Heritage Ranch pickup, to be exact. It was my dad's old truck that he loved almost as much as me. So when he died, as a tribute to him, I had a shop in

Dallas completely rebuild her, inside and out, add air conditioning and give her a sparkling new bright red paint job. She was beautiful and ran like a top.

Six days later, with the bed of Dad's old truck packed with three photo albums filled with pictures of Audrey and Rita, three suitcases of clothes, a box filled with Charley's toys, my old golf clubs, a tent and two sleeping bags, Charley and I jumped in and took off, heading north on I-45.

~

AFTER ABOUT AN HOUR of driving on that freeway, Charley started moaning and growling every time we would pass an exit.

"You have to pee already?" He didn't bark, so I knew that wasn't it. "Are you hungry?" He slowly turned his head and looked at me.

I took the next exit and stopped at the intersection. "What the hell is it, Charley?"

He turned his head to the right and barked. "You want to go that way?" He barked again, then turned back toward me and gave me that smile.

I pulled out the map, "You want to go to Palestine? What's in Palestine?"

"Woof."

I shook my head, shrugged and slowly headed down the two-lane road. Driving down the highway, we passed several beautiful farm-houses sitting a few hundred yards off the road, surrounded by perfectly aligned rows of lush green crops. We drove past ranches with acres and acres of beautiful green pastures stocked with horses that were grazing close to the white fences that lined the pastures, or that were running and playing in the fields.

Charley had been transfixed at the view, his tail constantly wagging as he stared out the window, occasionally barking at the horses and the cows. He was loving every minute of it. I finally understood what he'd been trying to tell me - it wasn't where we were going he cared about, it was the route we took to get there that mattered to him.

From then on, we took the scenic route, driving through the many small towns and communities along the way. I had no idea where we were going and honestly didn't care. As usual, Charley was right. We were in no hurry to get anywhere, so why not take the scenic route? And "scenic" was the perfect description. I had traveled through Texas, Louisiana and Mississippi many times in my life, but never that way. I had no idea of the majestic beauty and charm I had been missing, flying past all those small towns at seventy miles an hour on the freeway.

Every time we'd pull into a small town, I would pay close attention to Charley. Somehow, he always knew where the dog friendly restaurants were, and would start barking when we got close to one.

In those towns, we would spend a few days driving around, checking out the sights. If there was a good place to camp nearby, I'd pull out the tent, set everything up and build a fire. Charley loved camping in the woods. If we couldn't find a good place to camp, we'd start looking for a La Quinta Inn & Suites. Most of those hotels were dog friendly and Charley didn't seem to mind staying there.

For the next twelve months, Charley and I lived like a couple of hobo-nomads. In no particular hurry, we traveled from coast to coast, driving down the roads less traveled, discovering hidden gems - small cities and towns throughout the country.

In a few of these small, beautiful little communities, I would pick up a real estate magazine and check out some of the houses for sale. If I found something interesting, I'd drive to the house and Charley and I would walk around it, peaking through the windows. But at every single house, Charley would get bored, walk back to the truck, jump in and wait for me to come back and drive away.

"What was wrong with that one?" I'd ask him. "I liked it and I like this town."

He would lift his lip, exposing his teeth and growl. "Arrrrrrr."

We eventually made our way to Florida and discovered that there were several pet friendly camping sites that allowed us to actually set up on the beach and boy, did Charley love that.

In the morning, with him by my side, I would jog up and down those beaches. After my run, we would jump in the ocean, and play and swim for hours. At night, we would lie on the sleeping bags and stare up at the stars.

I'm not sure what it was about Florida, but those beaches, the sound of the surf, the warm ocean water and those stars at night seem to soothe my wounds. The constant aching pain in my heart began to heal. It didn't seem to hurt as much in Florida, so I began to seriously look for a place to settle.

I began looking for a beach house in the Florida panhandle and found several I could afford and really liked, but unfortunately, none of them were good enough for Charley.

"What about this one? It's really cool, Charley! And look at that water. Have you ever seen water that blue before?"

He did the same thing at every single house. He would walk around the property with me, turn around and look at the beach, raise his lip, snort and slowly walk back to the truck.

After rejecting fifteen or twenty beach houses up and down the Gulf Coast, I began to think that Charley didn't like Florida as much as I did. I drove all the way to Key West, with the same results. He didn't like it there, either, so I quit picking up real estate magazines and stopped looking for houses.

We spent the next few months wandering from island to island in the Florida Keys, then began making our way up the Atlantic Coast.

Driving up A1A, we drove through and explored every beach town from Miami to Daytona Beach, camping near the ocean when we could or staying in hotels along the way.

The official name of SR A1A is the Scenic and Historical Coastal Byway. It runs for 338 miles along the Atlantic Coast, from Key West to Amelia Island, just a few miles south of Georgia. While we were driving up A1A, Charley never looked at me when he could see the ocean out his window. The only time he looked away was when a large condo complex blocked his view. He didn't seem to mind the beach houses, but didn't like the condos. I didn't like them much, either.

At least once a day, I would stop at a public beach area that had bathrooms and an outside shower and we'd go for a swim in the ocean.

Then we'd shower off and drive with the windows down until we were dry. After those daily swims, Charley would usually take a long nap.

∼

I'VE ALWAYS LOVED PLAYING golf. I've never been any good at it, but I've always loved the game. That's why I had my clubs tucked away in the back of the old truck and was excited to get to our next stop–Saint Augustine. Not just because it's the oldest city in the United States, but because it's also the home of *The World Golf Hall of Fame.*

Charley was asleep, taking one of his naps when we pulled into Flagler Beach. Rather than turning on my blinker and taking the chance of the clicking sound waking him up, I rolled down my window and signaled the old fashioned way with my arm and made the turn toward I-95.

He must have felt the movement of the truck, because he raised his head and looked out his window. Then he looked at me, lifted his lip and grumbled.

"Come on, Charley, it's getting late. I want to see the World Golf Hall Of Fame before it closes! I-95 will save us an hour getting there."

He snorted, turned his head and stared out the window. It was his version of turning his back on me in the truck.

"It's about time you learn that you can't always have it your way." He snorted again, still not looking at me. "You know, sometimes you're a real pain in the ass."

"Arrrr. Woof."

He was still mad at me when we got to the Hall Of Fame and refused to get out of the truck. So I rolled down the windows and left him there to pout alone.

After my tour of the Hall Of Fame, just to aggravate him, when we got to the entrance of the interstate, I turned on my blinker like I was going to get back on the freeway. He stood up in his seat and started barking when he heard the first blink.

"Just kidding," I said, turning off the blinker. "You want to go check out Saint Augustine?" He smiled and wagged his tail.

It was almost 7:00 p.m. and I was starving, so we pulled into a Burger King and I bought us a Whopper and fries.

"What do you think so far, Charley? Does this look like the oldest city in America to you?"

"Woof."

"Yeah, I agree. So far all we've seen is modern shopping centers, gas stations and fast food joints."

Our first impression of Saint Augustine changed quickly when we made it to the historic district and drove down King Street. We got lucky and found a parking spot, put money in the meter and started walking down a square called Plaza de la Constitucion. It was more of a park than a typical town square. Four historic churches with very tall steeples that had some of the most beautiful stained glass windows I'd ever seen surrounded it.

Eventually, we made our way to Saint George Street. It appeared to be the main drag, with several restaurants, shops and bars where most of the tourists were walking.

At first, the narrow streets reminded me of New Orleans or Key West, but then I noticed all the children and the dogs. Everywhere you looked were young families walking with their children, pushing baby carriages with their dogs on leashes. Many of the restaurants had outside decks or patios and at almost every one of them, dogs were lying at their owner's feet.

It had been a long day, so after an hour or so of walking around, I loaded Charley in the truck and started looking for a dog friendly hotel. On a whim, I pulled into the first motel I saw. It was appropriately called the Bayfront Inn. Not only did they have a room available, they were dog friendly, so I checked us in for the night.

We slept a little late and missed the free breakfast, so with a cup of hot coffee in my hand, Charley and I walked across the street and watched the boats puttering up and down the Matanzas River. Across the river, I could clearly see the old historic lighthouse reaching high in the air, still standing after all these years on Anastasia Island.

I was getting hungry and wasn't sure where we should go, but Charley seem to, so I let him lead the way. We had only walked a few hundred yards when he turned and walked into a place called *O.C. White's*. It had a large outside patio and without stopping, Charley started pulling me toward a table.

"Wait, Charley!" I yelled. "We need to find out if they allow dogs first."

"Of course we do," I heard a voice say behind me. "You guys look hungry."

Charley sat up erect next to the table and actually let the server pet him on his head. "You are beautiful," she said. "Are you hungry?"

"Woof!"

"Good," she said, laying the menus on the table, "because we have the best dog cuisine in town."

When she walked off, Charley looked up at me and smiled. "Okay, smartass, I don't want to hear it. What do you want for breakfast?"

I read him his choices from the doggie menu and he selected chicken and rice with carrots. I'm not kidding, he argued with me, because he wanted those carrots.

When we had finished our meal and I was paying at the counter, I heard Charley bark. When I looked down at him, he was poking his nose against a magazine rack. After I got my change, I walked over to him, and he nudged the rack again and barked. His nose was poking a real estate magazine with a beautiful beach house on the cover.

I pulled it out of the rack and looked at it. "This is a beautiful house, Charley, but it's a bit out of our league." He barked and growled. "I'm serious. We can't afford this." He barked again and growled louder.

The cashier started laughing. "I think he likes that house!" she said, with a wide grin. "If you want to see it, go across the bridge and head south on A1A, it's only about fifteen miles away on Anastasia Island. Just follow the signs to Saint Augustine Beach."

I shrugged, held up the magazine and looked at the picture of the house again.

Arguing with Charley was something I did almost every day. It was normal for us, but I often forgot how *NOT* normal and strange it actually was. When I looked up, everyone sitting around the tables on the deck, including the servers, were staring at us with their mouths open in stunned shock.

I couldn't really explain it to them, so I didn't try. Instead, I just looked down at him. "I'm telling you, Charley, I can't afford this house." When he lifted his lip, exposing his teeth and growled at me, everyone in the restaurant burst out laughing.

When Charley heard the people laughing, he turned and looked at them. Then he lowered his lip, gave them that goofy smile and wagged his tail. He was loving all the attention. That made them laugh louder and start applauding, like he was doing a standup routine. What a ham.

# 5

# THE BEACH HOUSE

C harley was smiling and his tail was wagging at full speed as we drove across the bridge to Anastasia Island.

I held up the magazine with the picture of the house on the cover in front of his face. "I don't get it, Charley. Why this house? Why this city?"

He looked over at me. "Woof!"

I petted him on the head. "Why is this one so different from all the others?"

"Arrrrrr, woof!"

"Ok, but I'm telling you, it's gonna be too expensive."

He lifted his lip. "Grrrrr."

I threw up my hands. "Help me, help me! Somebody, please help me," I said, playing. "There's a ferocious mad dog in my truck!"

He lifted his lip further, showing me all his teeth. "Woof, woof, woof!"

"You know, Charley, your mad dog act would be a lot more convincing if you weren't wagging your tail."

The cashier was right. The house was only fifteen miles away, but when I pulled into the entrance, I realized it was a gated community. I wasn't sure I could talk my way in driving an old Ford pickup.

When the guard walked out of the building, he stopped instantly, admiring my truck. "Is this a 1954 Ford 100 Heritage Ranch?"

"Yes, it is," I said proudly. "It was my dad's truck."

"I haven't seen one of these since I was a kid! It's a real beauty!" he said, walking around her. "You here to see one of the houses?"

I held up the magazine. "I'd like to see this one."

"Really?" he said, surprised. "It's been a long time since anyone has come to look at that one."

I raised my eyebrows. "Why is that? What's wrong with it?"

"Oh, there ain't nothing wrong with it except that three million dollar price tag."

"Three million!" I looked over at Charley, but he turned his head and looked out the window.

"Yep, three million dollars! I keep telling Wilson, that's the realtor, he's asking way too much." He looked around to make sure no one was listening. "You didn't hear this from me, but I'm pretty sure he'd take anything even close to two and a quarter. But remember, you didn't hear that from me."

When we pulled up to the house, Charley started whining and jumping in his seat.

It *was* impressive and I instantly liked it. It sat in the middle of ten similar beach houses. Most were obviously smaller, but they were all built about three hundred feet behind a ten or fifteen-foot-high natural sand dune, covered with lush green perennial grasses and tall swaying sea oats. It was perched like a castle high in the air, built, I assumed, on several 15-foot-tall concrete posts. I wasn't sure, because the posts were not exposed like most beach houses - the entire ground floor was finished. It had three garage doors that met the driveway pavers, and there were large windows around the rest of the ground floor structure. The entire second and third floors of the house were surrounded with wide covered wooden decks and handrails. Two winding circular stair-cases led up to the ornate entry that featured two large cut glass entry doors.

When I opened Charley's door, he took off running at full speed, flying up the winding staircase. I could hear his excited barking as he ran around the deck; looking in the windows.

Between every two houses was a wooden walkway that was build up and over the sand dune, leading to the ocean. I was halfway up the staircase when Charley had apparently spotted the walkway and flew past me, running full speed toward it.

Watching from the back deck, I saw him run over the wooden walkway, fly down the sandy beach and jump head first into the ocean. Swimming and barking in the surf, it was easy to see…Charley had finally found our new home.

After a few minutes of playing in the surf, he walked out of the ocean, shook himself dry and headed back to the house.

The back of the house that faced the ocean was all glass, so it was easy to see inside. It was completely furnished and the interior decorator had done a great job. The very large back deck was also furnished with solid, redwood lounge chairs and tables. In each seat was a soft, bright yellow cushion, so I sat down at the table and for the next hour, Charley and I watched and listened to the sounds of the waves breaking on the beach.

I heard a voice and when I turned around, I saw a man standing there smiling. "It's quite a view, isn't it?" he said. "I'm Wilson James." He walked up to me, holding out his hand.

I shook his hand. "It's nice to meet you, Wilson. I saw your name on the sign out front. So you're a realtor?"

He smiled. "Yes, I am. I'm also the developer."

"You built this complex, all ten houses?" I raised my eyebrows and lifted my bottle of water. "My compliments to the chef. You did an amazing job! Please tell your architect he has a new fan. His use of space and exterior design...the way these houses seem to blend in with the seascape is nothing less than brilliant."

He took a seat next to me. "I agree with you. What he designed here is amazing. Unfortunately, he never got to see it. He passed away years ago. If it wasn't for his daughter, none of these houses would be here."

"Really? Why is that?" I asked. "Was there a zoning problem or something?"

He shook his head. "It's a long story. Are you sure you want to hear it?"

"Absolutely," I said, "but before you tell me, could you unlock the door and let us look around?"

The inside was exactly as I had expected. Not one square inch of wasted space, with sweeping panoramic views of the ocean from almost every room.

"What do you think, Charley?" He instantly took off, running around through the house for one more quick tour.

"Woof, woof, woof," he barked, then gave me that silly smile.

"Are you sure?"

His tail was wagging at hyper speed. "Woof!"

I looked at Wilson. "You heard him. We'll take it!"

He jerked his head up. "Don't you even want to know how much it cost?"

I grinned. "Let me guess. You're asking three million...I'll offer you two. You'll counter with two point seven. I will then tell you that this will be a cash deal and we'll settle at two point four."

He burst out laughing and reached out his hand. "Deal!"


To celebrate my purchase, Wilson and his wife, Connie, took Charley and me out to dinner at Cellar 6 that night. It was a nice up-scaled restaurant/martini bar located in the art district on Avila's street, supposedly the oldest street in America. I was stunned to find out that it was also dog friendly. We were seated outside on the deck under an umbrella, but it was a cool, clear night and Charley settled next to my feet and seemed to be very happy and content.

"You never finished the story," I said, "the one about the architect and his daughter."

Wilson glanced over at Connie. "You grew up with her. Why don't *you* tell him the story?"

Connie put down her fork and wiped her mouth with her napkin.

"It's a tragic story that we're all hoping is going to finally have a happy ending," she began. "The architect's name was Jacob Dean. He moved to Saint Augustine back in the 50's. Mr. Dean was a gifted architect and soon built a thriving business through out Florida. He designed many of the buildings you still see standing in downtown Jacksonville and literally hundreds more between Miami and here. He was extremely successful and bought the beach property your house is sitting on back in the 60's."

"What did he pay for the land?" I asked.

They looked at each other and smiled. "It's worth about ten million now, but he bought it for only three hundred thousand."

"Wow!" I said. "So why didn't he develop it back then?"

"It was just an investment for him at first. Jacob was the definition of a workaholic. It was one of the reasons he was so successful and wealthy, but it was also the reason he had never married."

"In the late 1980's, he received a huge offer to buy the beach property from a Miami condominium development company. They were going to pay him a small fortune for the land and also hire him as the architect to design it. So he drew up some quick plans and submitted them to the city planning commission.

"At that meeting, there was a young, beautiful environmentalist protesting the development of that property. Her name was Alice Cornelius, and she was there trying to save that very special stretch of natural untouched beach from being destroyed by condo developers, like they had done to the beaches in Miami and Fort Lauderdale."

"So she stopped the development?" I asked.

Connie grinned. "Yes, she did. It was a legendary town meeting that the old folks still talk about today. The ones that were there will tell you that it was obviously love at first sight for Jacob. He was so taken by Alice, that night in front of half the town and the city council, he announced that he was backing out of the condominium deal. He told them that he was going to keep his land and promised to design something very special for that property that would not damage the beach in any way. He made that promise under one condition: that

Alice would go out to dinner with him later that night and that she would also agree to help him with the design."

"Did she go out to dinner with him?"

"Yep," Wilson said. "And they got married a few months later."

"Really? That's so cool!" I said. "What a story, but that doesn't explain why he didn't develop the land. What stopped him?"

They glanced at each other and laughed. "Because they could never agree on what should go there," Connie said.

"They fought like cats and dogs over that for years," Wilson added. "So he never designed anything. At least, that's what everyone thought."

"This is where the story starts getting sad." Connie said. "There were ten years difference in their ages and they had waited years before they started trying to have a child; Alice was in her 40's and Jacob was in his 50's. After several miscarriages and warnings from her doctors not to try again, Alice was finally able to carry a child to full term. It was a girl they named Melissa. Unfortunately, there were severe complications with the delivery and Alice died, leaving Jacob devastated and alone to raise his daughter.

He shut down his business and dedicated the rest of his life to raising Melissa. She was a beautiful little girl and the apple of his eye. They were inseparable. You never saw Jacob without Melissa being somewhere close. Of course, he spoiled her rotten, but she never showed it. She grew up to be a sweet and loving person. In fact, we grew up together and she's one of my best friends."

"Where is she now?" I asked.

Wilson laughed. "Hold your horses, she'll get to that part in a minute."

"Ok," I held up my hand, "sorry for butting in. But Wilson already told me that Jacob died. Was Melissa young when that happened?"

"No not really, she was twenty-two and had just returned home from college."

"So she wasn't with him the last few years of his life?"

"No, she wasn't. He didn't tell her that he was sick and that bothers her to this day - that she wasn't there for him when he needed her the most."

"Unfortunately, that was just the beginning of Melissa's troubles," Connie said, frowning.

"There's more?"

"A lot more," she said. "It wasn't long after, that Jerry entered her life."

"Who's Jerry?" I asked.

"He's the no-good bastard that tried to steal all her money when she was sick!" Connie's eyes filled with tears. "I'm sorry, I haven't talked about this in a long time."

I glanced over at Wilson. He shook his head and shrugged. "Jerry's Melissa's ex husband. He's not from around here. She met him in college. When her father died, he showed up here and sort of swept her off her feet. Trust me, he's a certified prick." He took a sip of his beer and thought for a moment. "I guess it's one of those 'love is blind' things. Everyone around here that knows him sees him for what he is and can see all the damage he's done to her, but she just keeps taking it. At least, thank God, we finally convinced her to divorce his ass. But he's still here, hanging around."

Tears were running down Connie's cheeks. "Don't worry about it," I said, handing her my napkin. "I understand she's your good friend. We don't have to talk about this now. You can tell me the rest of the story some other time. I think Charley is getting a little restless anyway."

She wiped her eyes with the napkin. "Thank you, Grant."

We all stood and started walking out of the restaurant. When we got to the parking lot, Wilson stopped, reached into his pocket and pulled out the keys to my new house.

"You might need these," he said with a chuckle. "And I think there is one more thing you need to know before we go."

I took the keys and lifted my eyebrows. "Oh yeah, what's that?"

"Melissa is still beautiful...single...she owns a female Golden Retriever and...she's your next door neighbor."

# 6

## MELISSA AND DONNA

Melissa had noticed the man and his dog walking around the house next door earlier that day, but was shocked and a little concerned to see them back again that night sitting on the deck, so she took out her cell phone and punched in a number.

"Wilson, this is Melissa. I think you need to know that there's a man with a dog sitting on the back deck of the house next door."

"Yeah, I know," he said. "That's Grant Nash and Charley, they're your new neighbors.

"What? My new neighbors?" She heard Connie's voice in the background. "Yeah, he bought it today. Hang on, Melissa, Connie wants to talk to you."

The phone rattled in her ear and then she heard Connie's voice. "Have you seen him?"

"Seen who?"

"Grant, your new neighbor!" she exclaimed. "He's gorgeous and he's single!"

Melissa rolled her eyes. "Oh no, Connie. Not again."

"This is different. I had nothing to do with it. Wilson found him at the house this morning and he bought it on the spot. And he paid cash!"

Melissa bent down the blinds with her fingers to get a better look. "Cash?"

"Yes, cash. He wrote a check on the spot! It's so perfect!" she shrieked. "He's gorgeous, apparently rich, single...your divorce is final, you've got a dog, he's got a dog...I was just thinking..."

"I know what you were thinking and will you please stop it!" Melissa let go of the blinds, lifted her glass and took a sip of her drink. "Connie, I also have a daughter to think about and you know the nightmare I've just gone through with Jerry. The last thing I need in my life right now is another man. You know what Jerry would do if that happened."

Connie sighed. "I thought with the divorce being final...that maybe..."

"Jerry's never gonna leave me alone. Divorce or no divorce, we have a daughter together and until she grows up, that will always be his leverage over me, and he knows it."

"What leverage could that bastard possibly have over you? Melissa, with all you've gone through with your health problems... you are a living miracle and you deserve to be happy. Don't let that jackass stop you from living your life!"

"I wish it was that easy, but you know Jerry."

"Unfortunately, we all know Jerry. At least meet Grant and Charley. You will like them, I promise. Will you at least do that for me? Please?"

~

AFTER OUR DINNER with Connie and Wilson, I had stopped at Walmart and loaded up the truck with groceries and supplies, so when the sun came up the next morning, I rolled out of bed and cooked us some breakfast.

I was sipping coffee on my back deck when Charley and I saw my neighbor's dog for the first time. Actually, Charley spotted her first. When he saw her, he jumped to his feet and started wagging his tail.

"She's kinda cute, huh?" I said.

He turned around and looked at me. "Woof."

"Why don't you go introduce yourself?"

Surprisingly, Charley didn't take off running like I thought he would. Instead, he just plopped down and watched her every move through the posts of the deck railing.

A few hours later, after I had digested my breakfast, I decided to go for my first run on my new beach. After my run, Charley and I jumped in the ocean, splashing and playing together for a while.

On our way back to the beach house, walking on the wooden pathway over the dune, we ran into our new neighbors for the first time.

"Hi, I'm Melissa. You must be Grant and Charley," she said, smiling holding out her hand. "Welcome, neighbor."

"Hi," I said returning her smile, reaching for her hand. When our fingers touched, a cold chill shot through my body. Like electricity, it raced from my head all the way down to my toes. I wasn't sure, but I think it happened to her as well, because she gasped and jerked her hand away.

We both stood there staring at each other in awkward silence, not knowing what to say. Charley finally broke the silence when he barked, walked up to her and lifted his paw.

She instantly started laughing and dropped to her knees. "It's nice to meet you, Charley," she said, shaking his paw, "This is Donna."

Donna slowly walked up to Charley and sniffed him. He sniffed her back and then turned and looked up at me. "Don't look at me. It's your move, buddy."

He looked back at Donna. "Woof?"

Apparently, that was dog for "Want to go swimming?", because they instantly took off running toward the ocean.

Melissa and I sat down on the edge of the wooden walkway and watched Charley and Donna playing in the surf together.

"How did you know our names?"

Her smile glistened in the sun. I'd never seen teeth that white and perfect before. "Wilson and Connie are my two dearest friends. And

Connie, well she's sort of the town gossip, and she just couldn't wait to tell me all about you."

"Oh yeah? What'd she tell you?"

She was wearing a soft flowing bright yellow sundress and a large floppy hat, that almost covered her face, but I could still see her cheeks flush when I asked that question.

"She told me that you were rich, gorgeous and single."

I grinned. "One out of three ain't bad, I guess. I'm not rich and I own a full-length mirror. I know what I look like. But unfortunately, she was right about the single part. Actually, I'm a widower. My wife was killed in a plane crash two years ago. The money I used to pay for this house was from an insurance settlement."

"Oh Grant, I'm so sorry. That must have been horrible," she said, softly reaching for my hand. The second she touched me, I felt the cold chills, my heart began pounding in my chest and I broke out in a cold sweat.

Once again, she jerked her hand away and stared back at me with wide eyes. She parted her lips to say something, but stopped and turned away. It was obvious that she felt it, too, but it made no sense at all. We'd just met. I knew nothing about this woman, she knew nothing about me and yet...

～

THAT NIGHT I turned and tossed in my new bed for hours. There was nothing wrong with the mattress; my mind was spinning and I couldn't shut it off. Images of Rita, Audrey and Melissa constantly flashed over and over through my mind. Along with the images came deep, gnawing pains of guilt churning in my gut.

I kept asking myself how could I possibly have feelings for another woman this soon? Is that what that was? But if it wasn't...then what in the hell was it?

After lying there for what seemed like hours, I fumbled for my watch on the nightstand and was shocked to see that it was only 2:00

a.m. As quietly as I could, trying not to wake Charley, I slipped out of bed, walked to the kitchen and grabbed a beer out of the fridge.

Listening to the waves lapping on the shore, I sat there on the back deck sipping my beer, staring at the full moon glistening off the water.

He answered on the second ring. "This is Dr. Taylor, what's the emergency?"

"Marshall, there's no emergency. It's Grant."

I heard him take a deep breath and sigh. "Grant? What the hell?" he growled. "You better be missing a limb or something!"

"You told me to call you if I ever needed to talk," I said with a chuckle. "Remember?"

"I meant during office hours, asshole." I heard him fumbling for his glasses. "Is it really 3:30 am?"

"Well actually, it's 4:30 here."

In the background, I heard a woman's voice ask, "Is that Grant? Tell him I said hi."

"Is that Brenda? Whoa!" I said. "Are you two living together? That's great!"

"Shut up! That's none of your damn business," he barked. "What's so important you had to wake me up at this ungodly hour?"

"It's sure nice to hear your voice too, my brother. Get your ass out of bed and fix some coffee. I need to talk to you."

After he got some coffee down him, he came to a little and started acting sort of civil. "You bought a beach house? Are you serious? Where?"

"Saint Augustine, Florida. And I want you guys to come see it."

He put the phone on speaker. "Is it actually on the beach," Brenda asked, "or a few blocks away?"

"I'm sitting on my back deck now. Hang on, I'll hold up the phone, so you can hear the waves crashing on the beach."

"You don't have to rub it in, asshole. We believe you," Marshall said. "Congratulations on your poor choice of how to spend your money. We're very happy for you. Of course, a sane person would have waited and called us tomorrow to tell us about it, but no, not you, you whack job. Can we go back to bed now?"

"Nope! Not yet, there's more, much more. You might want to get another cup of coffee before I tell you about this. It's pretty weird."

I didn't know much about Brenda. I had only met her and talked to her briefly once before, but that night I found out that she was not only Marshall's girlfriend, she was also a psychologist.

When I finished telling them my story, there was no response. "Hello...are you still there?"

"Yeah, we're here. Hang on a second," Marshall said.

He took the phone off of the speaker and covered the mouthpiece with his hand. I could hear muffled talking, but couldn't make out what they were saying.

After a few minutes, he put it back on speaker. "Grant, I'm going to let Brenda take this. She thinks I'm too close to you to give you any constructive advice. I'm not sure I agree with her, but I guess it is more of her area, since she's a head shrinker."

I laughed. "A what?"

"Just ignore him," she said. "He's just an ordinary organist. I am a board certified psychologist."

"An organist?" he yelled.

"Shut up, Marshall. You know what I mean."

I started laughing. "Are you sure you guys aren't married? You kind of sound like an old married couple."

Ignoring my comment, she asked, "Can you describe the feelings in more detail? Was it just an emotion or were there physical symptoms as well?"

"The first time it was just a cold chill that ran through me, but the second time, I actually broke into a cold sweat and my heart started pounding and racing."

The sun was coming up and I could see the wooden walkway where we were sitting. "It was beating faster than it does when I'm jogging. What could cause that?"

"Is she pretty?" Marshall asked.

"Yeah, I guess. She has a pretty face, but I couldn't really tell much else. She was wearing this long dress and a big hat, but she's got great teeth."

I heard them laughing. "What I meant was...when she smiled, I saw her teeth. They were perfect...super white and...well, perfectly aligned."

"Grant," Marshal said laughing, "you've been out of the game a while. Normal people call that a great smile."

"So, you actually weren't attracted to her physically," Brenda said. "You have no real idea what she looks like under the dress and hat, other than her pretty face and smile."

"Yes, and that's the part I don't understand. If she was this super hot babe and I went nuts when she touched me, I'd get it. Male hormones would explain that, but this was not like that. It wasn't sexual. It was...almost spiritual."

Marshal snickered.

"What's so funny?" I asked.

"Grant, I love you, but come on...spiritual? You're making way too much of this. The touch of another woman has got you all fired up. That's all there is to it! I've known you since you were three years old. When, in your entire life, have you ever been physically touched that way by another woman, except Rita?"

I thought for a moment. "What about Betty Dockins?"

"What about her?"

"She did more than touch me."

"Grant, you were nine years old. That doesn't count."

"Of course it counts, she kissed me!"

"No, she didn't."

Yes, she did!"

"Where?"

"In the park."

"No, dumbass, on the cheek or on the lips?"

"Lips. Twice!"

"Well, that little slut! But it still doesn't count."

"Yes it does!"

"No, it doesn't!"

"Yes, it does!"

"No, it doesn't!"

"Boys, boys!" Brenda yelled. "Am I going to have to go get my belt?"

That got us all laughing pretty hard.

"Grant, I'm going to have to go with Marshall on this. He's told me about your lifelong devotion to Rita. And honestly, your lack of intimacy with other women is something that you should take under consideration. I *will* tell you that the intensity of these feelings you've described, along with the physical symptoms, is quite unique to me as a therapist. I'm not sure what to make of them.

I have a few weeks of vacation time coming and if I can force Marshall to take some time off, I'd love to come see you and your new beach house. We can talk more about this when we get there, but in the mean time, I have two suggestions for you."

"That would be great!" I said. "You'll love this place. It's probably a bit too laid back for Marshall, but I think you'll love it. So, what are your suggestions?"

"Grant, I think it's important for you to get to know Melissa better. Find out as much as you can about her and see if the feelings continue when she touches you. I also think it would be a good idea for you to start seeing a psychologist on a regular basis. I know you may not want to do this, but you've been through a tremendous tragedy...more than most people go through in a lifetime. I wanted to talk to you about this before, but I didn't know you that well and Marshall talked me out of it. But remember, you called us and woke us up this morning. You knew you needed help and I'm so glad you did. Sometimes opening up to a stranger, especially a trained psychologist, can help you solve problems you didn't even know you had. Will you do this for me?"

She was right and I knew it. I couldn't do this alone anymore. "Sure, I'll do it, but where do I find a psychologist here?"

"I'm not sure," she said. "You could call the local hospital or even try to google psychologist."

After I hung up with Marshall and Brenda I felt better, so I crawled back in bed next to Charley and slept until he woke up a few hours later. While he was taking care of his business around the back yard, I called the local hospital and they gave me three numbers of psychologists to call. Two of them were located in Jacksonville, about an hour drive away, but one was local, so I gave him a call and scheduled an appointment for the following week.

## 7

# DOCTORS ORDERS

Sitting in the dark on her back deck, Melissa watched Grant walk out of his house and lean against his rail. She thought about turning on her overhead deck light so he could see her there, but changed her mind and just sat there watching him for hours, hidden in the dark shadows.

Apparently, he couldn't sleep, either. She wondered if the reason was that he felt it too, that jolt or spark or...whatever it was.

She let her mind drift, remembering the moment their fingers first touched. It was like electricity and had actually shocked her. And then when he looked at her, it happened again–just from looking into his eyes.

"What are you, twelve?" she whispered to herself. "You're a grown woman, Melissa, this is not high school."

For the past two years, one of the unexpected benefits of her surgery had been sound un-interrupted sleep. She had fought with insomnia most of her adult life. She wasn't sure if it was because of her move to the beach house and the sounds of the crashing waves, or if it was the benefits of finally having good health, but whatever it was, ever since the surgery, she'd been able to sleep like a log...until tonight.

However, in the two years she'd lived in the beach house, it was the first time she had wanted the sounds of the crashing waves to be a little quieter. Eavesdropping was something that she would normally never do, but tonight she just couldn't help herself. Especially when she heard her name echo across the way from Grant's deck.

She had no idea who he was talking to on the phone, but it had to have been a very close friend, because it was 4:30 in the morning and he was actually laughing and talking, while he paced back-and-forth on the deck.

Finally after straining to hear his conversation, he stopped pacing and leaned against the rail at a close point to her deck where she was sitting.

"The first time it was just a cold chill that ran through me," she heard him say, "but the second time, I actually broke into a cold sweat and my heart started racing and pounding. It was beating faster than it does when I'm jogging. What could cause it to do that?"

That's when she knew for sure. He had felt it, too. But now the question was...what should she do about it?

∾

ALTHOUGH BRENDA RECOMMENDED that I only see a board-certified psychologist, it would've been an hour round-trip drive to Jacksonville, and I really didn't want to spend that much time driving on I-95 every week, so I decided on Dr. Jeremiah Ashford Hollingsworth.

His office was located in one of the old historic buildings in Saint Augustine, only a few miles from my house. When I opened the door, there wasn't a receptionist there to greet me as I'd expected. It was a small waiting room with comfortable chairs and magazines racks a few tables. In the corner, there was a small TV mounted near the ceiling. Staring up at it was a little girl, maybe six or seven years old, wearing shiny black patent leather shoes, white knee socks and a red lace covered frilly dress.

"Hello," she said, smiling, "I'm Molly."

"Hi, Molly. I'm Grant."

She slid off her chair, walked over to me and held out her hand. "It's nice to meet you, Mr. Grant."

I shook her tiny hand and smiled. "It's really nice to meet you too, Molly. Are you waiting to see the doctor?"

She frowned. "No, he's my daddy. I have to wait here until he gets off work."

"That doesn't sound like much fun. Where's your mother?"

She started nervously rocking her legs under her chair and stared up at the TV. "She's at her house, but I have to stay with Daddy for this month."

Before I could ask her more, the door opened. "Are you Grant Nash?"

"Yes," I said, following him into his office.

After I had made the appointment with Dr. Hollingsworth, I tried to Google him, but there wasn't much about him on the net. That bothered me a little, but I figured that maybe he was just old school and hadn't discovered the Internet yet.

I did google the other psychologist that had been recommended to me. I read a few comments from their patients trying to find out what I've gotten myself into. Almost all of the other doctor's patients' comments were positive, all of them talking about the instant bond and feelings of trust they had developed with their therapist.

Unfortunately, that didn't happen between me and Dr. Hollingsworth. Instead of developing an instant bond, I developed an instant dislike of the pompous ass. But I had promised Brenda that I would open up and tell him everything. So, over the next few weeks, I spilled my guts.

As the sessions went on over the next three weeks, I tried to accept what he was saying, but it got harder and harder, because his advice didn't seem right. I didn't argue with him. I assumed it was because what he was telling me wasn't what I wanted to hear, but deep down I felt it was wrong.

My sessions were on Tuesdays and Thursdays at 2:30. And every time I opened the door, Molly was there, staring up at the television. I always secretly brought her something: a candy bar, a cookie, a cupcake. As a result, we had become great friends in the last three weeks. Of course, she had to hide it from Daddy dearest–he didn't allow her to eat sweets. When she told me that, I didn't say it but I thought it, "What an asshole!"

~

FOLLOWING BRENDA'S OTHER ADVICE, I had made a point of trying to get to know Melissa a little better, but she had not made that easy. Three times I had invited her over for dinner, but she always politely rejected my offers, claiming to have other plans. We had talked a few times when we'd run into each other on the beach or when I would see her and Donna out on their deck. And she actually came over one afternoon to eat a hamburger with me, but she seemed in a hurry to leave. But in all of our encounters, we had never touched–not one time, so I had no idea if the feelings were still there. All I did know was when she was on my deck that day eating her hamburger...she looked me in the eyes, my heart fluttered in my chest and it took a few beats to return to normal, so I assumed those feelings were still there.

~

IT WAS A TUESDAY, my seventh session with Dr. Hollingsworth. I had finished my story at the last session, explaining my unusual attraction to Melissa. It had been a very emotional session for me. I had gone into detail of the gnawing guilt I was feeling deep inside me, because of the feelings I was developing for Melissa.

He had been unusually quiet during our last session. He seemed to actually be listening carefully to what I was saying. His head was up out of his yellow pad and he was staring at me as I talked. For the past five sessions when he wasn't talking, he was looking down, constantly writing. But during the sixth session, I had his full attention.

And when our time was up, he only said, "See you Tuesday."

When I walked in Tuesday, of course Molly was there, but Dr.

Hollingsworth was standing in the lobby waiting for me, so I couldn't give her the cookies.

When we sat down, he immediately started talking to me, but I couldn't get the image of poor little Molly out of my head. She looked a little upset and I was wondering what had happened. I kept thinking, *what kind of jackass would make his six or seven-year-old daughter sit in a waiting room all day, dressed up like she's going to church, all alone, watching TV, while he was seeing patients?* It was a beautiful day. She should be outside playing with her friends. What was she doing in that waiting room?

"Mr. Nash? I can't help you if you're not going to listen to me."

I looked up. He was glaring at me. "Sorry, Doc. I must have drifted away there."

"Its 'DOCTOR' HOLLINGSWORTH!" he shouted. NEVER CALL ME 'DOC' AGAIN!"

I gritted my teeth. It was all I could do not to come out of my chair and kick his pompous ass, but I knew Molly was in the lobby and even though he deserved to get his ass whipped, she was too young to understand that her daddy was a certified prick. I certainly didn't need a lawsuit, so I bit my lip and took a deep breath instead. "Sorry, *DOCTOR*," I said, "I didn't mean to offend you. My best friend is a doctor and I call him Doc all the time. It's meant as a term of endearment, not disrespect."

His exaggerated erect posture was one more thing I hated about the guy. And then there were his clothes.

One of the things I loved about Florida were the casual, friendly people who lived there. Flip flops, tee shirts and shorts seemed to be the state approved dress code. When the locals *did* dress up to go out, they wore shirts with collars and switched the flip flops for deck shoes, but the shorts remained. If you saw some one wearing long pants, they were either going to a funeral, a wedding, or it was their turn for jury duty. I'm exaggerating a little, but the dress code was very casual in Florida and I loved it.

However, Doctor Jeremiah Ashford Hollingsworth came to work every day, wearing $3,000 Armani suits, $1,800 Louis Vuitton shoes,

$500 Ermenegildo Zegna ties and flashed his $70,000 diamond studded gold Rolex or his $150,000 Audemars Piguet watch. Oh yeah, he also drove a new Jaguar.

How did I know this? The pompous ass always worked in *who* he was wearing that day during our session. Saint Augustine was a small town, and I assumed he'd heard that I'd paid cash for the house and was trying to impress me. It didn't.

After adjusting the crease on his pants and making sure his tie was perfectly aligned between the V of his suit jacket, he opened his notebook and looked over the table. "Mr. Nash, after our last session, I have gone back and reviewed all of my notes. I have spent the majority of my time in the last few days reviewing those notes, deliberating your situation, and have come to a conclusion."

I wrinkled my forehead and looked at him. "A conclusion in only six sessions? Of course, you're the expert, but from what I've read, I didn't think there ever were actual conclusions in psychology, just possible suggestions that took place over years of therapy."

His face flushed and his nostrils flared. "WHAT YOU'VE READ?" he shouted. "What did you do, Google psychology and now you think you're some kind of an expert?"

Gritting my teeth again, forcing myself to stay calm, I said, "As a matter of fact, yes, I have Googled psychology several times. Is that against one of your rules?"

He leaned back in his chair, took a breath and forced a smile, "Of course not, Mr. Nash, and you are correct. In most cases, there are no actual psychological conclusions that can be made in only a few sessions. However, your case is different and because of that, I feel I have to make one here. Please keep in mind that what I'm about to tell you is not based on a few Google searches. It's based on my doctorate degree in psychology and many years of practice. With that said, its my professional opinion that you are in a very dangerous and fragile emotional state. I know that you may not see it, but I'm afraid it may be getting close once again to being suicidal.

You are still in the early stages of the deep throes of grief from the loss of your wife and daughter. This will more than likely take you years to get over. These feelings you are having for this other woman are not real; they are simply warning signs of just how damaged you still are. The obvious signs to me are how hard you are trying to ignore those feelings of guilt. You want to ignore them, because part of you naturally wants to move on with your life. You are physically attracted to this woman, I understand that, Mr. Nash, but you are simply not ready yet. Those feelings of guilt are the correct feelings your brain is trying to guide you toward. Listen to them, embrace them."

He leaned forward, looking into my stunned eyes. "I know this isn't what you want to hear, but you have to trust me on this. Mr. Nash, pay very close attention, this is critical. I believe it is imperative that you immediately leave Saint Augustine. I'm talking about now, today. As soon as you leave my office, go home, pack up, drive away and never look back. Break all ties with this woman. It's my professional opinion that leaving and getting away from this woman is the only thing that will save you."

It took me a moment to realize that the session was over and he wanted me to leave, but eventually I got the hint when he stopped talking and began glaring across his desk at me. When I closed the door behind me and walked toward the exit, I was in a slight state of shock.

"Goodbye, Grant." I heard Molly's tiny voice behind me. I was so distracted I had forgotten she was there.

When I turned around, she was giggling and her eyes were sparkling up at me. "I don't believe it. You called me Grant," I said, smiling. "It's about time." For three weeks, I had been trying to get her to call me Grant instead of Mr. Grant and she had finally done it.

I walked over to her and handed her a candy bar. "You better hide this." Then I patted her on her head and walked out the door.

When I made it back to the truck, I didn't drive back to my house. I needed some time to think.

The only part of my 1954 Ford 100 pick up that wasn't original was the custom-made bed cover I'd installed before I left Texas. Locked inside, in the bed, were my golf clubs, so I headed to a driving range. I was angry and needed to hit something.

After sweating through my shirt and shorts, hitting two large buckets of balls, I locked the clubs back in the bed and drove to a Sonic drive in and ordered a giant Coke and a foot long hotdog.

Whacking the two buckets of balls had helped me take away my anger, but I was still utterly confused of what to do next. Was Dr. Hollingsworth right? Was I really still suicidal? How could that be? How could I not see that...or feel that?

My mind was whirling as I ate my hotdog and drank my Coke. I didn't want it to be, but it had to be the truth. Just because he was a pompous, arrogant prick and I didn't like him, it didn't take away the fact that he was an experienced doctor of psychology. What possible reason would he have to tell me something that wasn't true? And who am I to argue with a doctor? I did jump off that boat only one year ago...I did try to kill myself.

The reality of his conclusion was a very hard thing to accept, but I decided I had to do it. My only problem was...Charley.

I knew I probably wouldn't even have to tell him. He would more than likely know. And if he did, there's no way he'd ever agree with what the doctor was suggesting. On the drive back to the house, I decided to try to trick him, to somehow get him into the truck and drive away. I could have our stuff packed up and sent to us later. I just needed to somehow get Charley in the truck.

Before I unlocked the front door, I filled my mind with thoughts of the park. Charley loved going to the park, so I was hoping that if he could actually read minds, he'd think we were going to the park. But when I opened the door, instead of barking and spinning around like he normally did, he flew out the door, between my legs, ran down the staircase and stopped at the curb in front of the house.

"Charley, what the hell are you doing?" I yelled down at him.

As I said that, a taxi turned down our street and stopped in front of the house. When the back doors opened, Marshall and Brenda stepped out.

"Oh my gosh! This is beautiful!" Brenda gasped.

AFTER THEY GOT SETTLED in the guest bedroom, we all took a long walk on the beach. When we got back, I fired up the grill and threw on some steaks while Marshall and Brenda made a salad and opened a bottle of wine. Listening to nature's beautiful music of waves crashing on the beach as the sun went down, we had our dinner on the back deck.

Through out the meal, Marshall didn't say much, but I caught him staring at me several times.

"So what do you think?" I asked him.

"About what?" He said.

I frowned. "About the house."

He looked around. "It's great. Beautiful. But what do *you* think?"

"What?

"Its a simple question," he said. "What do you think about this house?"

"Are you serious? I love it! That's why I bought it!" I said this a bit too loud.

He raised his eyebrows. "Grant, don't forget that I've known you since you were four years old. I can tell when something is wrong with you. If you love this place so much, then why aren't you smiling? From the minute we got here, I could tell something wasn't right, and it has to do with this house. You could barely look at it when Brenda was going on and on about its design and how it was decorated. So...tell me the truth, what do you think about this house?"

I dropped my napkin in my plate, pushed my chair away from the table and stood, leaning against the rail. "Truthfully, I love everything about this house: the design, the furniture, the location, the ocean, but..."

"But what?" Brenda asked.

"I can't stay here. I have to leave." I shrugged and looked down at Brenda. "Doctor's orders."

"DOCTOR'S ORDERS?" They both shouted in stunned unison.

"What doctor?" Marshall asked.

"Dr. Jeremiah Ashford Hollingsworth."

"Is that someone's real name? Sounds like some pompous jackass you'd read about in a trashy romance novel."

I started laughing. "You got the pompous jackass right, but yes, it's his real name. At least that's what it says on his door. He's the psychologist I've been seeing for the last few weeks."

"Wait!" Brenda said. "Back up. Exactly how many sessions have you and Doctor Jackass had?"

"Seven, well actually six. Today wasn't a real session. Today, he just dropped the bomb on me with his conclusion of my case."

"Conclusion?" Brenda's eyes were wide. "Did he actually use the word conclusion?"

"Yes." I said, confused.

Brenda stood up. "Do you have more wine in the kitchen? I'm gonna need much more wine."

When she came back with a new bottle, she sat down, looked at me and took my hand. "Grant, trust me...you're not going anywhere. Now, I want you to tell me, word for word about Doctor Jackass' 'conclusion'."

# 8

# SECOND OPINION

**M**elissa had watched Grant and Charley greet the couple that arrived in the taxicab that afternoon, and had made a point of avoiding them for the rest of the day. She would liked to have met them, because they were probably some of Grant's close friends. But for some reason she couldn't explain she stayed hidden in the house in the dark, watching them through her blinds.

At least the insomnia had gone away and she had been sleeping well, but thoughts of Grant had continued to occupy her mind most of the days.

It had reached the point of frustration. She couldn't even read a book or watch television without her mind drifting back to that moment when she touched his hand, or that tingling feeling she had when he looked at her.

More than once, she had startled Donna out of a sound sleep shaking her head, screaming, "STOP THINKING ABOUT HIM!" It was driving her crazy, because it made absolutely no sense.

It was like an addiction. When she woke up in the morning, she would look in the mirror and promise herself she wouldn't think about him. Then she'd see him walking out his front door, or sitting on his back deck, or headed out for his daily jog on the beach...and her mind would instantly fill with those amazing feelings .

She had no idea why those feelings scared her so much, but they did, and until she figured out why, she intended to stay away from him. Fortunately, her daughter was coming back that morning from her court ordered four-week stay with her ex-husband. She knew that once she got home, her daughter's needs would take over and occupy most of her time and hopefully, her mind.

～

"ON THE BEACH? In the hot sun?" Marshall protested. "Are you trying to kill me?"

Come on, you wimp!" I said, throwing his running shoes at him. "Just a few miles along the shore. You'll love it. What could happen anyway, you're a doctor!"

Charley and I had to stop a few times along the way to let Marshall catch up, to catch his breath and cuss at me, but we eventually made it back to my walkway.

When we stopped, I heard a tiny voice yelling, "MR. GRANT, MR. GRANT!"

I looked around to see Molly and Melissa playing in the sand close to the ocean.

"Molly!" I screamed, holding out my arms as she ran up to me. "What are you doing here?"

"I'm building a sandcastle with Mommy," she said.

I looked at Melissa. "Molly is your daughter?"

Her shocked eyes were wide open. "How do you know Molly?"

"He's my friend," she said, holding my hand, pulling me down the beach toward where Melissa was sitting in the sand. "He gives me candy and cookies, but don't tell Daddy."

Melissa raised her eyes up at me and smiled. "Oh he does, does he?"

I shrugged. "I've been seeing Dr. Hollingsworth. You never told me your last name. I had no idea that he..."

She held up her hand. "That's okay, I understand. Molly was in the lobby, right?"

I nodded. "Yeah."

"That son-of-a-b..." she stopped herself from saying it. "He promised me..."

"Promised you what, Mommy?" Molly asked.

She looked down at her and smiled. "Don't worry, baby, its nothing. Let's finish the sandcastle. We still have to build the moat."

I stood there for a few more moments watching them dig in the sand, but it felt awkward, so I said goodbye, whistled for Charley, who was playing with Donna, and walked back to Marshall, who was sitting on the walkway waiting for me.

"Is that her?" he asked.

"Yes, that's Melissa and her daughter, Molly. And boy, do I have a story to tell you and Brenda about how I know her daughter."

When we walked over the dunes on the wooden walkway, I saw Dr. Hollingsworth glaring down at me from Melissa's back deck.

"Mr. Nash," he yelled down at me. "I see that you didn't heed my professional advice very well."

I looked up, covered my eyes from the sun with my hand and gave him my biggest grin, "Oh, hey there, Doc! Naw, I decided to get a second opinion."

"A second opinion?" His shocked eyes widened as he put his hands on his hips. "From whom?" he shouted down at me.

"From me!" Brenda said from my deck.

Shocked, he spun around and glared at her. "And whom, may I ask are you?"

"I am Dr. Brenda Reed."

He adjusted his tie and jacket, lifted his head arrogantly and glared back at her, "Humpt. And what exactly is your field of specialty, Dr. Reed?"

She smiled, "I am a board-certified doctor of psychology. I am licensed in the state of Texas, the state of California, the state of New York and," she dropped her smile, returning his glare, "in the state of Florida."

I could see his body stiffening twenty feet below. "Dr. Hollingsworth, I think you should know, I had a very long and detailed talk with Mr. Nash about your," she held up her hands making air quotes, *'conclusion'* concerning his case. I totally and unequivocally disagree with your finding. In fact, it's my opinion that your conclusion borders on malpractice."

His forehead instantly broke out in beads of perspiration. He pulled a chair out from the table and plopped down. All the blood had drained from his face and he was ghost white.

"And there is one more thing you need to know about me, Dr. Hollingsworth. I am a member of the Texas State Board of Examiners of Psychologists. I assume you know what that is."

Brenda walked slowly to the edge of the deck. She was only about fifty feet from him. He was glaring across at her, sweating profusely, gasping for air and having trouble breathing.

Brenda smiled at him. "What's wrong, Doc? You don't look so good."

He jumped to his feet and started to walk away.

"Wait, Doc, there's more. I just got off the phone with the Florida Board of Psychology."

When she said that, he stopped, turned around and stared at her. "I have an appointment to meet with them tomorrow. You know how that goes, professional courtesy between peers. They seemed very interested to talk to me. And unless I'm wrong I believe they will also totally and unequivocally disagree with your *conclusion*. Dr. Hollingsworth, if I have anything to do with it, you won't be calling yourself *doctor* much longer."

He yelped like a wounded animal, jumped up, ran into the house and slammed the door behind him.

"What did he tell you?" I heard Melissa's voice say behind me. "What was the conclusion she was talking about?"

I spun around. She was only a few feet behind me, but I had no idea how long she'd been there. "Ahh, well...he told me I needed to move, to get away from you."

She lifted her head and stared at me. "Get away from me? Why would he tell you that?"

I wasn't sure how to explain it. "I didn't know he was your ex-husband and...well...I told him about...this."

I reached out and grabbed her hand. She gasped and jerked her hand back.

"Did you feel that Melissa? I have to know. I felt something. It was like a bolt of electricity. I've felt it every time we've touched. Did you feel it, too?"

She locked eyes with me, then turned away and looked back at Molly playing on the beach, "I'm sorry, Grant, but I have to go talk to Jerry. Will you keep an eye on her for a few minutes? Please?"

Before she walked away, she took my hands in hers, stared up into my eyes and whispered, "Yes...I felt it too."

Watching her walk away, my heart was pounding like a jack-hammer inside my chest.

～

I HAD ORDERED a folding beach shade canopy from Amazon, but had never used it, so I pulled it out of the box and carried it to the beach.

After receiving some serious ribbing from Brenda for our apparent lack of construction skills and a few jokes like *how many doctors and architects does it take to set up a beach tent*, Marshall and I finally got it standing up next to Molly's sandcastle. For almost two hours, Brenda, Marshall and I baked in the sun or hid from it under the shade of the canopy, watching Molly play. Every ten or fifteen minutes, she would want to go jump in the ocean to cool off, so we all took turns taking her, and then carefully re-applying her sunscreen afterwards.

Eventually, we all got hungry, and walked back over the dunes to my house and had lunch around the bar in the kitchen, enjoying the wonderful coolness of the air conditioner.

When I saw Hollingsworth's Jaguar pull away, I called Melissa to tell her that I had Molly with me at my house. She was sound asleep in my lap.

Melissa's voice was soft. "Thank you, Grant. I'm so sorry; I didn't mean for it to take this long, but Jerry was...well, very angry and a little out of control."

"Don't worry about it," I said. "She was no trouble at all. I loved it and I think she had fun, too. Charley and Donna wore her out, she's down for the count."

When I hung up, I lifted Molly up off my lap, cradled her into my arms and walked her next door. When Melissa opened the door, I followed her to Molly's room, laid her down on the bed and tucked her in.

When I turned around, Melissa was grinning with a curious look on her face, her eyebrows were raised and her eyes were wide. "You've done that before."

"Done what?" I asked.

"Tucked in a child."

"Yes...I've done that many times."

"Do you have a child?"

I stared into her eyes, but this time she didn't look away. "I did...her name was Audrey, but she died. Melissa, we have a lot to talk about. I want to know everything about you, and I want you to know everything about me, but that's a long story. It has been one hell of a day and you look exhausted. How about this? Tomorrow, I would like for you and me to spend the day together, just the two of us. I've already talked to Marshall and Brenda, and they said they'd be happy to watch Molly and Donna."

She frowned. "I don't know, Grant."

"Melissa, what is it about me that you are so afraid of? Don't you want to..."

"No, Grant. That's not want I meant at all. It's just that I've never met your friends. I'm not comfortable leaving Molly with someone I've never met. I'm sure they're wonderful people and I know they're your friends, but..."

I smiled down at her. "I completely understand. Can I ask you one more question?"

"Sure. What about?

"Are you absolutely *'can't wait to get into bed'* exhausted, or are you just plain old *it's been a long day* exhausted? Would you be up for a glass of wine on your back deck? I'd love for you to meet my best friend, Dr. Marshall Taylor and his girlfriend, Dr. Brenda Reed."

She lifted her head and looked into my eyes. "Just plain old exhausted. I'd love to meet your friends, but before we do that, there's something you need to know about me first."

I put my arms around her, pulling her close. When our bodies touched, my heart began to race, "And what's that?"

"I don't drink," she said.

I frowned down at her. "What? Well, then forget it," I said, laughing.

"It's not that I don't like to drink. I love wine, but I'm not allowed to drink it anymore."

"Oh," I said. "Are you a recovering alcoholic?"

"No, it's a little more serious than that. A few years ago..." she paused and took a breath, "I had a liver transplant and I can't drink alcohol because of the immunosuppression medication I take daily."

I stood there, holding her in my arms with my mouth open, speechless.

She looked up at me. "Are you okay? I understand if that changes things between us."

I wasn't sure what to say, so I didn't say anything. Instead, I bent down and gently kissed her. When our lips touched...it took my breath away. It felt like I was floating and my entire body started tingling.

When I leaned back, her eyes were wet and tears were rolling down her face, "So...are you a Coke, Pepsi or Dr. Pepper kinda gal?"

～

MELISSA POINTED at the bottle on the table. "Either open that bottle of wine or get off my damn deck and go home!"

"Whoa! Grant, she's kinda of bossy." Marshall said, grinning. "I like her!"

"Me too," Brenda said.

"I'm serious. Just because I don't drink doesn't mean you can't," Melissa pleaded. "My friends drink around me all the time."

I opened the wine and filled Brenda and Marshall's glasses, but filled Melissa's and mine with Diet Coke.

Donna and Charley soon tired of our conversation, curled up together in the corner of the deck and fell asleep. Like I had hoped, Melissa, Brenda and Marshall bonded quickly and it didn't take long before he started telling her embarrassing stories from our childhood.

"They fell down at the finish line?" Melissa asked, giggling.

"Yep! It was the district track meet and the stands were packed. I was right behind him and saw the whole thing." Marshall was laughing so hard he could barely get out the words, "One minute he was running and the next minute, he was flat on his face with his gym shorts at his ankles with his bare white ass shining for the entire student body and everyone else in the stands to see! Including his own mother and father!"

"Ha, ha, ha," I said. "And you call yourself a doctor? You should be ashamed for laughing at a tragic event that could've damaged me psychologically for years. Ok...now, it's my turn." I lifted my hand to my chin and thought for a moment. "What about the time you filled your lunch thermos with your father's vodka, got half the football team drunk, and you and me expelled for three days?"

"You're the one that got us caught," he said, grinning, "You drank most of it and Coach Head saw you staggering down the hall!"

After an hour or so of laughing and hearing way too many of those stories, Melissa excused herself from the table to go check on Molly.

"I really like her."Marshall said.

"Grant, she's beautiful, brilliant," Brenda added, "and the attraction between you two is obvious. I guess I don't see the problem."

"There's really no problem, I like her a lot, but..."

"But what?" Marshall asked, leaning toward me.

I shrugged. "It's got to be more than a physical attraction. I can't explain it, but those feelings I told you about are still there...every time I touch her. Earlier today, I kissed her for the first time, and I honestly thought I was going to faint. I broke into a cold sweat, I got dizzy and light headed. Just from a kiss."

"I did, too!"

We all looked up to see Melissa standing in the doorway. "When you left, I had to go lay down and I cried for twenty minutes." She sat down at the table. "Marshall, I agree with Grant. This has to be more than just a physical attraction. Can you think of any medical reason this is happening?"

"When did it start for you?" he asked.

"The very first time we touched," she replied. "It felt like...like an electric shock."

I looked at her. "Exactly."

"Then it happened again when we made eye contact."

"Really?" I said. "You felt the shock just from eye contact?"

"Yes."

"I only feel it when we touch." I thought for a second, "Wait, that's not true. Once, my heart actually skipped a few beats when you looked at me. What the hell is it, Marshall? What could possibly be causing this?"

He looked over at Brenda and they both started laughing.

"What's so funny?" I asked.

Brenda reached across the table, took one of my hands and took one of Melissa's. "Are you listening to what you two are saying? When you touch, you both feel a bolt of electricity; when you make eye contact, your heart skips a beat and you feel a shock; when you kissed, you broke into a cold sweat, felt dizzy and got light headed, and you," she looked at Melissa, "you had to lay down and couldn't stop crying?"

She let go of our hands, sat back and took a sip of her wine. "As a board-certified doctor of psychology, it's my official medical opinion that what you two are describing is something that is very rare, but does happen. You may have heard of it before."

"What is it?" I asked.

"It's called..." she smiled at us, "...love."

"But we just met!" I said. "We don't even know each other!"

"You didn't let me finish," Brenda said, still smiling wide. "I said it was very rare, but it does happen. It's called...love...at first sight."

Melissa's eyes were sparkling when she looked over at me. "I guess that could explain it. After all, she is a doctor."

I leaned over and kissed her for the second time.

"Whoa!" Marshall yelled. "I think I felt a little jolt!"

# 9

# THE STAINED GLASS

I peeled the back off of the two round sticky back labels, attached one to her blouse and the other one to my tee shirt.

Melissa leaned in, squinted her eyes and read the small round label attached to my shirt. "Old Town Trolley Tours? Are you kidding? We're taking a tour of Saint Augustine? Grant, I grew up here."

"I know you did," I said, grinning, "but I didn't. This way, I can see all the historic sites, I don't have to drive and worry about finding a place to park, and we can jump off and on whenever we want."

Her smiling eyes glistened as she looked up at me. "Hmmm, I'm having second thoughts about you."

"Oh really? Why?"

"Well, if this is a Texas boy's idea of how to spend our first romantic day together...I can't help but wonder what you may have planned for tomorrow?"

"Well, ma'am, don't you worry your pretty little head about that," I said in my deepest Texas drawl, "I got that all planned out, too. I figured tomorrow we could do a little yard work, cuz your flower beds could use a good weedin'."

∽

"ARE YOU SERIOUS?" the uber driver asked. "I'm not sure I can do that. All the routes are supposed to be posted on the app, so they know where I am."

Dr. Hollingsworth rolled his eyes. "How much do you normally make a day doing this?"

"It varies, but usually a couple hundred a day...maybe three on a good day."

Jerry handed him four one hundred dollar bills. "Consider this your lucky day. Sign out of the app. I want to hire you for the day. Now that that's settled, stop talking to me and follow that trolly."

Jerry gritted his teeth when he saw Grant put his arm around Melissa, but his blood boiled when Grant leaned over and kissed her. But what shocked him the most was when Melissa, only a few minutes later, leaned over and kissed him back.

He followed them for over four hours that day. Every time they jumped off the trolly, he would get out of the Uber car, pull his baseball cap down low over his eyes and slowly walk behind them, watching their every move.

Their public display of affection was a disgusting sight, and it was not like her to do that sort of thing. She had dated other men before and this wasn't the first time he'd followed her, but this was the first time he'd seen her act like a common whore in public.

He wasn't sure how he was going to do it, but somehow he had to put an end to this.

The others were easy to bluff, chase away or buy off, but Grant was too smart, apparently rich and wasn't going to be easy to get rid of. But there was no way he was ever going to let it go. He'd worked too many years for it.

If it hadn't been for that damn transplant, it would have all been over by now, but...what were the odds?

Everything had been going exactly as he had planned since college, when he discovered it on their first date.

～

"WHERE?" Jerry asked.

"I promise, it will only take a few minutes," she told him. "I give blood every six weeks."

"Jake told me that you were rich. Why would you want to do that?"

She frowned up at him. "My father is rich, very rich, but not me. Anyway, I don't do it for the money, I do it because I have AB negative blood. It's extremely rare. Only 1% of people in the world have it, and I want to help them if I can."

Jerry was in medical school at that time and not doing very well, barely passing. He knew he wasn't really cut out to be a doctor, but he liked the idea and prestige that came with the title. He didn't have the stomach for anatomy and was repulsed at the sight of blood and surgery, so he decided that if he could somehow skirt through medical school, he would specialize in psychology. He figured he could bullshit his way through his psychology classes, but he knew he was never going to make any real money as a doctor.

He had met Melissa on a blind date as a favor to one of his fraternity brothers. She was part of a double date deal, so he agreed to take her out. When he first saw her, as he had expected, she did nothing for him. She wasn't his type; she was short, maybe five-foot, brown eyes, mousy short brown hair. She had a pretty face, but was just sort of plain. He liked them tall, blonde and leggy, with blue eyes and big boobs.

After he dropped her off at her dorm, he did some research on her father and discovered what she meant by *"very rich"*. He also found out that her father was in his mid-seventies, a widower and Melissa was his only child. He calculated that at the most, in maybe ten years he would be dead and…Melissa would then be the very rich one.

The next day, he began talking to some of his brainier fraternity brothers, who were also medical students, about just how rare A.B. negative blood was.

His plan solidified during one of those conversations. "Honestly, a person with that rare of blood would be wise to bank a lot of it for emergencies," his fraternity brother said. "If they did that they could live a normal life. The only real downside of having blood that rare would be if they ever needed an organ transplant."

"What difference would that make?"

"Come on, Jerry, just think about it. Only 1% of the population has that blood type. The odds of finding a healthy donor organ with that blood type would be astronomical, almost mathematically impossible. But of course, we're only talking about the heart or the liver; you can live on one lung or one kidney."

"But if they developed heart failure or liver failure?"

He shrugged. "I'm afraid that would be a death diagnosis for this blood type. The odds are just too high to find a matching donor."

For the next three years, Jerry dated Melissa exclusively, spending as much time as he could with her. He spent the rest of his time studying just enough to get through medical school, and what little time he had left, he spent doing extensive research on the causes and treatment of fatal liver failure.

∼

AFTER THE TROLLY TOUR, Melissa had me drive her to her favorite place. When I pulled up to the gate, she leaned over me, so the guard could see her. "Hi, Frank!" she called out.

"Well, hey there, Miss Melissa," he said, smiling. "I haven't seen you here in a while."

"Would it be okay if we go to the dining hall? I want to show my friend the glass."

We were at the back entrance to Flagler College, the part of the college that used to be the Hotel Ponce De Leon. And the glass she was talking about was the eighty-seven windows that Louis Tiffany himself had installed there in 1888. They are estimated to be worth today at about two hundred million dollars. We bought a Coke, found a table with a good view, and sat there in awe.

"You are the first person I've ever brought here," she said.

"I'm honored. Why is this place so special to you?"

"My father loved this place and used to bring me here when I was a little girl. And then when I got so very sick, I used to come here to pray and think. This has always been my private place to talk to God. I was here when I got the phone call. It was a miracle; he answered my prayers and told me about it right here." Across the table, I could see the rainbow of colors from the bright sunlit Tiffany glass reflecting in her eyes.

I took her hand. "You almost died, but God answered your prayers with the transplant?"

She looked down. "Yes I came very close, within days, maybe hours, but I wasn't praying for a transplant. Everyone told me that was impossible."

"I'm sorry, but I don't understand. You said God answered your prayers and it was a miracle. Wasn't that miracle the transplant?"

"I thought so at the time, but I'm not so sure of that now. I'm beginning to think there's more to his miracle. I've always had a feeling that there had to be more to it."

I tilted my head and lowered my eyebrows. "Miss Scarlett, frankly...you have lost me. You've got to keep in mind you're talking to a Texas boy. You might want to slow it down just a bit."

The corners of her eyes crinkled when she laughed. "I promise I will explain it to you some day, but in the mean time...are you always going to be this way?"

"What way?"

"Adorable."

"Adorable? Yuck! I was going for ruggedly handsome, suave and sophisticated. But you think I'm adorable...where did I go wrong?"

"You're doing it again," she giggled. "That's enough about me. I'd really like to know more about you. Were you born in Huntsville?"

I spent the next hour telling her about growing up in Huntsville and how I met Rita and Marshall. She was stunned to find out that I was an architect like her father, and even more impressed with Marshall for what he and his father did helping me start my business. She was also amazed when I told her a few of Charley's psychic stories, and burst out laughing when I told her the story about my father and the prison riot.

But when I told her about the plane crash, she crawled in my lap and cried with me as I held her in my arms.

~

WE WENT to dinner at a small little joint that specialized in gourmet hamburgers, then finished the day strolling along the beach.

"I don't know how to say this without it sounding rude or insensitive, but I just can't seem to put you and Jerry together. How did that happen?"

We found a good spot, spread out a blanket and sat down on the beach. "I never knew my mother; she died giving birth to me. My father raised me as best he could, but he was in his mid-fifties when I was born. I loved him and he was a great father, but he was very old-fashioned. I wasn't allowed to wear makeup, lipstick or even fingernail polish." She held up her hand, looked at her manicured nails and smiled. "He never did understand this."

I leaned back on my elbows and laughed. "When Audrey was five, she wrote a letter to Santa asking for the Barbie fingernail polish kit. I thought it was so she could paint her Barbie dolls' nails, but it was for *her* nails. I can still remember how excited she was when she opened that present. When Rita saw what I'd bought her she gave me one of those *'what in the hell were you thinking'* looks. It said right on the box for ten years or older, but I'd missed that. So Rita took her to the kitchen table, painted her nails bright red and hid the kit away. After that, ever so often, she'd pull it out and paint them again for her, but after a few months, she stopped asking for her to do it. It was a short-lived faze."

"I got my first manicure in college," Melissa said, smiling. "Don't get me wrong, he was a great father, just a bit too strict about certain things. I couldn't wear shorts either–only pants or knee-length dresses."

"What about when you went to the beach? You did go to the beach, right?"

She laughed. "Well, Dad would have preferred me to wear one of those long beach dresses you see in the old pictures from the 1930's, but I was allowed to wear bathing suits, but only unflattering one piece suits, never a bikini. As you can imagine, I was the brunt of a lot of jokes in school and wasn't very popular. Connie was my only friend."

"Is that why you went away to college instead of going here?"

"It was the only real argument I ever had with my father. He was a big part of Flagler College; their lead architect for any renovations that may be needed and he was a major benefactor. You're an architect, so I don't have to tell you how much he loved every square inch of that building. When he was there, he was always staring up at the rafters, studying its design. It was almost like a church in a way. So naturally, he had always assumed I would go there. When I told him I wanted to go to UCLA, well..."

I laughed. "I gather he didn't take the news very well."

"That's an understatement. For the first few weeks, he wouldn't even talk to me. Then he threatened to cut me off and not pay for it."

"So what changed his mind?"

Her eyes twinkled in the moonlight. "Wilhelmina Hickenbottom."

"Who is she?"

"Mrs. Hickenbottom was our oldest living resident at that time and also one of the richest. When my mother died giving birth to me, Dad stopped working. He closed his business and fell into a state of deep depression and if it hadn't had been for Wilhelmina, there's no telling what might have happened to both of us."

"What did she do?"

"One day, she knocked on our front door, dramatically barged in, and insisted that my father take over control of the renovation of an historic building she had just purchased. No matter how hard he tried, she wouldn't take no for an answer. I was just an infant, so I don't remember, but everybody tells me that it was that project and Mrs. Hickenbottom's insistence that pulled him out of his depression and saved both of us."

"She sounds like she was a very sweet lady."

Melissa started laughing. "Oh no, she wasn't. She was anything but sweet. She was always dressed like she was on her way to the opera, wearing way too much makeup, with painted on dark black, Groucho Marx looking eyebrows, too much red rouge on her cheeks and bright red lipstick. She rode around town in the back of this beautiful old Silver Shadow Rolls Royce limousine like Norma Desmond, chain-smoking cigarettes at the end of a foot long Tortoise shell cigarette holder. She was bigger than life. The most cantankerous, grouchy, disagreeable woman you would ever meet. And she gave my father absolute hell on that first project and the seven other historic renovations they did together over the years. She was the only person on earth he allowed to call him a moron or an idiot to his face in public, and she did it almost every day. She was the definition of a crotchety old woman, but Dad loved her anyway."

"How did she convince him to let you go to UCLA?"

"I'm not sure exactly what she said to him. Dad and I were still in the non-talking stage when her driver pulled up to our house and helped her walk up to our front door. Apparently, she had heard that I wanted to go away to college and took it on herself to talk some sense into Dad."

"How long did it take?"

"She was there about an hour. The only thing I heard her say before they closed the door was, "I've always known you weren't very bright, but I didn't know you were this stupid!"

"Is she still alive? I'd love to meet her."

"No, she died three years ago at 102. When she left that day, Dad came into my room and apologized. He admitted that he didn't really care that I wasn't going to Flagler College, it was just that he was going to be so lonely there all alone without me. When he said that, it broke my heart. I told him that I would stay and attend Flagler, but he insisted I go to UCLA like I'd planned. He said that it was finally time for him to let me leave the nest and sprout my wings and fly, just as long as I flew back home on every break."

"That's where you met Jerry?"

"Yes, it was in my sophomore year. It was on a blind date."

I raised up and looked at her. "So had you, how can I put this gently...changed your dress code?"

She grinned. "You could say that. When I showed up, I looked like a nun compared to the rest of the girls. Fortunately, I joined a sorority and the girls there took me under their wings and helped me learn how to put on makeup and took me shopping. But, I was still much more conservative than most of the girls on campus and because of that, I didn't date much."

I frowned. "That doesn't make any sense to me. You're beautiful; were the guys there blind or just dumb?"

She tilted her head and smirked. "That's sweet, but to quote you, Mr. Nash, 'I have a full-length mirror and I know what I look like.' Grant, I've never been beautiful. I'm not saying I think I'm ugly, but I'm not beautiful, and I'm okay with that. I'm short, my butts too big, and I'm constantly fighting my weight. If I gain five pounds, I start to resemble a sumo wrestler."

I grinned. "I bet you'd look pretty sexy in one of those thong diaper thingy's they wear."

She shot me a hard look. "Ha, ha, ha, very funny. Anyway, when I saw Jerry for the first time, I couldn't believe my luck. He was so tall and handsome. He drove a sports car and dressed so nice. He just sort of swept me off my feet. Boys like him didn't go out with girls like me."

"I'm sorry, but that sounds crazy. *'Girls like you.'* What does that mean?"

She reached out and took my face in her hands. "Oh Grant. You are so lucky you had Rita all those years in school. You are so naïve to how the real world works."

"Naïve? I'm not naïve!"

She let go of my face and laughed. "I hate to be the one to break it to you, yes you are. It may be changing now, but I don't think so. In high school and college, there are the pretty people and the not so pretty people. And they do not intermingle. So when I got the chance to go out on a date with Jerry..."

"It didn't matter to you that he was an arrogant, pompous asshole?"

She sighed. "He wasn't that way back then, or if he was, he was hiding it. He was charming and sweet."

I grinned at her. "We *are* talking about the same guy I met, right? Dr. Jeremiah Ashford Hollingsworth? Charming and sweet wouldn't be the words I'd choose to describe him."

She lowered her head. "I know, but he *was* back then."

"When did he change?"

"It started a few months after Molly was born. It was like he flipped a switch."

"In what way?"

"This is a little embarrassing to talk to you about, but he had no interest in me sexually any longer. We became more like roommates than husband and wife. He began to start," she made air quotes with her fingers, " 'working late' and would come in later and later. Eventually, he stopped coming home at all, staying away two or three days at a time. He claimed he was attending a doctor's conference or whatever, but I knew what was going on. This is a very small town."

"So that's when you divorced him?"

"No. It took more than that to finally open my eyes."

"What was the final straw?"

She looked down at her hands and nervously rubbed them together. "While I was unconscious, having the transplant surgery, Jerry hired a stranger to watch Molly and was partying in a hotel in Jacksonville with another woman."

"How did you know that?"

"Wilson was there at the same hotel attending a real estate convention. When Connie called him about my transplant, he ran to the front desk to check out and saw Jerry getting on an elevator. The guy at the front desk confirmed to him that it was in fact Dr. Jeremiah Ashford Hollingsworth and his tall blonde wife that had just checked in for the weekend."

"I'm so sorry. And I'm not trying to make excuses for him, but you knew he wasn't being faithful. You said earlier that your transplant was very sudden; he couldn't have known about the surgery. I really don't see the difference in this affair than any of his others, so why was this one so important?"

She wiped her eyes. "No, you're right, he didn't know about the transplant surgery, but he did know of my condition. I only had days, maybe hours to live, but he checked in that hotel for a three-day weekend. Don't you see? He was celebrating. He was celebrating my death."

I opened my mouth, but couldn't think of anything appropriate to say, so I just sat there quietly by her side, listening to the waves crashing on the shore and staring at the rising moon.

"Does Molly know?" I said, finally breaking the silence.

"Does she know what?"

"That her father is..." I caught myself. "I'm sorry, it's none of my business. I just hate that he's still in your life."

"Grant, I have no choice. He's the father of my child and he always will be. Can we please change the subject? I don't want to talk about him anymore."

I put my arm around her. "Sure."

"Were you hurt bad?" she whispered in my ear.

"What?"

"In the crash. How bad were you hurt?"

I sighed and dropped my head. "I've had nightmares about it for years. No one can explain why, I should have die, too, but I didn't even break a bone."

"Grant, you can't think of it that way. It wasn't your time. God has something more for you to do."

My heart skipped in my chest when she said those words. The one thing I hadn't been able to tell her about was my suicide attempt. I wasn't sure why, I guess I was embarrassed that I could've been so foolish, but I had held that back.

"Grant, are you okay? You look strange. What's wrong?"

"I'm okay," I said. "I was just thinking about what you said...about it not being my time and me having more to do. It's a little spooky, because someone else once told me the exact same thing."

# 10

## FALSE POSITIVE

W hen we got back to my house, I cradled Molly up into my arms, walked her back to Melissa's house and tucked her in. After Charley said his goodbyes to Donna and I kissed Melissa good night, Charley and I walked back to my house, I grabbed a beer out of the refrigerator and joined Brenda and Marshall on my back deck.

"Well?" they both said in unison. "How did it go?"

"It was fun," I said, petting Charley's head. "She's great and I like her a lot. She's had an interesting life."

"I can only imagine," Brenda said. "Growing up with a bad liver had to have been hard on a little girl."

"Actually, her liver problem didn't develop until she was an adult. It developed after she gave birth to Molly."

Marshall frowned. "Wait, back up. She never had any signs of liver problems before childbirth?"

"None," I said. "In fact, she was pretty athletic in school. She ran track and played softball.

Brenda leaned forward, resting her elbows on the table. "Were there complications with the delivery that caused the damage to her liver?"

I took a sip of my beer and leaned back in my chair. "I didn't really press her too much on that. She did mention something about having a scare, because she tested positive for hepatitis toward the end of her pregnancy, but after Molly was born, they discovered it was a false positive. Could that have anything to do with it?"

Marshall glanced over at Brenda. "Are you sure she tested negative for hepatitis after the childbirth?"

"Yes, I'm sure of it, because she was afraid she might have passed it on to Molly and was relieved to find out that she didn't have it."

Marshall leaned back in his chair and turned his head toward the ocean, but he was biting his lip. That had always been his tell. "Marshall...what is it? The last time I saw you this serious and biting your lip was when you found that melanoma on my mother's cheek."

He turned in his chair and looked at me. "It's probably nothing. It's just my suspicious nature, I guess, but there are just a few things here that don't add up to me. I'm an internal specialist, it's what I do. And I've got to tell you...the liver is a tough organ and damn hard to kill. It can be done, but it usually takes years and years...not two."

I raised my eyebrows. "What are you saying?"

"Grant, I don't know what I'm saying. All I do know is, other than liver cancer, it is extremely rare for someone's liver to go from healthy to fatal failure in less than two years. And here's the other thing that's bothering me. In today's world of computer testing, it's very unusual to get a false positive for hepatitis. It's difficult to explain, but usually false positives have to do with how the blood is drawn by the practitioner. It can sometimes get contaminated and show elevated levels of potassium, things like that, but not hepatitis. That would be very unusual and rare. And yet it happened to Melissa, who also in a very unusual and rare situation, lost her liver two years later."

"You don't think...Jerry..."

He lifted his beer, took a sip and stared over the table at me. "Well, he is a doctor...sort of. If he did have something to do with it, he would have left a trail. But he's not smart enough to fool me," he smiled. "I'd sure love to get a copy of her medical records. All of them, since she was a little kid through the liver transplant. You think you could talk her into giving me permission to looked at them? Tell her it's for a research project I'm working on."

"Speaking of Dr. Dirtbag," Brenda said, with a smile. "I met with the Florida psychology supervisory board today."

"Oh yeah? What'd they have to say?" I asked.

She shrugged. "Although they were appalled at his so-called conclusion, they didn't think it was sufficient grounds to revoke his medical license. However, it was enough to put him on their watch list. One more screw up and he's done. Apparently, he doesn't have much of a practice, anyway. They had to search for his name. He wasn't even in their top 100. That doesn't surprise me."

"I wonder how he can afford that fancy office, his new Jaguar and all his fancy duds?" I asked.

"With a prick like that," Marshall said, "I'd bet you anything that he's getting all his money from Melissa. Probably alimony or spousal support, or some shit like that. We know he's not making it as a psychologist. What a sleazeball. When I get back to Texas, I'll give O'Bannon a call and see if his father still has that private investigator working for his firm and see what he can dig up on Dr. Dirtbag."

"That's a good idea. Well, hopefully he got the message and he'll stay out of my life," I said. "I'd hate to have to whip his ass, but if I find out he had something to do with trying to hurt Melissa...I'm gonna do a lot more than just kick his ass!"

I looked down at Charley, who was curled around my feet. "He's the best judge of character I've ever met in my life. Hey, Charley, wake up." He jumped up and looked at me, "I want to ask you something. What do you think about Dr. Jeremiah Ashford Hollingsworth?"

He lifted his lip, exposing his teeth. "Grrrrrrrrrr."

We all laughed. "Is he a good guy or a bad guy?"

He shook his head. "Woof, woof, woof. Grrrrrrr!"

One more question. "Would you like to bite him in the ass the next time you see him?"

He looked over at Marshall and Brenda, then back at me and smiled. "Woof."

"Good dog," I said petting his head, "very good dog."

~

FOR THE NEXT FOUR DAYS, I rented a Cadillac Escalade, so the four of us and the two dogs would fit. We drove south all the way to Daytona Beach, and then north all the way to Amelia Island. On the last night of Marshall and Brenda's visit, since they had an early flight out of Jacksonville, we left Charley and Donna with a neighbor, and checked into the Double Tree Hotel at the Jacksonville Airport.

It was the first night Melissa and I had actually spent together. The first night we had ever made love. I must admit I was a little apprehensive. The electricity when we touched had not gone away; it was still there. We both laughed about it, but neither one of us was sure what was going to happen when we had sex. We wondered if all that electric shock might stop our hearts...it didn't.

At first, Melissa was very shy about her body, especially about her scars. But I insisted that I wanted to see every inch of her...kiss every inch of her...and before the night was over...I did.

After that night, our relationship flourished. We spent most of our days and evenings together, but because of Molly, we didn't sleep together. We had sex, but we were very discreet about it, not wanting to confuse her. She was too young to understand.

I made a point of hiding away or taking a long run every other Friday night when Jerry would come to pick up Molly for his weekend with her, and I made sure I was nowhere in sight when he'd drop her off Sunday night. The few times I miscalculated and did run into him, he always gave me his best cold stare. Charley would show him his teeth and give him his best growl, but I always waved and smiled, just to piss him off.

~

EVERYTHING SEEMED to be going great. Charley was head over heels in love with Donna and Molly, and I was getting that way over Melissa. The five of us - Melissa, Molly, Donna, Charley and me - were spending more and more time together and my life, for the first time in years, seemed whole again.

It was early Wednesday morning and Charley and I were heading out for a run on the beach while it was still cool. Jerry's Jaguar was parked in Melissa's driveway. I glanced at my watch to make sure it wasn't Friday, but even if it was, it was way too early for him to be there to pick up Molly.

"What the hell is he doing there?" I said, as I walked over the dunes to the beach.

When I got back from my run, his car was still there. For the next two hours, I kept checking, peeking through my blinds until I saw him drive away. I immediately picked up my cell and called Melissa, but she didn't answer. I left her a message, but she didn't call me back. After an hour, I called her again, left another message, but she didn't return my call.

Two hours later, I tried again. After the fourth try, I walked over and knocked on her door.

"Please go away. I don't want to talk to you," she said behind the door.

I stood there in shock. "What did I do? Why don't you want to talk to me?"

"I'm begging you. Please go away. I can't talk to you right now." I could hear her crying.

"What did that son of a bitch tell you? Why are you crying? What did he say to you?"

"Please, Grant. Just go away."

"Melissa, I thought we had something special together. You know we do. After all you've told me about Jerry. All the things he's done to you...all the times he's lied...why would you believe him now? Please, Melissa, talk to me."

I heard the door latch click. I pushed it open and walked inside. Melissa was sitting on the couch with Donna in her lap. Her eyes were swollen and bright red.

I sat down in the chair across from her. "What's wrong? Please, Melissa, tell me. What is this all about?"

She lifted her eyes and looked at me. "Will you promise to tell me the truth? Swear to God?"

"Of course. I've never lied to you and I never will. I swear to tell you the absolute truth, no matter what you ask me."

Her hands were shaking. "I promise I'll never tell anyone. Please just…just please tell me the truth. I have to know the truth."

"You have to know the truth about what? What are you talking about?"

"Did...did you crash that plane on purpose? Did you kill your wife and child just for the insurance money? Did you really?"

I jumped to my feet. I could feel the blood rushing through my body. I wanted to scream, hit something, but I didn't. Instead, I just stared down at her. "For you to even think that I could do something like that tells me more about you than I want to know. I used to feel sorry for you, because for years you didn't have someone good like me in your life. You had someone dirty and evil. You had Jerry, but now I realize that you deserve each other."

∽

FOR THE NEXT FEW DAYS, I sat in my house, stared out my window and wallowed in self pity. I couldn't get Melissa's question out of my mind. I didn't crash that plane on purpose. I loved Rita and Audrey with all of my heart...but I did just sit there. I didn't try to save them. Why didn't I do something?

For three days, I didn't eat or sleep. I just sat there, asking myself why I didn't do anything. I knew I was treading in dangerous waters that had almost killed me a year earlier, but couldn't seem to help myself.

I wanted to get drunk, but every time I reached for the Jack Daniels, Charley would bite my ankle and growl. Being the coward that I am, I waited until he had to go outside before I poured my first drink. But when he got back, he didn't bark or growl at me, he dropped my cellphone in my lap instead.

~

"Slow down," Brenda said over the phone, "and tell me exactly what she said."

I was trying my best not to sound drunk or cry, but I wasn't doing a very good job. I finally got out the words, *Did you crash that plane and kill Rita and Audrey just for the insurance money?*"

"Oh God, Grant. She actually asked you that?"

"Yeah."

"Where are you?" Marshall asked.

"On my back deck, why?"

"I just wanted to make sure you weren't at some bar somewhere that you had to drive home. You sound a little drunk."

"I'm way passed that."

"Grant, you know alcohol is not going to help the situation," Brenda said. "Do I have to jump on a plane, come down there and kick your ass?"

"Whoa! That doesn't sound very professional coming from a board-certified doctor of psychology," I said, laughing.

"Maybe not, but I will come kick your ass if you fall into that bottle again."

"Ok, ok. I swear, I've only had two Jacks, but I haven't eaten in a few days. I guess it's hit me a little harder than I expected. I promise I won't drink anymore. But what do I do now?"

"Grant, please listen to me, Marshall said, I know you're hurt, pissed and drunk. But you've got to promise me that you won't do anything tonight. Just stagger your drunk ass to bed and go to sleep. Get up tomorrow, eat some breakfast, go for a run and then call me. Brenda and I will talk about this and try to come up with a plan by then – a good one. Trust me, buddy, we're gonna make this asshole pay for this."

# 11

# BLUNT FORCE TRAUMA

T he next day, after my run, I saw Melissa sitting on her back deck. Charley ran up the stairs to say hello, but I didn't stop.

When I got back to my house, I made some lunch and had just settled around my patio table when my doorbell rang. When I opened the door, Brenda was standing there.

"What are you doing here?"

"Well, it's good to see you, too," she said, hugging my neck. "I'm here to put an end to Dr. Dirtbag once and for all, and hopefully try to patch things up between you and Melissa."

After she unpacked, she walked next door and spent almost two hours talking to Melissa.

When she came back, she walked to the refrigerator, pulled out a bottle of wine and popped the cork.

She filled two glasses, took one, and handed me the other. "Are you up for a little heart to heart?"

I followed her to the back deck, opened up the umbrella and settled next to her in the chair under the shade.

"Grant, if I thought for a second you were an alcoholic, I would never have poured you that glass of wine. I may be wrong and I've

only known you for a little over a year now, but you're not an alcoholic." She lifted her glass, took a sip and smiled, "You're an ostrich."

I raise my eyebrows. "A what?"

"An ostrich. They stick their head in the ground to hide. You do the
same thing with alcohol. You get drunk to hide from the things you
don't want to see."

I didn't respond and looked away.

"Grant, I'm not trying to hurt your feelings. I'm trying to help you.
I've wanted to talk to you about this for a long time, but Marshall was
afraid that…" she stopped in mid-sentence.

I looked back at her. "That what?"

"Do you know what everyone at the hospital calls me behind my
back?"

I shrugged. "No, I have no idea."

"Miss Blunt Force," she giggled. "As in Blunt Force Trauma."

I tried not to laugh, but I couldn't. "Why do they call you that?"

"I really don't mind, because it's sort of true. There are a lot of
different theories of how you should practice psychology. Some
doctors believe in babying their patient along, pampering them,
allowing them to slowly recognize their problems, pointing out the
error of their ways. I am not one of those doctors. I have had great
success by forcing my patients to face reality. By removing their
excuses or the shells and barriers they have erected to hide behind.
That's what Marshall was afraid of… 'my technique.'"

"Good lord, I'm not really that sensitive," I said. "Go ahead fire
away, Doc."

She leaned forward and took a deep breath. "One of your brain's
functions is to protect you from pain. If you cut off your arm, it will
immediately turn off the nerve endings so you can't feel it. That's why
a brain hemorrhage is the most painful thing humans will ever experi-
ence, because the brain can't numb itself."

"Ok…so what's this got to do with me, Miss Blunt Force?"

She smiled. "Grant, I've only known you a little over a year. In that
year, you have fallen in to what I would call a clinical state of depression two times, and for the very same reason. You are convinced that

your lack of action is what caused the crash. I know you don't want to, but I think it's time we finally talk about the crash."

I stood up and turned my back on her. "You're right!" I snapped. "I don't want to talk about it."

"Not that sensitive, huh? Ok, no problem. Marshall told me you wouldn't talk to me about it anyway. I guess he's right; you're not ready to face the truth."

I spun around and glared at her. "The truth? I'm not ready to face the truth? What fucking truth have I not faced?"

"Well, if you will stop cussing at me and sit back down, I'll tell you."

I plopped down in the chair and looked at her. "I apologize for my language."

She gently took my hand. "Grant, there's no need to apologize, but I have to tell you...I was pretty fucking offended." She burst out laughing. "You've got to be kidding, I live with Marshall, remember?"

I grinned. "Oh yeah, I forgot about that. What do you see in that trash mouth anyway?"

We laughed for a few minutes and then just sat there quietly, listening to the ocean, sipping our wine.

Finally, she broke the silence. "Are you sure you're okay to talk about the crash?"

"I guess so."

"I've heard you say many times that you froze, that you didn't do anything to prevent the crash, right?"

I dropped my head. "I can't really remember, but I don't think I did anything."

"Are you willing to try an experiment?"

"What kind of an experiment? Where?"

"Right here, now. Please?"

I shrugged. "Okay, sure."

"Does your phone have a stopwatch setting?"

"Yeah, I think so." I opened the app and handed her the phone.

"Ok," she said. "I want you to pretend you are flying the plane. On the count of three, the engine stops. Do what you think you should have done and yell *now* when you've finished the maneuver. Are you ready?"

I lifted my hands to the invisible pretend wheel and extended my feet out to where the pedals would be. "Okay, I'm ready."

"Three, two, one, GO!" she shouted.

I pushed hard on the left pedal while turning the wheel hard left. I also pulled out on the throttle trying to move at approximately the actual speed. "Now!" I yelled when I thought it was done.

"Try it once more," she said.

We did it four times. The average time was 3.3 seconds.

"Now I want you to read this." She handed me a file. It was the final FAA report of my crash. "Flip to the last page."

The last page was the data gathered from four test flights done on a flight simulator. All four tests were done under the same conditions of my crash, by four trained experienced pilots. Two of the pilots currently worked for commercial airlines. All four were unable to pull out and prevent the plane from crashing. Even when they knew ahead of time it was going to happen, they couldn't pull out. There just wasn't enough time. From the time the engine stalled to impact was only 2.8 seconds.

I wiped my eyes and read the report again. "This can't be right. It's seemed a lot longer than that."

"This is from the FAA's measurements and your plane's black box information. It's accurate."

"Really?" I whispered, looking at her. "Thank you."

"Don't thank me. Thank Marshall. He paid to have the simulator tests done. He wanted for you to have proof once and for all. Grant, you didn't freeze. You didn't have time to freeze, you didn't have time to do anything." She hit the stopwatch on my phone and we watched it count to 2.8 seconds. She stared into my eyes. "It wasn't your fault, Grant. Can you accept that now?"

After we had dinner, Brenda left once again, but when she came back she had Melissa with her. When I saw them walk in together, I frowned and turned to walk outside. "Stop! Turn around and sit down!"

"Yes, sir, Miss Blunt Force!" I said, with a salute.

I started to sit on the chair. "Oh no, not there. Sit next to her."

I shrugged and plopped down on the sofa next to Melissa.

"Now take her hand and tell her you're sorry for saying all those awful things you said to her."

"But..."

"No buts! You know you love her. And you know she loves you. You've just had your first fight, so stop all this wounded animal crap and lets get to the bottom of all of this. It's not her fault and you know it. Tell her you're sorry and kiss her. Now!" she yelled.

I kissed her and looked in her eyes. "Do you really think I could have done..."

Melissa stopped me, putting her finger over my lips. "Please don't say it. I'm so sorry. I don't know how I could have ever thought that of you. Please forgive me, but Jerry's always had this power over me. I can't explain it."

Honestly, I was still hurt and angry. I wasn't sure what to think, but she seemed sincere and when I touched her...well, you know.

"Melissa, have you ever talked to a psychologist or a psychiatrist before?" Brenda asked.

She shook her head. "No."

"I didn't think so. You need to understand that this power you're referring to is not uncommon," Brenda said. "Actually, it's very normal between couples. I've seen it many times in my practice. And although you may not think it's explainable, it is. It's logical, but only if you will accept some hard truths about yourself and...Jerry."

Brenda flipped a page of a yellow pad she had placed on the coffee table. "I made some notes on the plane and I hope you don't mind, but I think it's important that I do this with Grant here. If there's any hope for you guys, he needs to hear this, too. I wouldn't normally do it this way, but Jerry crossed the line and has forced my hand. You said you were willing to do anything to fix things between you and Grant, but I need to warn you, this is going to be a little brutal. But I think it's time you finally see the truth about Jerry – the truth that you have not been able to see or accept before." She took Melissa's hand. "If this is going to work, you have to answer these questions truthfully, even if they are painful to answer. Do you promise to answer truthfully?"

Melissa nodded her head. "I promise."

"Ok, the first question is...who has the most personal wealth between you two? I'm talking family inheritance."

"There's no question about that. Jerry's family had much more wealth than my father."

Brenda glanced at me and smiled. "Ok, the next few questions are a little more personal, but very telling. Who is smarter, you or Jerry?"

She dropped her head. "Jerry."

"Who is the most impressive and successful, you or Jerry?"

"Jerry."

"Who is the better looking one, you or Jerry?"

"Jerry."

"Who is the most dependent on the other? I realize you're divorced, but he seems to still be a big influence in your life. So in other words, do you need him in your life or does he need you?"

Melissa looked up at Brenda with tears in her eyes. "I guess I think I still need him."

"I know you don't drink, but I do." Brenda looked at me. "Grant, how about a little Chardonnay while I talk to Melissa?"

I poured Brenda a glass of wine and a Diet Coke for Melissa, then sat back down and listened.

"Melissa, your problem is you haven't let your reality catch up with your thinking."

Melissa took a sip of her drink and frowned. "I don't understand."

"I don't know anything about your past, but I bet I can guess," Brenda said, "You were very shy in high school and didn't date much, if at all. Did you have a date to your senior prom?"

Melissa looked down. "No."

"Don't feel bad, neither did I," she said with a smile. "When you got to college, it didn't change. All the hot guys didn't even look at you. Am I right?"

Melissa frowned.

"Then here comes Jerry in his little red sports car, his long blonde hair, his fancy clothes and he swept you off your feet, right?"

"Yes. He was so handsome."

"You didn't drink at all before you met him, but because he did, so did you. You had never smoked dope before you'd met him, but because he did..."

"I did," Melissa said.

"In fact, anything Jerry wanted, you did. Anything Jerry said, you believed."

"It's like you're reading my mind," Melissa said with wide eyes. "Did you have a Jerry, too?"

"No. My parents were poor. I went to college on scholastic scholarships. But for every rich girl I ever knew...there was always a *Jerry.* "

Melissa frowned. "Jerry was rich, he wasn't interested in my money."

"I know that's what he told you, but that's just one more of his lies. And one more reason that explains his dominance over you."

"Are you saying his parents were not wealthy?"

"That's exactly what I'm saying, but let's talk about that later."

Melissa's mouth was wide open in shock, her eyes filled with tears.

"Please, Melissa, don't get distracted. I need your full attention. Are you listening to me?"

She nodded her head slowly.

"Ok. Listen close, this is important for you to realize. When you first met Jerry, do you know why you were willing to do anything he asked and why you believed anything he said? The real reason you did it?"

Melissa sat quietly for a long time, then finally said, "I was afraid...if I didn't do what he wanted...he would leave me."

"And?" Brenda said. "Tell me the truth."

"And...I didn't think I'd ever find anyone that handsome that would even look at me again."

"So you did whatever it took to keep him."

"Yes, I guess so. I was very insecure back then."

"Back then? Melissa, do you really think you've changed? You are divorced, but you are still letting him control your thinking. In the last few days, Marshall and I have been doing some research, and remember you promised to answer truthfully. Who owns the building his office is located in?"

"I do."

"Who paid to have it remodeled?"

"I did."

"How much rent does Jerry pay you each month?"

She lowered her head. "He doesn't pay me rent."

"Whose name is the new Jaguar financed in?"

"The bank wouldn't finance him, so I..."

"If he is so wealthy, why would the bank turn him down, and why would he need to finance it anyway?"

"All his money is off shore, for income tax reasons..."

"Of course it is. Melissa, are you still with me?"

She was staring out the window with tears rolling down her face.

"Who owns his condo?"

She slowly looked down with understanding. "I do, but he pays me rent...sometimes."

"What was your grade point average in college?"

Melissa thought for a moment. "I think it was around a 3.4."

"It was actually a 3.7. Jerry's was a 2.8. He barely passed medical school and had to beg his way to get his degree in psychology. I talked to his professors. He was a terrible, terrible student."

Brenda stood up, walked to the couch and sat next to Melissa. "In college, you were shy and invisible. Jerry was handsome, flashy, flamboyant and fun. I can see why you may have thought you needed him then and that's okay; you were young. But you need to know that even then, you were the winner and he was the loser. And trust me, he knew that. He's always known that. That's why he's worked so hard all these years to intimidate you and keep you down. That's why he's so afraid of Grant. Because Grant is no loser and he knows it. Melissa, he is completely broke. His parents were never wealthy. His mother taught elementary school and his father was a plumber. They had to mortgage their house to put him through school. And he's never paid them back a cent. You are his golden ticket and he'll do anything to keep you. He took a confidential doctor-patient private and tragic conversation and twisted it to fit his personal needs. He broke doctor-patient privilege, one of the most sacred and protected rights in the medical profession, just to try to break you two up. He is a despicable and desperate man that you need to remove from your life."

Melissa covered her face with her hands and cried. "How can I do that?" she whimpered, "Jerry has shared custody with Molly?"

"I'm not a lawyer, but Marshall has talked to one of Grant's friends, who is a very respected attorney, and if you really want to get Jerry out of your life, these are his recommendations."

"It will be a long process, with several steps. Step one: I believe that if you will go with me today, both of you, and tell the medical board what he told you, I'm confident they will take away his medical license. Step two: you need to change the locks on his office and his condo, then call the bank and tell them you will no longer guarantee the loan on that car. You need to cancel any credit cards he has of yours and close any bank accounts he has signing privileges on as well."

"I can't do that, he'll go ballistic."

"Melissa, I know this may sound drastic and you're right, he will not take this well, but for it to work, you need to break him down to his knees. Unless he has some money hidden somewhere that we couldn't find, if you cancel his credit cards and close your joint accounts, he will only have a few thousand left in his personal account and that won't last long. Once that's gone, he'll be completely broke. That's when you do the final step and have your attorney offer him some cash with a few conditions. Number one: he must agree to pack up and leave town forever. Number two: he must agree to sign papers giving you non-contestable sole custody of Molly."

Melissa wiped her eyes with her sleeve and leaned back. "He's not a monster, he'll never sign that. He may have been a terrible husband, but he loves Molly...he's her father!"

"I hope you're right. I hope he refuses to sign the papers and take the money. I hope he proves us all wrong. If that happens, then you can decide what to do at that time."

"But Melissa," Brenda paused, took her hand and stared into her swollen, red wet eyes, "if he does take the money and signs the custody papers...that should prove to you beyond a shadow of any doubt that he's no good and is only after your money. I know you don't want to do this, but it's the only way to tell if he's any good, or if he's nothing but a leech. And if he is, you have to remove him permanently from your life, and Molly's life, especially Molly's, for her own good. And the only way to get rid of a leech is to smother its head."

# 12

# LOVE IS BLIND

B y the time the police arrived, the no longer "Doctor" Jeremiah Ashford Hollingsworth was lying on his back in a pool of blood behind my truck. He was bleeding profusely from three places: his left eye, his nose and his rapidly swelling upper lip. And although I had caused all of the damage, I wasn't in fear of being arrested because I hadn't started the fight, but I damn sure ended it. Fortunately, there were at least twenty or so people standing around me, in their front yards or in the street, that had witnessed the entire spectacle.

I am not a violent man. I've only had two or three fistfights in my entire life. My father taught me to avoid physical confrontation if at all possible, but if it came down to it and you had to fight...fight to win and fight dirty!

Jerry started his assault by crashing through the front security gate. Melissa had removed his name from her visitors list. It was the security guard who had called the cops.

He wasn't driving his shiny new Jaguar, he was driving an old rusty Chevy pickup truck and he let the entire neighborhood know why when he screeched into Melissa's driveway and ran up her stairs, yelling at the top of his lungs. "THE BANK REPOSSESSED MY JAG, YOU BITCH!!"

Melissa was at my house. I told her to stay inside, then I opened my door and stepped out onto my front deck.

"She's not there!" I yelled.

He glared across the yard at me. "Where the hell is she?"

By this time, the security guard had showed up, and some of the neighbors were opening their doors and watching from their decks.

"Jerry, she doesn't want to see you or talk to you."

"MELISSA!" he screamed, "GET YOUR ASS OUT HERE! NOW!"

I walked down my steps and jogged across the yard to Melissa's driveway where he was parked. "I have a card here she wanted me to give you." I held it up so he could see it. "It's her new attorney's card. You'll have to go through him from now on to communicate with her."

I stuck the card under the windshield wiper, turned and walked back to my house. I had just stepped onto my driveway when he grabbed my shoulder, spinning me around.

"Jerry, I'm warning you. Get off my property. Melissa doesn't want to see or talk to you. Just get back in the car and leave. Call her lawyer."

"Or what?" he said, defiantly. What are you going to do to stop me from walking up those stairs?"

I smiled. "Take one step and I'll show you."

"Please, Dr. Hollingsworth, you need to leave before the police arrive. You broke through the gate. I had to call them."

"You called the cops?" Jerry turned around, facing the young security guard. "You little bastard!"

He raised his arm to swing at the guard, but I grabbed his wrist, stopping him. By this time, there was quite a crowd gathered, and that's when Jerry made his big mistake. He jerked around and swung at me, but he missed.

I ducked his swing and countered with a left jab to his left eye, a right jab to his jaw, then stepped back and gave him all I had with a right cross to his nose. He dropped like a sack of potatoes, bleeding on my driveway like a stuck pig.

Jerry played the poor victim well, moaning loudly while they loaded him onto the ambulance gurney, but that quickly changed when they handcuffed him to the gurney and the police officer began to read him his rights.

"You are arresting me?" he shouted. "I'm the one who was assaulted and I want to press charges against him! I know my rights! Arrest this man!"

"Put a cork in it, Doc," the cop said, with a slight smile. "Everyone here told me you took the first swing. Your only problem is that he swung back and kicked your ass all over the driveway. So shut the fuck up. You better hope he doesn't want to file any charges against you."

∾

I *DID* FILE CHARGES, but only to keep him in jail long enough for him to meet with Melissa's lawyer. I told him that if he would at least have that meeting, no matter what he decided to do, I would drop the charges.

At that meeting, he was offered a one million, seven hundred thousand dollar check with only three conditions. Number one, he would sign papers giving Melissa full custody of Molly, and number two, he would leave the state of Florida permanently, only to return for two yearly supervised visits with his daughter. Finally, number three, he also had to relinquish any future alimony suits for financial compensation from Melissa.

Sadly, he didn't even think about it. He signed the papers immediately and the check cleared Melissa's bank the next day.

∾

MELISSA TOOK the news harder than I had expected. She locked herself away in her house for the next few days and didn't seem to want to talk when I called her.

I called Brenda and Marshall to talk about it. "It's going to take her some time to process this," Brenda said over the phone. "Give her a little space."

I sighed. "I'm trying, but I guess I don't understand the problem. I thought she'd be celebrating to be rid of that bastard, but the second he took off, she started backing away from me. I don't get it."

"Grant, have you ever heard the old saying, 'love is blind'?"

I laughed. "You must think I'm a complete hick or something. Sure, I've heard that saying before."

"Well, you are a bit of a hick," she snickered. "The clinical word for that is denial. We have forced Melissa to face the truth of that denial, and that is not an easy thing to accept. She's known the truth all along, but she has always been able to deflect it or simply ignore it until now. But when you can no longer hide...the truth can be very brutal and difficult to deal with. It can make you question everything you've ever believed. That's what she's going through now. She's a smart girl, she'll get through it. Just give her some space and time."

"Grant," Marshall yelled over the speaker, "next time you see her, tell her thanks for sending me the release forms for her medical records. I ordered them today. Her case still intrigues me. I can't wait to get her files and see what's in there."

∿

ONE OF THE things I hadn't done since the plane crash was sit behind a drafting table and draw. I'm not sure why, I just had somehow lost the desire. The truth was I hadn't even set up a design station in my new house. But when I got up the next morning, I suddenly needed to draw. I had no inspirations flashing in my head, no buildings or houses, nothing in particular. I just needed to hold a pencil in my hand again and see what happened. After a quick search of the house, I realized I didn't even have a number 3 pencil, so I loaded Charley in the truck and headed north to Jacksonville in search of an architectural supply store.

At the store, I bought a small drafting table, a comfortable stool with a back rest, the best mechanical pencil I could find and a few other supplies. After I loaded the drafting table and the stool in my truck, I walked back inside the store to get the rest of my supplies and

Charley. He was sitting by a computer workstation in the corner. I motioned for him to come, but he just sat there. When I walked up to him, he turned and looked at the computer.

"Yes, it's a computer, like the one I had in my office. I see it. Now let's go."

"Arrr, arrr, arrr," he said, touching the seat of the chair with his nose.

"What is it?" I stared down at him. "You like this chair better than the one I bought?"

He lifted his lip. "Gurrrr."

"You want me to sit down?"

"Woof!" he smiled and wagged his tail.

I knew better than to argue with him, so I sat down behind the computer and moved the mouse. The screen came to life displaying AutoCAD. It was the same computer aided design software I used in my office, but it looked slightly different.

The salesman walked up. "That's the latest version, but so far, no one can figure out what the new upgrades are."

It took me a few minutes, but eventually I found the changes and began pointing them out to the salesman. As I explained the changes to the salesman and showed him examples of how they worked and would actually improve a working design process, a crowd of customers began to grow behind us. Then my expanding audience began asking me questions about the AutoCAD software program and some specific architecture questions.

I was getting frustrated. I hadn't planned on teaching a class that day. All I wanted to do was get back home, set up my table and do some drawing.

I looked down at Charley and frowned, but he was loving it. He smiled up at me and wagged his tail. Something was up and I knew better than to argue with him. So I turned around and continued answering questions, giving graphic design examples on the large computer monitor.

This went on for almost an hour. When it was finally over, the owner walked up and handed me his card. "Mr. Nash, I really appreciate what you did there. You helped finally convince this old buzzard to convert his office to the new upgrade of AutoCAD." He pointed to an older man standing to his right.

I shook the man's hand. "I'm Grant Nash, nice to meet you. So I take it you haven't been an AutoCAD fan in the past?"

"I'm Les Patterson, call me Les. I'm sort of old school. I'm the only one in my firm that still does it by hand." He handed me his card. "Who are you with?"

I took his card and smiled. "No one at the moment. I had a small one-man shop in Texas, but closed that a few years ago, and moved to Saint Augustine. Actually, I'm not licensed in Florida."

He raised his eyebrows. "What's your name and number?"

I gave it to him and said goodbye. Then I loaded Charley in the truck and drove home.

That night, Melissa and Molly came over for the first time in almost a week and I grilled us steaks on the back deck. After dinner, Molly was sleepy, so I carried her back to her house and tucked her in. I opened two Diet Cokes, filled our glasses and we settled on her couch.

"Have you ever heard of someone called Lester Patterson?" I asked her.

She lifted her eyes above her glass as she sipped. "An older man, maybe 60's, tall with thick gray hair?"

"Yeah, that's him. Do you know him?"

"Yes, I've known him my whole life," she said with a smile. "He was one of my father's good friends. What about him?"

"I met him today in Jacksonville. He gave me his card." I reached into my pocket and pulled it out. "Is this a pretty big firm?"

"One of the biggest in Florida, maybe *THE* biggest by now. He was one of my dad's fishing buddies. I've known him since I was about twelve. I don't know him that well, but he was always very nice to me. Are you thinking about going back to work?"

"I don't know. I'm not really looking to go back to work, but I do miss drawing and designing. That's where I met Mr. Patterson. I drove up to Jacksonville today and bought a drafting table. I thought that would give me something to do while..."

"While what?"

"Ah, well…" I stammered, "While I wait for you to get over this Jerry thing."

"What Jerry thing?" She narrowed her eyes and glared at me.

I shrugged. "Melissa, please don't make me say it. You know what I'm talking about."

She stood up and put her hands on her hips. "Are you talking about what you and Brenda forced me to do? The thing that made Jerry do what he did? Is that the *'Jerry thing'* you are waiting for me to get over?"

I tilted my head and wrinkled my brow. "Excuse me? You blame Brenda and me for what your sorry ass ex-husband did?"

"What choice did he have? You forced me to close all of his bank accounts and take away his car. He had to sign the papers and take the money. He had no other choice. He was broke. He's not a monster!"

I stood and faced her. "Seriously? That's what you think, after all of this? After all we've gone through, that's what you've convinced yourself to believe? First of all, it wasn't his money in those bank accounts, it was yours! And they took away that car because he couldn't afford to pay for the damn thing and you know it. No, no he's not a monster, he's just a selfish gold digging asshole! Melissa, I was there; he didn't even think about it for a second. He would have signed anything to get his hands on that check. He's never cared about you or Molly! All he's ever cared about was your money! He's a worthless piece of shit! Why can't you see that?"

Her tear filled, bright red eyes shot daggers at me as she rushed out of the room. I stood there, furious in shocked silence trying to decide what to do next. I knew there was nothing I could do or say that would make any difference, so I walked out, slamming the door extra hard behind me when I left.

The next morning, my doorbell rang at 7:00 a.m. When I opened the door, Melissa was standing there.

I was a little shocked to see her, "Hey," I said smiling, "good morning. Come in."

She smiled. "No thanks, I just dropped by to ask you a favor."

"Ah, sure. What do you need?"

"I was going to ask you last night before..." she dropped her head and looked down.

"Melissa, I'm sorry. I shouldn't have said all that."

"No, Grant," she held up her hand, interrupting me, "you're right. What Jerry did had nothing to do with you. It's just so hard for me to believe he would just walk away from his daughter so easily, just for money."

"Hey," I reached out and touched her cheek, "I understand. Let's just forget about last night, okay? So, what's the favor? You need me to cut your grass, wash your windows, paint your house?" I said, grinning.

Her eyes sparkled for the first time that morning. "Well, now that you mention it, my windows could use a good scrubbing, but that's not the favor I was going to ask you. Molly and I are going away for a few weeks to visit my aunt in Savannah. She's allergic to dogs and I was wondering if you could look after Donna while I was gone?"

I felt Charley's wagging tail banging against my leg the second she said it. "Woof, woof," he said, smiling up at us.

"Sure, Charley and I would love to look after her. Is your aunt sick or something? This is sort of a sudden trip, isn't it?"

"No, my aunt is fine. In fact, she's only about ten years older than me. My grandfather's last wife was only twenty-one. It's a long story I'll tell you about someday, but it was quite the scandal. Anyway, she was my father's half sister and much younger than him. She is my only living blood relative. I'm going there to have her sign some papers."

"What kind of papers?" I asked.

She shrugged. "It's something my new lawyer has been trying to get me to do for a few months, but I kept putting it off. It's part of my will. Although I'm doing well, because I'm a transplant recipient, you just never know. Currently, my will states that if I die, all my assets would be transferred into a family trust for Molly...and the executor of the trust would be her blood relative. Right now, that blood relative is Jerry. I need to specifically select someone else to be the executor in front of Jerry. Actually, it could be anyone, but because there's so much family money involved, my lawyer believes it should only be a direct blood relative. And that's why I'm going there now, to have her sign the papers as Molly's executor."

My first instinct was to ask her if Jerry knew that if she died before she did this, that he would be in control of all her money? But I bit my lip and said nothing.

"Grant, after you left last night, I couldn't sleep. I thought about what you said over and over. And then I asked myself, what would happen to Molly if something happened to me? Would Jerry really use her money to make sure her future life was secure? Or would he waste it like he's wasted mine? And I had my answer."

Then she stepped forward, put her arms around my neck and kissed me. "I'm not sure why you showed up in my life, but I thank God you did. Please forgive me for being so foolish about so many things. I really am trying."

When she kissed me again, my heart started pounding in my chest and I felt the exact same electricity racing through me I had felt on the first day she had touched me.

As Charley, Donna and I watched them drive away on my front deck, I started laughing.

I looked down at Charley. "What is it about that woman? How can someone frustrate and infuriate me so much I want to break up furniture...and then almost stop my heart...with just one kiss?"

# 13

## BEVERLY BEACH

It was one of those damp, gray, foggy mornings. The haze was so dense I couldn't see the beach or even the ocean from my back deck. I was concerned about Melissa driving through this low hanging soup and tried my best to get her to wait until it lifted, but she insisted on leaving, concerned about making it to Savannah in time to have lunch with her aunt. She could be so stubborn sometimes. One more item on that list that infuriated me about her.

I looked at Charley and Donna, who were snuggled together, laying side by side on the deck. "What do you think Charley? Is she gonna be okay?"

He lifted his head and looked up at me. "Woof."

"Are you sure? This fog looks pretty bad."

"Woof, woof," he said, wagging his tail. Then he laid his head back down next to Donna. I relaxed a little after that.

When I finished my coffee, I walked into my home office and started opening up the box my new drafting table was in. When I finally got the parts unwrapped and out of the box, the pieces were scattered around the room, taking up most of the floor space. Charley and Donna were watching me from the doorway. They were both smiling and wagging their tails.

"What's so funny? You guys don't think I can do this, do you?"

It took me three hours and two beers, but I eventually got it together. Fortunately, the stool was already assembled, so after attaching and plugging in the boom arm lamp, I taped a sheet of paper to the slanted desk top and started sketching. It felt good.

I started with a small rough sketch of my new beach house. Then I gradually added more and more detail. Before I realized it, three hours passed by. When I finally stood up, both of my knees cracked loud from sitting there in one position so long, but I had loved every minute of it.

I pulled back the tape and held up my drawing. "What do you think?"

"Woof, woof, woof," Charley barked, smiling, spinning around in a circle.

"I agree. It's not bad. I guess I've still got it."

The fog had finally lifted, so I fed Donna and Charley and then we all took a short run on the beach. When we got back, my message light was blinking on my home phone. I had two messages. I assumed they weren't important, probably a salesman or something, because only a few people had that number and all my friends knew to call me on my cell, so I didn't listen to the messages. Instead, I grabbed a Diet Coke out of the refrigerator and plopped down in a chair under the umbrella on my back deck. The second I got settled, the phone rang again. I didn't get up to answer it, but listened to the message.

"Mr. Nash, this is Les Patterson. You are a hard man to get a hold of. I need to talk to you. I don't mean to be so persistent, I realize I've left you two messages already, but I'm in Saint Augustine and I was hoping I could meet with you tonight. It's very important. Please give me a call back as soon as you get this message."

I walked to the kitchen, wrote down the number on the pad next to the phone, then took out my cell and dialed it.

"Mr. Patterson, this is Grant Nash. You're in Saint Augustine?"

"Grant, thanks for calling me back. Yes, I'm here for the day and was hoping I could buy you dinner. Are you free tonight?"

I sat down on a stool next to the kitchen island and tried to gather my thoughts. The only reason I could think of why he would want to take me to dinner would be to offer me a job. My brain began to spin with several different scenarios. What would I say if he offered me a job? His firm was in Jacksonville. Did I really want to drive all the way to Jacksonville and back every day? Did I even want a job?

"Grant, are you there?" he asked. "Did I lose you?"

"No, sir, I'm still here." I said, "And yes, I'm free tonight. Where would you like to meet?"

We met at one of those trendy overpriced five-star restaurants called "*The Purple Olive.*" I only assume it was overpriced; I really didn't know because Les picked up the check, but any time I see a menu with no prices written next to the entrées, it's usually outrageous. It did have a creative dinner menu with a great wine selection, fresh baked artisan bread, homemade soups and made from scratch desserts. So at least the food held up to the advertised five-star rating.

Throughout dinner, Les didn't talk about business like I assumed he would. Instead, he filled me in, telling me the backstory of his life. The more I listened, the more I began to think that this dinner may not be about a job offer after all.

Les had grown up in a small town like I did. After graduating college with his degree in architecture, he married his high school sweetheart and had a child...again, just like I did. But when he told me what had happened to his wife and only son, I was beyond stunned.

"I never learned how to fly a plane myself," he said. "I was way too busy to take the lessons, so I hired a pilot. His name was Alexander Post, but when he became a Navy pilot, everybody started calling him Wiley. You know, like Wiley Post, the guy that was Will Rogers' pilot. Anyway, Wiley was a good one. He'd flown fifteen successful bombing missions in Nam, came highly recommended and worked for me for years. I trusted him completely, and that's the only thing I've been able to rely on and it's what got me through it. I know in my heart If anything could have been done, he would have done it."

He reached into his pocket, pulled out a white handkerchief and wiped his eyes. "Sorry. It's been almost forty years since I lost them and it's still hard to talk about. But somehow, knowing Wiley was behind that wheel and there was nothing he could do to prevent it helped me to accept that it was...their time. It hurt like hell...it still does, but I moved on with my life." He folded his handkerchief, put it back in his pocket and looked at me. "What about you, son? Have you moved on with your life?"

I put down my fork, lifted my glass and took a sip of wine. "How do you know about that?"

He smiled. "I've been in this business a long time and made a lot of good friends. Do you know Sterling Clark?"

"I know who he is; he owns a large architectural/design firm in Dallas, but I've never met him. Why do you ask?"

"Well, he sure knows a lot about you. We went to school together and he's a good friend. He said he's been following your career for years."

I tilted my head and lifted my eyebrows. "Why would someone like Sterling Clark in Dallas care about me and my little one-man operation in Huntsville?"

He grinned and leaned back in his chair. "Oh I don't know...maybe it has something to do with the fact that your designs from your little one-man shop, as you call it, have been featured in Architectural Digest five times?"

I shrugged. "I just got lucky on that."

He frowned. "Getting featured once might be considered lucky, but five times? Come on, Grant. We're in the same business, remember? You can drop the modesty act around me. From what I've heard about you, I'm impressed. Actually, I've been impressed with you since I met you three days ago."

"When Sterling told me about your wife and daughter, I knew we needed to talk." Looking over his readers perched on the end of his stubby nose, he stared into my eyes. "Grant, I don't believe in coincidence. Our meeting in that store was predestined. There is a reason for it and I think I know what it is."

I smiled. "Let me guess. We met because I'm supposed to go to work for your firm in Jacksonville, right?"

"Wrong. You are supposed to go to work for my firm here in Saint Augustine."

I sat up in my chair. "You have an office in Saint Augustine?"

"Yep," he said, smiling, "You want to see it? It's only a few blocks from here."

After he paid the check, I walked with him a few blocks through the old historic district. He stopped in front of an old two-story brick building, unlocked the door and flipped on the lights.

"Go on in and take a look around. There's a full kitchen, a small meeting room and a bathroom on this first floor. Your design station is on the second floor."

I tilted my head and looked at him. "*MY* design station?"

He chuckled. "Well, assuming you take the job. And I sure hope you do, because I've had to jump through a hell of a lot of hoops to get all this set up in two days. Before you say no, at least walk up the stairs and check it out."

Upstairs, I found two computer workstations, both with dual large screen monitors. They were positioned on the back wall next to two huge windows that overlooked King Street. The view was great. There was also a large drafting table, a stool, a large format printer for printing blue prints, a desk and chair, a small wet bar and a large full bathroom.

The blank walls smelled of fresh paint and the carpets still showed the tracks from the recent shampoo and vacuuming. I turned around and looked at Les. He was beaming, his eyes were sparkling reflecting the overhead light.

"How did you do all of this in three days?"

The corners of his eyes crinkled with his broad smile. "It was actually only two." He chuckled. "Like I said, I have a lot of friends. Okay, now that you've seen this part, before you say anything, I want you to look in the kitchen downstairs."

When I walked into the kitchen, I immediately knew what he wanted me to see. On the floor next to the sink were two silver bowls with bright red letters on them that said *"CHARLEY."*

I heard him laughing behind me. "I thought you'd want to know that it's a dog friendly building. So what do you think?"

I smiled. "I think I'm a little overwhelmed. Could I take a few days to consider this?"

"Of course." He reached in his pocket and pulled out some papers. "While you're thinking, would you mind taking a drive down the coast to look at this property? It's only about thirty miles from here at Beverly Beach. I'm thinking this would be perfect for your first project.

I opened up the paper and studied it. It was a land plot. "Is this oceanfront?"

"Yes," he said. "There's almost a quarter mile of beachfront there, plus all the land on the other side of A1A."

"Is this going to be private residences or a large condo project?" I asked.

"Condos."

"Humm, I don't know about that. Charley hates condos."

He raised his eyebrows and widened his eyes. "What? Who hates condos?"

I grinned at him. "I forgot, you only saw Charley, you haven't met him yet. How about a nightcap on my deck? It's a clear night and the ocean will be beautiful. I'd like you to meet Charley. If I'm gonna do this, I'll need to run it by him first."

I had no doubts Les was having some major second thoughts about me as he followed me to my beach house that night. Wouldn't you?

Charley and Donna greeted us at the front door with great enthusiasm. Donna actually jumped up on Les, something Charley never did. Fortunately, he was a dog lover and didn't seem to mind.

"I thought you only had one dog?" he said, petting Donna's head.

"She's not mine. I'm just watching her for a few weeks. Her name is Donna and she belongs to my next-door neighbor. I think you know her; her name is Melissa Dean Hollingsworth. She said you were a good friends of her father."

He thought for a second. "Are you talking about Jacob Dean's daughter? That Melissa?"

"Yes. She lives next door. She had to go to Savannah and asked me to look after Donna for her. And Charley here," I reached down and rubbed his head, "didn't mind that one bit. Isn't that right, Charley?"

He smiled and wagged his tail. "Woof, woof."

Les laughed. "I saw him at the store the other day, but I didn't realize what a beautiful dog he was. What is that color called?"

"He's mahogany red. He's a full blood Irish Setter. His parents were champion show dogs in Ireland. His registered full name is Sir Charles Radcliff the Third, but he doesn't like being called Sir Charles."

Les turned his head and looked at me. "How do you know that?

I grinned. "He told me."

"Okay, Grant. I can take a joke as good as the next guy, but don't you think this one's gone far enough?"

"I'm not joking. That's why I wanted you to meet him. I know you're gonna think this is crazy, it sounds nuts and hard to believe, but Charley understands English and..." I smiled, "he's psychic and knows the future. If it hadn't been for him, we'd never met. I went to that architectural store to buy a drafting table, that's all. But Charley wouldn't leave and kept barking for me to sit down behind that computer. To be completely honest, I hadn't even noticed it was there. I had already loaded my truck and was ready to go, but Charley wouldn't come when I called him. He was standing next to the computer and insisted I sit down. That's when you came in and saw me. I can't explain it, but Charley knew you were going to be there."

He threw up his hands. "Aw, come on, Grant. You don't really believe that, do you? How the hell could you possibly know that? Did he tell you that, too? I've had dogs my entire life and I know it seems like they understand you, but it's simply not true. They're just really good at reading our body language. That's all it is. Charley doesn't understand English any more than you understand Russian. And honestly, I don't know what to say about the psychic thing."

He smiled and lifted his eyebrows. "You keep talking like that, and they'll come and get you and put you in a padded room."

"Are you sure about that? I've got several friends, including a world renowned doctor, who would disagree with you. But I'll let you decide for yourself."

I walked to the kitchen, spread out and flattened the Beverly Beach land plot on top of the Island and opened a bottle of Mirlot. I grabbed a couple of glasses and directed him out to the back deck. The still ocean was glistening, reflecting the glow of the half moon on the water. It seemed extra quiet that night with hardly any wave action crashing on the beach.

After I filled our glasses and we spent a few minutes sipping the wine and admiring the view, I motioned for Charley to come sit between us.

"Charley, this is Mr. Patterson. His name is Lester, but he likes to be called Les. He's kind of like you. You don't like to be called by your full name either, do you, Sir Charles?"

Charley lifted his lip, exposing his teeth. "Gurrrrrrr."

I glanced at Les. "I told you he didn't like it."

He rolled his eyes. "Good trick. One of my dogs could smoke a pipe."

I laughed and sat back in my chair. "Okay, then *you* ask him something"

Les bent down and looked at Charley. "Grant thinks you understand English. I don't think you do. He also thinks you are some kind of a psychic. I personally believe he's one brick shy of a full load when it comes to that!"

Charley didn't move. He remained very still staring up at him, listening carefully.

"So I guess we're going to have to come up with some kind of a foolproof test." Les leaned back and sipped his wine. "Ok...if you understand English and you are also psychic, you should already know what we were talking about at dinner. Do you have any ideas how to ask him that?"

Les's last question was meant for me, but before I could answer him, Charley ran inside the house. When he came back, he dropped something in Les's lap. It was too dark for me to see what it was, but when Les picked it up and looked at it, his eyes flew open and he gasped.

"Well I'll be God damned!" was all he could get out, before he grabbed his glass and chugged down the rest of his wine—it was the Beverly Beach land plot.

~

LES DIDN'T MAKE it back to his hotel that night. He crashed at about two a.m. in my guest bedroom and that was a good thing, because neither one of us was in any shape to drive after finishing off that third bottle of Mirlot. I must admit I haven't had that much fun in years, listening to Les and Charley arguing about the new condo project. The more wine we drank, the funnier it got for both of us.

"Come on, Charley, just think about it." Les's words slurred more and more with each glass of wine. "We could only build a few houses on that property and only rich people would be able to buy them." He was very animated when he talked, waving his arms and spilling his wine as he made his point. "We don't want a bunch of spoiled rich assholes living there, but if we build condos, then anyone with a good job could afford them. Wouldn't that be a good thing? What's wrong with that?"

"Arrr, arrr, arrrrrrr."

"Grant, what the he...hell's he sayin'?'"

"How the heck do I know? I don't speak dog." We both burst out laughing and took another drink.

When I regained my composure, I looked down at Charley and rubbed his head. "I think it's because they blocked his view of the ocean when we were driving up A1A from Miami."

"Woof, woof!" Charley barked in agreement.

I poured myself another glass of wine and took a long sip. I hadn't been that drunk in a long time. I was just drunk enough that my normal filter that prevented me from expressing my true feelings was turned off. Trying my best to enunciate the words I blurted out, "Lester, I'll tell you what *I* don't like about friggin' condos...they're ugly as hell, butt ugly, and I don't like how they destroy the natural berm and sea wall. It always makes me sad to see a tall construction crane setting up on oceanfront property."

Les lifted his glass and finished it. Then he set it down on the table and after a few tries finally made it up to his feet. "Son, I haven't been this drunk in twenty-five years, but I think I'm done. So if you will point me to that guestroom you mentioned earlier, I would appreciate it. But before I go, I want to say this."

He looked down at Charley. "You, sir, are one hell of a dog! A little scary, but one hell of a dog!" Then he turned and looked at me. "Grant, I am absolutely convinced I was right and we are meant to work together. If you want the Beverly Beach project, it's yours. And if you don't want an ugly ass condo project there that destroys the natural berm, then design something that's not butt ugly and that doesn't harm the beach. I have no doubts that between you and Charley, you two can come up with something that will make us all proud."

When I woke up the next morning, Les was gone, but had left me a note on the island in the kitchen.

*Grant,*
*I had to get back to Jacksonville for an early meeting. I've left the keys to the new office and an employment contract on the island. I'm hoping you and Charley take the job. It was a very enlightening evening. I haven't had that much fun since the 1960's.*

*Let me know what you decide.*
*Les*

After breakfast, I loaded Donna and Charley into my old truck and drove the twenty-nine miles to Beverly Beach. When we got there, I took out the land plot and walked the property, including the full quarter mile of beach. It was untouched and pristine.

I felt sick to my stomach thinking about being responsible for destroying this beautiful natural piece of unspoiled nature. But I knew if I turned him down, he would just hire someone else to do it.

Watching out for the traffic, we walked across A1A and found the stakes marking the adjacent property that matched the land plot. Directly behind the land plotted on the map were several more flat, sandy empty acres. I walked that property as well.

I had an idea, so I loaded up the dogs and drove straight to the Flagler County Courthouse and found out who owned that property. Then I drove back to Beverly Beach and dropped in on a local realtor. I got the realtor to give me a ballpark estimate of what that property was worth. I discounted that price by about half, because he had no idea what was about to be built on the beachfront property in front of it that would block its view and drop its value considerably.

On the drive back, I called Les on my cell and asked him if he could come see me the next day in my new office. I called it 'my new office' to appease him.

The facts were I was going to take the job and it would be my new office...only if he liked my idea and agreed to my terms. If not, I was going to thank him for his confidence in me and for offering me the opportunity, then give him back his keys and walk away.

## 14

## FACE TO FACE

After checking out every square inch of the new office, Donna and Charley sprawled out on the floor behind my chair and I went to work. It was almost four a.m. when I finally flipped off the computer and headed home. My eyes were blurry from staring at the screen and my mind was numb, but I had a good start on the overall concept. Les wasn't going to be there until around six p.m., so after a little sleep, and some breakfast, we all headed back to the office.

When he got there at six, he was carrying a bottle of champagne and two glasses in his hand. "I thought we might want to officially christen your new office!" He said, holding up the bottle.

I smiled. "That sounds like a good idea, but before we pop that cork, I think you need to look at something."

I had printed out the plans and laid them on the table in the small meeting room. "I'm going to take Donna and Charley out for a walk. The plans are in there." I pointed at the table. "It's just a conceptual overview. I want you to look at the concept with an open mind, because I realize it may not be what you were expecting. When I get back, we can talk about it and I'll explain my ideas further."

I gave him almost thirty minutes before I came back. I wasn't sure what to expect when I walked in, but for the entire time I'd been walking the dogs, I'd been practicing my rebuttal speech, so I was prepared for just about anything.

"I'm starving," he said the second we walked in, "let's go get some dinner."

He grabbed Charley's leash out of my hand and took off walking. I locked the door, and Donna and I followed behind them.

He stopped at a small restaurant that was only a few blocks away from the office. "This is a great place. Fantastic food and they're dog friendly."

We settled around a table on the outside patio and ordered our food. Throughout the dinner, he never once said a word about my Beverly Beach drawings. I was beginning to lose my patience when he finally brought it up.

"If we don't build the condos on the beach, what are your plans for that property?"

Finally, I thought to myself. "To leave it untouched, natural and pristine."

He frowned at me. "Do you have any idea how much a quarter mile of ocean front property is worth?"

"As far as I'm concerned, it's priceless the way it is now, but if we destroy it and cover it up with concrete and steel, it's not worth much at all."

He stabbed the last bite of his steak and put it in his mouth. In between his chewing he said, "You ain't one of them damn tree huggers, are you?"

"I think the politically correct term is conservationist," I said, laughing, "And yes, I guess I am a little bit of a tree hugger at heart. Don't get me wrong, I understand our growing population problems and the need for more housing, but come on, Les, building $400,000 condos isn't really part of that problem and you know it. All I'm trying to do here is save a quarter mile of beach. That's all."

"I understand, but this all comes down to business. How am I supposed to convince the owners of this property and the investors of the development that your concept is going to make them the most return on their money? It's a cruel world, son, and that's really all it's going to boil down to. Dreams are nice to have, but money is money, and that's what rules the world and gets projects built."

"Les, I'm not some kid fresh out of college. I'm not naïve to how the real world works. Remember I asked you to look at this with an open mind. Are you willing to at least listen to my ideas?"

He yelled for the waitress and ordered a double scotch, "Sure, I'm willing to listen," he said, "but hang on until I get my drink. I think I'm gonna need it."

I gathered my thoughts while we waited for his scotch. After he took a few sips I began, "When was the last time you saw a Florida beach front condo complex featured in *Architectural Digest* and talked about on all the news channels?"

Les frowned, wrinkling his forehead as he considered my question. "I don't think I've ever seen that before."

I smiled. "You know why? Because they're all exactly the same. Some are bigger, some are smaller. They may look completely different and have unique designs, but in the end, they are all the same and were built for the same reasons you just talked about – to make the most profit possible for the investors, with absolutely no consideration for what that development might do to the environment and ignoring the permanent destruction of the natural beach line.

"Simply put, they are all the same and therefore not newsworthy. But what if a group of investors did it differently? This will be one of the largest developments in the entire state. What if these developers were willing to sacrifice a small percentage of their profits to develop something that was environmentally friendly? Something that served exactly the same purpose, but didn't destroy the natural pristine beach, but instead preserved it forever...for the tenants and the rest of the world to enjoy? What if this project goes out of its way to take advantage of the newest green technology, like solar and wind to power the project? What if this development was actually concerned about its impact on the environment? And there's one last thing I'd like to do that if we could pull off I'm sure would seal the deal."

Les frowned. "Oh lord...there's more?"

"I want to build it with American made products. From the steel super structure to the carpets. All American made. I don't know about you, but I think a project like this just might be newsworthy, especially considering the growing worldwide concern of global warming and the current movement to bring jobs back to the U.S."

I paused to let my words sink in and sipped my Diet Coke. "And one last thing. What if the architect for this project just happened to have a close connection with one of the contributing editors of *Architectural Digest*, who has already expressed an interest? And...what if this architect graduated college with one of the producers of the *Today* show on NBC? You think that might help sell this to your investors?"

Les leaned forward and sat his Scotch down on the table. "How much more per unit would all this take?"

I grinned. I had his attention, "Well, that would depend on how good your guys are at resourcing and purchasing the materials. But if we do it this way, the amount of recognition and free advertising should offset the increased costs of construction."

Les looked at Charley, who was lying at my feet. "Charley, is all this your idea, or is he really this smart?"

He jumped up and put his paw on his knee. "Woof, woof."

∾

WHEN THE RESIDENCES of Beverly Beach first heard about the plan for a large condo project coming to their area, they were angry. A few of them actually protested at the planning commission, but when they realized what we were doing and how concerned we were with preserving the natural beach line and only using American made materials, they changed their minds and got onboard. And because of this support, the plans and building permits were expedited, approved quickly and in less than six months, the project broke ground.

It was quite the celebration. Les had pulled a few strings and twisted a few arms, so on the day of the groundbreaking, every news channel you could name was represented, with their station logos on their cameras aimed at the platform. On that platform standing behind the gold-plated shovels were the CEO of NEW-SKY, the development company, Les, the governor, the mayor, me and Charley, and Savanna Guthrie from the NBC *Today* show. My producer friend had pulled that string. A photographer from *Architectural Digest* was also there, taking pictures for the promised cover and featured article that would be published when the project was completed. I had been correct. This project *WAS* newsworthy.

To complete the designs and drawings, I had been working almost round the clock for the past six months, sleeping on the sofa in my office most nights. To be honest, I was thankful to have the work to keep my mind occupied.

I wish that I could tell you that over the past six months, my relationship with Melissa had improved and flourished, but unfortunately, it had taken an unusual turn and as a result, we had drifted further and further apart.

～

SIX MONTHS EARLIER, the day I got the call from Les telling me that the Beverly Beach project was a go, was the same day Melissa was supposed to get back from her trip to Savannah.

I was standing in the kitchen when Donna and Charley suddenly jumped up and ran to the front door, barking. The doorbell had not chimed, but I knew what was going on. When I opened the door, Donna and Charley flew out and ran down the front steps to greet Melissa and Molly, who had just pulled into the driveway.

I was not surprised when Molly jerked open the door and jumped in the middle of the two dogs, rolling on the ground, laughing and giggling at the top of her lungs. But I *WAS* surprised when Melissa opened her door, ran up my steps, jumped into my arms and kissed me.

"Oh, Grant." She purred in my ear, "I've missed you so much."

In the two weeks she'd been gone, we'd only talked a few times, so I wasn't sure what to expect, but I was loving it. As usual, the chills were racing through my body and my heart was pounding in my chest with each kiss. It was great to feel her back in my arms again. I just hoped it would last this time and we could finally move to the next step in our relationship, but that just didn't seem to be in the cards for us.

For the following three weeks, my life resembled something you might read in a romance novel, because it was very sexy and extremely romantic.

It started the very next day when she offered to help me decorate my new office and before I knew it, the lights were out and we were making love on the floor.

I took her out to the most romantic restaurants in town and after these dinners, we walked barefoot, hand in hand, along the beach shore. We'd had sex before, but it seemed different. Now, we couldn't stop looking into each other's eyes and we couldn't seem to stop snuggling afterwards.

Those strange jolts of electricity that continued to run through us that used to confuse and bother us no longer seemed inexplicable. We decided that they must simply be jolts of love. What else could it be, because we were both falling deep, hard and fast!

We had just come in from one of those moonlit walks when my cell phone rang. It was Marshall.

"Hey, what's up?" I asked. "Isn't this a little past your bedtime?"

"Yeah, a little." His voice was not cheerful. "Is Melissa back from her trip?"

"Yeah, she's sitting right here next to me. What's wrong?"

He hesitated before he spoke. "Will both of you be home this weekend? I need to talk to you. Both of you."

I looked at Melissa and raised my eyebrows, "We're both here listening, why can't you just talk to us now?"

"I don't want to tell you this over the phone. It's...just too important. I need to tell you in person, face to face."

"Well, to be honest with you, Marshall, I love you, buddy, and would love to see you, but I'm already behind schedule with this new Beverly Beach Project and I don't really have time for company. Can't this wait?"

He put the phone on speaker. "Grant, this is Brenda. We know you're busy, but no, this can't wait. We'll be there tomorrow night about six p.m. We'll rent a car, so don't worry about picking us up. Just make sure you guys are there when we arrive. This is very important."

Melissa and I stared at each other in silence for a long time after they hung up wondering what in the world could be so important that they had to fly all the way from Houston just to tell us face to face.

"I have no ideas, do you?"

"No. I just hope it's not something else about Jerry."

Their phone call had created a dark black cloud that hung directly over both of our heads and killed the mood. Neither one of us felt like doing anything else, so I walked her back to her house, paid the babysitter and kissed Melissa good night, or perhaps I should say…goodbye.

I dropped off to sleep quickly, but woke up at about three a.m. My mind was whirling with possible scenarios. I couldn't stop wondering what in the world Marshall was coming all that way to tell me. I knew I'd never go back to sleep so I woke up Charley and headed for the office. Since I knew I would have to quit working at five-thirty to make it home by six, I thought I would make up the time by getting to the office early.

Fortunately, I am one of those one-track mind guys, so once I got into the project, my brain took over, and the thoughts of Marshall never entered my mind except for the hour that I took off for lunch and the few times I had to take Charley out to pee.

Surprisingly, I had gotten a lot done and had a productive day. I was running late and the traffic had been unusually heavy, so I had just pulled in to my driveway when Marshall and Brenda pulled in behind me in their rental car. It was one of those smart cars, the smallest vehicle I'd ever seen in my life. I couldn't help but start laughing, watching Marshall work his 6'4" body out of that door.

"Where are your big shoes and red nose? What kind of friggin' clown are you?" I yelled.

He frowned back at me. "What?" He didn't get the joke, but Brenda burst out laughing. "What's so funny?"

"Never mind, honey," Brenda said to him, grinning at me. "You'd have to have a sense of humor to understand."

"I have a sense of humor!" he retorted as he struggled trying to get the suitcases out of the tiny back storage space.

"Of course you do," I said, "but unfortunately, yours is warped."

He jerked hard on the handle of his suitcase, finally freeing it. Then he pulled up the sliding handle, flipped me the bird and rolled past me down the sidewalk to my front staircase.

After he'd climbed the stairs up to my front door, he turned and yelled back at me, "Hurry the hell up and let me in, asshole! I need a beer!"

After they were unpacked and all set up in the guest room, the three of us met on my back deck and settled around the patio table.

"You want me to call Melissa?" I asked.

Marshall shook his head. "Not yet," he said, sipping his beer and gazing out at the ocean. "Let us enjoy this view for a little while longer."

## 15

## ISONIAZID

I knew Marshall well and through the years, I thought I'd seen all of his emotions and body language, but what I was looking at was something new. Although he was trying hard to conceal it, there was a level of concern inside him that was screaming from his eyes and showing in every move he made with his body.

Instead of putting his feet up in the empty chair and leaning back, like he'd always done before, he was leaning forward, slightly rocking back and forth nervously. His wrinkled forehead seemed to be locked in a permanent scowl and his eyes never stopped moving. I didn't know Brenda that well, but she appeared to be equally stressed.

"What in the hell is wrong with you two?" I asked.

Marshall glanced over at Brenda and then looked back at the ocean. "You'll find out soon enough. Go ahead and get her on the phone. I want to talk to her."

She answered on the first ring. "Hey...yeah, we're out on my deck, but Marshall wants to talk to you before you come over."

I handed the phone to him. "Hi Melissa...yes, it was a smooth flight. Would you do me a favor? I need you to gather up all of your medications and bring them with you. I need to see exactly what you are taking now. No, there's nothing wrong with your health, I promise.

I just need to check something. And if you have any old prescription bottles of something you used to take, even if it's been years, before the transplant, I'd like to see that too. Okay, see you in a few minutes."

Even though Melissa didn't mind, I never drank alcohol around her, so when she got there, I poured out my beer and fixed us two Diet Cokes.

Marshall suggested we talk in the living room, so we all settled in there around the coffee table. Melissa and I were sitting together on the couch and Marshall and Brenda were facing us in chairs.

I couldn't believe how many prescription bottles were in the sack she had brought over. For almost thirty minutes, we all sat in silence, watching Marshall methodically take out each bottle one at a time, carefully read the prescription, popped the cap and inspect the pills inside. When he finished with a bottle, he would set it on the table in a specific row and make a note on a yellow pad.

When he was through, the top of the coffee table was almost covered with brown prescription bottles of various sizes.

"I need to talk to Brenda for a second," Marshall said. "We'll be right back." They walked outside to the deck and closed the door behind them.

"Do you know what's going on?" Melissa asked, looking up at me. Her hands were trembling.

"I have no idea; he wouldn't tell me anything. But don't worry, remember he said it has nothing to do with your health."

Her eyes filled with tears. "Then what's this all about?" She pointed at her medicine on the coffee table. "It has to be about my health!" She leaned forward, holding her face in her hands and whimpered. "God, not again!"

I put my arm around her and pulled her close. "Whatever this is, we'll get through it."

When they came back and saw Melissa crying in my arms, Marshall didn't sit back down in his chair. Instead, he walked around the table and sat next to her.

"I didn't mean to frighten you with all of this. This has nothing to do with your current health situation. In fact, I talked to Dr. Shad yesterday and he told me that you are in perfect health. You are showing no signs of rejection and you have made a steady, upward, positive climb since the transplant. Please forgive me if I scared you. I never meant to do that."

Melissa looked up at him and smiled. "Thank you, Marshall. I'm sorry for acting this way, but you *did* scare me."

Although I was relieved to hear she was okay, I was angry at both of them for putting her through such a scare.

"If she's perfectly healthy, then what in the hell is this all about? Marshall, she almost died two years ago! And then you two come in here with all the secret cloak and dagger shit checking out all her medicine and scare the ever-living crap out of her. Will you just stop with all the secret meetings between you and Brenda and just tell us what the hell is going on?"

Marshall glared at me, stood, walked back to the chair and sat down. "Just shut up for once in your life, calm down and let me do this my way, okay?"

Trying to lighten the mood, I looked back at him. "You know, Doc, your bedside manner sucks!"

"God damn it, Grant!" he screamed. "This is not a joke. It's very serious! Please, for God's sake, just shut up and let me talk!"

Marshall had never raised his voice at me in anger before, so I stopped talking and listened.

He picked up a prescription bottle off the table and held it up for her to see. "How long did you take Isoniazid?"

Melissa thought for a moment, "Ah...I'm not exactly sure, maybe four or five years. That's an old prescription. I haven't taken it since my transplant. Why do you ask?"

Marshall shook the bottle. "Do you know what this medicine was for?"

She thought about it a second. "Not really, I can't remember. Truthfully, I don't know what most of them are for."

He smiled. "That's what I thought." He opened a bottle and took out a pill and laid it down on the table. With his index finger, he pointed at the lined-up bottles. "This row is what you're taking now.

This row, minus a few bottles, was what you were taking before the transplant. In my opinion, you don't need most of what you're taking now and we'll talk about that later." Then he picked up the Isoniazid pill. "But you never needed to take this one."

Her eyes widened. "Really? Why not?"

"Because you never had hepatitis and have never been clinically depressed. That's what this is prescribed for and one of the reasons Brenda and I are here today."

"You came here because of that pill?" I asked. "Really?"

He dipped his head. "It's one of the reasons." He picked up three other prescription bottles and handed them to me. Then he handed me the Isoniazid bottle. "Read the prescriptions on these bottles and I think you'll understand."

I looked at the first three bottles and read the prescription carefully. Then I read the Isoniazid bottle and saw it immediately. I glanced up at Marshall. "Is this the only one he prescribed?"

"Yes. Out of all of these, it's the only one."

"It's the only one what?" Melissa asked, "What are you talking about?"

I handed her the bottle. "It's Jerry's prescription. Of all of your prescribed medicines, this was the only one he prescribed...and...the only one you didn't need to take." I looked back at Marshall. "What are the side effects?"

He took a deep breath and sighed. "Before I get into that, I need to ask Melissa something."

He leaned forward and stared into her eyes, "Melissa, I hope you understand that we're here because we care about you. So please don't get upset at my questions. But if we're going to get to the bottom of this, I have to know the absolute truth, even if it's embarrassing or painful to admit. I can't express how critical it is for me to know the truth."

She looked up at me with wide eyes, then turned back to face Marshall. "The truth about what?"

"According to your medical records, when you were pregnant with

Molly, in your 28th week, you tested positive for hepatitis C, is that correct?"

She dipped her head. "Yes, but that turned out to be a false positive."

"Yes, I know," he said. "After the birth, you tested negative. Now think hard. Was that about the time you started taking Isoniazid?"

She opened her eyes wide. "Yes, I remember now. Jerry didn't trust the tests that showed I was negative and insisted I take it in case the tests were wrong. I can't believe I forgot that."

"I think I know how that could have happened. It wasn't long after that you started showing signs of liver failure, correct?"

She tilted her head and lowered her eyebrows. "Are you saying taking Isoniazid caused my liver to fail? Jerry poisoned me? He was trying to kill me?"

He held up his hand. "Hold on, you're getting ahead of me. Before I explain, I need to ask you the question I was talking about earlier, the one that you have to be completely honest about. Are you ready?"

She looked at him and nodded. "Yes."

"Isoniazid is not a poison. It's actually a very good medicine when used properly. And that's what I have to ask you about. I know you don't drink alcohol now, but after you gave birth to Molly, did you drink then?"

"I've never drank much, and didn't drink at all when I was pregnant, but after she was born, I would have a glass of wine after dinner with Jerry and maybe one or two drinks when we would go out."

"Jerry saw you drinking and didn't try to stop you or say anything?" Brenda asked.

She raised her head slowly and stared at Brenda. "Stop me? Why would he stop me? I wasn't pregnant. Why couldn't I drink?"

"I'll explain in a minute," Marshall said, "but do you swear that's all you drank? You have to trust us; we are not here to judge you. Were you drinking more, and I mean a lot more, during this time...maybe drinking privately and hiding it from everyone?"

She gasped and her mouth flew open, horrified. "No, I swear! I'm telling you the truth, I've never been drunk in my life! Not even in college!"

"That's what I thought. I'll be right back. I have to get something out of my carry on."

When he returned, he had a blue folder in his hand. "Melissa, before I show you this, I want you to know that Brenda and I believe you. We do not believe one word of what is written in this file. But before you read this, you need to understand more about Isoniazid. When you take this medication, especially at this strength, you cannot drink alcohol. None. Not even a glass of wine. If you do, it can cause severe damage to the liver."

The three of us sat in silence as Melissa slowly studied the files in the folder. When she finished, she handed it to me, stood up and excused herself. "I need to go to the bathroom." Although she had closed the door, we could hear her crying through the walls.

When I opened the folder and scanned the reports, I couldn't believe my eyes. I didn't comprehend most of what I was looking at, because they contained a lot of numbers of liver and blood test results, dating back four years, but the handwritten notes on the bottom of the pages from her doctor were easy to understand. I read most of them, but the last one, one week before her transplant, said it all.

*This patient has obviously continued to ignore the warnings I have discussed in detail with her husband, who is also a medical doctor, of the dangers of taking the drug Isoniazid and the consumption of excessive amounts of alcohol. As a result, it's my opinion her liver will fail soon. Unfortunately, due to her obvious alcoholism, I cannot in good faith place her on any national liver transplant list.*

I handed the folder back to Marshall, leaned back against the couch and sat there in stunned, shocked silence. The only sounds in the room were Melissa's muffled whimpers coming through the bathroom walls.

"I'll be back in a minute," Brenda said. We heard her knock on the bathroom door and go in.

"I think I need a break, "I said. "Lets go outside and give them some privacy."

About thirty minutes later, Brenda and Melissa appeared in the doorway and joined us on the deck. Melissa wasn't crying anymore, but her eyes were red and wet. She forced a smile and squeezed my hand when she sat down next to me.

"I'm sorry, I didn't mean to..." her words choked off. She dropped her head to hide her embarrassment.

I lifted her hand and kissed it. "Hey, it's okay. We all understand."

Her tear filled eyes glistened in the moonlight. "It's just that...it's not every day you find out your husband has been trying to kill you."

For almost five minutes, no one said a word. We all just sat there quietly, listening to the waves crashing on the beach, absorbing her astounding, atrocious, but unfortunately accurate words.

"Marshall," Melissa said breaking the silence, "How could he have done this? I mean, the alcohol part. How did he do it if I didn't drink it?

"When your liver started showing the first signs of failure, did they put you on an IV drip?" he asked.

Her eyes flew open. "Yes! Jerry said it was to help build up my immune system. It wasn't all the time, maybe three or four days a week."

"He did it at night, right?"

"Yes."

"Do you remember feeling groggy or sluggish the following day?"

"Yes. And I always had a terrible headache. Jerry said it was just a side effect of the medicine." She frowned and stared across the table at Marshall. "But was that really a hangover?"

"I think so. That IV bag was more than likely a mixture of glucose and vodka."

Her eyes filled with tears again and she grew quiet, thinking. "May I ask you a medical question?"

Of course." He said.

"What is my true life expectancy? How many years will this transplant give me?" She sat up erect and stared at him. "The truth. Please Marshall, tell me the truth."

He glanced over at me before he answered. "Melissa, there's no real way to know for sure, but I can tell you what the statistics say. You were thirty-one when you had the transplant. The studies show that for both men and women patients that are liver transplant recipients, between the ages of 17 and 34, once they pass the critical six-month period, they live an average of twenty-eight years."

She wiped her eyes and looked down at the table. "That means...I won't live to see sixty. And I may never get to meet my grandchildren."

I took her hand and squeezed it. "You can't think about that. And I know it doesn't seem fair, but the truth is, none of us are even promised a tomorrow. My dad used to tell me 'It's not how *long* you live, it's how *well* you live.'"

"I'm sorry, Grant, but I'm not in the mood for another dear old Dad story right now," she said, jerking her hand away. "I've heard all that before. I *am* thankful for this transplant and the years it's giving me, but don't you understand...I did not have to have it! Jerry did this to me!"

When I looked into her eyes, I didn't recognize her. I'd seen her angry many times before, but what I was looking at was much more than anger, it was rage.

She looked across the table at Marshall, clinching her fists. "Jerry has taken away twenty years of my life. How can I make him pay for this?"

"Melissa," Brenda said, "look at me. I don't think you are in any frame of mind to make a rational decision about this right now."

"OH MY GOD! PLEASE STOP WITH THE PSYCHOANALY-SIS!" she screamed, jumping to her feet. "I love you guys, but seriously how did you expect me to react? *'I'm not in the right frame of mind to make a rational decision?'* Are you serious? You come here and tell me my husband tried to kill me and in the process destroyed my liver. What frame of mind would *you* be in?"

Suddenly, she collapsed to the floor and curled into a fetal position, crying. Wailing through her tears, she whimpered, "I want him to pay for this! I want him to suffer!"

I jumped up, lifted her off the floor and carried her to my bed. "Molly..." she whispered.

"Don't worry, I'll send the babysitter home and go get her right now. You just rest."

When I got back with Molly, I put her to bed on the couch in my home office. I told Charley to watch her, so he and Donna curled up together, lying next to the couch on the floor. When I stuck my head in my bedroom to check on Melissa, she was sound asleep and Brenda was sitting in a chair next to the bed reading a magazine.

When Brenda saw me, she held up a finger to her lips. "Shhhhh. Quiet, she's asleep. I'll watch her for a while."

I walked to the refrigerator, grabbed two beers, walked outside and plopped down in the chair across from Marshall. I handed him a beer, popped the top of mine and chugged it.

When I finished, I crushed the can in my hand, tossed it in the trash, leaned back and smiled at him. "Enjoying your trip so far?"

He grinned. "Now you see why I couldn't tell you all this on the phone?"

"Yes...I sure do." I said, nodding. "So, is she gonna be all right? She freaked out there pretty bad."

"Actually, she handled it much better than I expected," Brenda said behind me.

I turned around to look at her standing in the doorway. "Really? What did you expect?"

She handed me a bottle of wine and an opener. "I don't know how to use this new wine opener. You do it."

I popped the cork and filled her glass.

"I expected much more anger and rage," she said.

I lifted my eyebrows. "More than that?"

She smiled. "Oh yeah, much more directed at Marshall and you."

"Me?" I said shocked. "Why would she be angry at me? What the hell did I do?"

"Because she loves you and you love her. You were trying to

comfort her and she was in a rage. She needed to smash something, hurt something. So she lashed out and tried to hurt you, and then she tried to hurt me. It's a basic human reaction, but it's not her true nature and she couldn't really do it, so instead, she broke down emotionally."

"So what's going to happen when she wakes up?" I asked.

"She's not actually asleep right now. It's like a sleep, but more of a brain rest more similar to a coma. It's a healing process. That's why she went out so quickly. Melissa experienced a slight emotional break-down. In the old days, they called them 'nervous breakdowns', but that's not an accurate description. The body can only handle so much stress, anger and rage. When it gets to a breaking point, something *will* happen. That can manifest in many different ways, depending on the individual. Stress is the number one cause of heart attacks and strokes. Long-term uncontrolled stress that turns to anger and then rage is why you hear about normal people that just seem to snap one day and do uncharacteristic things, like smashing up their property or shooting strangers. Stress or rage is a characteristic all humans possess, but fortunately, most never see. We all got to see a small part of Melissa's tonight."

"If she's not asleep, how long will she be out?" I asked.

Brenda sipped her wine and shrugged. "No way of knowing. No one really knows what's going on during this process, but I think the brain is organizing all this new and shocking information she learned tonight and putting it in the proper places so she can process it better. That's just my theory from dealing with other patients who have gone through this. Most of them, when they wake are no longer in a rage and can think more logical. They are still angry, but not raging. That's what I'm hoping will happen with Melissa."

"Me too," I said.

"And Grant," she grabbed my hand and looked at me, "I doubt she will remember what she said to any of us. So just let it go. We all love your dear old Dad stories."

"Really?" Marshall said. "You like 'em? I'm sick of them!"

We all burst out laughing. It felt good to smile and relax for the first time that night.

# 16

## AN AUGUST HARVEST

I didn't want to disturb Melissa, so I slept on the couch in the living room that night and woke early with the morning sunrise. Its golden beams streamed brightly through the windows and lit up my face like a stage spotlight.

I was at least two days behind on the Beverly Beach foundation plans, but I wanted to see how Melissa was, and it *was* Saturday, so I decided to cook breakfast instead of heading to the office.

The second my feet hit the floor, Charley and Donna ran into the living room, so I opened the deck door and they both shot down the back deck stairs like a couple of rockets. I hit the button on the coffee maker and got my first cup going, then filled Donna and Charley's bowls with food and water. With my coffee in my hand, I walked out on the back deck and watched Charley and Donna playing in the surf.

"You're up awful early," I felt Melissa's arm slip around my waist. "Sip?"

I smiled and handed her my coffee. "Mmmm," she said with delight as she savored it. She took another sip and pointed her finger. "Is that Donna and Charley?"

"Yeah. It looks like they're having fun." I took her hand holding the coffee cup, pulled it up to my mouth and took a sip. "Are you hungry?"

"Are you cooking?"

"Yep."

"Then yes," she chuckled, "I'm starving."

It's truly amazing what the smell of sizzling bacon can do to even the deepest sleepers. I hadn't even flipped over the first batch of bacon before Molly, Brenda, and Marshall were crowding around me in the kitchen.

"I like my bacon crisp, my eggs over medium and be sure and not lace the edges." Marshall shouted his order. "I hate it when cooks lace the edges."

I rolled my eyes at him. "Got it, Doc. Bacon rare, two scrambled hard, coming right up." Actually, I went all out and even made them my world famous pancakes, and I did not lace any edges.

After we cleaned up the dishes, we all took a long slow walk and talk on the beach, but what had taken place the night before never came up. It was as if it never happened. The main subject during our stroll was my new job, my new office and the Beverly Beach Project.

When we got back from our walk and Molly's babysitter arrived, we all crammed into Marshall's tiny rental car, drove to my new office and I showed them around the space. After the tour, we walked down the alley to *Harry's Seafood Bar and Grille* and had lunch.

During our meal, we all agreed that we'd never survive the long drive to Beverly Beach in that tiny Smart car, so while Marshall paid our tab, I called Hertz and rented a human size car. With all of us sitting upright with actual room for our legs and feet, we drove the twenty-nine miles south to the construction site.

"Are the barges out there in the ocean part of this project?" Marshall asked.

"Not officially, but the work they are doing is being funded by the generous donations to the government from the developers of this project."

Marshall raised his eyebrows and looked over the top of his

glasses. "What kind of bullshit answer is that? What the hell are they building out there, some kind of secret underwater government lab?"

I glanced at Melissa and we both started laughing. "No, it's nothing like that. Have you ever noticed that the beach behind our housing complex is much larger than it is just a few hundred yards away in either direction? And have you noticed that the water is calmer and the waves are smaller?"

Brenda looked at Marshall. "I don't think I've ever paid any attention to that before. Have you?"

Marshall lowered his forehead, thinking. "No, I've never noticed that."

"Check it out when we get back tonight, it's very obvious. In Melissa's father's original plans for the houses on that property, he had also designed an artificial reef to be built a few hundred yards out from the coastline. He was way ahead of his time; no one had ever done anything like that before or even thought of it. It was truly a revolutionary concept that unfortunately, he never got to see work."

Brenda looked at Melissa. "Your father died before the project was completed?"

"Actually, he never tried to develop the project when he was alive," she said. "He hid the plans away and never showed them to anyone. After he died and I was going through his office, I found them. At first, I thought they were just another set of his many unfinished designs, but when the lawyer read his will and I realized I had inherited that beach-front property, I remembered the name of the property written on the top of the plans. When I showed them to a few of my friends in the construction business, they all told me that they were way overdesigned and would cost too much to build. They said that no developer would be willing to take the financial risk, because it wouldn't make enough profit, so I built them myself...exactly to Dad's plans and specifications."

"But her friends were wrong," I said. "Because of his revolutionary ideas, the houses sold quickly and have survived three major storms, including one hurricane with minimal beach erosion and zero structural damage. Her father's *'overdesigned'* plans were genius. And that's why I borrowed his exact reef design that they're building out there."

Marshall looked back at the barges. "An artificial reef to protect the beach. Great idea, so why the mystery on who's funding it? What difference does it make where the money comes from?"

"It shouldn't make any difference at all," Melissa said, "because you're correct, it will protect the beach from erosion. Personally, I think every beach project should be required to do it, but unfortunately, getting a permit to build a reef has become political."

"The permits come from the U.S. Army Corps of Engineers in federal waters," I added, "or the Florida Department of Environmental Protection in state waters. Due to the liability connected to placing materials on the sea floor these permits are not issued to private individuals. So basically, they are owned and maintained by the government, either state or federal, depending on the location of the reef."

Marshall frowned. "And to get the government permits..."

"That's where all the politics come into play," I interrupted, finishing his sentence. "And unfortunately, the politicians use these permits like poker chips in the big game they're all playing.

"The real questions should be will it help the environment? Will it actually help save the beach and what materials will be used? What is its stability and its storm impacts? Will there be long-term studies of reef community succession, residency of benthic species, juvenile fish recruitment, and will there be comparisons of artificial reef fish communities with those on adjacent natural reefs? But instead, it all comes down to who is in power, the Democrats or Republicans, and who the people asking for the permits supported in the last election."

∾

WE SPENT a little over an hour walking the site as I showed them the plans, explaining where each structure would be located. They all seemed impressed, nodding their approval.

It was a beautiful day, so we stopped at a convenience store, bought something cold to drink, rolled down the windows and took our time driving back to my house, admiring the ocean view and the beautiful beach houses along the way.

When we got home, the girls decided to take a nap while Marshall and I returned the rental car. On the way back, we stopped by a seafood market to pick up some fresh fish to grill for dinner. As usual, Marshall and I argued our way through the seasoning and grilling process of the grouper, but the end result was fantastic.

A slight cold front had moved in and as a result, the temperature had dropped into the low 70's, but with the ocean breeze, it felt much colder. Just cold enough to fire up my new round brick fire pit I had installed.

Once everyone was settled around the fire pit I said, "I'll be right back, don't go anywhere." I ran up the deck stairs and returned with four long metal prongs with wooden handles, a bag of marshmallows, a box of graham crackers and a sack full of Hershey's chocolate bars.

"S'mores?" Brenda yelled. "I haven't done this since I was a kid!"

Although the grouper was amazing, I'm pretty sure everyone liked the S'mores best of all.

"What time is your plane tomorrow?" I asked.

"It's tomorrow afternoon," Brenda said, "2:30 or 3:00, I think."

Marshall lifted the wine out of the ice bucket and filled his glass. "This has been such a terrific day, I hate to bring this up, but Brenda and I came here for two specific reasons, and we've only got to one of those. And that first one is something we're all doing a good job of ignoring, but we can't do that. I'm sorry, Melissa, I know you don't want to, but we really need to talk more about it."

Melissa's body stiffened. "I'm fine, Marshall, really I am."

"No, you're not," Brenda said. "No one would be and none of us believe you. So stop this now. If you weren't furious at him, if you weren't incredibly angry, something would be wrong with you. It's okay. Don't deny it and let it out, but use that anger constructively."

Melissa lifted her head. "How do I do that?"

"By being very careful about what you do next. If it was just *you* to consider, I would strongly suggest you file attempted murder charges against him and put him in jail. But it's not just you. You have Molly to consider, too. What will all that do to her?"

None of us had any answers to that question, so we just sat in silence, listening to the crackling fire and the ocean crashing on the beach on the other side of the tall berm behind us.

"So if I file charges, Molly will hate me for putting her father in prison," Melissa whimpered, "but if I don't...the bastard gets away with it. Is that what you're saying?"

"Molly is what, six, almost seven?" Brenda said. "She's too young to comprehend any of this. And speaking as a psychologist, this kind of trauma to a child her age could have a severe effect on her development."

"So I just try to forget what he's done, smile and act nice when he comes to visit Molly? How can I do that?"

"I don't know what else to tell you, Melissa, but I personally believe there are worse things you can do to Jerry than to send him to prison. But you do need to know that the statute of limitations for attempted murder in the state of Florida is four years. If you are going to file charges against him, you need to do it soon, but first, please consider what that might do to Molly. I would hope you would allow her to grow up and develop a few years before you tell her the truth about her father. She needs to know the truth about him, but she's too young now. Soon she won't be and you can explain it to her then."

Melissa wiped her eyes and stared at Brenda. "What could I do to him that's worse than going to prison?"

Brenda looked over her shoulder at Marshall, then back at Melissa. "Do you have any idea where Jerry is now? Have you heard from him?"

"No. He hasn't even called to talk to Molly," she said softly.

Marshall leaned forward. "When I discovered all this in your medical files, I panicked and hired a private detective to track him down. I wanted to make sure he was nowhere around you and Grant. I don't trust him as far as I could throw him. Anyway, we found out that he's living in Asheville, North Carolina and spending that million, seven he got from you like water. He paid cash for a $700,000 house and a new Jaguar. He has a fancy new office in the most expensive high rise in downtown Asheville and is somehow practicing psychology again, and he is running with the super elite high society circles there. He's become a real big shot. However, he's almost broke. His bank account is showing less than $200,000. At the rate, he'll go broke in six months."

"That doesn't surprise me; he's spent that much money in a month," Melissa said. "But I don't understand what that has to do with getting him back for what he's done to me?"

Brenda smiled. "Being rich and living high is Jerry's true God. It's all he's ever cared about. It's why he tried to kill you, so he could get your money. If he was ever broke, and I mean completely broke, disgraced, left penniless, homeless, forced to live on the street...that would be much worse for him than to have to go to prison where he would get food, clean clothes and shelter."

Melissa tried not to smile. "So what do I do?"

"I'm confident when he runs out of money, he will call you," Marshall said. "Who else could he call?"

We all nodded our heads in agreement. "You are the only one he *could* call. And when he calls for money, say yes." Marshal said. "But tell him you'll only give him the money in the form of a loan. Before he shows up, have your lawyer draw up an iron clad agreement that puts his house, his furniture, his Jaguar, basically all of his possessions, up for collateral. This document will also have a payment plan that states that if he misses a payment, you can foreclose and take posses-sion of his property immediately."

"Why would he sign something like that?"

Brenda laughed. "Because when you say yes to giving him more money, he will believe that he still controls you, and that you would never actually enforce it.

"Even after all I've done to him?"

"Melissa, think about it from his point of view," Brenda said. "What have you really done? You took away his custody of Molly, his office, his apartment and his car, but in return, you gave him almost 2 million dollars. And now, you are agreeing to give him more money.

He'll gladly sign the papers, but with absolutely no intentions of ever paying you back a cent. And that will be the worst mistake he will ever make."

In the moonlight, Melissa's eyes twinkled above her wide grin. "I hope you're right. And if he does this, I think I'll let him get three months behind before I lower the boom on the sorry bastard."

I stood and poked the fire to get it going again. "So, was that the second thing you guys came here to tell us?"

Marshall lifted his glass and sipped his wine. "No, it's not. There's something else I need to tell you, and it concerns both of you."

I sat back down in my chair and stared over the fire pit at his face, but I couldn't read his expression. "Am I going to need more than this Diet Coke for this? Maybe some wine or perhaps a shot of Jack Daniels?"

He gave me a blank look. "To tell you the truth, buddy, I have no idea how you're going to react to this."

That didn't sound good to me. "I'll be right back," I said. I ran up the steps and poured myself two fingers of Jack Daniels, then slowly walked down the steps and sat in the chair. "Ok, tell us."

Marshall nervously ran his hand through his hair and sighed. "When I received Melissa's medical records, I was actually stunned to discover that her blood type was AB negative. That's extremely rare. In fact, it's the rarest blood type of all – only 1 or 2 % of the entire human race has that blood type. That got me thinking about how incredibly lucky she had been to find a healthy liver donor with AB negative blood on that exact day. Her doctor told me that she more than likely would not have survived another twenty-four hours without the transplant…it was that close."

He sipped his wine, glanced at Brenda and then back to me. "Grant, do you know what day it was that Melissa received her transplant?"

I looked at Melissa. "What day was it?"

Confused, she shrugged and said, "It was two years ago on February 17th."

My body froze and my heart began pounding in my chest when I heard the date. I turned and stared at Marshall. "What was Rita's blood type?"

He lifted his brow and dipped his head slowly. "AB negative."

I gasped. My jaw slacked and I felt light headed. I tried to speak, but couldn't form words.

"What does that mean?" Melissa asked, still confused.

I stared into Marshall's eyes. "How?" Was all I could get out.

Marshall leaned forward. "Before we actually unplugged her, we harvested her vital organs. She had checked the donor box on her drivers licensed. Since we didn't need your permission, I didn't tell you. You were in no condition to talk about that. Grant, she not only saved Melissa's life, she saved two other people, with her heart and lungs."

The chair tumbled behind me, skidding off the brick patio into the sand when I jumped up and ran away. I have no memory of this, but that's what they tell me I did. The next thing I actually remember was running barefoot down the beach. I wasn't sure what had happened to my shoes or how far and how long I had been running, but I was out of breath. When I stopped, I fell to my knees on the sand, gasping for air, crying. Out of the corner of my eye, I saw Charley. He was only a few feet away, standing there quietly watching me.

I held out my hand. "Hey, buddy." He slowly walked up to me and nudged my hand with his nose. "I'm okay," I said, petting his head, "don't worry."

I turned over and laid down on my back in the sand, staring up at the stars. Charley curled up next to me, resting his head on my chest. "You've known all along, haven't you?"

He lifted his eyes and stared up at me. "That's why you didn't like all those other beach houses. You were bringing me here...to Melissa...because you knew all along. What are you, Charley? Are you my guardian angel?"

"Thank God! You finally stopped running!" I looked up to see Marshall standing over us, holding his side and breathing hard. "Are you all right?"

I sat up. "I don't know," I said. "I don't feel much of anything right now. My mind is blank and my body is sort of numb."

He sat down on the sand next to us. "Well, you sure scared the shit out of everybody when you jumped up and took off running like a friggin' rabbit. Why in the hell did you do that?"

I sighed and laid back down on the sand. "I don't know. It just seemed like the thing to do. To be honest, I don't remember doing it. I remember what you said, and then the next thing I know, I'm sitting here petting Charley. I guess I owe everyone an apology for taking off like that."

"I think that would be a good thing to do."

"How is Melissa?" I asked.

He sighed. "I don't really know. When you took off, she didn't know what to do, so she went home. Brenda's with her now."

I wasn't sure what to say, so I stopped talking and stared up at the sky. Marshall took the hint, rolled onto his back and stared up at the sky with me.

After a few minutes of silence, he said, "This reminds me of when we were kids, laying on those blow up floats out on the lake at Huntsville State Park. Remember that?"

I chuckled. "Yeah. That seems like a million years ago. Sometimes I wish I could go back. We didn't know it, but we had it made back then."

"Yes, we did," Marshall said, "but I wouldn't want to go back. I like where I am now."

"I don't blame you," I said, grinning, "you were pretty geeky back then with those coke bottle thick horn rimmed glasses and all those pimples."

He sat up and threw a hand full of sand at me. "You weren't exactly a babe magnet yourself. I never could figure out what Rita saw in you."

We both laughed. "I never figured it out either. She could have dated any guy in school, but she chose me." My voice cracked and my eyes filled with tears. I turned away, wiping my eyes with my sleeve.

"I'm sorry, Grant. I didn't mean to bring up bad memories."

"It's okay," I said holding up my hand. "Those are not bad memories, those are the best memories I have, and the ones I hope I never forget. The ones I love to think about. I do it all the time and I know how lucky I was that she chose me."

We laid there quietly not saying a word, staring up at the sky for ten or fifteen minutes.

"Marshall, I'm not upset. I'm glad you did it."

He frowned. "Did what?"

"I'm talking about the harvest. Rita would have wanted that. And I know why you didn't tell me about it when it happened. I was such a mess back then I couldn't have handled it, but I got better and moved on with my life. The only thing I don't get is, it's been over two years. Why haven't you told me before now?"

He raised up, knocking the sand off his back. "I've wanted to tell you for a long time. When Brenda and I came to visit you here in Saint Augustine that first time, I had planned on telling you then, but it never seemed to be the right time."

"I understand, but I wish you'd told me."

"I wish I had, too. The last thing I'd ever want to do is cause you more pain in your life. And I'm really sorry for that."

"Marshall, I'm a little stunned to find out about Rita's harvest, but you need to know that at the same time, I'm happy about it. There's no question in my mind...she would have definitely wanted it. It's just the other part. Hell, I can't think of a word to even describe it. The odds are just so...so impossible that Melissa..." I couldn't finish the sentence. "Are you absolutely sure?"

"Yes. I've double-checked. When her liver was harvested, it was flown directly here. I've talked to her surgical team. It was Rita's liver."

"Do you think that's why...when we touch...the shock?"

He shrugged his shoulders. "I don't know, maybe, but that doesn't make any sense, either."

I didn't respond. I just laid there quietly, slowly shaking my head, dumbfounded at the impossibility of it all.

"Grant, I know you well," Marshall said. "I can almost hear your thoughts whirling around inside your head from here. You're trying to apply logic to this, but none of this is logical...it's spiritual. That's the only explanation."

"What's the old saying, 'God works in mysterious ways'?"

Marshall smiled. "You really want to know what I believe happened here?"

"Well, old buddy, you've always been the smartest one between us," I said, grinning, "So absolutely yes, please, Doc...help me understand all of this."

He stood up and looked down at me. "I'm a man of science, a doctor of medicine and not supposed to believe in things like God, spirits and angels. To most of my colleagues, this would be explained simply as a huge coincidence. And maybe it is, but it's too impossible for me to believe that. I'm convinced that there has to be more to this than simple coincidence. It's bigger than that, the odds are too astronomical." He pointed up at the sky. "Grant, I believe that this was an au-gust harvest."

"A what?" I said, confused. "August? Rita died in February."

"I didn't mean August like the month. I meant *au-gust*, like something marked by majestic dignity, something very, very special...magnificent. That's the definition of au-gust."

He put his hands in his pockets and looked at me. "Grant, no one can explain why, but it *was* Audrey and Rita's time. But it *was not* Melissa's. If Rita hadn't died that day, Melissa would have. And as hard as that is to hear, it *has* to mean something. It has to be God's plan for you. I believe this was an au-gust harvest and you are supposed to be here...now...with Melissa."

I sat silent on the beach processing what he had said. "An au-gust harvest," I whispered slowly as I stood and brushed the sand off my clothes. "I'm still not sure I understand any of this, but I think this might be what Rita was trying to tell me when I was drowning in that water. I guess I do have much more to do. Let's go find out what that is. I think I'm ready to go home now."

When we made it back to the house and walked in the door, the second Melissa saw me, she burst into tears, ran up to me and jumped into my open arms.

# 17

# IT DOESN'T MATTER

M elissa and I didn't talk much for the rest of that night. Instead, we just held on to each other tightly and listened to Marshall and Brenda, when they could think of something to say. Truthfully, they didn't talk much either, but the long periods of silence between us wasn't awkward, it was peaceful, something we all needed. The blissful peace between all of us continued the next morning through breakfast and our long walk together, strolling through the shallow water from the waves crashing on the beach.

All the tension that had been so obvious in Marshall's eyes was gone, and he was back to his old self. He was actually smiling when he shook my hand and hugged my neck. Then he followed Brenda down the front staircase, squeezed into his tiny rental car and left for the airport. After I waved goodbye to them and turned around, Melissa was standing in the hallway with a somber expression on her face. She was holding Molly's hand and Donna's leash.

"We're gonna go, too," she said softly. "You need to get back to work and I've got a lot to do around my house."

"Yeah, you're right, I do need to head to the office, but before I go, I was hoping we could talk a little. I know I should have talked about this last night...I'm sorry, but I was just too overwhelmed to think straight. But I'm better now and I thought..."

"I'm sorry, Grant," she said, stopping me, "but I don't want to talk about it right now. I need some time to think about it...alone."

"Sure," I said a little surprised, "Take as much time as you need. I guess I was wrong, because...well, the way you were acting around Brenda and Marshall, I...I thought you were okay with all of this."

She dropped her head. "I didn't want to upset them and you know Brenda. I love her, but she just can't stop psychoanalyzing me."

I bent down and kissed her. "You don't have to explain. She does it to me, too."

"But I *want* to explain. I *am* okay with it...I think," she said. "Honestly, I don't know *what* I think. Please, Grant, it's a lot to take in. It's not just about the transplant, it's all this crap about what Jerry did to me, too. I need some time to absorb it and figure out what I'm going to do next. Please, just give me a few days. Do you understand?"

Melissa's *"three days"* turned out to be almost three weeks. During that time, we saw each other occasionally, waving back and forth from our decks, but we never got close enough to touch, and we never talked.

∼

I HAD SPENT the three weeks catching up with my work on the Beverly Beach Project, working almost around the clock, sleeping more nights on the couch in my office than in my bed at home, so the time had actually flown by before I realized it.

Being so busy had kept my mind occupied, but not completely. Out of nowhere, more than once, the thoughts of Rita's organs being harvested, Au-gust or not, caused me to lose it and break down. When I did this, Charley would either lay his head on my lap and let me cry, or bring me his leash and bark until I took him out for a walk. He always seem to know exactly what to do that would bring me back.

On our walks, my mind would drift with thoughts of Rita and Audrey and the life we had spent together. Then it would jump to thoughts of Melissa and Molly and what my life might become with them. When I thought of Audrey and Rita, it was never bad or sad; I had somehow successfully locked those horrible memories away. I only recalled the good ones, the fun ones, the happy ones. I guess it was therapeutic, because it always made me feel better, stronger somehow.

After many of these walks with Charley during those three weeks, I only had one unanswered question in my mind, and it's not what you may be thinking. Now that I knew that there was a part of Rita alive, living inside of Melissa, the question wasn't *was it Rita, or was it Melissa that caused that shock that rushed through my body when we touched?* The question was...was I truly in love with Melissa...and if I was...did it matter where those sensations were coming from?

~

I HADN'T SEEN Melissa in almost a week. I had finally caught up with my drawings and was actually ahead of schedule on the Beverly Beach project. It was Saturday morning and instead of jumping up, rushing around and leaving for the office, I hit the snooze button on the alarm clock when it went off. Unfortunately, Charley didn't have a snooze button and wasn't about to let me sleep. I could feel his presence, and when I opened my eyes, he was standing next to the nightstand about a foot away from my face staring at me. "Woof!"

"Charley, it's Saturday. We're not going to the office today. Go back to sleep."

He didn't move. "Woof, woof, woof." He nudged me with his nose. "Woof!"

"Come on, Charley, let me sleep just a little longer."

He bit down on the sheet and drug it off me to the floor. "Woof!"

I knew it was a losing battle, so I rolled out of bed, walked to the kitchen and made some coffee. I was barefoot, only wearing my boxers. When I lifted the cup out of the coffee maker and turned around, Charley was standing behind me, holding my jeans in his mouth.

"What in the hell is your problem this morning? What's the big rush to get dressed? I told you we're not going to the office today."

He dropped my jeans at my feet. "Woof!" he said, nudging them closer to me with his nose.

"Okay, okay, you crazy mutt! I'll put them on, for God's sake."

The second I pulled them up and got them zipped, the doorbell rang. It was Melissa and Donna.

"Hey, good morning!" I said, opening the door. "What's up?"

Donna ran up to Charley and after a few excited circles and sniffs, they both took off running through our legs, down the staircase toward the beach.

"Come in," I said, "want some coffee?"

"I'd love some," she said with a shy smile, "and maybe a little breakfast?"

"Is that some kind a hint that you want me to cook?"

She lifted her eyes." I've been thinking about your world famous pancakes since I woke up this morning." She handed me a plastic grocery sack. "I even brought the ingredients, just in case you were out of something."

I took the sack and she followed me to the kitchen. "Where's Molly?"

"I just dropped her off at a play date with one of her friends from school."

I pulled out my recipe and together we measured the ingredients and mixed the batter. When we finished, I turned on the stove and heated up the griddle.

"Whose handwriting is this?" she asked, holding up the old, worn 3 by 5 recipe card in her hand.

"That's my grandmother's. I loved her pancakes so much, she wrote the recipe on that card and gave it to me when I was about twelve."

"And you've kept it all these years?"

I set a plate stacked high with four steaming hot pancakes in front of her. "You bet I have. I even have a Xerox copy of it in my safe." I picked up the card and looked at it. "I probably should be using the copy, but I like holding it when I cook them. It reminds me of watching my granny singing and cooking in her kitchen. I loved that. This card is priceless to me."

She smiled. "One more," she said.

"One more what?"

She took a bite and moaned. "Oh my God! These are amazing."

Talking with my mouth full, I mumbled, "Yummy!"

The room fell silent while we gorged ourselves eating the hotcakes. When I finished and pushed my plate away, I said, "You didn't answer me. One more what?"

She put down her fork, wiped her mouth with the napkin and grinned. "You weren't supposed to hear that."

"Too bad," I said with a chuckle, "because I did. Come on...spill it. One more what?"

She looked into my eyes. "One more reason on my list to love you and another reason I know you are the right one."

I raised my eyebrows. "You have a list?"

"Sort of," she said shyly. "It's not written down or anything, but yes, it's a list of reasons why or why not."

"Is it a long list?"

"It's getting longer."

"May I ask...what was the item you just added? What was the 'One More' thing?"

She reached down and picked up the recipe card. "It's this card. Grant, I don't think you kept this card all these years just for the recipe that's written on it. You kept it because of whose handwriting is on it. You are sentimental. That's not a common trait for a man. And just one more thing I love about you."

"What else you got on that list?"

"You really want to know?"

"I think I can handle it. Go ahead, but tell me the good stuff first."

She reached across the table and took my hand. "That's my problem. There's only good stuff."

I laughed. "That's because you haven't known me very long. Just wait, you'll see."

"Well, here's what I have so far. You love Molly, you are smart, kind hearted, a hard worker, a great cook and apparently sentimental."

I threw up my hands. "That's it? That's all you've got. What about the ruggedly handsome and amazing lover part?"

She stood up, walked around the table and sat in my lap. "That's the best part." She took my face in her hands and kissed me on the lips.

"Do you still feel them?" she whispered. "I do."

I took her hand and pressed it over my heart. "Feel that? It's jumping like crazy."

She laid her head against my chest. "I can hear it." Then she raised up and stared into my eyes. She wasn't smiling and her eyes were full of tears.

"What's wrong?" I asked softly,

She looked away, "I love you, Grant, I really do, but..."

"But what?"

"Now that we know whose liver is inside of me…that changes things. I'm not sure I can do this."

"Changes what?" I jerked my head up, frowning at her. "What's that supposed to mean? What can't you do? If we're not supposed to be together, then how do you explain these feelings when we touch?"

"That's sort of my point. Can you look me in the eyes and swear to me that what you feel when you touch me...is because of me...and not because Rita is part of me?"

I didn't answer and held her gaze for a long time until she finally looked away. "That's what I was afraid of."

She tried to move away, off my lap, but I held her there. "I didn't say it was Rita. I didn't answer, because I don't know where it comes from. Does it really matter?"

"Yes!" she shouted. "It matters to me." She pulled away harder, so I let her go.

She walked outside to the deck and leaned against the rail. I followed her and put my arm around her waist. "Please don't cry. I didn't mean it that way. I know it sounded harsh, but I've thought about this a lot, and apparently you have, too. I can't explain where these feelings come from and neither can you. Maybe it does have something to do with a part of Rita living inside of you, who knows, but what I was trying to say was...it doesn't matter to me. It's *you* that matters to me now."

With my hand, I wiped the tears away from her cheek and pulled her into my arms. "Isn't that enough?"

"I guess it should be, but it's not," she whispered. "When you touch me, kiss me, make love to me...as a woman, I have to know that you are feeling me...and only me. And...when I touch you and I feel that shock inside of my body...I have to know...is that coming from me or is that somehow coming from her? I know that may sound crazy and foolish, but I can't help the way I feel."

She stared up into my eyes. "There are so many reasons to fall for you, but until I know for sure...I don't think I can."

"Melissa, I'm doing my best to understand, but I don't know how we will ever know the truth about this."

"Grant, I've known there's something special about you since the day Molly ran up to you on the beach. It was how you lit up the second you saw her, the way you looked at her, the way you talked to her. You were a complete stranger, but I instantly knew you were meant to be a part of our lives, a big part. And I've loved every second I've spent with you since then. I truly believe that everything we've done, all we've shared together was meant to be. But now that we know about my connection to Rita...where we go from here...to be honest, I just don't know, but something inside of me feels different."

I wasn't sure how to respond to her. My feelings for her had not changed. I knew I loved her, but I couldn't lie to myself, either. When I touched her now and felt that shock, I instantly thought about Rita. I took her hands in mine and smiled. "I know I love you and I'm supposed to be part of your life, so how about this? Let's just take things slow from here on and see where it goes. Something brought me here to you and I believe the love we have for each other will someday, somehow, make everything clear to us."

We followed that plan and over the next few months our relation-ship flourished, spending as much time as we could together. We had date nights almost every weekend and always spent Sundays with

Molly, either playing on the beach or just hanging out. We never once talked about the continuing sparks, shocks and tingly sensations we always felt when we touched. I wasn't sure about her, but I had hoped that they would eventually go away, but they never did. I *did* learn how to not react when they happened.

~

THE BEVERLY BEACH PROJECT was going great. It was on schedule and so far, under budget. It was a huge project that kept me hopping. It had become almost more than I could handle, but I got lucky and found a great assistant to help me stay organized. I met her by accident...well, sort of. It was another one of those Charley things.

My office was located in the heart of Saint Augustine's historic district. It was literally surrounded by great restaurants. After trying most of them, I soon found my favorite three or four to have lunch. The main requirements were good food, quick service and they had to be dog friendly, because Charley was usually with me. It was never my decision of which restaurant we went to; that was up to Charley. I would just follow behind him holding on to his leash and he would take me where he wanted to go.

The day I met Annabelle, my assistant, Charley didn't lead me to one of our regular lunch spots. Instead, he drug me almost a mile, with me complaining behind him all the way. He took me to *O.C. White's*. We'd been there before, but it was too far away from my office, so it wasn't one of our regular lunch hangouts.

When I realized where he was taking me, I pulled on his leash to make him stop and look at me. "*O.C. White's*? Why here, Charley? They're always packed and their service is too slow. I don't have time for this today. I need to get back to the office,"

He stared up at me. "Woof." Then he turned and continued walking, pulling me behind him.

When we got to the entrance to the outside patio, I stopped, let go of his leash and started to ask the hostess if she had an open table.

Charley didn't wait for the answer and walked past the hostess to an empty table near the back.

The hostess laughed and motioned for me to follow Charley. "We have several open tables, but it looks like he wants to sit there."

I smiled at her, shrugged my shoulders and walked to the table Charley was now sprawled under. Although there were five or six tables available that were not surrounded by other diners, apparently Charley wanted me to sit there, in the middle of the most crowded area on the patio.

When I reached to pull out a chair, he stood up and growled at me. "What? You don't want me to sit down?"

He looked over at the chair behind the table and barked. "You want me to sit back there?" He gave me his goofy smile and laid back down.

I actually had to slide the table forward a little to get the chair out far enough to sit down. I was only inches away from a group of young college girls sitting behind me.

When the waitress came, I bent down and read out loud to Charley his choices. When I got to what he wanted, he barked his approval. This did not go unnoticed.

"No way!" I heard someone say behind me. It was one of the college girls. She was staring down at Charley. "He didn't really do that, did he?"

I smiled and looked at her. "Do what?"

"Did he tell you what he wanted?" she asked.

"Sure. He loves carrots, so he chose the chicken." I said nonchalantly.

That started the whole thing. The next thing I knew, the girls had pulled their chairs over to my table and were making a fuss over Charley. That's when I knew something was up, because he just stood there smiling, letting them pet him. That was not his normal reaction to strangers who tried to pet him.

"Who has the birthday?" I asked, pointing at what was left of a cake on their table.

"That's not a Birthday cake, it's a celebration cake for Annabelle," one of the girls said.

ize

I introduced Charley to them and got their names as well. "Well then, congratulations, Annabelle," I said smiling, holding up my Coke toasting her, "What are we celebrating?"

Her face lit up. "I just graduated college. Finally!" she said.

"Wow! That *is* something to celebrate. Did you graduate from Flagler University?" I asked.

"No," she said shyly. "I wish. I went to Appalachian State University. That's in Boone, North Carolina. That's where I'm from. I'm just here visiting my friends."

"What was your major?" When I asked that, her friends burst out laughing. "What's so funny?"

She dropped her head, embarrassed. "My major wasn't what you might think. That's why they're laughing. They all think it's a dumb major."

"How can any major be dumb?" I said. "You got a college degree, right? So tell me, what was your major?"

"Construction management. But I also got a minor in business."

Her friends laughed again, but I didn't. "So what are you planning on doing with your degree?"

"That's really why I'm here in Florida," She said. "There are limited opportunities in North Carolina, especially for a woman in the construction industry. I'm hoping that here in Florida, I could get a job working with a large construction company, maybe starting out as an estimator or whatever. My goal is to one day become a project manager on a large construction project."

Her words were not spoken with confidence and her body language screamed her shyness and reluctance to talk about herself. It was almost as if she was embarrassed to tell me her goals. And her friends didn't make it any easier for her, with their snickering and constant eye rolls.

Annabelle excused herself and went to the ladies room, leaving me alone with her friends. I turned and looked at them. "So, what are 'your' majors?" I asked with a smile.

They were all attending Flagler University. Two of the four were theater art majors, one was majoring in graphic design and one was studying psychology.

Trying my best not to sound too condescending, I said, "So you two want to be movie stars, you want to design websites and you want to be a guidance counselor?"

They looked at each other and shrugged, but I got no responses from any of them.

"How do you know Annabelle?" I asked.

"We grew up together," the two theater arts majors said. "We went to the same high school."

"She's been your friend a long time, right?"

They smiled and shook their heads. "Yes," the graphic design major said, "she's one of our best friends."

I leaned back in my chair and shrugged my shoulders. "Then I don't get it. I know we just met and it's really none of my business, but if she's one of your lifelong friends, why are you all making fun of her and hurting her feelings like this? I don't understand what's so funny here. Personally, I'd bet she's going to do really well with her degree."

"In construction?" they all said in perfect unison.

I smiled and nodded, "Yes, in construction. Florida is booming these days."

When Annabelle got back and sat down, I checked my watch. I'd been there almost an hour and needed to get back to work. I stood, walked to the table they were sitting at before they slid over to mine, and grabbed their check.

"Oh no, you don't," Annabelle said, reaching for the check in my hand. "We're gonna split this between us."

I pulled the check back out of her reach and smiled. "Please, it's my pleasure. Consider this as my graduation gift to you."

They all thanked me profusely. "That's so nice of you," Annabelle said, "But we don't even know your name. We know Charley's, but not yours."

I reached into my pocket, pulled out my business card and handed it to Annabelle. "It's Grant, Grant Nash. Ahhh, look, Annabelle, I have to get back to my office, but when you get finished here, I would like you to come by there. It's only a few blocks away. I would like to talk to you. I may be able to help you on your job search."

Her jaw dropped when she read my card. "You're an architect?" she said with wide eyes. "Are you serious? You know someone who might give me a job?"

I grinned as I clipped the leash to Charley's collar. "Yes, I just might know someone. Come see me later and we'll talk about it."

It was almost an hour before my office doorbell rang. I hit the intercom button to unlock the door and told her to come in. "Go get her," I said to Charley, who was standing at the top of the stairs wagging his tail. I heard her laughing when he ran down the stairs to greet her.

"What a beautiful office," she said when she walked in the room. "Is this only for you? You work here alone?"

"Hang on one second, I need to send this to the printer. Have a seat," I said, pointing at the couch.

When the printer started making noise, I stood up from behind my work station and walked over to her. "Yes, I'm sort of a one-man shop. Would you like something to drink? Follow me, I'll give you the five cent tour."

After I showed her around the office, I got her a Coke, poured myself a cup of coffee, and we settled around the meeting table. "What do you think of this?" I tapped the plans to the Beverly Beach Project that were spread out on the table. She looked down and began studying them, flipping through the pages slowly.

When she finished, she looked across the table at me. "Are these your designs, your drawings?"

I nodded. "Yes. What do you think?"

For the next hour, she grilled me on every aspect of my designs. I expected most of her questions, because they were obvious, but I didn't expect some of her others. It didn't take me long to realize that this small town girl from Boone, North Carolina knew her stuff.

"Where did you learn all of that?" I asked her with a grin. "I'm pretty sure it wasn't in college."

Her eyes lit up. "My father was a contractor. He built houses and a few small office buildings around Boone, so I grew up around construction sites. I'm an only child. Dad was hoping for a boy, but got me instead. So, I grew up playing with toy hammers and saws, instead of Barbie dolls. I was an expert at taping and floating sheetrock at ten years old and knew how to handle a skill saw as good as anyone."

That day, I learned Annabelle's father had a heart attack when she was seventeen, her senior year of high school, and had to close down his construction business. After she graduated, she wanted to go away to college, but her parents couldn't afford it, so she applied to Appalachian State University there in Boone.

"Because it was a local, I received a special rate," she said. "At first I was disappointed, not getting to go away to college like my friends, but I soon grew to love Appalachian State. And when I saw they offered a degree in construction management, it just seemed to be a natural fit for me."

I leaned back in my chair and smiled at her. "I think you made a very wise decision."

For the past few months, I had been talking to Les about hiring an assistant if I could find one qualified, so I hired Annabelle on the spot.

With her incredible organizational skills and uncanny ability to spot potential problems, within months, she had the Beverly Beach Project whipped into shape and every detail in its proper place. With her taking care of all the tedious required paperwork for the permits and help with organizing the timing schedules of the different trades and sub-contractors, the project progressed without a hitch.

I know that some of you may find this hard to believe, but I hired Annabelle because first, Charley obviously wanted me to and took me to her and second, because of her skills. The fact that she was a young, beautiful woman never entered my mind. As silly as it sounds, I was so wrapped up and busy with the Beverly Beach Project, I never paid any attention to what she looked like...but apparently Melissa had.

That became very obvious the day I invited her over to my house to spend a day on the beach with Melissa, Molly and me. Again, being oblivious to her appearance, I paid no attention to what she was wearing when she showed up, but when we got everything set up on the beach and she took off her coverup, exposing the tiny pink bikini underneath...I noticed. Her perfectly proportioned, muscular toned body was stunning. Around me at work, she had always dressed very conservatively and until that moment, I honestly had no idea she had a body like that.

To make matters worse, I opened up my big mouth and asked if she had ever been a dancer or something.

With her amazing body glistening in the sun, shining from the sun tan lotion I had watched her apply, she looked up at me, smiled and said, "Yes, I took ballet when I was young and I was a gymnast in high school and college."

I wanted to say, "Well no wonder you're so smoking hot", but thank God I didn't. Instead I just smiled and forced myself to look away. When I did, I made eye contact with Melissa, but to my surprise, she wasn't giving me a dirty look, she was grinning.

Molly instantly fell madly in love with Annabelle and for the rest of the afternoon, Melissa and I watched the two of them play together like children, building sand castles, splashing and laughing in the surf.

After Annabelle went home and Molly went inside to take her shower, Melissa and I had our first real conversation about her. It was a conversation that completely baffled me.

"You two make a cute couple." She said with no real emotions showing on her face.

"Couple? For God's sake, Melissa, she's only 22 or 23 years old. I'm not attracted to her. She's way too young for me! You have nothing to worry about."

"Did I say I was worried? But I'm not blind, Grant. I saw the way you were looking at her. You almost swallowed your gum."

I started laughing, put my arms around her and kissed her, "I wasn't chewing gum."

She tried to pull away, but I held her tightly in my arms. "It's a good thing you weren't. You might have choked to death."

That night we made love for the first time in weeks, and I did everything I could to try to convince her that she had nothing to worry about when it came to Annabelle.

"I didn't hire her for her looks. I hired her because she's really good at what she does, and she is doing an amazing job for me."

"Grant, relax. I'm not worried about Annabelle. I really like her. She's wonderful. I will admit to being a little jealous of her body. She looks like a friggin' Victoria's Secret model. And me with all my scars...."

"Look at me," I said. "I'm in love with you, not her. You have to know that by now, don't you?"

She nodded. "Yes, but..."

"There're no buts. I love you. It's just that simple."

That's what I told her that night and I meant it. But from that day forward, things began to change and our lives weren't so simple.

# 18

# THE MARK OF THE DEVIL

S taring at his reflection from the glistening door of his brand new black Jaguar, Dr. Jeremiah Ashford Hollingsworth adjusted his tie and smoothed back his hair. In the mirrored walls of the elevator, riding up to his penthouse office suite, he checked his appearance once more. When he was sure everything was perfect, he stepped out of the elevator and walked quickly past his receptionist.

"Good morning," he chirped, nodding his head as he walked past.

In his office, he sat down behind the very large, one of a kind, designer glass and bronze desk and checked his phone messages. There were only three. One from the general manager of his country club, letting him know that his dues were late again, and two from his banker demanding a return call.

"Dr. Hollingsworth?" He looked up from the message to see his receptionist standing in his doorway.

"I'm sorry to have to bring this up," she said nervously, holding a small piece of paper in her hand, "but my paycheck bounced."

"That's impossible!" he shouted. "Run it through again. The bank must have made a mistake."

Her hand trembled, as she held up the check, "I tried, but my bank said it's written on an account that has insufficient funds. They said I need to have you write me another check from a different account."

He jumped out of his chair and rushed up to her. "Give me that!" he shouted, jerking the check out of her hand. "I'll take care of it. Go back to your desk."

"But I really need the money. I'm overdrawn in my account and..."

I SAID I WOULD TAKE CARE OF IT!" He screamed, "GO BACK TO YOUR DESK, NOW!"

He locked his door when she left, walked back to his desk and sat down. Reluctantly, he dialed the number for his banker.

"I need to speak with John Willy. This is Dr. Jeremiah Ashford Hollingsworth calling."

"Yes, Doctor," an obviously young, female voice said, "he's expecting your call. Hold on, I'll put you through."

The phone clicked in his ear and began to ring. "Dr. Hollingsworth, I need to see you, today." John Willy, the bank president, said immediately. "We have a serious problem. All three of your accounts are overdrawn. The bank examiners are breathing down my neck and this needs to be corrected immediately. Today, this morning!"

"John, I am so sorry to have put you in this situation. There must have been some glitch in the offshore money transfer. Let me check into that and I'll get right back with you."

"Jerry, I'm not going to fall for that again!" he shouted. "That's exactly what you told me last week and you never called me back. I'm not sure what kind of game you're trying to play here, but it's not going to work with me. I will give you exactly forty-eight hours to get this cleared up. If it isn't, I will be forced to take serious legal action against you. I am through playing your game! Forty-eight hours! Not one second more!"

Jerry started to respond, but the phone clicked in his ear before he could say a word.

He leaned back in his chair and stared up at the ceiling. *How the fuck did I go through all that money so fast?* he said to himself. The more he thought about his situation, the angrier he got.

"Bitch!" he screamed out loud. "How could she have done this to me! I've never had to worry about money before."

He stood and began pacing his office. "It's beneath me," he spat. "A man of my status should never have to worry about such trivial things!"

~

MELISSA and I were eating lunch at a small restaurant near my office when he called. Her body stiffened when she read the name on the caller ID. "Oh my God, It's Jerry. What do I do?" She stared across the table at me with wide eyes.

"Calm down. You know why he's calling. Act surprised when you answer."

"Hello?" she said meekly, "Jerry, is this you?"

She locked eyes with me as she listened. "Yes...we're doing fine. I wish she was here, she would love to talk to you." Her forehead wrinkled and her lips tightened,' as she listened to his response. "Sure...I'll tell her. So...if it wasn't to talk to Molly, then why are you calling?"

Staring into my eyes, she moved her head from side to side as she listened. "Jerry, I don't know, that's a lot of money. My accountant, and especially my attorney, won't like it. When do you need it?"

She actually smiled when he told her. "How in the world did you get overdrawn that much? Don't you balance your checkbooks?" She pulled the phone away from her ear. I could hear him yelling from across the table. "Jerry...Jerry...stop yelling at me or I'm hanging up!"

She listened for a few minutes, "I understand. You've never been good with money. Now listen to me. This is serious. If I do this, you have to understand that it will be the last time. If you blow this money, don't call me again. I'm serious. Do you understand?"

I couldn't make out the actual words he was saying from the other side of the table, but his groveling gratitude was obvious by the way Melissa was smiling at me. "Ok, I'll call your banker today and have my lawyer draw up a loan agreement."

She paused, listening. "Because it's the only way I will give you this money. It has to be a loan, not a gift. My lawyer will insist on it. And you're going to have to pay me back. That's the only way I'll do it. Take it or leave it, it's up to you."

That afternoon, Melissa's attorney had the loan documents overnighted to Jerry's banker, John Willy, with instructions to have the documents signed by Jerry, witnessed and notarized in his presence. Once that was done, his bank would receive a wire transfer of one million dollars. After the overdrafts were covered, that would leave Dr. Jeremiah Ashford Hollingsworth with a little over $870,000 left in his account.

The collateral for the million-dollar loan was Jerry's house, his furniture and expensive art collection, his Jaguar and his office furniture – basically everything he owned with any value. Melissa didn't add any interest on the loan. All that was required was payments for five years of $16,666 per month.

When the lawyer showed Melissa the loan documents, she started laughing. "Isn't 666 the mark of the devil? How appropriate."

∽

I HAD GIVEN Jerry five months, in our unofficial pool, on how long it would be before he blew through the money or stopped making the payments.

Surprising all of us, his $16,666 payment arrived a day early, for seven months, before he called Rob Waterson Melissa's attorney, asking for an extension.

After a quick phone call to John Willy, the president of Jerry's bank, inquiring about the status of his remaining bank balance, Rob sent a registered letter to Jerry's office telling him no, reminding him that if he missed two payments in a row, the loan would officially be in breach and foreclosure proceedings on all of his collateral would begin.

As we all expected, the second month's payment did not arrive. After that, Jerry simply ignored all of the registered letters he received over the next several months, informing him of his breach of contract and the imminent foreclosure he was facing.

Jerry wasn't worried in the slightest, and just laughed and tore up the documents when they came. It was all just a bluff. He realized that the documents were real, but he knew that it was just her lawyer doing his job to keep earning his monthly retainer. Melissa would never actually go through with a foreclosure. She would be furious, but she'd never allow that to happen to him. She was still under his spell. The same spell he put her under when she was young. She had no real backbone to go through a foreclosure. And she wasn't smart enough to realize why she could never actually hurt him. She was his sheep and would do anything he asked. And although he had done it again and was running low on money in his bank account, he knew right where to go to get more.

No, Dr. Jeremiah Ashford Hollingsworth wasn't worried at all, so when he didn't have a patient, which was often, he spent his days playing tennis at the country club and his nights eating at the finest restaurants in town with his good friends. Life was good.

# 19

# GONE WITH THE WIND

"Yes!" Dr. Jeremiah Ashford Hollingsworth shouted, running toward the net. It was the best serve he'd hit in months — a smoking ace that just hit the line, winning the match.

He jumped over the net, holding out his hand. "Sorry, old man," he said grinning, shaking his opponent's hand, "maybe next time."

He walked to the bench, picked up his towel and sat down, wiping his face.

"Doctor Hollingsworth?"

He turned around to see a young woman standing behind him. She was wearing a navy blue Lakeside Country Club golf shirt, so he assumed she was one of the employees.

"Yes, I'm Doctor Hollingsworth." He said.

"I think you need to go to the parking lot," she said hesitantly.

He frowned. "The parking lot? Why on earth would I need to go out there?"

"They're hauling off your car."

"Who's hauling off my car?" he yelled, jumping to his feet.

She stared down at the ground, shuffling her feet nervously. "I don't know who he is, sir. I've never seen him before. He said he was hired to pick up your car, that was being repossessed."

Jerry ran past the young girl to the parking lot. His beautiful new Jaguar was sitting on the back of a large wrecker. "STOP!" he screamed, running up to the driver, who was bent over attaching a chain to the undercarriage of the Jag.

He grabbed the man's arm and pulled him back. "I SAID STOP!"

The large, burly wrecker driver grabbed Jerry's hand and jerked it away from his arm. "I'm just trying to do my job, sir," he said, glaring down at him. He walked to the cab, opened the door and picked up some papers. "Read this."

Jerry took the repossession papers and scanned them. "I don't give a shit what these say," he shouted throwing the papers to the ground. "This is some kind of a mistake and I'm not going to let you take my car!"

He grabbed the driver's shoulder and pulled him back away from the wrecker. The driver took Jerry's hand, squeezed it hard and bent it backwards. Jerry screamed in pain and fell to the pavement on his knees.

Twisting his wrist further, the driver growled, "If you touch me again, I'm gonna consider that as an assault. What I'll do next will be considered self-defense. Trust me, sir, you won't like that one bit. Do you understand?"

Jerry didn't respond. "Now, sir, I'm gonna let go of your hand and what you do is up to you, it's your call. But I suggest you let me do my job and leave me alone. If this is a mistake, I think you need to pick them papers back up off the ground and call that number on the letter head and talk to them.

Jerry didn't move, staying on his knees when the driver let go of his hand and walked back to the wrecker. The driver carefully checked the chains and straps securing the Jag to the truck bed, jumped back in the cab and slowly drove out of the parking lot.

~

WHEN THE CAB driver turned on the street to his house, Jerry couldn't believe his eyes. The street was blocked off by two police cars with their blue lights flashing, and there was a large moving van backed up to his front door.

From the back seat of the cab, he could easily read the word 'EVICTION' written in large red letters on the paper that was taped to his front door.

"Don't stop," he said to the cabbie, "take me to my office."

When he walked into the lobby of his office building, he was stopped by two security guards. "We're sorry, Dr. Hollingsworth, but we have orders not to let you in the building."

"But I have to get to my office," he shouted. "I need to make a phone call!"

"I'm sorry, Doctor, but we can't let you do that. You couldn't get in anyway; they changed all the locks this morning. I'm sorry, but you have to leave. You're not allowed to be in this building."

He stormed out and walked across the street to the Starbucks. He ordered a frappuccino. and a slice of banana nut bread, but when he tried to pay for it, his credit card was rejected. Furious, he slammed the cash down on the counter and took a seat in the back.

～

ROB WATERSON, Melissa's attorney, had just hung up his phone when his secretary opened his door. "It's him, and boy, is he pissed," she said, grinning. "He's on line two."

He lifted the receiver, punched line two and said, "Rob Waterson."

"Mr. Waterson, this is Dr. Jeremiah Ashford Hollingsworth calling."

"Hey, what's up, Doc?"

"You know what is up, you son of a bitch. How dare you embarrass me like this in front of my friends and colleagues?"

Rob punched the speaker button and hung up the receiver, so his secretary and his partner could hear the conversation. "Sorry about that, Jerry, but you didn't leave me much choice. You are four months behind on your payments. When you didn't answer my three registered letters, you forced me to do what I had to do to secure the collateral."

"Does Melissa know about this?" Jerry screamed. "Get her on the phone! I want to talk to her right now! I've been trying to call her, but she hasn't answered. Get her on the phone now!"

"Sorry, Doc, but that's not going to happen. Melissa doesn't want to talk to you. And yes, she does know about this. In fact, I'm following her instructions."

"That bitch! I'm going to kill her for this!"

"Dr. Hollingsworth, I think I need to inform you that you are on a speakerphone, my secretary and my partner just heard you make that threat. You might want to calm down and think about what you're saying."

"I don't give a shit who is listening," Jerry shouted on the phone. "As soon as I talk to Melissa and get this straightened out, you will all be fired. I promise you that!"

Rob smiled. "Is that a fact? Well, in that case I guess it would be a good time to explain to you the rest of this shit storm you're in. Are you sitting down, Doc? You might want to find a chair. Tell me when you're all settled in."

"I *am* sitting down, you fucking asshole!" Jerry barked.

"Hey, watch your language. There's a lady listening," Rob said, grinning. "Doc, have you ever heard of a drug called Isoniazid? I bet you have. I think you need to know that we have all the evidence we need to have your ass arrested for attempted murder. You see, Doc, we all know what you did. We know that it was you that suggested Melissa take Isoniazid. We also have copies of all those prescriptions you wrote and filled. And we know all about the vodka and the store where you bought it, that you put in her IV trying to damage her liver. And you would have gotten away with it, too, if it hadn't had been for that transplant. Boy, I bet you were pissed about that. "

Jerry wiped the sweat off his forehead with his sleeve. "You can't prove any of that!" he snarled.

"I think you're wrong there, Doc. I'm confident I have enough to convince a jury to convict you, but don't worry. Melissa doesn't want to put you in jail. She'd rather see you flat broke, homeless, living under a bridge somewhere. That's what this is all about, but don't worry, it'll be over soon. You won't last long living on the street. We all know what kind of a pussy coward you really are. Somebody will kill you, or you'll kill yourself."

Rob stopped talking, waiting for him to say something, but he didn't say a word. "Doc, are you still there? I hope so, because I've got a lot more to tell you. Yesterday, we had a meeting with a local judge. I showed him everything, all of it. Of course when he saw it, he wanted to have you arrested, but again, Melissa wouldn't let him. However, she did allow him to put a restraining order against you. That means that if you try to make contact with her, in any way, you'll be held in contempt of court. If you do that, you *will* go to jail."

He paused again. "What's the matter there, Jerry? Cat got your tongue? I sure hope you heard what I just said, because this is not a joke. If you get within a thousand feet of her, I'll make it my life goal to put your ass in prison.

He paused and waited for him to say something, but all he could hear was his breathing. "Are we clear on that, Doctor? Say something, damn it! I want to make sure you are getting this."

"I heard you," Jerry whispered.

"Good. I have a few more things to tell you. I think you need to know that the state of Florida has revoked your medical license...permanently. And as a result, the state of North Carolina has banned you from practicing psychology in their state as well. That's why you are locked out of your office. So from now on, Dr. Jeremiah Ashford Hollingsworth...you're just plain old Jerry.

"And finally, just in case you get any bad ideas about revenge or something stupid like that...you are no longer in Melissa's will, and you have been replaced as the executor of Molly's trust. Your free ride is over...you're done."

They could hear him breathing hard, whimpering and crying over the speakerphone. "How could she do this to me?" he said barely above a whisper, "What am I supposed to do now? I don't have any money and my credit cards have been canceled!"

"She didn't do this to you", Rob said. "You did it to yourself you greedy, selfish bastard. I think the word is 'karma'...and it's a bitch. When it comes to what you do now? To paraphrase Rhett Butler, *'Frankly, Scarlett, nobody, and I mean nobody, gives a damn!'*"

# 20

# THE TRUTH ABOUT ANNABELLE

The green-eyed monster of jealousy that I had expected from Melissa toward Annabelle never reared its ugly head. It was just the opposite; the two of them had gotten close and had become good friends over the past few months.

I will admit that Annabelle's looks had become a slight distraction to me at times. It was especially difficult when she wore short skirts or tight fitting dresses that accentuated her body. On those days, I tried to stay away from her as much as possible, burying my head in my drawings and staying busy doing whatever I could think of to keep from walking down the stairs past her workstation.

Of course, avoiding her completely was impossible, because often she needed to talk to me about one thing or another pertaining to the project. When those impromptu meetings occurred, I forced myself to look into her eyes, not at her body. What I was trying to do was to make her feel safe and respected around me, and I thought I had done a good job of it, but apparently my actions had caused a reverse effect.

"Do you have a minute?" I looked up from my computer monitors to see her standing in my doorway.

It was one of those days. She was wearing a very short skirt and a tight midriff knit blouse that exposed her tan flat belly and accented her breasts. She was barefoot, which made it even worse.

I have this thing about feet. No, I do not have a foot fetish, just the opposite. I don't really like feet much. I don't like them, because most people's feet are ugly as hell, with bent gnarly toes. But for as long as I can remember, it's usually the first thing I notice about people, especially women. It's one of the first things I look at. I know it's a little weird, but I can't help it.

The day I first met Annabelle at the restaurant, she was wearing flip flops. After she and her friends slid over to my table, she slipped them off and was barefoot. I know I said that I didn't really pay much attention to her looks that day and that's true, but I did notice her feet. They were small, perfectly shaped, manicured and, well...beautiful. In my entire life, there has only been a handful of women that I thought had beautiful feet. Unfortunately, Annabelle was one of them.

So there she was, in her tight blouse, barefoot with her tanned muscular legs shining in the light wanting to talk to me. It was a breathtaking image. "Sure," I said smiling, staring directly into her eyes. "What do you want to talk about? Do we have a problem with the project?"

"No, it's not about work," she said softly, sitting down on the couch, "It's...it's about something personal."

"Personal huh?" I grinned. "Are you having boy troubles?"

She tucked her legs under her body, actually sitting on them. Then she tugged at her short skirt, trying to adjust it down a little, but it didn't work. I could easily see her pink panties peaking out from underneath, so I looked away.

I gave her a few moments to hopefully readjust her skirt before I looked back, but she hadn't readjusted anything, so I made a point to look into her eyes.

Her forehead was wrinkled and she was frowning. "It's not boy trouble," she whispered. "I don't have a boyfriend."

I raised my eyebrows. "Seriously? Why not?"

She sighed deeply. "I had one for a long time. His name was Drake

Davis. I met him in the first grade and we dated all through high school, but I broke up with him when I went to college."

"Why did you do that?"

"I really don't know. He was just so immature. He never grew up and I couldn't take his crap one more day. It broke his heart, and he called and begged me to go back with him for years, but I couldn't do it."

"What happened to him?"

"He finally stopped calling me and moved away. I haven't heard from him, or anything about him, in a few years. He was really sweet and a good guy, but just didn't want to grow up and I did."

"It sounds like you really cared about him for a long time. And it also sounds like Drake was madly in love with you."

"Oh yeah, he was, and I really did hurt him." She dropped her head. "I was pretty mean. I think about him often. I really do hope he's met somebody that makes him happy. I hope he's doing okay."

"First loves never go away. They'll always hold a piece of your heart and you'll always wonder about them. What about other guys?"

She smiled. "Well, I do get asked out a lot, but boys my age are...again, so immature."

I laughed. "Annabelle, you need to give 'em a break. They're young and supposed to be immature. Maturity comes with age. You can't force it on someone. It doesn't come overnight. Don't worry so much about that. Just go out and have fun. That's the biggest problem about being young like you. You can't appreciate how great it is to be young...until you're not."

"Did you just make that up?" She was staring into my eyes, "That was very profound. You are amazing."

I chuckled. "No, I'm not. I'm just old. It will happen to you one day and then you'll understand exactly what I'm talking about. What I said wasn't profound at all. It's just the simple truth."

"You are not that much older than me," she said softly, gazing into my eyes. You are the perfect age." She looked down. "I think you are amazing."

I turned in my chair and looked out the window. My mind was

spinning. The depth of my naïveté had been astounding, but suddenly, like being hit on the head with a hammer, I got it, and everything became clear and made sense. Annabelle was falling for me. That explained her gradual change of wardrobe and appearance.

When she first started working for me, she usually came to work wearing jeans or pants with a simple blouse. She rarely wore makeup, maybe a little eyeliner and lipstick, but not much else. The first time I saw her all dolled up, in full makeup, was at a party thrown by the developers of the Beverly Beach project. When she walked in, a hush fell over the crowd and every eye in the room followed her through the doorway. She was absolutely stunning. And, I foolishly made it clear that night how amazing I thought she looked.

Molly had come down with a fever that day, so Melissa couldn't come and missed the party. So that night, Annabelle jokingly announced that she was my date for the evening. I didn't think anything of it at the time, but apparently Annabelle did. That night, she never left my side, holding on to my arm, and would laugh and smiled wide when people would tell us what a great looking couple we made.

That party was almost a month ago. Thinking about it now, I realized that was when her transformation began, when she started coming to work with full makeup and began wearing sexy shoes, short skirts and tight blouses.

"Grant, have I done something wrong?" She asked.

I spun my chair around and looked at her. She had tears in her eyes. "Of course not. You are doing a great job. Why would you ask me that?"

She wiped her eyes and stared down at the floor. "This isn't about my work," she said so softly I could barely hear her. She slowly lifted her head and looked at me. "It's...it's about me."

I thought I knew exactly what it was about, but didn't have a clue of how to respond, so I played dumb. "About you? Annabelle, what are you talking about?"

She wiped her face with her hand and stared back down at the floor. "Do you think I'm ugly?"

"Ugly? Are you kidding?" I said. "Annabelle, look at me." She lifted her head. Tears were rolling down her cheeks. "Come on now, don't cry. Of course I don't think you're ugly, you're a beautiful girl. What's this all about?"

She took a tissue out of her purse and wiped her eyes. "Then why do you ignore me all the time? Why won't you look at me? It's like I'm invisible or something."

I leaned forward. "Annabelle, you are a young and very beautiful woman, but I'm your boss. I *can't* look at you."

She wrinkled her forehead. "So...you're doing it on purpose? That's why you never look at me?"

I nodded and smiled. "It would be improper. It might even be considered sexual harassment."

She stared into my eyes and smiled. "Even if I want you to?"

"Especially if you want me to. Annabelle," I said with a sigh, "we shouldn't even be having this conversation."

"I know and I'm sorry to bring it up." She dropped her head. "This may sound awful, but I want you to look. I spend hours every morning trying to pick out what to wear so you *will* look. Is that wrong of me to want that?"

"Annabelle, you've put me in a very awkward position here. I don't want to say the wrong thing and upset you. If I do, I apologize, but I have to tell you the truth. As long as you are working for me, especially since there're just the two of us in this office, I have to treat you no different than if you were a man. It's actually against the law for me to treat you any other way. I can't even make a comment on how you look. That's considered sexist and sexual harassment."

"That's stupid," she said.

"I don't disagree, I think it is too, but that's the way the world is these days. So, if you want to keep your job here with me, that's the way it has to be. Do you understand?"

She grinned. "So...no more short skirts?"

"That would make my life a whole lot easier," I said with a grin.

She stood up and walked to my doorway. "So...you *were* looking," she said excitedly, obviously flirting. "Actually, I have a skirt even shorter than this one. I think I'll wear that one tomorrow, but don't you dare look." She giggled and hopped down the stairs.

When she left, I looked down at Charley. "This is all your fault. You took me to her. What am I supposed to do now?"

~

FROM THAT DAY FORWARD, Annabelle stopped trying to hide her attraction to me. But thank God, she never showed it around Melissa. However, when she came over to spend a beach day with us, her bikinis seemed to get smaller and smaller.

I fought it off with all my might, but my attraction to *her* grew slowly as well. I wanted to talk to Melissa about it, but never got up the nerve – she had gone through so much in her life, I just couldn't do it.

For the next several months, my life got more and more confusing. My feelings for Melissa continued to grow and our relationship got stronger, but unfortunately, my feelings for Annabelle, although very confusing, grew as well.

My physical attraction toward her was obvious and easy to understand, but that wasn't what was doing it. It was working with her so closely every day and realizing just how brilliant she was; watching her interact with other people on the job site; listening to her conversations on the phone with her friends and family, hearing her sincere concerns for them... I could go on and on, but the more I got to know Annabelle, the more I adored her. She was truly genuine, a good person with only love and kindness in her heart. The only thing that contradicted all the good things I had learned about her was her obvious and blatant attraction to me. Knowing about my relationship with Melissa and just ignoring it didn't fit who she was.

The fact that she no longer hid her feelings toward me, and could continue to be, or at least very convincingly, pretend to be a good friend to Melissa, and at the same time seem to be absolutely head over heels in love with Molly...absolutely confounded me. It kept me up at night, jarring me awake. I knew I had to do something about it, but because nothing had actually happened between us, other than her obvious flirtations, I just let it go on.

~

ON THE WEEKEND of the grand opening of the first phase of the Beverly Beach Project, Brenda and Marshall flew in for the big celebration. Melissa was my date that night and Annabelle came alone.

When Annabelle arrived, she immediately went into hostess mode and did her usual amazing job of making sure everything went smoothly. She was constantly switching from greeting the arriving VIP guests with her dazzling smile, to making sure the buffet table was replenished and clean, to filling everyone's glasses with more champagne. She was incredibly efficient that night. She also looked like she'd just finished a shoot for *Vogue*, in her long form fitting Emerald Green gown and her very sexy, sparkling matching stiletto heels. Melissa and Brenda had both commented on how beautiful she looked. When they said that, I nodded. I had to agree, because she did look amazing.

The next morning, I fired up the grill and cooked a brisket. I invited Annabelle over to join us for a beach day and dinner. I wanted her to get to know Brenda and Marshall better. That day, she wore one of her larger bikinis, but when she took off her cover up and ran into the water, I thought Marshall's eyes were going to pop out of his head.

"Holy shit…" he whispered under his breath.

I shot him a quick look. "Amen, brother," I said, grinning.

Fortunately, I had trained myself well and was able to take a few quick looks and not get caught by Melissa, but Marshall wasn't so lucky.

"Would you like me to go get the camera?" Brenda said, glaring at him, "The one with the telephoto lens?"

He smiled and shrugged his shoulders. "Naw, I'll just put on my shades, so you won't catch me again."

That night after everyone left, the three of us - Marshall, Brenda and I - settled on my back deck to talk and catch up.

"Has Melissa heard anything about Jerry?" Brenda asked.

"Not a peep. He's disappeared. Her lawyer hired a private detective agency to keep an eye out, but they lost track of him. The only thing they're sure of is that he's not in Asheville, North Carolina anymore."

"I don't like that," Marshall said. "We need to know where he is. There's no telling what a guy like that might do."

"I don't like it either, but wherever he is, he's staying off the grid. The detective agency her lawyer hired is a big company with offices all over the country. So far, they can't find any signs of him. They think he must be living on the street somewhere. I just hope it's not somewhere in Florida."

"Me too. I think that guy could be dangerous. Do you own a gun?"

I frowned. "A gun? No, I don't. You think he might come after me?"

"Well, just think about it. He was living pretty high on the hog until *you* showed up. I don't think it would be a bad idea to buy a gun, just in case. At least until this agency can track him down."

"May I change the subject?" Brenda asked. "I don't like guns."

"Sure, I don't like them, either," I said. "So what would you like to talk about?"

She gave me a funny look, tilting her head, grinning wide. "Well, how about Annabelle? I'd like to know a little more about her."

"Ahh, well, there's not much to tell. She's from Boone, North Carolina, she just graduated college with a degree in Construction Management...and she's my assistant."

"And..." she chimed, stretching out the word.

"And what?"

She rolled her eyes, "Come on, Grant. It's me. Spill it. What's going on between you two?"

I grinned. "Nothing! There's nothing to spill. What on earth gave you that idea?"

She moved her hand up and touched her chin, exaggerating a thinking pose. "Hmm, let me think. Maybe it's the way she looks at you with stars in her eyes every time you talk. Or, perhaps the fact that you never once looked at her today on the beach. Remember I make my living studying people's body language and actions. I know for a fact that you are not gay, but only a gay man would not have stared at her in that bikini, but you didn't even look...not once." She lifted her eyebrows and smiled wide. "Grant, you can't fool me. So come on...spill it!"

I leaned back in my chair and sighed. "Is it really that obvious? Do you think Melissa knows?"

"She didn't say anything to me, but she's not blind. It only took me about ten minutes to see it, but that's what I do. Grant, it's obvious Annabelle's head over heels for you. What I want to know is what's going on inside of *your* head? Do you have feelings for her? Has something happened between you two?"

I looked away. "No, I swear, absolutely not. Nothing has happened." I turned and looked in her eyes. "But to be completely honest with you...I think she's amazing, but..."

"But what?" Marshall asked.

I shifted in my chair and looked down. "I couldn't do that to Melissa. She's been through so much in her life. I just couldn't do something like that to her."

Brenda glanced at Marshall then looked back at me. "Do something like *what* exactly? Follow your heart? Tell her the truth? Grant, you've done nothing wrong. You can't stop love."

"I didn't say I was in love with Annabelle. I've never even kissed her!" I shouted. "I'm supposed to be in love with Melissa!"

"*Supposed to be?*" Brenda repeated with wide eyes. "What does *that* mean?"

"Hell, Brenda, I don't know what that means. I don't know what anything means anymore. I'm so confused. If I'm not supposed to fall in love with Melissa, then why in the *hell* did Charley bring me here, to Florida, to this house, next door to the woman who has Rita's liver inside of her? That has to be my fate. What else could it be?"

"Grant, I can't answer that. I don't think anyone can, but I agree with you. I believe you are here for a specific reason. Maybe your fate is to be with Melissa, but what if it's not? What if you're here for some other reason?"

"What other reason could it possibly be? And why would we both have those feelings when we touch, the shocks and tingles? What about that?"

"I haven't a clue. I've never understood why that happens, anyway. The only thing I know for sure is time will eventually reveal the truth to both of you. Grant, if you have feelings for Annabelle, you need to be honest and tell her. It's not fair to either one of you to hide them. She has the right to know what's going on in your heart."

Brenda lifted her wine glass and took a sip. "And so does Melissa. You especially owe that to her, because of what she's lived through in her life. Grant, you can't lie to her. She's lived through Jerry's lies all these years. I know it would be very hard on her, but I believe she's strong enough to get over losing you. But I know for sure she would never survive knowing that another man she loved has lied to her. That would completely destroy her."

I stood, grabbed my beer off the table and leaned back against the rail. "Don't you think Annabelle's too young for me?"

Marshall laughed. "Not really. Do you think Brenda's too young for me? They're almost the same age."

I looked at Brenda. "No way! How old are you?"

"Thanks for the compliment!" She fired back with a frown. "How damn old do you think I am?"

"I didn't mean I thought you looked old, but you're a doctor, you have to be at least thirty something, right?"

She smiled. "Wrong. I graduated medical school at twenty-two, got my doctorate in psychology at twenty-six. I'm twenty-eight years old."

"Holy shit!" I yelled. "How old were you when you graduated high school?"

She lifted her eyes and smiled. "Thirteen."

I looked over at Marshall, "Well, I know *one* thing for sure; she may not be too young for your old ass, but she's *way* too smart for you!"

Marshall shrugged. "Interestingly, I don't find her all that intelligent." She gave him a good whack on his arm and we all laughed.

"Can I be brutally honest with you?" Brenda asked, setting her wine glass down on the table.

I sat back down in my chair and faced her. "Absolutely. Fire away."

"When I first laid eyes on Annabelle and realized that this was the girl you had been telling us about, the young girl you had hired as your assistant, the brilliant one, the super efficient one...her image didn't fit the picture I had conjured up in my head. Oh, I had assumed that she would be young and pretty, but I was not expecting Christie Brinkley. And to be honest, I took an instant dislike to her. And it didn't help that your friend there," she reached over and whacked Marshall again, "almost dropped his champagne glass when she walked up and introduced herself to us."

"She did look pretty good that night," I said, grinning at Marshall.

He lifted his glass and clinked it against my beer. "Oh yes, she did!" he said.

Brenda shot him a hard look. "She looked a bit *too* good and that's why I didn't like her at first. Then I began to study her. I can't help it, that's what I do. And after watching her a while, it became very clear to me that I was completely wrong about her. Annabelle doesn't know how beautiful she is on the outside. She knows she's pretty, but has no idea *how* pretty. It's not something she seems to care about. You would think she would be shallow and selfish, but that's not who she is at all."

"You learned all that, just from watching her at the party?" I said, amazed.

She nodded. "Yes, from the party, and from talking to her today. I believe she is one of those rare people, who are as beautiful on the inside as they are on the outside."

"Tell him what I told you," Marshall said, "what we talked about last night."

"Why don't *you* tell him?" she said.

I glanced at Marshall. "What'd you say?"

He lowered his brow and thought for a second before he spoke. "I don't want this to come out wrong. You know how much I care about Melissa, how much I like her, right?"

I nodded. "Of course I do."

"Melissa is a special person who's lived through hell. Hopefully, now that she's finally rid of Jerry the asshole, her life will be a lot better and happier than it has been, but..." he paused and took a deep breath, "her life will never truly be normal. Her transplant saved her life, but for how long? There's always the possibility that, for no apparent reason, her body will start to reject her new liver. You heard what I told her. It's possible she could live to see sixty, but the harsh reality is that more than likely...she won't...and she knows that."

I looked away, staring up at the dark sky. "Yeah, she definitely knows that. We've talked about it often. She's convinced she'll never see fifty."

Marshall's expression dropped. "I think she's probably right. And that's what Brenda and I were talking about last night. Again, I don't want this to sound wrong, but although I love Melissa...I love you more. You are my brother, blood relative or not, that's who you are to me. From the moment this all began, and you told us about your feelings for Melissa and about her condition, my stomach has been in a knot. I never thought I would say this out loud to you, but I'm afraid for you.

"I can't stand the thoughts of you having to live through the death of someone else you've allowed yourself to love with all your heart. I'm not sure you're strong enough to survive that again. I know *I* wouldn't. But when I saw Annabelle and how you lit up when she walked in, the knot in my stomach relaxed. I know you were doing your best to hide your feelings toward her, but you didn't fool me. The exact words I said to Brenda last night were 'I sure hope Grant sees what I see in her. She's absolutely perfect for him.' I know that may sound..."

I held up my hand stopping him. "I hear you, and don't worry, it didn't come out wrong. Unfortunately, it's way too late. I'm already in love with Melissa. So...when she dies...well, I guess I'll have to deal with that then. I can't allow myself to think about stuff like that.

"And, I'm not going to lie to you, of course I have feelings for Annabelle, I'm only human," I laughed. "As usual, my life is totally and utterly confusing."

Marshall sighed. "Buddy, I wish I had the answers for you, but I don't. I have no idea why Charley brought you here, why you were supposed to meet Melissa. And I don't have a clue of what you're supposed to do next, but I believe there's also a very good reason you met Annabelle. She has to be part of what Rita was telling you when you were drowning in that water. What was it she said, 'You have much more to do?' I'm convinced Annabelle is a big part of that. Grant, please listen to me. I know it's very confusing and this may not be what you want to hear, but I think it would be a huge mistake for you to ignore your feelings and the truth about Annabelle."

# 21

# PREMONITIONS

I wasn't sure if Brenda talked to them before she left and flew back to Houston, but I suspect she did. Knowing her the way I did, I was confident she couldn't have gotten on that plane if she hadn't. Another reason for me thinking this is because of how things changed.

Annabelle suddenly stopped with her obvious flirting. Her wardrobe didn't change; she still dressed trying to kill me everyday, but she seemed much more relaxed and calmer somehow. She was constantly smiling and singing around the office; always in a great mood and happy, no matter how stressful or difficult the day may have been. She seemed very content with the situation and never once mentioned her feelings toward me again.

I could sense no real change from Melissa when it came to us. In fact, our relationship couldn't have been much better. She also seemed happier and somehow calmer. She stopped flying off the handle and losing her temper like she had done so many times in the past, and her overall attitude and outlook seemed more positive.

The only obvious change was between Melissa and Annabelle. As strange as it may sound, with every passing day, they seemed to grow closer and closer. They talked on the phone constantly and started spending more and more time together. If I had to work late, Melissa and Molly would come to the office, and the three of them would go out to dinner. If I had to go away on a business trip, Melissa would call Annabelle to come over and stay with them until I got back. Melissa even took Annabelle to Savannah one weekend to meet her aunt.

Over the next few months, they became inseparable best friends. And although I was happy for Melissa to have such a close friend and especially happy for Molly, who absolutely adored Annabelle...the reality of it all was surreal and very confusing to me at the same time.

Unfortunately, my feelings for Annabelle had continued to grow, but my feelings for Melissa had grown as well. I was in a ridiculous predicament. I had somehow let myself fall in love with both of them and it was driving me nuts. The dumbest part of it all was that my deep growing feelings for Annabelle were just in my heart. She didn't know about them, and I wasn't even sure she still felt the same about me.

"You are such an idiot!" I said out loud, waking up Charley. It was almost ten p.m. I was working late, alone in my office trying to finish up the final plans for phase two of the Beverly Beach project, but I was having a hard time keeping my mind on my work.

Charley got off the floor, walked up to me and laid his head in my lap. "What do I do about all of this, Charley? I'm all twisted up inside. How could I love two women at the same time?"

I got up, walked to the bar and poured two fingers of Jack in a glass. Charley growled. "Don't worry. I'm not gonna get drunk. I just need to relax a little and talk this out. Are you okay with that?"

He looked up at me and wagged his tail. "Woof."

I petted his head, walked to my window and looked out at the lights. "What should I do Charley? Do I tell Melissa about my feelings for Annabelle?"

I took a sip of Jack and laughed. "Maybe I should tell Annabelle first. If she's changed her mind and doesn't feel the same, then none of this matters anyway."

I took another sip. "Yeah, I guess that's what I need to do. I can't go on like this any longer. I have to know what she's feeling." I finished what was left in my glass and set it on my desk. "Tomorrow, Charley, I'll ask her tomorrow."

"Why don't you ask her now?"

I turned around and Annabelle was standing in my doorway. "How long have you been there?"

She smiled. "For a few minutes. I came back to get my laptop and heard you talking." She took a few steps toward me. "Do you do that a lot?"

"Do what?"

"Talk to Charley, up here alone at night?" She moved closer, standing only a few feet away from me.

The room was dark except for the soft glow coming from the lamp on my desk, but her face was highlighted and her eyes were glistening, reflecting the outside lights streaming through my window. "I've been doing that a lot more lately."

She took another step, standing only inches away from me. "And why is that?"

"It's all because of you," I whispered, staring into her eyes.

She raised up on her tiptoes, put her arms around my neck and moved closer. I could smell her perfume and feel her breath on my lips. It was intoxicating.

"What did you want to ask me?" she whispered.

When we kissed, I didn't close my eyes. I couldn't stop looking at her. It was a great, tender kiss, but I didn't feel anything, nothing. I kissed her again, but longer this time, savoring the feel of her tongue against mine, and the taste of her lips. But again, I felt nothing.

However the confusion in my heart and in my head about my feelings toward her instantly disappeared and everything became crystal clear. There was no question that I cared about her, absolutely adored her, and loved her...but I wasn't "in love" with her.

But now that we'd crossed that line, my mind was spinning trying to come up with the correct words to gently explain to her my true feelings.

Before I could come up with anything, she looked up at me, smiled and whispered. "Did that answer your questions?"

I smiled back. "That answered a 'lot' of my questions. And now I know exactly what I have to do."

"And what's that?" She purred.

"Well first, I have to tell Melissa about this."

She wrinkled her forehead. "Grant, you don't have to, she already knows."

I let go of her and took a step back. "What?"

"Grant, she's known for a long time, and she knows how I feel about you, too. You don't think I would have let this happen if she wasn't okay with it, do you? I would never do anything behind her back. She's my friend and I love her, too."

I threw up my hands and walked around her. "Whoa! What are you saying? Melissa knows about this? About us? Did you two plan this?"

"No, of course not!" She walked around my desk and put her arms around my waist. "What happened tonight wasn't planned. I really did come back to get my laptop. I swear."

"Then how do you know she's okay with it?"

"Because we've talked about it. She knew it would happen some-day. I wasn't so sure, but she was."

I sat down on the couch. My head was swimming. "How could she be okay with this? I don't get it. You two talked about this? Do you know how wrong that sounds? If she doesn't love me, why didn't she say something? Why let me go on and on like some love struck fool?"

Annabelle sat down next to me. "You are jumping to the wrong conclusion. She's all right with this…because she *does* love you. She's doing this for you."

I tilted my head, confused. "What are you saying?"

"Grant, she came to me when she heard I was leaving."

"You were leaving?"

She looked away. "Yes, I was going to tell you after the grand opening of phase one. I did tell Brenda. That's how she found out." Her eyes filled with tears, "I knew I couldn't stop the feelings I had for you, and when I saw you two together at the party with your friends…I realized I couldn't break you up. It wasn't right, no matter how much I loved you. I couldn't do it, so I decided I had to go away somewhere."

"Melissa stopped you from leaving? Why would she do that?"

"She's been having premonitions and doesn't think she's going to live much longer. Grant, she begged me to stay. For you...and for Molly."

"What kind of premonitions was she having?"

"She doesn't know how or when, but she's sure it has something to do with her transplant. She believes her liver is going to fail again soon."

"That doesn't make any sense," I said, shaking my head, "She's doing great with that. Marshall told her there're no signs of her body rejecting it and because it's been over two years, she's well past the critical stages. Why would she believe that?"

"At first, I didn't believe her and said no, absolutely not. What she was telling me was too farfetched to accept. But she wouldn't give up. She kept begging me to believe her. I did admit to her that I had feelings for you, but could never do anything about them, because I could never hurt her. When I said that, she just smiled, hugged me and told me that she already knew how much I loved you...and because I was willing to walk away from that love for her...proved that I was the right one."

I tilted my head. "The right one?"

"I know it may sound crazy, but she knew you were going to fall for someone else. She thought it was me, but wasn't completely sure. She knew this was going to happen because she saw it in a dream. A dream she's been having over and over for months. In that dream, she's hovering over her body, looking down at us. We're all there – you, Marshall, Brenda, Molly and someone she thinks is me - and we're crying." Annabelle wiped her eyes with her sleeve. "I know it sounds crazy, but she believes it's a premonition, so she can die in peace knowing that Molly will be all right."

"Is that in the dream, too?" I whispered.

"Yes. She sees the three of us together, you, Molly and someone she believes is me. We're walking on the beach, holding hands with Molly...laughing."

"Oh God," I whispered, looking at her. "I don't know what to say."

She reached over and touched my hand. "Grant, I know this may be impossible to understand, but she believes it. And maybe I went along with all of this, because I wanted to believe her. At that point, I was willing to do anything to be with you." She squeezed my hand and stared into my eyes. "Was that wrong?"

I held her gaze for a long time before I spoke. "Annabelle, you don't know much about me, about my life. Someday, I'll tell you everything. And when I do, you'll understand why this is *not* hard for me to believe. So many things have happened to me in the last few years..." I laughed and nodded. "Nothing is *too* farfetched for me. And no, I don't believe anything you've done was wrong... just misguided."

She jerked her head up. "Misguided? What are you saying?"

I took her hands in mine. "Annabelle, I've been very confused, but now I think I know. What I'm feeling for you inside my heart right now *is* love. I know without any shadow of a doubt that I love you, I really do," I said, smiling, "and in a different life...you never know what may have happened between us. But I also know that I'm in love with Melissa, and I don't believe her premonition. I think she's wrong about the future and about the two of us. There was a reason she and I were brought together." Her eyes instantly filled with tears. "Please don't cry, let me finish.

"Annabelle, I know you think you love me, but it's just infatuation. I know you want to believe her and this premonition, but she's wrong. I'm the wrong guy. I'm too old. You are so young, beautiful, smart and kind. You deserve more than I can give you. There is someone else out there that can give you back the love you deserve. The question we have to figure out for the three of us now...is where do we go from here?" I took my hand and wiped the tears away from her face, "So, what do *you* think we should do now?"

The corners of her lips curled slightly, making a small smile. Then she leaned over and kissed me. "I'm sorry, Grant, but I don't agree with you and I'm not giving up. I know I love you and only you. So does Melissa and we both think you're the right guy. So, I guess we need to go talk to her and see what she thinks."

~

BOTH OF OUR cars were parked in the office lot. On our walk there, I pulled out my cell and called Melissa to warn her that we were coming over, but she didn't answer. "That's weird, she didn't pick up."

"It's almost midnight, she's probably asleep and didn't hear it," Annabelle said, "Try her cell. She keeps it next to her bed. She should hear that."

Melissa didn't answer her cell, either. "Maybe she took a sleeping pill or something?"

"Maybe," Annabelle said, thinking, "but she's not supposed to do that. It effects the other medication she takes." She looked at me, frowning, "Grant, this doesn't sound right, something's wrong. I'll follow you in my car. If she did take a sleeping pill and we can't wake her up, I'll go home and we can talk to her tomorrow."

On the way, I tried Melissa's home and cell several more times, but she never answered. Every time I would hang up, Charley would whine. "What's wrong? You need to go?" He didn't bark back, so I knew that wasn't it. The closer we got to Melissa's house, the louder he whined. "What the Hell, Charley? What is wrong with you?"

When I turned on the road to our houses, I figured out why he was whining and why Melissa hadn't answered her phone. There were three police cars, with their blue lights flashing parked in front of her house.

I skidded to a stop in my driveway and ran next door. "What's happened?" I yelled. "Is she all right?"

One of the police officers walked up to me. "Do you know Mrs. Hollingsworth?"

"Yes, I live here, I'm her neighbor." I shouted, "She's a good friend of mine. What's happened to her? Where's Molly?"

He raised his eyebrows. "Who's Molly?"

"Her daughter! She's only seven years old. Where is she?"

I tried to step around him, but the other officers blocked my way, "You can't go up there, sir, it's a crime scene."

"A CRIME SCENE!" I screamed, "WHAT HAPPENED?"

"Calm down, sir. We don't know what happened. We're waiting on a detective now. I'm sure he's going to want to talk to you when he gets here."

"Are they up there?" I heard Annabelle ask behind me. I reached for her and pulled her close, hugging her in my arms.

"No ma'am, no one is up there," the cop said, "the house is empty. The silent alarm went off, that's why we're here. When we pulled up, the front door was standing open. Does Mrs. Hollingsworth own a car?"

I looked at the garage. Both doors were open, but her car was gone. "Yes, it's a gold Lexus. A new one, she just bought it a few months ago."

"I'll be right back, I'm going to run her car" the cop said, rushing away.

"Where are they?" Annabelle shouted. "They should be here. We were supposed to go to lunch tomorrow."

I hugged her in my arms and squeezed. "I don't know where they are, but this looks bad."

After the forensic team finished, the detective finally let us go up and walk around her house. He was hoping we might see something that was missing or out of place. We checked every room, but nothing was wrong. It looked like she'd just walked out for a few minutes. All of her rejection medicine was perfectly lined up on the bathroom cabinet. The only thing that caught my eye and seemed out of place was the unmade beds. Making the bed was the first thing Melissa did when she got up and had trained Molly to do the same thing .

The detective wrote that down on his pad. "Always? Without fail she makes her bed?"

"Yes. It's the first thing she does in the morning."

The detective raised his eyebrows. "And how would you know that? Were you two...involved?"

"Yes," I said. "We've been dating for a while."

"Really?" I heard a voice behind me say.

I turned around to see a woman standing there. "I'm Detective Reynolds, Detective Johnson's partner on this case," She pointed at the other detective, "Did you say you and Mrs. Hollingsworth were dating?"

I nodded. "Yes, for over a year now, almost two."

"Humm," She mumbled, writing in her small note pad, "Was it a bad break up?"

I frowned down at her. "What?"

"When you two broke up, was it cordial, or did it get pretty nasty? It must have been tough living next door to each other like this."

I stared at her. "We didn't break up? What are you talking about?"

The two detectives shot each other looks. "What about her?" She pointed at Annabelle. "Didn't I see you two hugging outside. And I'm pretty sure I saw you kiss her. So again I'll ask you, what about her?"

I finally got it. I understood what she was getting at, but I wasn't exactly sure how to explain it. I smiled, "She's my assistant, she works for me and..."

She lifted her hand, "No need to explain, I get it."

"No!" I shouted, "It's not what you're thinking."

"Mr. Nash, isn't it? I've been a detective for a long time. I'm pretty sure it's exactly what I'm thinking. All I want to know is...what did, Mrs. Hollingsworth think about it?"

I held up my hands. "Look, please stop this. You are jumping to the wrong conclusion here. I love Melissa and Molly, and I did not have anything to do with this. My relationship with Annabelle is...well, it's complicated and Melissa knew all about it."

I tried my best to explain the situation to them, but they had already made up their minds. The next thing I knew, I was being loaded into the back of Detective Johnson's car and Annabelle was being loaded into Detective Reynolds'.

Four hours later, after being relentlessly grilled by the two detectives, I was finally allowed to make a phone call. I called Rob Waterson, Melissa's attorney. He told me to stop talking to the detectives. "Not one more word! Do you understand?"

"Yes, I got it," I said, "but that's not going to be easy."

"Sure it is. Just tell them your attorney is on the way and you'll be glad to answer any more questions they may have when he gets there."

"Well, Grant, of course that's your right," Detective Reynolds said with a smirk, "but it makes me wonder why you'd think you'd need a lawyer? If you don't have anything to hide, then what's the problem?"

"The problem is..." I caught myself and stopped. I lifted my hand to my mouth and zipped my lips.

"Ok," she said, shrugging her shoulders, "but it doesn't make you look very innocent in my eyes."

I smiled at her and did the lip zipping motion with my hand again.

Rob stormed in the room an hour later. "Let's go!" he said the second he walked in."

"Hold on!" Detective Reynolds said. "We're not through questioning him."

Rob walked up, bent down and put his face next to hers, nose to nose. "Detective, I'm going to walk Grant and Annabelle to my car, then I'm going to take them home. When I'm done, I'm coming back here to talk to you and Detective Johnson and trust me, you'll like what I'll be telling you. You see, I know who took Melissa and Molly, and it wasn't Grant and Annabelle. I have proof. I can get you the security camera footage of them walking into and out of their office. It's time stamped. Also, I can show you a video of Melissa, Molly and a man wearing a hat pulled down hiding his face, driving her Lexus through the security gate at exactly 11:55 p.m. Just in case you're wondering where Grant and Annabelle were at that exact time...you guessed it, they were walking out of their office door together. If you two were real detectives, you would know that, too."

He motioned for me to leave. When we got to the door, he turned and looked back at the two stunned detectives. "Who was the man in the hat? Here's a hint, since you guys are so good at jumping to conclusions, I want you to think about this a second. If it wasn't her boyfriend who has an iron clad alibi, maybe she had an ex-husband...a crazy one who hates her. But like I said before, real detectives would already know that. And FYI, it only took my private detective an hour to find out all of that." He squinted his eyes and leaned toward them. "Is that really a gold shield clipped on your jackets? I think you need to polish 'em up. They're looking a little tarnished."

～

THE HIGHWAY PATROL located Melissa's Lexus in a rest area 15 miles south of Jacksonville. None of the other travelers that had stopped there were missing their cars, so apparently Jerry, or whoever had taken Melissa and Molly, had a different car there waiting to switch to.

We had set up camp at my house, waiting to hear something from the police. Rob frowned when he hung up the phone. "The police think that whoever this is has a partner that's helping him, or he somehow hitched a ride to her house here in Saint Augustine. They're checking the video footage of the rest area's security cameras now."

"What about the front gate here?" I asked. "If someone drove him here, it should be on that tape."

Rob nodded. "They're checking on that, too. They're also contacting all the cabbies and Uber drivers."

"That's a thirty or forty dollar ride. If this is Jerry...where did he get the money? I think I agree with the cops, he had to have help with this." I stood up and paced the room. "Did your private detectives find out if he has a girlfriend? I'm talking about when he was in Asheville."

"He had several," Rob said, "but we know he wasn't living with any of them."

"How could they know that for sure?" I argued. "How long did they keep them under surveillance? I guarantee you it's one of those women. That slimy bastard is doing it again, laying on his charm, sucking some woman out of her cash." I stopped pacing and plopped back down on the couch next to Annabelle.

"They'll find them," she said tearfully. "I just know they will."

"Who will find them?" I shot back. "The cops? They still think I did this! They couldn't find their own asses!"

Her eyes widened. "After all of this? They still suspect Grant?"

Rob nodded his head. "Probably," he said, "It's how they all think. If the story doesn't add up...go for the obvious. Grant's the last person to see her, and their number one suspect. It wouldn't surprise me if they're thinking that Grant's the one helping Jerry."

"That's crazy!" she shouted, "Why on earth would they think that?"

He lifted his eyebrows. "Annabelle, all they can see is a middle aged man with a middle aged girlfriend...and then there's you."

"Me? What's wrong with me?"

He laughed. "Seriously? You don't get it? Are you really that naïve?"

She looked up at me. "Naïve? Grant, what's he talking about?"

I glared at Rob. "That's enough! If we're going to find Melissa and Molly, *we* have to do it! We both know the cops aren't going to do a damn thing but look at me for this. *We* have to find them and I can't do it without your help. We have to work together, so If you want to know what's going on between me and Annabelle, just ask."

"Ok," he said, nodding, "I think it's pretty obvious. All I want to know is...when did it start?"

For the next hour, I sat quietly and let Annabelle explain while Rob listened.

When she finished, Rob looked over at me. "I owe you two an apology. I jumped to the same wrong conclusion the cops did and I'm sorry."

He leaned back in his chair and rubbed his face. "I have to admit, it sounds like something she would do. I just wish she'd told me about her premonitions. She was in my office last week and never mentioned anything to me. She seemed fine...really happy. She looked great, better than I'd seen her look in a long time."

"What was she there for?" I asked.

He sighed. "I didn't think much about it then, but now...it's...it's not going to look good."

I frowned. "Why was she there?"

"She made a few changes to her will," he said, shaking his head. "It made sense to me, so I did it. I thought you two...well, I just assumed you two were about to get married."

"What did you change in her will?" I shouted.

"She had me remove her aunt and named you as her sole beneficiary. If she dies, you get all of her assets."

"Do the police know this?"

"It's public record. I'm sure they do. It explains why they zeroed in on you."

Annabelle sighed. "If the police know that, then they probably also know Grant already has a lot of money. Do they really think he could be involved with whoever took her? Just to get more money?"

"Unfortunately, I know how this district attorney thinks," Rob said. "He's a real jackass. I can see him now, putting all the pieces together."

"What pieces?" Annabelle asked.

Rob shot me a knowing look and I nodded in agreement. "He's going to try to tie this to my first wife's death."

"What are you talking about? How could he connect this to your wife's death?"

I took her hands in mine and looked into her eyes. "Because that's the reason I have money. I was paid almost six million dollars because of it."

"But it was an accident!" she yelled. "Wasn't it?"

She stared at me with fear in her eyes. "Yes, it was a terrible accident, but no one can explain why it happened. None of the experts have a single clue why that engine stopped." I dropped my head and stared down at my feet. "There's more."

Rob lifted his head and stared at me. "Grant, look at me. This is critical." I looked up at him. "What haven't you told me about that crash? I need to know everything, every detail."

I looked at Annabelle. She was staring at me with wide eyes. "What did you do?"

I shrugged. "Because all the experts couldn't find a definitive reason for the engine to stop, my attorney was afraid that they would blame me. Call it pilot error...or claim that I did it on purpose." I looked into her eyes. "I swear on my mother's grave that I didn't do it on purpose. The engine just stopped, but..."

"But what?" Rob asked, shifting in his chair.

"Rather than going through a long trial and letting them bring up these kinds of accusations, and they had made it clear to my lawyer they would, he convinced me to take a small settlement instead. He advised me to put an end to it, so I agreed."

I looked at Rob. "If they dig into the crash, you think they'll find out about that? I swear Rob, I didn't do anything wrong. It was an accident."

He didn't respond. He just sat there quietly, looking down, thinking. After a few minutes, he looked up at me. "I'm sure they already have."

# 22

# WHERE ARE THEY

For the second time in three years, I watched my life disintegrate before my eyes.

The Saint Augustine district attorney made a phone call to the District Attorney in Huntsville and convinced him to take another look in to the plane crash. I know this, because I got a phone call from Mike O'Bannon. He told me that someone in his father's law firm heard a rumor that I might get indicted by a Texas grand jury on suspicion of causing the plane crash and murdering my wife and child.

One day after that, I *was* indicted by a Florida grand jury on suspicion of kidnapping and child endangerment. They arrested me at my house the following day. Sitting in that cell, waiting to be arraigned, although I was in a complete state of shock, frustration and rage were the real emotions I was feeling. Melissa and Molly had been missing for four days and no one seemed to even care about that.

Before my arraignment, Rob met with me in a small private space, just outside of the courtroom. "Grant, listen to me carefully. Keep your mouth shut. I'll do all the talking. Do you understand?"

"Yes, I understand," I said. "Have you heard anything about Melissa and Molly? Is anyone even searching for them?"

"I don't think so," he said, frowning. "But I am. I've hired two different private detective agencies to track them down."

"Why aren't the police looking for them?"

"They believe they're already dead, and they're convinced you know where they are buried."

"What?" I yelled.

He glared at me. "Shhhh! Keep your voice down. We only have a few minutes to talk. Grant, that's their entire case against you, that's it. They have zero proof of anything. I know this judge and he's a stickler for evidence. I think I can get you out of here on bail. So again, keep your mouth shut and let me do what I do."

Rob convinced the judge that the entire case against me was nothing more that some bizarre story that the D.A. had concocted in his head.

"I don't want to hear any more!" the judge said, slamming his gavel down. "Mr. Rutherford, You have forty-eight hours to gather some real evidence against this man. If you fail to convince me, I'm throwing this case out. In the meantime, I'm granting Mr. Nash's requests for bail." He glared down at the Assistant District Attorney. "Tell your boss, he's skating on thin ice on this one. Forty-eight hours, not one minute more!"

∼

ROB WAS LEANING against his car at the bottom of the steps when they finally let me walk out of the jail. I jumped in and we drove away.

"Any new developments? Have they found them?"

He shook his head. "Not yet."

"No sign of them at all?"

"I'm re-applying pressure on the district attorney to, at the very least, put out a BOLO on them. The jackass said he'd think about it."

"He's still convinced they're already dead...and I killed them."

Rob nodded. "I'm afraid so. Without the help of the police, we just don't have much to go on. That's something I wanted to talk to you about. I'm thinking about going to the press with all this, maybe offering a reward to any verified sightings. What do you think?"

"I like that idea. I'll even put up the money. Let's do it!"

"You can't be involved, not until we resolve this case against you. The judge would go nuts and immediately drop a gag order on you!"

"So how do we do it?"

"I talked to Les Patterson this morning," Rob said. "Actually, it's his idea and he's putting up the money."

I sighed and looked down. "I was hoping he hadn't heard about this yet. I assume he's already replaced me on the Beverly Beach Project."

"No, I don't think so. He told me that Annabelle was on top of everything." We stopped at a red light. He turned his head and looked at me. "She's very impressive. I really like her."

"Yes she is. She's...very special." I took a deep breath and let it out. "I can't imagine what's going through her head about me now."

The second we pulled up to my house, I could hear Charley barking. I was only halfway up the front staircase when the door opened and he flew down the steps to greet me. When I looked up, Annabelle was standing in the doorway. She wasn't smiling, she was crying. When I took that last step and walked up to the door, I didn't know what to do, so I stopped a few feet from her and just stood there staring.

She ran to me and jumped into my arms. "Thank God you're here! They wouldn't let me see you. I tried, but they wouldn't let me."

Her face was wet from her tears. "Don't cry. It's okay. I'm glad you didn't see me in that place." I wiped her face with my hand. "I'm just glad you're here now. I wasn't sure you would be."

She wrinkled her brow. "Why would you think that?"

I took her hand, walked inside and closed the door behind us. "I wasn't sure what you thought of me now."

Before she could answer, Charley jumped up on me, knocking me down on the floor and between his whines and barks, soaked my face with his sloppy kisses. Then Donna and Annabelle joined in, piling on top, welcoming me home.

I took a much-needed shower to wash off the stench of the jail and all of Charley and Donna's kisses from my face. After I dried off and slipped on jeans and a tee shirt, I found Annabelle on the back deck. She was sitting there quietly, staring out at the ocean.

"Boy, do I feel better," I said. She turned and smiled up at me. "I need a beer and I know this may sound dumb, but do you drink? I can't believe I don't know the answer to that question, but I've never seen you drink anything but tea or a Coke."

She stood up and pulled out a chair. "Sit. I'll get the beer."

When she returned she had two beers in her hand. "You are going to have to open them." She handed me the bottles, sat down across from me and gave me a wide smile. "I like beer, wine and on special occasions, a little tequila. But my favorite is Jack Daniels."

I started laughing. "What's so funny?" She asked.

"One more thing," I said, sipping my beer.

"One more thing?" she asked. "What's that mean?"

"It's just one more thing I love about you." The minute those words left my mouth, I realized where I'd heard those words before.

Annabelle sensed my instant mood change. "What's wrong?"

"That was something Melissa said to me once. I can't remember what I had done, but she said it was just one more thing she loved about me."

Her face dropped and she looked down at the table. "Where is she, Grant? And where's Molly? We have to find them."

I reached across the table and took her hand. "I promise you I'm going to. Somehow...I'm going to track them down and bring them home. I swear I will."

For the next hour, we sat there silently, thinking about Melissa and Molly.

"What did you mean earlier?" she asked. "You said something about not knowing what I thought about you now?"

I stood up. "Are you hungry? I'm starving?" I slid open the door and walked to the kitchen.

She followed me. "Grant, what did you mean? Why did you say that?"

I leaned against the bar, looked at her and shrugged. "You really don't know?"

"No, I really don't."

"Annabelle, you don't know my story. Not the whole story. Actually, we've never had the chance to get to know each other much at all. I know you think you know me, but you really don't. How could you?" I opened the refrigerator and pulled out another beer. "You want another one?"

"Maybe later."

I twisted off the cap and took a sip, "Did you know about the plane crash, about my wife and Audrey?"

"Yes, Melissa told me about it."

"Did she tell you that I was flying the plane?"

"Yes, I knew that."

"But you didn't know that some people suspected me of crashing that plane on purpose, did you? You didn't know it, because I've never told anyone about that, not even Melissa."

"No, I didn't know that," she said softly, "but I know you. And I know you a lot better than you think I do. What do you think Melissa and I have been talking about all these months? We've been talking about you. Melissa wanted me to know everything." She walked around the bar and wrapped her arms around my waist. "Grant, I may not know every detail of your life, but I know enough to know that you couldn't have done that. You may not love me, but nothing has changed for me."

I couldn't find anything to cook, so we ordered a pizza and brownies, and devoured every slice and half of the brownies on the back deck.

"Pizza, beer and brownies," I said with a chuckle, "You are definitely my kind of girl."

She smiled at me, but not with her eyes, only her lips. "That's what I keep trying to tell you."

～

WHEN ANNABELLE LEFT THAT NIGHT, I tried my best to sleep, but I couldn't. My mind kept coming up with horrible scenarios of what Jerry was doing or had already done. I kept asking myself why would he do such a stupid thing? Jerry was lazy, greedy, arrogant, but he wasn't stupid. He did try to kill her before, but he did it because of her money. He had to know he couldn't get to it now, so why would he do this? What could he possibly gain? It made no sense.

I got out of bed, slipped on my jeans and headed to the beach. Walking barefoot with Charley and Donna by my side, I strolled down the sand, along the shore talking to myself and Charley.

"Charley, the cops think they're dead, but they're still alive, aren't they?"

"Woof," he barked.

"Yeah, I think so, too. Do you have any idea where they are?"

He lifted his eyes and gave me a sad look.

"Why on earth would he do this? He has to know he'll get caught. Is it just for revenge?" Charley snorted.

"It has to be about the money! That's all he's ever cared about."

"Woof."

I stopped walking and looked down at him. "Do you think that's it, too? It's all about the money?"

"Woof, woof," he barked and spun around.

"But Charley, she changed her will. If he kills her, he won't get anything and he'll go to jail!"

I sat down on the sand and looked him in the eyes. "Why would he do this, kidnap her, risk going to jail just to get her money? He's a smart guy, Charley. He took them for a reason."

He lifted his eyes and growled. "I don't know what he's trying to do, but I promise you I'm going to find out and somehow, I'm going to stop him, or die trying.

∽

HIDING IN THE DARK, behind the tall sea oats in the berm, Detective Anastasia Reynolds froze, holding her breath as Grant Nash walked by.

One of the two dogs he was walking with, broke away and ran up to her. "Woof," he barked.

"Go away," she whispered. "Get out of here!"

The dog didn't move. "Woof, Woof," he barked again.

"Charley!" She heard Grant yell. "Come on!"

The dog moved closer and looked at her. Then he lifted his lip, exposing his long, sharp, white teeth. "Woof," he barked, then turned and ran away.

Her entire body was shaking and she was breathing hard, gasping for air. After she calmed down and caught her breath, she stood and slowly walked down the beach. A few hundred yards away, she could see them walking in front of her, highlighted in the moonlight. She followed them, but kept her distance.

When she got back to her car, she dug in her purse, pulled out a cigarette and lit it with her shaking hand. It was only her fourth one for the day, but as she drew in her first drag, she knew that as soon as that one was out, she would light up another one. She would quit again tomorrow.

That was too close. She'd almost gotten caught, or worse, attacked by a big dog. She wondered what would have been worse, getting caught or bitten? She smiled, thinking about it. If she'd gotten caught and her captain found out what she'd been doing, his bite would have hurt a lot more.

Even her partner didn't know what she was up to. She didn't tell him, because she knew what he would have said. Johnson was a good cop, but a little too by the book for her tastes. He wouldn't even *bend* a rule, let alone break one. No, this was something she had to do alone. And besides, what she did in her off time was her business...sort of. Yes, it was an official case and what she was doing could be considered by some asshole lawyer as police harassment, but only if she got caught. Putting an unofficial tail on him wasn't the problem, but eavesdropping and listening to his conversations might be. She wasn't sure about the exact constitutional right she might be breaking, but at this point she didn't care. The assistant district attorney told them that they only had forty-eight hours to dig something up, and that was fourteen hours ago. Of course, this wasn't the first time she'd done something like this on a case, but it was the first time what she had discovered in the process made her have to back up and rethink everything.

When her surveillance had began that afternoon, she was absolutely convinced she was right about Grant Nash. Detective Johnson, her partner wasn't so sure, but there was no question in her mind that he was guilty. Her suspicions started with her first impression of him standing there at the crime scene pretending to be concerned, hugging on that young girl at the same time. And it wasn't just *some* young girl. She remembered thinking that she was probably a stripper with a body like that. Maybe eighteen or nineteen, twenty at the most. When she found out she was twenty-four with a college degree, it was a bit shocking, but it didn't change her mind about him at all, because...she was his, quote unquote, assistant. Right, sure she was. Then she did a little digging into his background and it became obvious to her. All she had to do was add up the facts. What were the odds of lightening striking twice in less than two years to the same guy? How unlucky could one person be?

His wife and child are killed in a mysterious plane crash that none of the experts can explain. A plane that he was flying...a plane he crashed in such a perfect position that killed everyone else, but he was barely hurt? Six million dollars later, here he is again, kissing his bombshell assistant on the same night his girlfriend and daughter wind up mysteriously missing. And if they are located somewhere and, God forbid, they are found dead, guess who's the beneficiary of their multi-million-dollar estate...Grant Nash. What a coincidence.

In her mind, Grant was either cursed with incredibly bad luck, or he was a very smart, greedy serial killer. Unfortunately, they had nothing on him but that theory, no real evidence, just her gut feelings and her years of busting scumbags just like him. So when the assistant district attorney told them they only had forty-eight hours to find something, she knew what she had to do.

Earlier in the day, when she had parked her car and walked the two blocks over to his house, she had assumed it would be empty and had almost gotten caught placing the bug under the patio table when she found out it wasn't. She was under the table placing the bug when Annabelle slid the glass door open and walked out on the deck. Under the table, she could see Annabelle's bare feet and legs as she walked up and leaned against the rail. She froze and held her breath. Then a phone rang in the house and Annabelle ran back inside. As quietly as she could, she crawled out from under the table, backed down the stairs and ran to her car.

When she got back to her car, she turned on the receiver and put on her earphones to check the signal she was getting from the bug. She couldn't hear anything but the sound of the crashing waves of the ocean, but figured if she could hear that, she'd be able to hear them talking when they were sitting around the patio table. She had planned on placing three more bugs inside the house, but with Annabelle staying there, that was out. As it turned out, the one bug would be all she needed. She remembered smiling when she first heard the ocean sounds coming through her headphones. "I'm gonna get you, you son of a bitch," she had said out loud. "You just wait and see."

That was her big plan. But now, ten hours later, sitting in her car, watching the sun come up, thinking about all she had heard...she realized that she had been wrong about Grant Nash. He was an innocent man, just trying to live through his unbelievable misfortunes.

The big question now was, what could she do to help him?

# 23

# EVERYONE YOU HAVE EVER LOVED

W hen his phone began to ring, Detective Mark Johnson groaned and rolled over on his back. He opened his eyes and tried to focus on the small digital clock sitting on his night table. "5:45?" He grumbled. "Hello?"

His sleepy voice crackled in her ear. "Did I wake you up?"

"Of course not, Detective Reynolds," he growled, "I was just sitting here, drinking my morning coffee and enjoying the sunrise. Anastasia, what the hell are you calling me about this early? It's five fucking thirty!"

"Actually, it's five fucking forty-eight," she said in a cheerful voice, "and I'm calling you about the Nash case."

"Hold on," he said, sitting up, pulling back the covers, "let me get up. I don't know what you've been up to, but I'm pretty sure I'm gonna need some coffee to hear about it."

She laughed. "That might be a good idea. This is pretty big news."

"Oh shit!" he snorted, getting to his feet. "What in the hell have you done now?"

LOOKING out at the heavy downtown morning traffic through the passenger window, Melissa counted on her fingers. It was the sixth day she had not taken the critical medication that helped prevent her body from rejecting her transplanted liver. She wondered how long it would take before the rejection process would begin. Would she be able to tell? Would she feel it?

At 9:00 am Jerry pulled up to the curb in front of the bank and stopped. He held up the knife in front of her face and pushed the button. The sharp stainless steal blade popped out of the handle. "If I see one cop, one patrol car...she's dead." His dark, cold eyes pierced hers. "Understand?"

She nodded and turned her head, looking in the back scat into Molly's frightened eyes. "Don't be afraid, everything will be okay soon."

"I'm going to do exactly what you asked," she said, glaring at him. "Please don't hurt her." She clutched the handle of the briefcase and opened the door. "I have no idea how long this will take, so please don't panic if it takes a while. I'll be back as fast as I can."

Inside of the Jacksonville branch of the Chase Manhattan bank, she nervously fiddled with the latch on the briefcase while the bank president read the instructions.

When he finished reading her note, he frowned and looked over his glasses at her, "Mrs. Hollingsworth, are you in some kind of trouble?"

"Jack, please no questions, just do it," she said firmly.

He glanced around the lobby of the bank through his office glass walls. "Melissa, are you being watched? My finger is on a button under my desk. One push and we'll be surrounded by armed guards."

"No!" she screamed. "Please, Jack, that would not help me. Just do the transfer and act like nothing is wrong." She stared into his eyes. "You can do whatever you want after I leave, but not until I'm out the door and safely away. Please, no more questions, just do this as fast as you can."

Thirty minutes later, she walked out of the bank and waited by the curb. A cab pulled up and stopped. Jerry and Molly were sitting in the back seat. "Get in!" he yelled.

When she got in, she handed him the briefcase and the receipt for the wire transfer. Fifteen minutes later, when he was sure they weren't being followed, he directed the cabbie to a side street only a few blocks away, where he'd parked the car. Five minutes later, he pulled on to I-95, heading north.

"Where are we going?" Melissa shouted. "I did what you asked, now let us go. You promised."

He turned and glared back at her. "Are you really that stupid? I lied."

"You promised!" she shouted, "At least let Molly go."

He gave her an evil smile and shook his head. "Oh no, she's all part of my plan."

"Please, she is scared to death. Let her go. Have you gone completely crazy? You have my money and me, what else do you want?"

With the back of his right hand, he reached over and hit her as hard as he could, bloodying her lip. "I am not crazy!" he screamed, "Don't you ever call me that again. And tell her to shut the FUCK UP!"

Molly was crying in the back seat. "She can't help it, Jerry. She's just a little girl and she's frightened. Please, I'm begging you, let her go."

"MOLLY!" he screamed, "STOP CRYING!"

She stopped and stared up at Melissa with terrified eyes. "It's okay, baby. Mommy's all right."

No one talked or made a sound for the next hour. In the dark, she could see Jerry's expressionless face illuminated from the blue dashboard light. She looked over the seat at Molly. She was finally asleep.

"Why are you doing this?" she whispered. "You know they will catch you and put you in jail."

He shot her a hard look. "Maybe. And then again, maybe not."

"I just don't understand this. You haven't really done anything wrong yet. I swear to you, if you let us go. I won't tell them anything. You have all this cash and the money I transferred... just drive to an airport, get on a plane and fly away."

He turned and looked at her. "You have no idea, do you? What you've put me through…what you've made me do just to survive." He turned back and stared forward at the road, "It's not just about the money anymore. No, I can't jump on a plane and fly away yet. Not until I've paid you back for what you did to me. You tried to destroy me, so now I'm going to destroy you."

She lifted her head and looked over at him. He was smiling. "I will get on that plane someday and fly away, but not until I know that you are finally going to die…and have lost everything and everyone you have ever loved."

∼

I HAD JUST STEPPED out of the shower when my doorbell rang. I assumed it was Annabelle, so I wrapped the towel around my waist and walked to the door. When I opened it and saw the two detectives standing there, I frowned and held out my wrists. "Would you mind if I put on some clothes before you cuff me?"

Surprisingly, Detective Reynolds smiled at me. "Mr. Nash, we're not here to take you in, but we *would* like to talk to you. Would you mind if we come in?"

I opened the door wider and motioned them in. "I need to put on some clothes. There's a coffee maker in the kitchen if you want some. I'll be there in a second."

I ran to my bedroom, slipped on jeans and a shirt and walked to the kitchen. When I got there, Detective Johnson was standing by the coffee machine smiling at Detective Reynolds, who was backed up against the glass patio door staring down at Charley. He was growling at her only a few feet away.

"Charley!" I yelled. "Be nice, back off!"

He lifted his lip and exposed his teeth, "Arrrr," he growled, then backed away from her.

"What is wrong with you?" I said, scolding him. "She's a nice person, Charley. Leave her alone. She's just doing her job, so be nice, okay?"

He looked up at me and snorted, then he walked out of the room.

"I'm sorry, Detective Reynolds, he's not normally like that. But don't worry, so far he's never actually bitten anyone," I said with a grin. "Up till now anyway."

Cautiously, she walked to the kitchen bar and sat down on a stool. "I think I could use some of that coffee now," she said.

"You got it," I said, dropping in the coffee pod and hitting the button. "So what do you want to talk about this time? I know you don't believe me, but I really have told you everything I know."

When her coffee was ready, I picked up the cup and set it in front of her. "There's Coffeemate and sugar in here."

I pointed at the silver containers in the middle of the island. While she was doctoring up her coffee, I looked over at Detective Johnson. "So what's this all about?"

He shrugged his shoulders. "I think I'd rather have her tell you what's going on."

I looked at her. "Ok, Detective Reynolds, what's up? Do I need to call my lawyer?"

"No, you won't need him anymore. That's what I came here to tell you."

I frowned and tilted my head. "Why wouldn't I need my lawyer anymore?"

She sighed and took a breath. "We just left the District Attorney's office. He's dropping the charges against you."

My heart started pounding in my chest. "Oh God! Did you find them? Are they alive?"

"I'm sorry, but no, we haven't found them."

"Then why did he drop the charges?"

"I convinced him that you were innocent."

I pulled out a stool and sat down across from her. "How did you do that? What did you tell him?"

She held up a small digital recorder. "I let him listen to this. That was all it took."

"What's on it?" I asked, totally confused.

She punched a button and I heard my voice. Then I heard Annabelle's. The stool bounced on the tile floor and crashed into the wall behind me when I jumped up. "You bugged my house?" I screamed. "Who the hell do you think you are, the CIA? I'm not a lawyer, but I know you can't do that!"

Detective Johnson slid off his stool and held up his hands. "Calm down, Mr. Nash. Trust me on this, she knows she was wrong. She may even lose her job over it. I guess that's sort of up to you and what you do about this, but if I were you, instead of screaming at her, I would be thanking her."

"What? You want me to thank her for trying her best to destroy my life? And now for invading my privacy? Why in hell would I do that? Do you have short-term memory loss? Wasn't it just yesterday I was sitting in a jail cell because of her and you? And just a few days before that, both of you were screaming at me?"

He shrugged, but he didn't respond. What could he say?

"I was just trying to do my job," she said softly. "I'm a good cop, but sometimes because of what I have to deal with, and what I see every day...I guess I've gotten jaded. I forgot that there are still good people out there in the world. When I saw you with Annabelle, I immediately assumed the worst. Mark didn't, but I did. Maybe it was because I'm a woman and she looks...well, you know. Anyway, I was wrong about her...and especially wrong about you, so very wrong." She lifted her head and looked at me. "I know it probably doesn't mean anything to you, but I'm sorry. I really am."

She lifted her cup and took a small sip of coffee. Her hands were trembling. "The D.A. is worried that you'll try to sue the city for false arrest and ruining your reputation. I wouldn't blame you if you did, but I'm not here because of that. I'm here to personally apologize for being so stupid and close-minded. I want to make it up to you if I can." She actually had tears in her eyes.

I took a few deep breaths to calm myself, thinking about what she'd just said. I wanted to be angry at her and tried to think of something harsh and hurtful to say to her for what she'd done to me and Annabelle, but the rage inside me wasn't there. All I felt was relief that it was over.

I looked at her somber face. "So whatever's on that tape convinced the D.A. I'm not involved?"

"Yes, that and some other evidence that has surfaced."

"What other evidence?"

"Yesterday morning Melissa walked into the Chase Manhattan Bank in Jacksonville. She was alone, but the bank president was sure someone was watching her."

"Why was she there?"

"She withdrew a million in cash and transferred everything else to an offshore numbered bank account. Earlier that morning, she had called her broker and instructed him to sell all of her stocks and bonds and transfer that money to the same offshore account."

"All of it?"

"As far as we can tell. The bank security camera showed her getting out of a car when she went in the bank and getting into a cab when she left. There was a man and a little girl in both cars that matched Molly and Dr. Hollingsworth's descriptions."

"Don't call that sorry piece of shit doctor!" I yelled. "He doesn't deserve that. So that's what this is all about...her damn money."

"Yeah, it looks like it," she said. "Hopefully now that he's got it, he'll let them go."

I looked at her. "I sure hope so, but I doubt it. What about all the crap the district attorney stirred up about me with the D.A. in Texas?"

"He was making that call when we left," Detective Johnson said.

"My lawyer tells me he's a real piece of work. A certified asshole who hates to lose. I bet he was pissed to find out it was Jerry and not me."

He nodded and grinned. "You could say that. But now to cover his ass, he's making this case a top priority."

I picked up my stool and sat back down. "In what way?"

Detective Reynolds looked up at me. "He's ordered a nationwide BOLO and he's bringing in the FBI."

Finally, I thought to myself. I looked across the bar and studied the remorse in her face. She was either the best actress in the world or she was showing me the other side of her, the human side, not the cop.

"You know, Detective Reynolds," I said, handing her a napkin to wipe her eyes. "I don't know much about your profession, but I'm pretty sure a hard ass, tough detective like yourself shouldn't be crying on the job."

She wiped her eyes with the napkin and gave me a small grin. "I'm not on the job. I got suspended."

"Well, to be honest with you, you probably deserved it," I said, smiling. I picked up the digital recorder and held it up. "I don't suppose you were following me this morning on the beach? Maybe close enough to record me with this?"

She nodded her head. "That's why your dog hates me. He saw me hiding in the berm."

I laughed. "Now I understand, but don't worry about Charley. He doesn't hate you. And I'm sure he knew you were there all along. If he thought you were a real threat, he would have let me know." I handed the recorder back to her. "And I wouldn't worry about your job much. You've met my lawyer. I'm going to call him and ask him to come over here to talk to you. After I tell him what you've just done for me, Melissa and Molly...I'm going to sic him on the D. A."

# 24

# TRAIL OF DEATH

Even though the FBI were now involved and there was a nation wide BOLO out on Melissa, Molly and Jerry, Rob went ahead with his plan to release their pictures to the press, offering a $20,000 reward for any verifiable sighting. It didn't take long for the phones to start ringing after that.

~

JERRY FLIPPED off the television and stared at Melissa. Then he pointed his finger at Molly. "You, in the car, now!"

"Please, Daddy don't hurt Mommy again," she whimpered.

"I said get in the car NOW!" he shouted. Crying, Molly ran out the door.

"You don't have to do this!" Melissa yelled. "I swear I won't tell anyone what you've done. Just leave us here and go."

Jerry glared down at her as he ripped the long strip of duct tape off the roll. "Shut the fuck up," He yelled, covering her mouth with the tape. "Do you really think I'm that stupid? I'm in charge now, bitch, not you. How does it feel to be completely helpless and under someone else's control?"

He flipped her over onto her stomach and jerked the plastic ties securing her feet up to the middle of her back. Then he took another long plastic tie and bound her wrists and ankles together behind her. She tried to scream, but the duct tape muffled the sound.

"Scream all you want, nobody will hear you," he smirked. "I'll be back in a few minutes."

The second the door closed, with every ounce of strength and energy she had Melissa tugged against the plastic ties. She screamed from the pain of the thin plastic strips slicing her skin. Crying and gasping for air, breathing through her nose, she tried again and again and again. Terrified and exhausted, she tried to yell, but the duct tape blocked the sound.

In the car, Jerry grabbed Molly's arm and squeezed it hard. She screamed and started bawling. "Stop crying or I swear I'll go back in there and kill Mommy!" He yelled. "STOP IT!"

She immediately stopped and froze, terrified. "That's much better," he said backing out the car. "We're going to a gas station. When we get there, if you say one word or cry, when we get back, I will kill Mommy. Do you understand me?"

She didn't look at him, but shook her tiny head yes.

"That's a good girl," he said, smiling.

After Jerry filled the car with gasoline, he went inside the store, leaving her alone, sitting in the back seat. On the other side of the pumps, a car pulled up and a man stepped out and began filling his car. When he went to retrieve the windshield squeegee, he saw Molly sitting alone in the back seat with all the windows rolled up.

It was a hot day, almost ninety degrees. He smiled at her. "Aren't you hot in there?" Molly looked up at him, but quickly turned away. "You need to roll down the window or at least crack the door open," he said.

Molly didn't respond, keeping her head down. "Hey, little girl, can you hear me? You need to roll down the window. It's too hot out here, it's not safe."

When she didn't respond, he walked around the pumps and opened her door. "It's way too hot in here for you, baby. At least keep this door open."

Molly looked up at the stranger. "Help me," she whispered.

"What?" The man said. "You want me to help you? Are you in trouble?"

"He's gonna kill Mommy."

"Who's gonna kill your mommy?" he asked.

He felt something push against his back, so he jerked around to see a man standing behind him. Then he felt something brush against his neck. He reached his hand up to feel what it was. When he pulled his hand away, it was covered with blood. He tried to talk, but nothing came out. Suddenly he felt lightheaded and weak. Then he fell to the ground between the pumps and the car.

~

MOST OF THE calls that came in to the police were bogus, from people making up stories trying to get the $20,000 reward, but two of them turned out to be real. They both came from Kingsland, Alabama. The first was from a waitress in a small cafe who recognized Molly's picture. She said that she was with a man wearing a baseball cap, but she didn't pay him much attention to him and couldn't positively identify Jerry. But she remembered wondering why Molly seemed so sad when she waited on them. The second tip came from a small rundown motel there.

Kingsland was a tiny little town thirty-four miles north of Jacksonville, just over the Florida state line. Because they had crossed that state line, it was now officially in the FBI's jurisdiction, allowing them to engage all of their vast resources in the search.

They had been staying in one of the rooms at this shabby motel for almost two weeks. The manager recognized Jerry's picture on his television and called the police. But by the time the FBI and the local police had surrounded the motel, the room was empty.

"This is usually a sleepy little town," the Kingsland Sheriff said to the FBI agent, "but with this, and that murder yesterday, we're having quite the crime wave around here."

"What murder?" the FBI agent asked.

"Some guy got his throat cut over at the Kangaroo Mart yesterday afternoon. He died right there by the gas pump. It was my first murder investigation. In fact, it was the first murder in this town's history."

"Did they see who did it?" the agent asked.

"No, sir. Louise was working there by herself and didn't see anything. I figure it was some kind of road rage thing. The Kangaroo is right there at the I-95 exit. Yeah, I figure it probably started on the freeway and ended there at the pump."

"Does the Kangaroo have video surveillance?"

The sheriff took off his hat and scratched his head. "I'm pretty sure they do, but I figured whoever done this is long gone by now, so I didn't check 'em."

~

MY HEART SUNK in my chest when the FBI agent in charge of the investigation called and told me that the motel manager had not seen Melissa. He had only seen Jerry and a little girl when they checked in.

"Mr. Nash, we assume that either Mrs. Hollingsworth wasn't there with them, or he had her locked out of sight," he said. "Our forensic team is in there now. I'll let you know what they find."

"Were there any other sightings? Maybe at a restaurant or a store there?"

The agent sighed. "Yes, we think so. We're running a surveillance video we received from a gas station through facial recognition software at Quantico as we speak. We're pretty sure it was Mr. Hollingsworth and Molly."

"Did the station attendant recognize him?"

"No, but we think someone there did," he paused. "If it's Mr. Hollingsworth and the little girl on that surveillance tape, then this case has escalated substantially."

"Escalated?" I asked. "In what way?"

"Whoever's on that tape cut another customer's throat and drove away. If it's Mr. Hollingsworth, this is now a capital murder case."

When I heard that, my knees buckled under me and I had to sit down. My head was swimming. "I just don't get it. Jerry's a coward, a greedy asshole, but murdering a stranger? Cutting his throat...that just doesn't sound like something he would do."

"Mr. Nash, you'd be amazed at what people can do, especially when they're on the run. At least we believe we have his car. We got the plates and model from the surveillance tape. We're sure it's stolen, but if he's still driving it, we'll get him. I sent a car to talk to the registered owner. She lives in Savannah."

"Did you say Savannah?" I gasped. "What's the name of the owner?"

I could hear him flipping pages in his notebook. "It's registered to an Mrs. Eileen...

"Forester?" I interrupted. "It's registered to Eileen Forester?"

"Yes, do you know her?"

"Oh God, it's Melissa's aunt in Savannah! You said you have a car on the way?"

"It's there now. They knocked on her door, but she didn't answer. We figured she's probably at work."

"No! "I yelled. "She's retired, she should be there! You need to check inside, break down the door if you have to. They could be in there hiding!"

"We need a warrant to do that. Let me hang up and get to work on that now." He paused for a moment. "I know this is hard, but, Mr. Nash, give us a little time. We'll find them. We know what he's driving, he won't get far."

～

THE FBI RECEIVED the warrant thirty minutes later and broke down Eileen's front door. At first look, they thought the house was empty, but after a more thorough search, they found her. Her body was stuffed inside of a black garbage bag in the freezer. She had been strangled.

Because her corpse had been frozen, the autopsy was inconclusive on the exact time of her death. But the medical examiner was confident that she had been dead for several weeks, perhaps even a month.

"So he wasn't living on the street?" Annabelle asked me with wide eyes, "He was there at Melissa's aunt's house all this time?"

"Looks like it, but no one knows how long he was there. The FBI canvassed her neighborhood and apparently no one's seen Eileen for months. They said that a man claiming to be her nephew had told them that Eileen had taken a long cruise and while she was gone, he would be housesitting for her. They all identified his picture and said that he showed up a few months ago. I'm guessing he killed her then."

Annabelle started shaking her head. "No, that can't be right. Remember? Melissa and I were just there." She pulled out her cell phone and started checking her calendar. "Look," She said, holding up her phone, "we flew there May 14th. That was only six weeks ago."

I looked at her phone and counted the weeks. She was right. "Did Eileen seem okay to you? Was she acting strange in any way?"

She thought for a moment, then lifted her head and locked eyes with me. "Oh my God, Grant!" Her hands began to tremble.

"What is it? What's wrong?"

"He was there! Oh God! That's why she wouldn't let me go down there!"

"Down where?" I asked. "What are you talking about?"

"Molly left her doll there on their last visit. She made me promise I would find it and bring it back. I looked everywhere, but I couldn't find it. When I opened the basement door to go look down there, Eileen screamed at me and told me to stay out of the basement. It surprised me, because she was kind of rude." Annabelle looked up and stared into my eyes. "I thought she didn't like me for some reason, but that wasn't it at all. Oh God, Grant, he was there the whole time, and she was just trying to protect me."

I hugged her. "I think you may be right. And if you are, she probably saved your life, and Melissa's."

She dropped her brows. "I don't understand. If he was there, why didn't he kidnap Melissa then?"

I thought about what she'd said a moment, then shrugged my shoulders. "I don't know. Maybe it was because Molly wasn't there and he wanted them both."

We called the FBI agent and told him about their trip. "So you're saying they were there on the fourteenth and left on the fifteenth?" he asked.

"Yes, they got there Saturday afternoon about two and left Sunday around noon."

"That fits. I think you're right. If he wasn't in the house, he was close by. We just uncovered a video showing Eileen and a man that fits Jerry's description standing behind her at her bank the next day, on the sixteenth. She cleaned out all of her accounts and left with about $60,000 in cash. What we know so far, from talking to her neighbors, is that he had apparently been living there for at least three months. So yeah, I'm sure he was there. She's lucky."

"Yeah, she was," I said, "but I'm thinking he wanted Melissa and Molly."

"Mr. Nash, I'm about to get on a plane heading your way. I need to know more about Melissa and Molly. Anything you can tell me that might help us find them." He paused. "Can I call you Grant? This Mr. stuff is a bit formal."

"Sure, call me Grant."

"Great, I'm Jordan." He paused again and took a breath, "Grant, we found the car and...it had blood in the trunk. It's Melissa's."

"Oh, no," I said, leaning back in my chair and staring into Annabelle's eyes. "How much blood?"

"Not enough to be considered a mortal wound, but she's injured and bleeding. We found the car abandoned on the side of the road at somewhere called Franklintown, a few miles north of Amelia Island."

"That's only a few hours away from here," I shouted. "When did you find the car?"

"I just got the call. I'm guessing a few hours ago."

"You don't think he's coming back here, do you?"

"That's why I'm heading your way. We don't know where he's going. It doesn't fit into any scenario we've ever seen before. The car didn't break down, it was full of gas and started right up. He abandoned it on purpose and tried to hide it; it was off the road about thirty feet in the woods. If a hunter hadn't come across it, we wouldn't have found it for months. We assumed he hitched a ride with someone. Grant, to me it looks like he's heading toward something close, maybe to you, or maybe to somewhere else, but I'm certain he's heading to a specific destination. Otherwise, he'd be going in a different direction far away from Florida."

When I hung up, I walked into my bedroom to my closet and opened my gun safe. When I turned around, Annabelle was standing behind me.

"I didn't know you owned a gun. What are you planning on doing with that?"

"Annabelle, listen to me. This is very important. I want you to put Charley and Donna in your car and drive nonstop to your parents' house."

Her eyes flew open wide. "What?"

"Don't argue with me. I think Jerry is coming back for me, and I don't want you or Charley anywhere around here when he shows up."

"No, Grant!" she shouted. "I'm not going to leave you here alone."

I wrapped my arms around her. "He's already killed two people. And he may have already killed Melissa and Molly. I can't have you in danger, too. Please don't argue with me. Take the dogs and go. *Now.*"

I had to drag Charley down the stairs and shove him into her car. He knew something was up and did not want to leave me alone. I could hear him barking and Annabelle crying as they pulled out of the driveway and drove away.

## 25

# A TOOTHBRUSH

nnabelle's apartment was only seventeen miles from Grant's house, and although he made her promise she would drive straight to her parents in Boone, she didn't even have a toothbrush with her. It would only take her a second, she thought, to pack her toothbrush and some clothes in a bag, so instead of turning toward the freeway, she turned right and headed to her apartment.

As she made the turn into her complex parking lot, Charley began to whine. When she pulled into her parking space, he whined louder. "Stop that," she said to him, "It will only take me a few minutes. I'll be right back."

When she opened her door to step out, Charley jumped across her lap, out the door and took off running. "Charley, come back here!" she screamed, running after him. By the time she ran to the street, he was gone, nowhere in sight.

She knew where he was going; back to Grant's house. She ran back, jumped into her car and cranked the engine, but instead of putting the car in reverse and backing out, she changed her mind and turned off the key. It didn't make any sense not to go get her toothbrush and some clothes while she was there. After that, she could drive back to Grant's, pick Charley up again and drive on to Boone.

⁓

WRAPPED IN A BLANKET, hiding in the tall sea oats, beach grass and railroad vines in the berm behind his beach house, Grant sat quietly, holding his new Glock in his right hand. He had turned on every light in the house and garage. He'd even turned on the four exterior flood-lights that lit up his front, sides and back yards. From the berm, he could easily see someone approaching.

When he heard the noise, he froze and searched with his eyes. When he saw the source of the sounds, he couldn't believe what he was seeing. It was Charley, and he was running toward him barking.

"What the hell are you doing here? You're supposed to be with Annabelle!"

Charley started spinning in circles, barking, crying and whining. A cold chill ran through his body remembering the last time he had seen him acting this way. It was Valentine's Day morning, two years ago, when he had walked down the stairs with Rita and Audrey heading to the airport.

"Where's Annabelle?" he yelled. "Is she in trouble?"

Charley turned and ran around the house. He jumped up and ran after him. When he got there, Charley was standing beside his truck, whining and barking. He pulled out his keys, unlocked and opened the door. Charley jumped in first, then he got in, cranked the engine and took off.

When he stopped at the light at A1A, Grant looked over at him. "She went to her apartment, right?"

"Woof, woof, woof."

⁓

DETECTIVE REYNOLDS KNEW she shouldn't be anywhere near there. She'd only been reinstated for a few weeks, but she couldn't stop herself. It was a feeling in her gut she'd had all day long. Something told her she needed to be there, so after her shift ended, she drove to

Grant's neighborhood and backed her car off the road into the woods across the street from his house.

From there, she had watched Grant load the dogs into Annabelle's car and wave as she drove away. An hour later, she watched as all the lights outside his house began to come on. Then she watched him walk down the steps and walk around the side of his house. He was carrying a blanket and something black in his right hand. Curious, she slipped out of her car, ran to the adjoining house and watched him wrap the blanket around him and crawl in between the tall sea grasses in the dune behind his house.

"What the hell is he doing?" she whispered to herself. "Why is he hiding there?"

After a few minutes, she left him and walked back to her car. Thirty minutes later, a car slowly pulled into the cul-de-sac. She couldn't make out the driver, but whoever it was drove around the circle and backed into a driveway of an empty house with a for sale sign in the front yard.

She pulled out her cell and punched in a number. When Detective Johnson answered, she whispered, "Mark, something's going down here."

"Down where?" he asked.

"At Grant Nash's house. There's a guy backed up in a driveway at a vacant house."

"What the *fuck* are you doing there? Do you want to get fired this time?"

"Damn it, Mark, I'm telling you something's going down! Grant's hiding in the bushes, in the berm behind his house, and I think he's got a gun."

She heard him sigh. "Anastasia, call the FBI. It's their case now. You don't need to get involved. Call them and get the hell out of there now!"

"Whoa, what's he doing here?" she whispered.

"Who is it? Who are you talking about?"

"The dog. Grant's dog. He just ran around the house."

Frustrated, he yelled. "Anastasia, the dog lives there. Will you please get the hell out?"

"I know that, but Grant loaded him into Annabelle's car an hour ago. I'm telling you, something is wrong here."

"For God's sake, crank your car and leave!" Mark yelled. "I'm calling the FBI."

"Wait, hold on," she whispered, "They're getting into his truck!"

Sliding down in her seat, not to be seen, she watched Grant and Charley speed away. A few moments later, she saw the mysterious car slowly pull out of the driveway and follow them. As the car drove by, she recognized his face.

"Oh shit, its Hollingsworth!" she shouted as she cranked her car and backed into the road.

"Hollingsworth is there?" Mark shouted, "I'm on my way. Don't do anything until I get there."

"I can't do that, he's on the move. I'm going to follow him. He's driving a white Ford sedan, I think. I'm going to see if I can get close enough to get the plates."

"No, God damn it!" Mark yelled. "Hang back. Don't let him see you."

～

FOLLOWING the old pickup a few cars back, Jerry smiled as they made the turn, because he knew where they were going. "Don't worry, Grant, you'll all be together soon," he said with a chuckle. "You, Melissa, Molly, and your new one. It should go down pretty easy," he said out loud. "What's the old saying? Like shooting fish in a barrel."

～

GRANT SLID to a stop in Annabelle's apartment parking lot behind her car. Her driver side door was standing open and the inside lights were on, shining bright, illuminating the empty interior. Annabelle and Donna were nowhere in site.

He opened his truck door and followed Charley running up the four flights of stairs. He was gasping for air when they finally made it to her apartment and banged on the door. When the door opened, he got the shock of his life. Standing in front of him was Molly.

When she saw him, she burst into tears and jumped up into his arms. "Mr. Grant! Help us!" she cried.

Holding her in his arms, he walked into the room and looked around. It was empty, but Charley barked and ran toward the bedroom. When he walked into the room, he saw Melissa and Annabelle, side by side lying face down, hog-tied with their wrists and ankles bound behind them with plastic ties. They both had silver duct tape covering their mouths.

He put Molly down and ran to the bed. Melissa didn't move, but when Annabelle heard him, she opened her eyes and started struggling against her bindings. She tried to talk, but the tape muffled the sounds. As gently as he could, he peeled back the tape from her mouth.

"Jerry!" she screamed. "He did this."

"I know, don't worry, I'm here now," he said softly. "Don't struggle. Let me cut you loose. I'll be right back, I'm gonna go get a knife."

He ran to the kitchen and frantically began jerking open the drawers, searching for a sharp knife.

"You won't find anything in there." Grant jerked around to see Jerry standing in the doorway, smiling.

When he saw him, his blood boiled and he ran toward him, but stopped when Jerry held up a long switch blade knife. "Not one more step," he said. "I've gotten quite good with this."

Grant glared at him. "Yeah, I've heard all about it."

Out of the corner of his eye, Grant saw movement. It was Charley, standing only a few feet away from Jerry. He lifted his lips and growled deeply. "No, Charley!" Grant shouted. "Back off!" He stopped growling, but didn't move.

"The gun. Give me the gun," Jerry snarled. "I saw it. It's stuck in your belt, behind your back. Put it on the bar."

Grant smiled. "You saw that, huh? Yep, it's a gun all right, but I'm not going to put it on the bar. I think a better idea would be to see if I can pull it out of my belt and shoot you with it, before you stab me with that knife."

Jerry smiled back. "I'm afraid you're a little too far away, but I bet I could kill him before you can shoot me." He took a step toward Charley.

"No, Daddy! Don't hurt him." Molly ran up to Charley and put her arms around his neck.

Before Grant could make a move, Jerry jerked her by the arms and pulled her beside him. Holding the knife to her neck, he yelled, "PUT THE FUCKING GUN ON THE COUNTER! NOW!"

Slowly, Grant pulled the gun out of his belt and laid it on the counter.

"Over there," Jerry said, pointing to the couch, "and take the dog with you."

Grant grabbed Charley by his collar, drug him to the couch and sat down. Jerry picked up the gun and shoved Molly toward the couch. "Go sit with them and be quiet, or you know what I'll do."

Obediently, she walked to the couch and sat next to Grant.

"If anybody moves, I swear I will slit their throats." He glared down at Grant. "Do you understand?"

Jerry left them alone and walked into the bedroom. A few minutes later, he returned with Annabelle. He had cut off her ties and was pointing the gun at her head. "Go sit by your boyfriend." He shoved her forward and shot Grant a hard look. "If anybody moves, everybody dies!"

He left them alone again for a few minutes. When he returned, he was holding Melissa under his arm. He dragged her unconscious body into the room and dropped her down on the floor. He shook her hard. "Wake up, bitch!" he yelled. "You're gonna miss the party!"

Melissa moaned and slowly opened her eyes. When she saw Grant sitting on the couch above her, she opened her mouth and tried to talk, but no sounds came out.

Grant stood and moved toward her. "DON'T MOVE!" Jerry yelled, pointing the gun at his head. "Sit your ass back down and don't even think about it."

Grant held up his hands and sat down. He looked down at Melissa's skeleton thin body and gave her a gentle smile. Her red bloodshot eyes were sunk back deep into her sockets. Her red eyes made a stark contrast against her greenish yellow skin on her face and neck. He'd seen that look before on his mother's face the day she died – it was a death mask.

~

SILENTLY, the parking lot of Annabelle's apartment complex began to fill with black FBI vehicles, local police units and two large SWAT team vans.

Detective Reynolds explained everything she had seen take place at Grant's house to Dan Hathaway, the special agent in charge.

With thermal energy cameras attached to a drone, the FBI determined that they were all in the front room of the apartment.

"One standing, one lying on the floor and three are sitting side by side on what we assume is a couch," the agent reported to Hathaway. "It also appears that there is a dog sitting next to the people as well."

Hathaway nodded his head. "That makes sense. Grant Nash left with his house with a dog. What about a sniper?"

The SWAT team leader nodded his head and said, "We're bringing in three bucket trucks. They should be here soon. I think we may be able to get the shooters high enough for a shot with those."

"Let me know when you have that in place. I'll wait to make the call then."

# 26

## SIT IN DADDY'S LAP

J erry bent the blind down with his finger and peered out the window. "Oh my," he smirked, "the calvary has arrived." He let go of the blind, backed away from the window and grinned. "All the Saint Augustine boys in blue must be down there. It's quite an impressive showing. It'll be big news tomorrow."

Grant lifted his head and glared at him. "You did all this for press. Going out in a blaze of glory so you'll be famous?"

Jerry didn't respond. He just smiled, sitting patiently as if he was waiting for something, fiddling with his knife – folding the blade back into the handle, then pushing the button, watching it snap back open.

"It's not real fame, Jerry," Grant said. "You of all people should know how humans react. Oh, the world will all hear your name, but they will soon forget it. And if your name ever comes up again, they'll just say, 'Is that the crazy ass doctor who killed all those innocent people? The guy who got his head blown clean off his shoulders by the SWAT team sniper?'"

Jerry closed the knife and frowned at Grant. "You really think that's what's going to happen?"

"I know that's what's going to happen. As soon as they have a shot, your head will suddenly explode like a ripe melon and your brains will be splattered all over the room. But don't worry, Doc, you won't feel a thing," he said with a smirk, "I just hope I get to see it."

Jerry jumped out of the chair and pointed the gun at Grant's head. "You won't be able to see anything, because that's not going to happen. You don't think I've gone to all this trouble without having a plan, do you?" He lowered the gun and laughed. "What's really going to happen is, you will all be dead and I will be on a plane heading to some faraway island...a very rich man."

Grant started laughing. "Come on, Doc, that's your big plan? You are disappointing me. I've never liked you. I've always thought you were an arrogant, lazy, greedy bastard, but at the same time, I've always thought you were very intelligent. Don't you watch TV? At the first shot, they'll crash through that door and take you out. They'll never let you walk out of here alive."

Jerry lowered himself back down into the chair. "Molly, come here," Jerry said.

As if she was in a trance, Molly obediently slid off the couch and walked up to him. "Sit in Daddy's lap."

Without hesitation, she crawled into his lap. "That's a good girl. Now hold on to Daddy's neck real tight and don't let go." He looked her in the eyes, "If you don't hold on tight, you know what I will do, don't you?" She dropped her head and nodded. "That's a good girl."

Cradling Molly in his arms, he stood up and leaned back against the kitchen counter. "You're right. *I*, of all people, *do* know how humans react. Do you really think they will take a shot at someone holding a little girl in his arms?" he grinned. "Not even if it's a clean head shot, they won't take it. Not as long as her head is close to mine. And another thing...they won't hear any gun shots." He pushed the button on the knife and the sharp stainless steel blade popped open. "We'll be using this."

"You think I'm just going to sit here and watch you slit their throats...and mine?"

Jerry gave him a sinister look and pointed the gun at Molly's head.

"I won't be doing the slitting," he pressed the gun against her temple and smiled. "You will."

Grant and Jerry both jumped when the phone on the kitchen counter rang. They locked eyes and listened to it ring again. After the fifth ring, Jerry lifted the receiver and put it to his ear.

"Dr. Hollingsworth, this is Don Hathaway, I'm a special agent with the FBI. Will you talk to me?"

"Special Agent Hathaway, I'm afraid I don't have much to talk about," Jerry said, smiling, "Actually, I'm a little busy now, could I call you back?"

"I'm afraid not, Doctor. And I think we have a lot to talk about. I need to know the condition of your hostages? Are they alive? Is anyone hurt or in need of medical assistance?"

"Not yet," he chuckled, "but they all will soon if you and the rest of the gang down there in the parking lot don't back off and drive away."

"Doctor Hollingsworth, I want you to understand that I am in charge of this operation and have full authority to make decisions to help you get out of this situation, but backing off and driving away will not be a decision I will be making. Do you need anything? Is anyone there hungry or thirsty?"

Jerry laughed out loud. "Agent Hathaway, I'm assuming you know that I am a doctor of psychology. I am not your typical criminal. So stop with the good cop bullshit act. I will not be falling for any of your tricks."

Trying not to lose his cool, Hathaway bit down, gritting his teeth. Then he relaxed, took a breath and thought about his next move. He was standing, unarmed, only a few feet away from the front door of the apartment, breaking every rule he'd ever learned about hostage negotiations. But it was a dangerous volatile situation, and he knew he was dealing with someone that knew more about human psychology than he did. All of his training wouldn't work anyway, so he was winging it.

"Ok, Doctor, let's cut to the chase. The building you are in is surrounded by thirty local police and five FBI units. There are also two SWAT teams here with snipers positioned and in place. We know that you are currently standing in the kitchen, holding a little girl in your arms that we assume is Molly. There is another adult standing three feet away from you. There are two more adults in the room, one lying on the floor and one sitting on the couch. And finally, there is also a large dog lying next to the couch. Is that a correct assessment?"

Jerry's eyes widened, stunned at the accuracy. "Yes," he whispered, "that is correct."

"We know the adult on the floor is alive, from her thermal heat, but we don't understand why he or she is lying there. Is this person injured?"

"No, she is not injured," Jerry said, "but she's not doing very well. I suspect she is dying of acute liver failure."

Hathaway glanced up and frowned at Detective Reynolds and Detective Johnson, who had broken rank and were moving down the walkway toward him. He cupped the phone in his hand and lifted his finger to his lips. "Shhhh, Not a sound," he whispered. "Melissa is down."

He took a breath and lifted the phone back to his mouth. "Doctor Hollingsworth, as a sign of good faith, would you allow me to send in an EMT team to take Melissa out? She obviously needs medical attention and is no good to you in there."

Jerry frowned. "I think I'll pass on that. That would be a complete waste of everyone's time anyway. She's too far gone, nothing can be done for her now."

"I'm sorry to hear that. Okay then, if I'm going to be able to help you, I need something. How about Molly? She's certainly no threat to you. Let her go and I'll consider that as your act of good faith."

Jerry laughed again. "You are good, Hathaway, but we both know that's not going to happen. She's my get out of jail free card – my get away girl. And I'm going to keep her very, very close to Daddy." He hung up the phone in his ear.

He looked over at Grant and grinned. "Change of plan. This has escalated faster than I had assumed. I'm afraid this development has accelerated my time schedule." He pushed the button on the knife. When the blade popped out, he flipped it in his hand, holding on to the blade. Then he reached out his arm toward Grant, "It's time to do the deed. Take this and kill Melissa first."

Grant took a step back. "I'm not killing anyone!" he yelled.

Jerry flipped the knife back around in his hand and pressed the blade against Molly's neck. "Ok then, I guess I'll have to do it. I think I'll start with her."

The phone rang again. Jerry sighed, put the gun down on the counter, picked up the receiver and said, "Dr. Jeremiah Hollingsworth."

"Doctor, we got disconnected," Hathaway said in his ear. "We weren't finished talking."

"I think you said quite enough, Agent Hathaway. I have nothing more to say."

"Ok, that's fine. You don't have to talk anymore. I'll take it from here. Are you listening carefully?"

Jerry frowned, rolling his eyes. "Yes, I'm listening."

"Good. I will only say this one time, so listen carefully. We can see and hear everything you're saying. There will be no more killings with that knife. So you might as well put it down on the counter."

Jerry jerked his head up, searching the room for a camera, but saw nothing.

"Doctor, I am standing a few feet from your front door. I am alone and unarmed. I want to talk to you face to face. You are a very intelligent man. There is no way out of this and you know it. This has gone on long enough and I'm not going to wait until you do something. Whatever you may have planned is no longer going to work, but there's no reason for anyone to die today. I want to help you. Please, Doctor, let me help. Let me save your life. Put the gun and the knife down on the counter and open the front door. You have exactly thirty seconds."

"FUCK!" Jerry screamed. He dropped the knife on the counter and pulled Molly up, holding her head close to his.

"That's good, Doctor. Now hang up the phone, walk to the door and open it slowly."

Jerry hung up the phone, but picked up the gun. He walked toward the door and opened it. "Talk to me!" he yelled.

"Drop the gun, Doctor, and step out of the doorway."

Holding Molly up with her head next to his, he said, "Agent Hathaway, I'm sorry, but I can't do that and this is as far as I'm going. Do you have something to offer me?"

# 27

# LIKE A RIPE MELON

A nnabelle's apartment was on the top floor, in the middle of the four-story building. There were stairways on each side that connected to a long, eight-foot wide concrete walkway that ran in front of the apartments on each floor. The outside edge of the walkway had a black metal ornate four-foot tall handrail.

The one hundred-fifty-foot walkway in front of Annabelle's apart-ment was empty, except for the two detectives and Hathaway standing next to Annabelle's apartment door. But on the third and fourth flights of each stairwell, on every other step, dressed in black riot gear, were SWAT team members ready to advance. On the roof of the building, connected by body harnesses and long ropes, were seven more.

"Go away," one of the SWAT team guys said softly to Donna as she slowly climbed the stairs past him. Several more SWAT officers quietly tried to shoo her away as she continued to climb the steps.

In his ear, Hathaway heard, "There is a large dog coming your way." He looked down the walkway and saw Donna slowly moving toward him. She was crouched down, in a hunting position, slowly inching forward.

"Doctor Hollingsworth!" he yelled. "There is a large dog on the walkway coming my way. I believe he is going to attack me. This is not a trick or a police dog. I don't know where he came from, but if he does attack, please do not react. Let me handle the dog. Don't do anything stupid."

Jerry leaned forward and glanced down the walkway. When Molly saw her, she screamed, "DONNA!"

Instantly, Donna bolted, running as fast as she could, flying down the walkway.

Hathaway reached for his gun, but remembered that it wasn't there. He had not lied; he was unarmed. He braced himself for the attack, but instead of attacking him, when Donna reached the door, she turned and leaped up at Jerry, biting, snapping and growling ferociously.

Jerry screamed when Donna clamped down on his wrist. He dropped Molly, who fell hard on the walkway, rolling head first toward the railing, screaming and crying.

Fighting off Donna's attack, Jerry swung the gun down hard against her head. She whelped loudly and fell to the floor unconscious.

Detective Johnson rushed to Molly, scooping her up in his arms and ran toward the stairs, pushing his way through the SWAT team, who was running toward the apartment.

When Charley heard Donna's whelp and saw her fall to the floor, he jumped up, leaping into the air growling and snarling, knocking Jerry backwards out of the door. He kicked Charley in the chest, knocking him back inside the apartment door.

Suddenly exposed on the walkway, Jerry turned and saw the SWAT team rushing toward him. He knew it was over, so he lifted the gun and started shooting randomly inside the apartment.

Coughing up blood from the kick, Charley pulled himself off the floor and attacked him again. Jerry was still firing at random into the apartment when Charley jumped up on his chest, knocking him back against the rail, chomping down hard on his neck, literally hanging in the air by his teeth.

Everything had happened in a few seconds, but to Grant, it seemed like he was watching the sudden horror and chaos in slow motion. He looked at Annabelle and locked eyes. He could see the frightened panic and terror. He ran toward the door and stepped onto the walkway to see Charley hanging in the air, snarling and biting Jerry's neck. Jerry leered at Grant, then raised the gun and pointed it at his chest. Bracing himself, Grant stared back into Jerry's cold, dark eyes.

Suddenly…his eyes were gone. One second they were there…and the next…there was just a red, cloudy mist. Grant blinked his eyes trying to comprehend what he was seeing. It took him a second to understand. The snipers bullet had disintegrated the top of Jerry's head.

He leaped forward, grabbing Charley, pulling him back into his arms only seconds before Jerry's headless body toppled backwards over the railing, crashing into a bloody heap on the patio deck four stories below.

Grant looked down at Charley in his arms. His eyes were closed and he wasn't moving. His coat was covered with blood, which was running down his back. He had been shot. "Charley!" he screamed, "GOD NO! WAKE UP, CHARLEY! OPEN YOUR EYES, BUDDY!"

His lids fluttered, then opened. He lifted his eyes up to Grant for a second, exhaled…and then went limp in his arms. "NOOO! PLEASE, GOD, NOT CHARLEY." He pulled him close to his chest and cried.

"I've got him!" He looked up to see Detective Reynolds kneeling beside him, "He's breathing, so he's still alive. I know a great vet. He's the best, I promise. He'll fix him up."

She lifted Charley out of his lap, cradled him in her arms and took off running. Grant, still on his knees, watched her run down the walkway and disappear down the stair well.

"Are you hit?" He looked up at Hathaway standing over him. "No, I don't think so." Hathaway held out his hand and helped him up.

"I'm Don Hathaway with the FBI. Are you sure you aren't hit?"

Grant looked down and patted his body, "No, I think I'm okay." His head was swimming, barely noticing the multiple sirens blasting loudly below him, piercing everyone's eardrums. The hot stale air was still full of smoke and reeked of the lingering pungent smell of gunpowder. He leaned over the rail and looked down at Jerry's body splattered on the deck below, lit up by the bright patio floodlights.

In his dazed state, he watched seemingly in slow motion as Detective Reynolds carefully loaded Charley into her car and speed away with her lights flashing and her siren blasting. Then he watched four EMT attendants hurriedly unload two gurneys from two ambulances in the parking lot. When they were set up, he watched them running with the gurneys toward the stairway. His senses gradually began to return and finally realized that they were coming with two gurneys. "Annabelle!" he shouted, running toward the apartment door.

She was lying on the couch, surrounded by two men. He couldn't see what they were doing to her. All he could see was their backs with the large white SWAT letters printed on their black shirts. He looked down and saw two more leaning over Melissa.

Someone touched his arm. "You're gonna be in the way. Come over here." Hathaway said, pulling him toward the kitchen."

Trance like, Grant slowly turned his head and looked at Hathaway. "She got hit?" he whispered.

He nodded grimly. "Yes, twice."

"Oh my God...is she gonna be all right?" His eyes pleaded up at him.

Hathaway shrugged. "I don't know, she's hit pretty bad."

"Could someone do something with this dog?" Grant looked down at the SWAT guy. He was trying to pull Donna back away from Melissa.

"Donna," Grant shouted, "Come here, girl." She looked up at him and ran to his side, trembling and shaking. He squatted down and petted her head. When he touched her, she yelped in pain. "I'm sorry, girl, is that where he hit you with the gun?" He said, hugging her.

After they loaded Melissa and Annabelle on the two gurneys, he and Donna ran behind them, down the walkway and followed them closely down the stairs.

They loaded Melissa in one ambulance and Annabelle in another. Grant stood behind them both, holding Donna by her collar, watching the two EMT teams frantically working trying to stabilize them."

"Do you know her blood type?" Annabelle's EMT guy yelled.

Grant ran up to the back of the ambulance. "No, I don't."

The attendant looked at him grimly. "Are you sure? She's lost a lot of blood. If we knew her type, we could call for a chopper. She'll never make it to the hospital without some blood."

In the other ambulance, Melissa lifted her head and whispered, "AB negative,"

The EMT attendant working on her bent over and put his ear close to her mouth. "What did you say, ma'am?"

She opened her eyes and whispered again, "She...has...A...B...negative. Same...as...me."

"Are you sure?"

"Yes."

He jumped out the back of the ambulance and ran up to the other one. "She has AB negative," he yelled, "That's what my patient said. I'll call for a chopper!"

Grant watched the two EMT attendants lock eyes with each other and shake their heads. "What does that mean?" he asked.

The attendant looked down at him with sad eyes. "I'm sorry, but there's not enough time. She'll die before the chopper gets here."

Grant collapsed to the ground, pulling Donna close to him and hugged her in his arms.

"Do you have a transfusion kit on board?" Melissa's EMT guy asked.

"Yes, why?" the other one asked.

He bent down, squatting next to Grant and Donna. "My patient said that she has the same blood type. Are they sisters? Could that be true?"

"They're not sisters," Grant said, "but I know for a fact that Melissa has AB negative blood."

Grant help them load Annabelle's gurney into the other ambulance next to Melissa. They immediately closed the doors and sped away, leaving him standing there with Donna in the parking lot.

A car pulled up next to him. "Get in. We'll follow them." It was Detective Johnson, and he was holding Molly in his lap. She was sound asleep. "You might want to take her back there with you."

With Molly asleep in his arms and Donna curled close by his side,

Grant stared out the window, frozen in place. His body was numb and his mind was blank. In his dazed state, he didn't hear the two blaring sirens echoing through the air, or see the bright red and blue flashing lights as they flew down the road at a hundred miles an hour only a few feet behind the ambulance.

# 28

# THE MARINE

A t the hospital, Grant called Marshall and Brenda to let them know what had happened.

"What's their condition?" Marshall asked.

"All I know is that they were both still alive when they arrived, but they wouldn't tell me anything else."

"Have you called Annabelle's parents?" Brenda asked.

"No, not yet. I was hoping to hear something to tell them before I called."

"They need to know, Grant. Do you want me to call them?" Marshall asked. "I'm used to delivering bad news to parents. What's their number?"

"Thanks, but I got her in to this. I'll call them."

"What about Charley?" Brenda asked, "Have you heard anything yet?"

Grant wiped his eyes. "No. I don't even know where he is. Detective Reynolds took him to a vet somewhere. I haven't heard from her...but...he was hurt pretty bad."

"We're on our way. We should be there in four or five hours," Marshall said. "I don't know what to say, buddy. I guess all we can do now is pray."

Grant didn't hesitate and dialed Annabelle's father's cell phone as soon as he hung up with Marshall and Brenda. Somehow, they already knew and were on the road driving there. He didn't ask how they found out, but told them he would call them if he heard anything.

Next, he called Connie and Wilson, Melissa's best friends. Fifteen minutes later, they walked into the hospital waiting room and found him. He filled them in on what had happened and after a few mutual tears had been shed, they volunteered to take Molly and Donna home with them.

When they left, he walked to the desk and asked the nurse once more if they knew anything else. If she did, she didn't tell him. When he turned around, he saw Detective Reynolds sitting next to Detective Johnson in the waiting room. She had a somber look on her face. He didn't really want to know, but somehow, he forced himself to walk over to her.

She looked up at him with tears in her eyes. "Is he gone?" he asked softly.

"No, he's still alive, but it doesn't look very good. Would you like me to take you to him?"

Grant sat down next to her and sighed. "I would love that, but I can't leave now. I have to stay here. Charley will understand."

"How about some coffee?" Detective Johnson asked. "I could use some. I'm sure there's a cafeteria around here somewhere."

On their way to the coffee shop, they came across a small chapel. Grant stopped at the door and motioned to them. "I'll meet you in a few minutes." He opened the door of the chapel and stepped in.

The room was small, only about twelve feet wide and twenty feet deep. There were four rows of eight chairs, four chairs on each side, with a center aisle leading to a small wooden pulpit, bookended by two beautiful all white flower arrangements. Behind the pulpit was a wall of multicolored stained glass, glowing softly, backlit by florescent lights.

In the front row, kneeling by the pulpit, was a soldier, a Marine, and he was praying.

Sitting silently in the back row, Grant studied him. The pain the

Marine was feeling was obvious, radiating through his body. His young face was stern. His eyes were closed tight, his brow furrowed and wrinkled. His sun-tanned cheeks were wet, dripping from his tears. Grant could almost feel his pain and wondered what terrible consequence had brought him to that small chapel that day, but he doubted whatever the marine was living through could be as bad as what had brought *him* there.

When the Marine stood, wiped his eyes and walked out, Grant move to the front, nearer the pulpit. He stared at the stained glass with images of the angels hovering over a crucified Jesus Christ nailed to the cross. He felt something hit his fingers. He held up his hand and inspected it, surprised when he realized that it was a tear, his tear. He was so numb, he was crying and didn't even know it. When he touched his face and felt the wetness, he lost control. Leaning forward, rocking in his chair, hugging his body, he let it all out and wept from the depths of his soul.

Through his tears, in a gravelly voice he spoke out loud. "God...what have I done to you? Why are you so angry at me?" He wiped his eyes and looked up at the image of Christ. "I can't think of anything I've done that would have offended you so...but you keep taking away everything and everyone I love."

He stood, walked closer to the stained glass and put his hand on the image. "I know it's been a long time since I've talked to you, but... after Rita and Audrey...I was so angry. I just had nothing to say to you."

He gently touched the stained glass image of Christ's face with his hand. "But I do now. I have a lot of questions for you and I sure hope you're listening."

"He's always listening," a deep voice said behind him.

Grant spun around. The Marine was standing in the aisle. "I apologize, sir," he said gently, "for eavesdropping, but you were praying out loud."

Grant smiled at him and nodded. "I guess I was, sorry. I thought I was alone. No need to apologize."

The Marine walked to the front row and picked up his cap. "I left my cover," he said. "I didn't mean to interrupt you, sir."

"I hope you're right," Grant whispered, "about Him listening."

"I am, sir. I know He is real." The Marine folded his cap and held it in his hand. "At times it may not seem like it, because he doesn't always answer our prayers...but He loves you, sir, and He is always listening." The Marine nodded, turned and walked out of the chapel.

Grant walked back to the row of chairs and sat down, staring up at the stained glass. "Very impressive young man. I bet You're proud of him," he said, smiling. "So, how do we do this? Where do I start?"

He sighed, leaned back in the chair and ran his hand through his hair. "I'm not going to ask You why You took Rita and Audrey from me. We've been over that a million times already and You haven't answered. So, let me ask You this. What's the deal with Charley? I believe he may be one of Your angels. Is that it? You sent him to me to help me get through losing Rita and Audrey? If that was it, I'd like to tell You that he's done a hell of a good job." He lifted up his hands, "Sorry, that slipped out. Is hell a bad word? I never have figured that one out. If it is, again, sorry. Back to Charley. If he's one of Your angels that you sent to me, why take him now? If I've ever needed an angel," his eyes filled and tears rolled down his cheek, "God, now is the time. Please don't take him. I love him and I need him desperately."

Fighting his emotions, he sat upright and wiped his eyes with his sleeve. "I know You work in mysterious ways, but why save Melissa once, just to let her die like this? That's Your plan for her, really? And Annabelle? What has she ever done? Lord, she's so young and inno-cent...and good. Why her?"

He broke down again and cried hard for a long time. Finally, he stopped and lifted his head. "I know I probably shouldn't say this to You, but aren't You supposed to be a loving God? If You are, I'm not seeing much of that love. If I've done something that's offended You, please forgive me. Show me what it was and I swear I'll never do it again, or take me, punish me, God, not them. I may deserve Your wrath, but they are so good...they do not deserve this. Please, God, I'm not asking You to give me anything, but I'm begging You...work Your miracles...give them their lives, don't take them, not now. Please, Lord, let them live...if You need to take someone...take me instead."

～

"MY FIRST NAME IS ANASTASIA," Detective Reynolds said when he sat down.

"And mine is Mark," Detective Johnson said.

Anastasia took his hand and squeezed it. "I think we're beyond formalities at this point. We've been through a lot together."

"We sure have," he whispered. "I don't think I've told you how much I appreciate what you both did back there with Charley and Molly. Thank you."

"She has to be traumatized," Mark said softly. "I have a grand-daughter about the same age. Poor little thing."

Grant looked down. "I can't imagine what he's done to her. She's in for a long road ahead." He looked down at the table and sighed. "Especially if Melissa doesn't make it. But if I have anything to do with it, Molly's going to be okay, eventually."

"If there's anything we can ever do to help, just ask," Mark said. "If you ever need a babysitter, my wife and I would love to watch her. We could set up a play date with my granddaughter."

"I may take you up on that."

"There you are!" a voice said. "They told me you may be in here." Rob pulled up a chair at their table and sat down. "What the hell happened?"

For the next twenty minutes, Grant sat quietly sipping his coffee, listening to Detective Reynolds fill him in with the gory details. He didn't have the energy to add anything to the conversation, so he kept quiet.

"How long have they been back there? In the E.R.?" Rob asked grimly.

"A few hours," Grant answered, finally speaking, "but they won't tell me anything."

"They can't. You're not a relative. The HIPAA patient privacy laws are very specific and strict. What about Molly? Where is she?"

"She's safe, thanks to Detective Johnson here. He was the one that got her out of there to safety. She's with Connie and Wilson James. They're two of Melissa's close friends; they grew up together."

"How is she doing? Was she hurt at all?"

"Not physically," Grant said. "We were just talking about that. I'm sure Jerry has done some severe damage to her, but we won't know how much that is for a long time, maybe years."

Rob sighed and leaned back in his chair. "I can't help but wonder if I didn't have something to do with all this."

"What are you talking about?" Grant asked, frowning, "What could you have to do with this?"

"The last time I talked to Jerry, I may have stepped over the line. He was such a pompous jackass, I just couldn't hold back."

What did you say to him?"

"I was almost laughing at him. Rubbing it in his face. He had just lost every single thing he cared about in his life...and I was laughing about it." Rob looked over his glasses at Grant. "I should have known better. I knew he was probably unstable, but I never dreamed he would do something like this."

"Rob, we all thought Jerry was just a selfish, arrogant greedy bastard. No one knew he was crazy. You or no one else could have predicted he was capable of doing something like this."

"You'd be surprised at what seemingly normal stable people are capable of," Detective Johnson added. "You wouldn't believe what I've seen in my career. Sometimes people just snap and do unthinkable things. It happens every day." He looked at Rob. "I've had years of dealing with this sort of thing. Trust me, Mr. Waterson, I know for a fact, it was not your fault. No one could have known he'd do this."

~

WHEN THEY GOT BACK to the waiting room, Grant saw an older couple he assumed could be Annabelle's parents, standing in front of the reception desk, talking to the nurse. He walked up to them. "Excuse me, but are you Annabelle's parents?"

The woman's eyes were red and swollen. She lifted her eyes up at him and said, "Yes, we are. I'm Sue Douglas, her mother. Are you Grant Nash?"

He nodded yes, but before he could say anything, she burst into tears, reached out and pulled him into a hug. "She thinks so much of you," she said, sniffing back her tears. "She's always telling us about how talented you are, and how wonderful you treat her."

Her father held out his hand. "I'm Albert Douglas, Annabelle's father. It's nice to meet you."

Grant reached around her mother's hug and shook his hand. "I'm so sorry this happened. Have they told you how she's doing? They wouldn't tell me anything."

Her mother released her grip and backed away. "They said she's stable, but still in grave condition."

"Will they let you see her?"

"No," Albert said, "they won't let us see her yet. They said maybe in a few hours. But if she's stable," he said loud enough for the nurse to hear, "then I don't see why we can't at least peek in and look at her!"

"I don't, either." Grant said, motioning toward the waiting room. "You guys have had a long hard trip. Why don't we go find some place to sit down?"

They found a seat across from Rob and the two detectives. Grant made the introductions and sat down next to them.

"Mr. Nash," Albert said, "could you tell me what happened to my girl?"

"Please call me Grant," he said. Then he took a deep breath and looked Albert in the eyes. "Simply put, Annabelle was in the wrong place at the wrong time. And to be completely honest with you, it's all my fault this happened to her, because I put her there."

As gently as he could, for the next hour, he told them the entire story. The only part he left out was his true feelings for Annabelle and their growing relationship. He didn't tell them to protect himself; he did it to protect Annabelle. They were an old-fashioned couple from

Boone, North Carolina. There was no doubt in his mind that Annabelle had not confided her true feelings about him to her parents. As far as they knew, he was just her boss. They would never understand how a man of his age could fall for their very young and innocent daughter. Especially a man who had just spent the last hour telling them about another woman that he was in love with.

"Grant," Annabelle's mother said, taking his hand in hers, "we don't blame you for this. It's obvious to me and Albert that you cared a lot about our daughter. You tried your best to get her away from the danger. It was *her* decision not to drive straight home to us. She didn't listen to you and went to her apartment instead. What happened to her is not your fault. It's in God's hands now. You are a good man who has been wonderful to our daughter, and we thank you for everything you've done for her. So please stop blaming yourself for this."

"Thank you. Annabelle is a special person and everything I've done for her she has deserved. She is the talented one between us." He turned and looked at Albert. "She knows more about construction than I ever will. And she learned that from you. You both have done an amazing job raising her."

"She knows more than me, too," Albert said, wiping his eyes.

"Is there a chapel here in the hospital?" her mother asked.

"Yes," Grant said, "follow me. I'll take you there."

He led them down the hallway and left them alone in the chapel to pray. He needed a break from people and wanted to be alone, so he walked to the cafeteria, bought a cup of coffee and found a seat in the back corner.

Across the room, sitting alone was the Marine. He was staring out the window, talking to himself.

Grant watched him a few minutes, then got up and walked over to him. "Mind if I join you?"

The Marine jump to his feet, standing at attention. "No, sir. I could use the company."

Grant pulled out a chair and sat across from him. "I wanted to personally thank you for your service. How long have you been in the Marine Corps?"

"Two years," he said, sitting in his chair, "but I just re-enlisted."

"Seen any action?"

"Yes, sir. I just got back from my second tour of Afghanistan."

"I can't imagine what that must be like. I never served in the military, but I am a patriot and hold all of our soldiers serving around the world in the highest regard. When I see one like you, I feel proud."

"Thank you, sir. I am very proud to serve."

"You have someone here in the hospital, I assume," Grant said. "Is it serious?"

"I don't really know. I'm not part of her family, so they won't tell me how she is. But I'm pretty sure it must be very serious. She was rushed here in an ambulance."

"Is she your girlfriend?"

The Marine lifted his eyes and shrugged his shoulders. "She used to be, but we broke up. I haven't seen or talked to her in three years."

"But you've never gotten over her, right? That's why you're here, waiting alone. And she was who you were praying for in the chapel."

He clinched his jaw. "I love her, sir. And I always will."

"You didn't have to tell me that. It's pretty obvious," Grant said with a smile. "Why did you two break up?"

He looked away and stared out the window. "It was because of me. I chased her away because I was stupid. She was always very smart, a lot smarter than me, always at the top of the class, ever since first grade. But I was always at the bottom. I hated school, but she loved it. She tried to help me, but I didn't care about my grades. All I wanted to do was smoke dope, ride my skateboard and play video games."

Grant took a sip of his coffee and thought for a second. "How long were you two together?"

"From the first grade through her first year of college," he said softly.

"I know this is none of my business, but she must have seen something in you to stay with you all those years. You must not have been all *that* stupid."

"Oh yes, I was. When I look back now, I don't understand why she stayed with me that long. But she finally had enough and told me that she didn't love me anymore. She said I was just too immature for her."

"Ouch," Grant said, "that had to hurt."

"Yes sir. I wanted to die. I tried to get her back, but she stopped returning my calls and then she changed her number. That was three years ago. I haven't talked to her since then."

"So you joined the Marines to forget her, to see the world. To get a different woman in every port, right?"

He shook his head. "No, sir. I joined the Marines for her. To prove to her that I could grow up. That I could be someone. Someone she could be proud of."

"I don't get it, soldier. If you love her this much, why haven't you called her and let her know that you're not the same guy she broke up with three years ago?"

"I didn't have her number and I couldn't make myself call her parents to get it. They never liked me much."

"But you're here, at this hospital. How did you know where she was?"

"I called one of her high school friends. It took me a while, but she finally gave me her address. I got off the plane this morning and drove straight there, but when I got there, they were loading her into an ambulance. I followed it here."

"Grant!" He heard someone's voice yell behind him.

He turned around to see Brenda and Marshall running toward him. When he stood, they both grabbed him and hugged him tight.

"I'm so sorry," Brenda said tearfully. "Have you heard anything?"

When he told them no, Marshall frowned. "They'll tell me!" He growled. "Let's go, follow me. We're going to find out something right now!"

Grant grinned, "Attaboy, Doc. Let's go get 'em"

The Marine stood. "Good luck, sir."

"Thank you. Wait. Marshall, could you find out about my friend's girl when you're back there? They won't tell him anything, either."

Marshall nodded. "Damn straight I will. What's her name, soldier?"

"Annabelle Douglas," he said.

They all froze, shot each other looks and then looked back at the Marine. "No way…" Grant said. "Are you Drake?"

The Marine's eyes flew open wide. Jumping up to attention, he said, "Yes, sir. I'm Private First Class Drake Davis. How do you know my name?"

Grant grinned. "Annabelle told me all about you. I'm Grant Nash, her boss."

# 29

# ANASTASIA

When Marshall and Brenda walked into the waiting room, they were not smiling.

Grant jumped up out of his seat. "How are they?" he asked.

Marshall gave him a strained look. His eyes were squinted and his forehead was wrinkled. "Are Annabelle's parents here?"

Albert and Sue stood, holding on to each other. "We're Annabelle's parents," they said guardedly.

"I'm Doctor Marshall Taylor and this is Doctor Brenda Reed. We're friends of Grant's. I just saw your daughter and had a long talk with her attending physician. She's stable at the moment, but classified in grave condition."

"Yes," Albert said, "That's what they told us before. What exactly does that mean, Doctor? How serious is it?"

"She was shot twice, in her arm and in her chest. She lost almost 40% of her blood volume before the EMT team could begin a transfusion between her and Melissa."

Sue looked up at Grant. "*Your* Melissa?"

He nodded yes.

"So Grant's Melissa saved her life?"

"Yes," Marshall said, "but the transfusion with Melissa's blood may have caused other problems."

Grant took a step closer to him. "What kind of problems?"

Marshall looked him in the eyes. "Melissa's liver is failing. There are traces of Isoniazid in her blood and puncture wounds in her arms, obvious signs that Jerry had her hooked up to an IV. I guess stopping her anti-rejection medication wasn't working fast enough for him, so he went back to his old tricks to finish the job."

Sue and Albert looked at each other, confused. "We don't understand. Please, Doctor, tell us what's wrong with Annabelle."

Drake walked up and stood behind Sue and Albert, towering over them. "Is she going to die?" he asked with a quivering voice.

"I can't answer that," Marshall said. "we won't know for a while, but she's young and strong."

"I don't get it," Grant said. "How could Melissa's blood be causing more problems? It was the same type, right?"

"Yes, amazingly they both have AB negative, but because Melissa's liver hasn't been functioning correctly for some time..." he paused and thought for a second. "It's difficult to explain in laymen's terms, but I'll try.

"The liver does many things for the body. With the help of Vitamin K, it produces proteins that are important in helping the blood to clot. It's also one of the organs that breaks down old or damaged blood cells. The liver plays a central role in all metabolic processes. It converts the nutrients in our diets into substances that the body can use, stores these substances, and supplies cells with them when needed. It also takes up toxic elements and converts them into harmless substances and makes sure they are released from the body.

"The liver also plays an important role in the metabolism of proteins: liver cells change amino acids in foods so that they can be used to produce energy, or make carbohydrates or fats. A toxic substance called ammonia is a by-product of this process. The liver cells convert ammonia to a much less toxic substance called urea, which is released into the blood. Urea is then transported to the kidneys and passes out of the body in urine."

Grant held up his hands, frustrated. "English, please."

Marshall sighed. "I told you this is hard to explain. Okay, think about the liver as a filter that cleans the blood removing poisons. All of you have heard about ammonia. You've probably all used it to clean your kitchen or bathrooms. It's extremely poisonous. All of our bodies produce it, but the liver filters most of it out of our blood to non-toxic levels when it's working right. But if the liver is damaged and isn't filtering out the ammonia, it can cause severe damage to other vital organs in your body. And it doesn't take very long to do that damage."

"So you're saying that Melissa's blood they put into Annabelle had toxic levels of ammonia?" Sue asked.

"Unfortunately, yes," he said with a grim expression. "It was a double-edged sword. Without Melissa's blood, she would have certainly died, but because of it..."

"It may kill her as a result of it," Grant finished his sentence. "Is there any way to save her?"

"The second they discovered it, they began a complete exchange transfusion. That's what they're doing now, replacing the toxic blood with new clean donor plasma. It's a slow process that can take up to four hours to complete. Unfortunately, the longer the toxic blood remains in her body, the more damage is done."

Marshall ran his hands through his hair, took a deep breath and looked at Drake. "That's why I can't answer your question if she will survive. Until the exchange transfusion is complete, we won't know the extent of what damage, if any, has been done to her other vital organs." He looked down at Sue and Albert. "All we can do now is wait and pray."

Drake put his arms around Sue and Albert's shoulders. "If you need me, I'll be in the chapel," he said, walking away.

Without saying a word, Albert reached down and took Sue's hand. Together, walking hand in hand, they walked away, following Drake to the chapel.

When they were gone, Grant looked up at Marshall. His face was blank, expressionless. "How long does Melissa have?"

Marshall shrugged his shoulders. "Honestly, I don't know how she's alive now. I just checked her vitals and somehow, they're not all that bad, considering her liver is only functioning at about 20%. Miraculously, she is stable for now. But being realistic, I doubt if she'll survive more than a few more days"

"Can you take me back to see them?"

"They're not conscious, they won't know you're there."

"I don't care," Grant said. "I need to see them."

∼

THEY MADE Grant put on a sterile surgical gown, mask, cap and gloves before they led him back to Melissa's bed. In the months since Jerry had kidnapped her, she had lost a lot of weight. Looking down at her frail, skeletal body, he barely recognized her. Her thin arms and bony arms, that only a few months earlier were healthy, shiny, toned and golden brown, were now dull and greenish yellow. He could see dark blue veins through her almost translucent skin running down her arms and on her hands. Her eyes were closed, almost hidden behind the large mouthpiece of the respirator that was taped to her face.

Grant stood there silently beside her bed, taking it all in. He looked at the multiple video monitors that were mounted on the back wall behind her bed, watching the line on the screens jump, marking her heartbeat. He stared at the screens for a long time. Finally, he took her hand in his and squeezed. Instantly, his heart skipped and began to race, and he felt the familiar cold chill race through his body. The inexplicable shocking sensations were still there and felt just as strong then as they had the first time he had touched her, almost a year ago.

"Did you feel that?" he whispered. "I sure did." Tears were dripping off his chin, soaking the bed sheet under him.

He leaned over the bed and gently kissed her cheek. "Melissa, I don't know if you can hear me or not, but I hope you can. I wanted to tell you that Molly is okay. She's with Connie and Wilson, and they tell me that she is doing well. Brenda and Marshall are here, too. Brenda is going to go see Molly today and talk to her. And Brenda promised me that she would find the best child psychologist in Florida to help her get over all of this. She's gonna be fine, don't worry. I promise I'll take care of her and make sure she grows up to have a happy life."

His voice cracked, slurring his words through his tears. He leaned back and wiped his eyes, fighting back his emotions. "I hope you know that you saved Annabelle's life. I met her parents...you would like them. Annabelle is the image of her mother. I'm sure they would want me to thank you for them. I'll be sure to tell them I did.

"Poor Charley is hurt and I don't think he's going to make it. I'm going to go see him tonight...to say goodbye. I'm sure gonna miss arguing with him."

He squeezed her hand tightly. "Do you know how much I love you? Did I say that enough? I hope so, because I do. Before I met you, I was lost. After Rita, I never thought I could fall in love again. I didn't believe there was any room left in my heart to love someone else the way I loved her, but then I met you and I instantly knew that I was wrong. I've loved you since that first touch. I hope you know that."

The curtain was pulled back and Brenda walked up to the bed. "Annabelle just opened her eyes," she whispered. "Tell her that."

He leaned over and whispered in her ear. "Did you hear that? Annabelle is awake." He kissed her on the forehead and said, "I love you," and walked away.

When he pulled back the curtain surrounding Annabelle's bed, he was shocked to see her smiling up at him. "Well, hello there. How are you feeling?"

She opened her mouth and said something, but it was so soft he couldn't hear her it. He leaned down closer. "I couldn't hear you. What did you say?"

She took a breath, licked her lips and forced out the word. "Melissa?"

He forced a smile. "She's two doors down. She's stable."

"That's good," she whispered.

"I met your parents. You look just like your mother."

Her face lit up. "They're here? Can I see them?"

Grant smiled. "I think we can arrange that. There's someone else here, too. Someone I think you'd like to see."

"Who is that?"

Grant grinned down at her. "I think I'll let that be a surprise."

On his way out of the ICU, Grant passed Marshall, who was leading Annabelle's parents to her bed. Their faces were glowing.

Grant looked around the waiting room, but didn't see the Marine. He walked down the hallway to the chapel and then to the cafeteria, but he wasn't there.

He ran back to the waiting room to the reception desk, "Have you seen a soldier, a Marine?"

The nurse looked up from her desk and said, "Yes. He just left."

"Which way did he go?"

The nurse pointed at the double doors. "That way."

Grant ran out the doors and search the parking lot and saw a car backing out. He ran to it, yelling and waving his arms.

"Where are you going?" he said, when Drake rolled down his window.

"I don't know, sir," He said. "I guess back to the airport."

"Why in the hell would you do that? She's awake. Don't you want to see her?"

"I would love to, but I doubt she wants to see me. The doctor said that she's probably going to be all right." His face lit up with his smile. "That's what I was praying for. That's enough for me."

"Bullshit! Park this car and come with me. That's an order, soldier!"

When he saw the look on Annabelle's face when she first laid eyes on the new and improved Drake, it was all he needed to know.

Quietly, he backed out of the room, pulled the curtain closed and walked out of the hospital. He had noticed his old truck parked in the lot when he'd stopped Drake earlier. He didn't know how it had gotten there, but he was glad it was. He jumped in, cranked it up and slowly pulled out of the parking lot, on his way to see Charley.

~

WHEN GRANT PULLED into the veterinarian hospital, the parking lot was empty. He tried to open the front door, but it was locked. Glancing at his watch as he read the sign on the door, he realized they had closed thirty minutes earlier. He knocked on the door and waited, but no one answered. A few minutes later, he knocked again with no results.

Back in his truck, he took out his cell and called the number, but only got a recorded message. Angry with the thoughts of Charley laying inside that building injured and alone, he pulled out his wallet and searched for Detective Reynolds' card. When he found it, he punched in the number. She answered on the second ring.

"What the hell!" He screamed in her ear. "This place is closed! Charley is in there alone!"

"Calm down, Grant," she said. "He's not there."

"Where the hell is he?"

"Don't go anywhere, I'll be there in fifteen minutes and I'll take you to him."

Grant rolled down his windows, stretched his legs out under the brake and clutch pedals, leaned back against his seat and closed his eyes. It was the first time he'd relaxed in almost forty-eight hours. Thinking about Charley, he instantly drifted off, sound asleep.

$$\sim$$

HE FELT someone touch his face and say his name. He stirred in his seat and opened his eyes. He saw red hair flowing in the wind, backlit from the sun. He blinked his eyes and tried to focus. When his vision cleared, he saw beautiful blue eyes staring into his.

"Rita? Is that you?" His sleepy voice was husky and gravelly.

Still groggy from his unexpected deep sleep, he squinted his eyes, and saw white teeth glistening, framed by large pouty red lips of a beautiful smile. "No, I'm not Rita, I'm Anastasia. You know, Detective Reynolds. Are you all right?"

He sat up in his seat, trying to shake off his sleepiness and clear his head. "Was I asleep?"

She giggled. "More like a coma. I've been trying to wake you up for about ten minutes. I don't think I've ever seen anyone sleeping that hard before," She laughed again. "I was just about to fire off my gun."

He smiled up at her. "You have a great laugh. I like it. You should laugh more often."

She blushed. "Thanks," she said, smiling wider. "Are you ready to go see Charley?"

"Yes, I would like that. How is he? Have you heard anything?"

Her expression dropped. "I checked on him an hour ago. He's the same."

"If he was here, why did they move him?"

"He wasn't here. He's at the veterinarian's house. Do you want to ride with me in my car or follow me?"

"I don't want to leave my truck here. It's a classic and somebody might steal it, but there's no sense in taking two vehicles. Why don't you ride with me? I'll bring you back here later."

He watched her walk to her car, lock it, walk back to his truck and jump in. She wasn't wearing her normal clothes. Every time he'd seen her before, she was wearing a dark pantsuit, heavy black shoes and a gun. She had also always worn her hair pulled back into a tight bun.

"Were you going out on a date or something?" he asked, trying not to stare at her cleavage, tanned legs and sexy shoes.

"Oh no. After I left you at the hospital, I stopped at the precinct a few minutes to check my messages and then drove home. I had just gotten there and changed my clothes when you called."

"Really?" he said with a grin.

"Yes, really. Why do you ask?"

"Never mind; it's none of my business."

"What are you talking about? What's none of your business?"

"Well, I just have to ask. Is this what you normally wear around the house?"

She laughed out loud. "No it isn't. I'm usually in sweats and a t-shirt, but before you called, I was thinking I might go check on Charley."

"Ohhhh, I get it now," he turned, looked at her and wiggled his eye brows, "You're a little sweet on the vet."

She blushed and looked away. "Am I really that obvious?"

"Hey, I'm sorry, I didn't mean to hurt your feelings. It's just that I've never seen you dressed in anything but cop dark drab. You look great. I'm serious, you look amazing."

She turned back around and smiled. "Thank you, Grant. That's really sweet of you to say. I don't get to hear that much. At the precinct, I'm just one of the boys."

"Yeah, sure," he mocked. "I doubt that. Trust me, they all know different. So, what's up with the vet? Does he know how you feel about him?"

She frowned. "No, it's always been strictly business between us. In my work, it's not unusual for me to run across orphaned pets at a crime scene. I just can't leave them there or let them take them to the pound to be destroyed, so when I find them, I take them to Jake. He checks them out and finds them a new home with one of his customers."

"How long have you known him?"

She sighed. "A few years."

"And he's never asked you out?"

"No. I'm not even sure he realizes I am a woman. To him, I'm just Detective Reynolds."

"Well, Detective Reynolds...if you dress like this around him and he doesn't notice that you're a woman, he's either a friggin' dick...or he's batting for the other team."

Listening to her infectious laughter as he drove had lifted his spirits and given him strength to face what he had to do next.

~

Dr. Jake Atkins, the veterinarian, greeted them at the door and took them back to see Charley. He was lying on a mattress in the corner of a small room. He was hooked up to an IV and had a long clear tube coming out of his mouth. It was secured to his snout by white tape. His chest was moving up and down from his rapid breathing. When they walked in, Charley's tail moved slightly, but he didn't open his eyes.

Grant sat down next to him and petted his head. "Hey, buddy, how are you doing?"

The tip of his tail moved again, but his eyes remained closed and his chest continued to pump up and down from his breathing. Grant looked back at Jake. "Is he having trouble getting air?"

"Not really. It's not unusual for dogs to breathe rapidly when they are injured. It's part of their healing process."

Grant turned back around and petted him. "Is he sedated?"

"No, he's not sedated, but he's been non-responsive like that since I removed the bullets."

"Bullets? He was shot more than once?"

He nodded. "He was shot three times, but they didn't hit anything vital."

"Then why is he like this?"

"I'm not exactly sure. I've done two MRI's on him, double-checking to see if I've missed something, but there was nothing there. The only thing he seems to be able to move is his tail. It's possible that he is paralyzed, but if that was the case, the MRI should have shown me the injury that caused it. My other thought is that he's not fully conscious. He could be in what is called a 'minimally conscious state', partially awake and partially asleep. That would explain the tail wag when someone is near him. Unfortunately, it's very difficult to diag-nose. There's just no way to know for sure."

Jake tightened his lips and lowered his brow. "There is one other possibility and it's the worst case scenario. Charley had lost a lot of blood before I got it stopped," He paused and took a deep breath. "It's possible that the severe blood loss has caused some brain damage. The tail movement could be involuntary."

Grant looked down at Charley and petted him gently. "Is he in pain?"

"No, I don't believe he is, or I would suggest that we put him down. But I'd like to wait a few more days before we talk about doing something like that. Detective Reynolds tells me that he's a unique dog, extremely intelligent. I wanted to give him special treatment. That's why I have him here with me on the feeding tube. Here, I can keep a close watch on him. The only good news I can tell you is that his vitals are getting stronger every day."

"Thank you, Doctor. And you are right, he is a very special dog. Would it be okay if I stay here with him for a little while longer?"

"Of course."

They turned and walked out of the room, closing the door behind them, giving him some private alone time to spend with Charley. He laid down on the floor, pulled him into his arms and gently stroked his head with his fingers, listening to his rapid breathing.

"Charley," he whispered in his ear, "can you hear me?" His breathing slowed and Grant felt his tail move against his leg.

Grant lifted his head and stared down at Charley's body. "Could you do that again, so I know for sure you are hearing me?"

His tail did not move. "Come on, Charley, you can do it. Wag your tail, just a little."

He watched his tail closely, but it didn't move. Grant's hands were trembling, tears were rolling down his cheeks and his heart was racing. "Please, God, help him, heal him, give him strength." He buried his wet face in Charley's soft coat, hugging him tightly. "You can't die, Charley. I need you. Please don't die, buddy. Fight this, open your eyes and let me know you're still there."

Charley's breathing slowed again. Against his leg, he felt his tail move and he saw his eyelids twitch. Grant sat up and wiped his face with his sleeve. "Good boy," he whispered, "Try that again. Open your eyes for me."

Charley's tail moved and his eyelids twitched. "Doc!" he yelled. "Come look at this!"

When Jake and Anastasia came back into the room, Grant tried to get him to move his tail and eyelids, but it didn't work. He remained completely still.

"I swear, his breathing slowed down, his eyelids twitched and his tail moved when I was talking to him. He did it twice," he explained. "Do you think he knows I'm here?"

Jake looked down at him and shrugged. "Maybe, but I honestly don't know. It's possible, but it's too sporadic to know for sure. It's just as likely that it's involuntary muscle movement. I hate to say that and I know that's not what you want to hear, but I'm just trying to be realistic. Unfortunately, there's no way to know for sure."

Grant dropped his head and looked down at Charley. "He heard me. I know he did. Would it be okay for me to stay here with him tonight? I want to be with him. I'll sleep here, on the floor. I just can't bear going home to my house without him being there."

"No problem," Jake said. "I'll get you a pillow and a blanket."

"Grant, I'm sorry," Anastasia said, "but I need to go home. I have to work tomorrow. Would you mind taking me back to my car and then coming back here?"

"I can take you," Jake said, handing Grant a pillow and a blanket.

She looked up at him and smiled. "Are you sure you don't mind? I'm parked at your clinic."

"Of course I'm sure, Detective Reynolds," he said. "It's not a problem at all. Let me go get my keys."

When he walked out of the room, Grant raised his eyebrows and grinned at her.

She grinned back. "It's just a ride to my car."

Jake walked back in the room, jingling his keys. "Are you ready to go?"

Grant pulled himself off the floor and held out his hand, "Thank you, Doctor, I really appreciate this."

Jake smiled and shook his hand. "You're welcome. I just wish I could tell you more."

When they turned to leave, Grant said, "And by the way, Doc, her name isn't Detective Reynolds, it's Anastasia. And she hasn't had dinner. I bet she's hungry."

Jake grinned and looked at her. "Are you hungry?"

"A little," she said shyly, blushing.

"Me too," he said, glancing at his watch. "If we hurry, we can make it to this great place on the beach that makes amazing grilled shrimp."

Following behind him, Anastasia glanced back at Grant and gave him a frown. He returned her frown with a wink and a wide smile. "You're welcome, Detective," he said, wiggling his eyebrows.

# 30

# LIVING DONOR

The next morning, after doing some extensive tests with great results, they moved Annabelle from the ICU to a private room. Marshall and the rest of her doctors were shocked and astounded by her remarkably quick recovery. They attributed it to her youth and the fact that she was in such great physical condition when she was shot.

When Grant walked into her room, she was sitting up in her bed, watching television. "I think this must be the wrong room," he said, grinning. "I'm looking for Annabelle Douglas' room. Is she around here somewhere?"

Her face lit up. "Are those for me?" she said reaching for the flowers. "They're beautiful."

Grant glanced around the room, but it was empty. "Where are Drake and your parents?"

"My parents are at their hotel. I just called and told them that I'm out of ICU. They're on their way." She looked down and nervously fiddled with the flowers. "I don't know where Drake is. I haven't seen him today."

"Don't worry, he'll show up."

Annabelle shot him a stern look. "I'm not worried. I don't care if he shows up or not."

Grant sat on the edge of her bed and smiled. "I think you do." He took her hand and squeezed it. "Annabelle it's okay. I like him. He's impressive and certainly not the same guy you described. He's changed."

"I guess he has," she said, looking away. "He told me that he joined the Marines because of me...to help him grow up."

"Yeah, he told me the same thing. So, what did you tell him?"

"It doesn't matter what I told him. I really don't want to talk about that right now. How is Melissa?"

He slid off the bed, sat down in a chair and rubbed his face with his hands. "She's alive, but just barely. She's still in a medically induced coma, but they told me she's stable for now."

"Isn't there anything they can do?"

He dropped his head. "Not really, other than another transplant. They're searching for a donor now, but Marshall isn't hopeful. The odds of finding someone with her blood type is astronomical."

Suddenly, the door swung open, and Sue and Albert ran in the room, rushing up to her bed. They were both crying and laughing at the same time.

"Oh, my baby girl!" her mother shouted tearfully, leaning over her bed and hugging her. "Look at you! You look so much better!"

Albert leaned over from the other side and joined the group hug. He didn't say a word, he didn't have to...his tears said it all.

"I'm gonna be all right," Annabelle said, sniffing and wiping her eyes. "Please stop crying. I'm going to be fine."

There was a knock on her door and the attendant brought in her breakfast. She placed it on the small table and rolled it in front of her. "Bon appétit," the attendant said as she walked out.

For the next few minutes, they all sat quietly watching her eat. "Will you guys stop staring at me? You're making me nervous."

"I'm sorry, but I can't help it," her mother said. "I almost lost you and I can watch you if I want to. I'm just so happy you're alive."

Grant stood up and waved at Annabelle. "I think I'll go check on Melissa. I'll be back later."

Walking toward the ICU, Grant passed Drake in the hall. "Good morning," he chirped with a smile. "Annabelle's doing great today. She's waiting to see you."

Drake looked down and shuffled his feet. "Mr. Nash, could I ask you a question?"

He turned to face him. "Sure. What's on your mind?"

"Annabelle told me that she wasn't sure how she felt about me anymore. She said that it may be too late, because she had met someone else. Do you know who that is? Would this guy be better for her than me?"

Grant wasn't sure what to say and stood there staring at him. If he told him the truth, it would shatter him and he would probably leave and never return. It would be an honor thing for the Marine. Although he had only known him a couple of days, he knew that it would be impossible for Drake to come between him and Annabelle. Forty-eight hours earlier, that would have been exactly what he wanted, but now he wasn't sure about anything. The only thing he knew for absolute certainty was that Annabelle deserved to be happy.

He nodded. "Yes, I know who she's talking about. It's an older man that she's become infatuated with. Nothing has happened between them, so don't worry."

Grant leaned against the wall and put his hands in his pockets. "Is this guy better for Annabelle than you? Well, I guess that depends on if you've really changed and what your intentions are for you two in the future. You told me that you just re-enlisted. Are you planning on making the military your career?"

"No, sir. If things work out between me and Annabelle, I plan on finding a job as soon as I finish this tour, and then go to college at night until I get my degree." He lifted his head and looked Grant in the eyes. "Mr. Nash, I will do whatever it takes to make her happy and give her a good life."

"I have no doubt that you will," he said with a smile. "Look, keep this between me and you, don't ever tell Annabelle I said this. Don't worry about this other guy and don't let anything stop you. And one more thing, soldier...her favorite flowers are yellow Calla Lilies. They don't sell them in the flower shop here in the hospital, but there's a florist a few blocks away. Go get her some. She'll love them!"

~

GRANT ONLY SPENT a few minutes with Melissa. She was still unconscious and he couldn't stand looking at her like that, so he kissed her and walked to the cafeteria. He bought a banana nut muffin, a cup of coffee and found a table in the back corner of the room. He had just finished off his muffin when Brenda and Marshall walked in and sat at his table.

"I got to spend some time with Molly yesterday," Brenda said. "She's very confused at why her daddy would have been so mean to her, but I think time with a good child psychologist will get her through this. She's very smart and sweet."

Grant smiled. "Thank you for doing that. I just can't imagine what she's had to endure and what she's seen. I just hope that she's young enough that she may forget everything she saw."

"No, that's not what we want. The worst thing she could do would be to block the memories away. Repressed memories can be very dangerous. She needs to keep the memories on the surface and, with professional help, learn how to deal with them. As she gets older, she'll be able to understand what actually happened and realize that it was not her fault. She may not like it, but one day she'll understand that some people do terrible things. And that's what her father did. When she understands that, I believe she'll be okay."

"I hope so," he said softly. "But what will it do to her if her mother dies, too?"

She looked over at Marshall. "I think you need to tell him."

"Tell me what?"

Marshall leaned forward and looked at him, "I didn't want to tell you until we knew for sure, but we may have found a donor."

"Really?" he gasped. "That's great! Who is it?"

"Don't get your hopes up yet. It may not happen. Yesterday a sixteen-year-old woman in Chicago had a brain hemorrhage. She's AB negative and on life support now. She's showing no brain activity at all. The doctors have told her parents that she is brain dead and trying to convince them to donate her organs, but they are resisting."

"Do you remember how you felt when I said those words to you about Rita? Just imagine if it was Audrey I was talking about instead of Rita? We both knew what Rita would have wanted, but a child?"

Grant looked down. "Knowing what she would have wanted didn't make it any easier. She was there, breathing. I could touch her, kiss her...how could she be dead? I know exactly what they're going through."

"That's why I didn't want to tell you. They may not agree," Marshall said with a sigh. "And if they don't agree soon..."

Grant looked up. "How much time does she have?"

"Honestly...none. I don't know why she's alive now," he said grimly, "but somehow she is."

～

IN AN ALMOST ROBOTIC, numb state, Grant left the hospital and drove to his house. He didn't know exactly why he was going there, but he knew he had to get away from that hospital.

When he pulled into his driveway, he didn't open the door and get out. Instead, he sat there quietly, admiring his beautiful house. It truly was spectacular. The memory of the first day he had seen it flashed through his mind. The day Charley had insisted on him driving there. The memories of Charley running up the stairs, peeking in the windows and barking made him smile.

"I still don't get it, Charley," he said out loud, "what was it about this place? Why here? How did you know?" He opened his door and stepped out. "Why did you bring me here, Charley?"

He headed to the wooden walkway over the dunes. At the bottom of the steps, he took off his shoes and walked to the shallow water rolling up on the beach. *What now?* he asked himself as he strolled along the shore. The water was cold on his feet, but it was stimulating and shocked his numbed senses, clearing his head.

As he slowly walked along the shore, he began to recount the last years of his life. He thought about Rita and how she looked when he first saw her holding Audrey in her arms just moments after the delivery. She was absolutely radiant. Her blue eyes were glowing, reflecting the overhead lights, glistening from her tears of joy. It was a sight he never wanted to forget.

With that memory, the floodgates opened and his mind filled with more and more wonderful memories of Rita and Audrey. It was the first time he had allowed himself to actually look back. He had repressed those memories, but now, for whatever reason, he had let them out. Perhaps it was because Brenda had mentioned how dangerous repressed memories could be earlier, he thought. He really didn't know why, but whatever the reason, those memories didn't make him sad like he had feared; they made him feel happy and blessed to have experienced them.

His thoughts turned back to Charley, Melissa, Molly and Annabelle. As he continued to stroll along, he tried to recall every moment he'd spent with them as well. Again, it made him feel happy and blessed.

He walked back to his house and took a hot shower, changed clothes and headed back to the hospital. On the drive back, he felt revived, stronger somehow. He thought he had finally figured out what Rita was talking about. What she meant when she said that he had "much more to do." He had no idea what the future may hold for him, but whatever it was, he would somehow survive and get through it. He had no choice. It was all about Molly now. He was all she had.

~

HE HAD TIMED IT RIGHT, Annabelle had just finished her lunch when he walked into her room. Her parents were both dozing in their chairs and Drake, always the Marine, was standing at attention next to her bed.

"Whoa, check out the Calla Lilies," he said, pointing at the yellow flowers.

"Aren't they beautiful!" she beamed, pulling herself up in the bed. "Drake brought them. I love Calla Lilies; they're my favorite flowers."

"Oh, really?" he said, grinning at Drake. "How'd you know she liked Calla Lilies?"

He grinned. "I remember everything about her."

He laughed. "Good answer, soldier!"

Grant found a chair from an empty room next door and ignoring the dirty looks from the nurses, he drug it into Annabelle's room and sat down. For the next hour, he sat quietly, listening to all of them swapping stories about growing up in Boone.

"You wouldn't know it now by looking at him, but Drake was sort of a runt and skinny as a rail," Her father said, laughing. "And you never saw him without that damn skateboard, flying down the road, jumping off of tables and rails all over town."

Yeah," her mother added, "he was a living Dennis the Menace!"

"Do you still have it?" Grant asked. "It's an Olympic sport now."

"No, my mother sold it at a garage sale when I joined the Marines."

"Maybe you should buy a new one," Grant said, "You never know. You might be in the next Olympics."

After several more old, embarrassing stories, the conversation lulled and everyone got quiet.

The door swung open and Marshall and Brenda walked in. Their faces were dark and gloomy.

"We lost the donor," he said.

"The parents wouldn't agree to the organ harvest?" Grant asked.

"No, they wouldn't," he said, shaking his head. "However they did agree to unplug her from the life support equipment. I just got off the phone with the doctor in Chicago. She died ten minutes ago."

"What about another donor?" Annabelle asked.

Marshall looked at her with sad eyes. "I think we're out of time."

Annabelle's mother began to cry. "That poor girl, what's going to happen to her daughter? She'll be an orphan."

Grant stood up and looked at her. "If they'll let me, I'm going to adopt her. But even if they won't, I'm going to take care of her for the rest of her life."

Everyone stopped talking and the room grew silent and sad. Grant gave his chair to Brenda and sat on the edge of Annabelle's bed.

Grant looked at Marshall. "So what do we do now?"

"Pray and wait, I guess," Marshall said softly.

"Can I ask you a medical question?" Annabelle asked.

Marshall lifted his head and looked at her. "Sure."

"Does the donor have to die?"

Marshall glanced at Grant. "Well, actually there is something called 'living-donor transplants.'"

"How does it work?" she asked, pulling herself up further in her bed.

"A portion, about two thirds, of the living, healthy donor's liver is removed and given to the recipient patient. The liver is one of the few organs in the human body that will regenerate. The portion that is removed from the healthy donor will grow back to the original size in a few months and the same will happen to the recipient."

"So are you saying I could give Melissa part of my liver?" Annabelle said. "I'm the same blood type, right? What are we waiting for?"

Marshall held up his hands. "Hold on! I said 'healthy living donor.' You almost died three days ago. You are in no condition to be donating anything. Your body is not strong enough to handle the stress. Even if the donor is in perfect physical condition, which you are not, there is serious risk with this kind of surgery. I'm sorry, Annabelle, but you could die."

She looked around the room at her parents. "Melissa saved my life. If she hadn't given me her blood in that ambulance, I would have bled to death."

They both looked back at her. "We know," her father said, "and we understand why you want to help her, but you're not strong enough to do it."

"Neither was she. She was barely alive, but she insisted they take her blood to save me." She threw back her sheet and swung her legs over the side of the bed. Then she slid off the bed and stood. "I know I may not be in perfect condition, but I can't just let her die. I'm standing here because of her. She saved my life and now I have a chance to save hers."

On unsteady legs, she slowly walked up to Grant. "Don't you understand? I have to do this."

Grant took her hand and led her back to her bed. "I understand why you think you have to do this, but I also know that Melissa wouldn't want you to do it. It's just too much of a risk."

She turned and looked at Drake. "What would *you* do?"

He thought for a long time before he answered. "Annabelle, I don't want you to do this. I just got you back in my life and...well, I don't know where this might lead, but I've been dreaming about having another chance with you for years. And when I thought you might die...I wanted to die, too. I was devastated, so absolutely not, I don't want you to do it."

He walked to her bed and took her hand in his. "But that wasn't your question, was it? You asked what 'I' would do and I have to be honest. If someone saved my life and I had the chance to save theirs...I would do it. No matter what the risk."

Annabelle smiled at him. Then she turned her head and looked at Marshall. "Will you do the surgeries?"

"I wish you would listen to me. If you do this, you could die," Marshall argued. "Your body is still trying to heal from the gunshot wounds. You are too weak to survive this kind of surgery."

"I realize that," she said softly, "but I have no choice. I have to at least try."

He sighed deeply. "Transplants are not my specialty, so if you do this, no, I won't be the one doing the surgeries."

"But you'll be there, right? Just in case something goes wrong?" she asked.

Yes," he said, "I can be there as an observer if you want me to...but if something goes wrong...there won't be much I can do."

# 31

# A PROMISE TO MELISSA

The next morning, Grant sat silent and stoic between Annabelle's parents, holding their hands as they watched the medical team wheel her out of the room on her way to surgery. They had already said their goodbyes, crying and telling her how much they loved her, but when they wheeled her out, her mother burst out crying again, but her father held it back.

"If it's okay with you," Drake said, "I would like to wait this out in the chapel." He held out his hand. "Mrs. Douglas, would you like to join me?"

With his arm around her shoulders, Drake and Sue slowly walked down the hall to the chapel, while Grant and her father followed close behind.

When they got there and walked in, they didn't sit in a group. Sue and Albert sat holding hands a few rows back from the pulpit on the right side, Drake sat alone on the front row on the left, and Grant sat in the last row by the door. No one talked. They just sat there, silently praying to themselves.

Grant kept checking his watch, but time seemed to have stopped. After a few hours, he couldn't take it any longer, so he left them there and walked to the surgery waiting room. When someone would walk out of the double doors, he would jump up and ask if they knew how the transplant was going, but none of them seemed to know anything.

~

THE TRANSPLANT SURGERY was going well. Although Melissa was barely alive by the time they got her to the table, she remained stable throughout the long surgery. Annabelle's body was weak, but she sustained the trauma as well.

The five-hour simultaneous surgeries took place in two different surgical theaters and everything went as planned.

Standing as close as possible without being in the way of the surgical team, Marshall first observed the removal of Melissa's damaged, shriveled liver. Then he walked to the other theater and watched the precision of the surgeon as he dissected Annabel's healthy liver. He removed two thirds of it and carefully laid it on a tray, and then went back and skillfully began closing her wound. To close the final layer of skin, Marshall had called in the best plastic surgeon he knew to do it. It took him longer, which added a slight more risk to the operation, but because of his expertise, in a few years Annabelle and Melissa's scars would be virtually invisible. When it was over, he scanned the machines displaying her vitals before he walked back to the other theater to watch the final process of attaching the loaf of Annabelle's liver into Melissa's body.

When the plastic surgeon had finished closing up Melissa's wound, everyone stood silently, holding their breath, watching the video monitors.

~

MARSHALL HAD TOLD him if it went well it shouldn't take more than four hours. So as hour four approached, Grant grew more and more anxious and fearful. He wanted to leave, maybe go for a run to calm his nerves, but he was afraid he wouldn't be there when it was over, so he just paced the room instead. After five hours, forty-five minutes, he knew something had to be wrong, so he walked back to the small chapel to be there with Annabelle's parents when the bad news eventually came.

~

MARSHALL WAS STANDING next to Melissa, holding her hand, when he heard the alarm go off in the other theater. When he rushed into the room, he saw the flat line scrolling across the screen.

"Clear!" the surgeon yelled, pressing the two paddles against Annabelle's chest. When the current hit her, her entire body lurched upward. Marshall stared at the screen, but there was no blip.

"Clear!" the surgeon yelled, trying once more. Again, he saw Annabelle's body jerk upward, but the flat line continued rolling across the screen. On their third try without success, Marshall's heart sunk in his chest and he began to pray. When he heard the second alarm go off, he lifted his head and began searching the monitors to see what it was. When he heard the third one, he realized that it was coming from the other room.

He rushed back to Melissa's theater in time to see the surgeon make the incision on her chest. He watched them cut her breast bone and spread her ribs wide, allowing the surgeon room to reach in and start massaging her heart with his hands.

His first instinct was to push everyone out of the way and do it himself, but he fought it back. Instead, he just stood there and watched in horror.

"Clear!" He heard the surgeon yell again from Annabelle's side. There was nothing he could do for Melissa, so he walked back to Annabelle and stared up at the flat line that was still rolling across the screen.

"Two forty five, Doctor!" He heard a nurse yell. The surgeon looked up, made eye contact with him and shook his head.

"Again!" Marshall yelled. "Do it again!" On the sixth attempt with no pulse, he knew it was over and his worst fears had come true...they had lost them both.

He checked his watch, and although both teams were still frantically trying to revive them, he knew too much time had passed. He untied his mask, pulled it off his face and slowly walked out of the double doors. He looked around the waiting room, but no one was there. On the elevator he punched the ground floor button and rode it down to the lobby. When he reached the door of the chapel, he stopped and took several deep breaths to clear his head. "How do I tell them this?" he whispered.

When he opened the doors and saw them looking at him, he froze and his mind went blank. He tried to say something, but he couldn't make a sound. Overcome with emotions, he walked to the front, fell on his knees and began to pray.

A few minutes later, the chapel doors opened and a nurse rushed in and ran up to him. Whispering in his ear, she said, "We have a pulse."

He jumped up and ran back to the elevator. When he got there, he couldn't believe his eyes. Miraculously, they had both been revived and were still alive.

When he walked out of surgery through the double doors this time, they were all there in the small waiting room. No one spoke, but they all stared up at him with fear in their eyes.

He pulled the blue surgical hat off his head and said, "It's been touch and go. They've both had serious complications and I can't really explain why, but they are alive."

"Thank God," Sue cried, hugging Albert.

Marshall looked into Grant's worried eyes and put his hand on his shoulder. "It was pretty rough and we're not out of the woods yet. The next forty-eight hours will be critical."

～

OVER THE NEXT TWO DAYS, Marshall kept a close watch on them. Annabelle, for the second time in her life, had made an amazing recovery. She seemed to grow stronger with each passing hour and was soon strong enough to receive visitors. Unfortunately, Melissa's recovery had not gone as well. Although her new liver was functioning properly, her vital signs were not improving.

Dressed in green sterile hospital scrubs, including the hat, mask and latex gloves, Grant walked up to her bed and took her hand in his. The greenish yellow tint of her skin was still there, but had faded slightly. She had lost even more weight and looked like a small child lying there.

"She *is* showing active brain waves," Marshall said softly, "but I have to be honest…it's not good. Her oxygen levels are falling."

Grant looked down and gently touched her cheek with his gloved hand. "I wish I could see her face. Does she still need the respirator?"

"Yes, she's not breathing completely on her own. For now, it's keeping her alive."

For almost an hour, Grant stood there, holding her hand, looking at her. Then he bent down, kissed her forehead and walked to the lobby. Rob was sitting in the waiting room.

"Hey Rob, thanks for coming," Grant said.

Rob shook his hand. "How's Melissa doing?"

"Not so good," he said. "She flatlined after the surgery, I guess her heart couldn't handle the stress of the transplant. The surgeon had to crack her chest and manually massage her heart to revive her. We almost lost her."

"Could I see her?" he asked. "I really need to see her."

"Sure. I'll take you back."

They walked to the elevator and Grant punched the button. "Grant, after I see her, would it be possible to meet with you and her doctor for a few moments?" Rob asked. "We need to talk about something. It's important."

Rob spent thirty minutes with Melissa, then walked to the coffee shop to meet Marshall and Grant.

"So, what did you want to talk about?" Marshall asked him, sipping his coffee. "Grant said it was important."

"It is," he said, reaching into his coat pocket. He pulled out some papers and laid them on the table. "I really don't want to do this, but I have no choice. I promised Melissa."

Grant frowned and tilted his head. "Promised her what?"

He sighed and flattened the papers on the table with his hand. "Melissa was having a reoccurring dream. I know this will sound a bit strange to you, but I believe she somehow knew this was going to happen." He looked at Grant. "Remember when I told you she had come to me a few weeks before Jerry kidnapped her and changed her will?"

"Yes, I remember," he said.

Rob leaned forward in his chair and took a deep breath. "When she was there, she asked me to do one more thing for her. She had me draft this DNR."

He handed the papers to Marshall. He read them slowly, then handed them over to Grant.

"I only have one question," he frowned and looked at Marshall. "Is she being kept alive by machines?"

Marshall dropped his head and said. "I can't answer that. We won't know until we disconnect the respirator. When that happens, she will either continue breathing on her own or…" He didn't finish his sentence.

Rob sighed, leaned back and ran his hand through his hair. "That's what I thought and I hate this, but she was very specific. She did not want to be kept alive by a machine. I promised her, if that ever happened, I would force the hospital to take her off life support."

~

DRAKE HELPED Annabelle out of the wheelchair and held her hand while she said goodbye to Melissa. Next was Annabelle's parents, who thanked her for saving their daughter's life. Then Connie and Wilson took turns kissing her gently on her cheeks and telling her how much they loved her. Rob could barely stand and couldn't seem to stop telling her over and over how sorry he was, but he was just doing what she had asked him to do. He was a complete wreck.

After everyone had left the room, Brenda and Grant brought Molly in and stood next to her, trying not to cry as they listened and watched.

Grant had been honest with her and told her everything, explained to her how her mother looked and let her know that if she didn't want to see her that way, everyone would understand, but Molly wanted to tell her goodbye.

They had no idea how she would react, but she was incredibly brave when she walked up, stood next to her mother's bed and took her hand, trying her best not to cry. "I love you, Mommy," she said. "I wish you didn't have to die, but Mr. Grant said you were going to go to heaven and would be real happy there, so I guess it's okay, but I'm sure gonna miss you." Molly looked back at Grant. "Can she hear me?"

He nodded. "I don't know honey, but I think so."

She held out her hands. "Would you lift me up?"

Grant picked her up and held her close to her mother's face. She kissed her on the cheek. "Goodbye, mommy," she whispered, finally breaking down and crying. "I promise that I will never, ever forget you."

It was the saddest thing Grant had ever witnessed, and his heart broke hearing Molly cry so hard, but he knew that some day when she was older, she would be glad she had been able to say those final words to her mother.

After everyone left and it was just Grant in the room, Marshall walked in, put his arm around his shoulders and said, "I've got it from here, old friend."

"No." Grant said, "I want to be here when she crosses over. Not being there with Rita has been one of the biggest regrets in my life. So no, I'm staying."

Grant took her hand in his and squeezed it. "We're ready," he whispered.

"You don't need the gloves," Marshall said, motioning toward his hands. "It's okay to touch her."

Grant slipped off the latex gloves and took her right hand in both of his. He was hoping that when their skin touched he would feel the shock run through his body, but there was none. He looked over at Marshall with sad eyes. "I guess she was right all along."

Marshall lowered his brow. "Right about what?"

"The shocks. They're gone. She always believed they came from Rita, not her."

The nurse removed the tube from her mouth, cleaned her face and backed away. Grant leaned down and gently kissed her on the lips. "I don't care where they came from...I've loved you since that first touch." He kissed her one last time and leaned back. Squeezing her hand, with tears rolling off his chin, he stood there silently...waiting.

# 32

# SIR CHARLES III

To prepare me, Marshal had explained that when someone is taken off life support, usually because they are brain dead or terminally ill, one of two things will happen. They will die, or their bodies will stabilize and they will live. In the best-case scenario, if their bodies stabilize, the patient eventually wakes up, gets better and resumes their life. In the worst case, they don't wake up and remain in a coma. This coma can be the results of many things and last for weeks, months and in some cases…years.

When they removed the endotracheal tube from Melissa's throat and turned off the respirator, she did not die as everyone had expected. Instead, she began breathing slowly on her own and her oxygen level began to rise. Her heart rate, although slow at first, increased steadily and within twenty-four hours, all of her vitals were at life sustaining positions. But unfortunately, she did not wake up.

After fourteen days without her showing any signs of regaining consciousness, she was moved from ICU to the rehabilitation floor.

~

WITHOUT TELLING ME, Jake decided to take Charley off the feeding tube and try an experiment. After several hours of no food, Jake laid on the floor next to him, forced his mouth open and placed a spoonful of baby food on his tongue. He instantly swallowed the food. After two more days of baby food, Jake tried canned dog food and he swallowed that as well. Although Charley couldn't move his body, his tongue and digestive track apparently was still working.

Every time Jake laid on the floor next to him with his food, Charley's tail wagged and his eyelids would flicker, so Jake no longer believed that his movements were involuntary. He was convinced Charley was still in there, conscious, but paralyzed for some reason he hadn't discovered yet.

He took him to a Jacksonville hospital and convinced one of his doctor friends there to do another MRI on Charley using their *human* MRI machine. It was a much more sophisticated device than the one he had used to do the other two. Finally, this machine revealed the problem. One of the bullets had glanced off Charley's spine and had moved two of his vertebrae just enough to press against his spinal cord, causing the paralysis. Unfortunately, the MRI was inconclusive on the amount of damage done to the spinal cord and couldn't make out if it was completely severed or not. All it showed for sure was that the disks were severely out of place.

With a grim look on his face, Jake stared in my eyes and told me the news. "Grant, I think it's time to put him down. To repair this damage, it would cost thousands and thousands of dollars, with no guarantees Charley would even live through the surgery...or improve at all if he survived."

I found a chair, sat down and rubbed my temples. After a few moments of pressing against the throbbing veins, I looked up at him. "So...you're saying this can be repaired?"

He nodded. "Yes, but it would be tricky. But Grant, it's also possible that when they get in there, they could discover that his cord is severed."

"But what if it isn't?" I said.

He shrugged. "The best case is by removing the pressure against the spinal cord, he could recover and maybe even walk. But I'm confident he'll never be able to run again."

I shook my head. "This is the third time in my life I've been asked to kill someone I love with all my heart. Why me, Jake? Why does this keep happening to me?"

He shook his head and shrugged his shoulders. "Grant, I wish I knew what to say to help you. Life has dealt you some terrible cards."

"No shit!" I snorted "And I am sick of playing this game!" I could feel the anger building up inside of me. I wanted to smash something, but I didn't. I just rubbed my temples again, trying to stop the pain in my aching head. "Jake, I don't care if it cost a million dollars," I whispered, "I can't put him down if there's even the slightest chance."

I stood up and looked at him. "And who cares if he can run? Go do it, Jake. Go find the best of the best to do this surgery. I don't give a shit about the money. Go do it, Jake. Go fix Charley."

~

AFTER THIRTY MORE DAYS WITH no change in Melissa's condition, I was given one more impossible task. Because Melissa had given me medical power of attorney in her new will, I was faced with...what now?

I had been avoiding Rob, but he finally cornered me and forced me to make some decisions about Melissa. The first decision was to answer his legal question. In her signed DNR, she had been very specific about not being kept alive by any medical machines. The question was, did that include a feeding tube?

She had good brain wave activity, was breathing on her own, her blood pressure was good, her heart rate was perfect, her liver had regenerated to an almost normal size and was functioning perfectly. She was alive and according to her doctors, surprisingly healthy. The only thing wrong was...she was unconscious. She was in a deep coma and no one had any idea why.

Technically, a feeding tube was considered mechanical life support and without it, she would certainly die, but her death wouldn't be because she was sick or one of her vital organs failed...she would die from starvation. And that was something I couldn't accept. No matter what her signed DNR said, I couldn't believe that it would be her intent for me to allow her to starve to death.

I couldn't do it. I could not make a life or death decision again – not by myself, so I called Marshall to get *his* advice. "If I don't do anything, how long could this last?" I asked him, the second he answered the phone.

"There's no way to know that, it could be years." I could hear him shuffling papers. "I was hoping you'd call me. I've done some research on coma patients and I know this isn't going to help you much, but last year, a man in Michigan woke up after nineteen years."

"Really? He was in a coma for nineteen years and then...just woke up?"

"Yes, but that's a very rare case. Most coma patients don't do that. Most eventually die, never regaining consciousness."

I sighed and took a sip of my wine. "If their bodies are healthy, I don't get it. Why do they die?"

"There's a myriad of reasons, but simply, the human body is not designed for inactivity. Walking helps pump the blood and assists the heart. Inactivity slows the entire digestive system. Without physical movement, blood clots can form and cause a stroke. The list goes on and on. I know this isn't what you want to hear, but the end result with most coma patients...is usually death."

I didn't respond. He was right, that was something I didn't want to hear.

"Grant, Brenda thinks it's really important for you to accept the fact that most coma patients, especially after this much time, never wake up. She believes that you shouldn't base your decision on a fantasy that someday, Melissa might wake up."

"Marshall, I'm not asking Brenda. I know she's worried about how all this may psychologically effect Molly as well as me." I paused and took another sip of my wine, "I called *you*. I need you to tell me what to do. There's nothing left inside of me. I've cried all the tears I can cry, and I've prayed all of the prayers I know. God, Marshall, how many more times in my life am I going to have to do something like this? Please, Marshall, I just can't do it this time. I have to know. What would *you* do? Please...tell me what to do."

Marshall was silent for a long time. I could hear him breathing, contemplating. Then he said, "Grant, I honestly believe that one day, without any warning, she will quietly die. That's what all the statistics point to. The odds of her ever waking up after all this time are impossible. But..." he laughed softly, "we *are* talking about Melissa. The fact that she's still alive...well, statistics and odds don't seem to apply to her." He paused and took a deep breath. "If I was in your shoes and this was Brenda, I'd make sure that she received aggressive physical therapy that included electrical muscle stimulation every day. That will strengthen her bones and keep her muscles toned. But at the same time...I would prepay for her funeral."

The next day, I had Melissa moved from the rehabilitation unit...to my house.

∿

IT COST me over a hundred thousand dollars to find out that Charley's spinal cord wasn't severed, but I didn't care about the money. The doctors couldn't tell how severe the damage to his spinal cord had been and had no idea if it was permanent or not. But three weeks after the surgery, Charley still hadn't opened his eyes or moved his body. He only moved his tongue when he was eating, and his tail and eyelids when someone laid down next to him.

Every day, I stopped by to see him at Jake's house on my way to work each morning. Although Jake told me I could have, I didn't bring him home.

Brenda absolutely insisted that I didn't. "Oh sure, that's exactly what Molly needs," she snapped at me. "Her mother in a coma in one room and Charley paralyzed in another. How much more psychological damage do you think she can take?"

Brenda had made her point well, and Jake didn't seem to mind, so I made arrangements for one of his assistants to come to his house and spoon feed Charley three times a day. It wasn't the greatest situation, but it was all I could think to do, and I knew Charley would understand.

⁓

I THANK God that I have a one-track mind, especially when it comes to my work. Most architects farm out the boring, mundane, detailed drawings like plumbing, HVAC and electrical to draftsmen, and only concentrate on the more creative parts of the design. It's a much more efficient use of time and in the past on some projects I had done that, but time was something I had too much of these days, so for the past few months, when I wasn't sitting next to Melissa praying she would wake up, I had spent eighteen to twenty hours a day buried deep into drawing plumbing, HVAC plans and electrical schematics...anything to keep my mind occupied.

I would draw non-stop until my eyes grew too blurred to see, or when Donna would bark for me to take her outside. I rarely went home, usually sleeping on the couch in my office. I knew it was wrong. I needed to be home spending time with Molly, but there were nurses there for Melissa and I had hired a nanny to look after Molly and she seemed to be doing okay. Truthfully, she was doing much better than me...I had grown to hate that house.

When the urge hit me, I stood up behind my work station, stretched and walked to the bathroom. When I had finished and washed my hands, I glanced at my watch, it was almost 1:00 a.m. It had been several hours since I had heard a peep out of Donna. I looked around the room, but she wasn't laying in any of her usual spots, so I walked downstairs searching for her.

"Donna? Where are you, girl?"

I heard a faint whine coming from the kitchen. When I rounded the corner, I saw her lying in the floor, curled up into a ball. She was panting and her body was trembling. I fell to my knees and petted her head, "What's wrong, girl? Are you sick?"

She opened her eyes, looked at me and whined softly. "NO, NO, NO!" I screamed, lifting her off the floor. "You can't be sick!"

I ran out my door to the parking lot and carefully loaded her in my truck. Driving like a maniac, flying through red lights and stop signs, I made it to Jake's house in fifteen minutes, sliding to a stop in his driveway.

Holding Donna in my arms, I yelled at the top of my lungs and kicked on his door. I wasn't sure what time it was, one or two a.m., and the house was dark. "Jake! Wake up!" I yelled. "I need you, it's an emergency!"

The porch light came on and the door cracked open. "Jake, Donna's sick and I think she's dying. I found her like this on the floor."

"I'll take her," he yelled, pulling her out of my arms, running toward the back of the house. "There's a Keurig coffee maker in the kitchen. I'll check on Donna, you make the coffee," he said, running away.

I found the Keurig, dropped in the pod and hit the button. When that one was done, I made one more. I picked up the cups and headed toward the back, searching for him. "Where are you?" I yelled.

A door opened and Jake stepped out. He was smiling, "Ahhh, coffee," he said, reaching for the cup.

"What's wrong with her?"

"Calm down, she's not sick." He took a sip of the coffee and motioned toward the door. "Have a look."

I looked in the door and saw Donna lying on an exam table. She was panting harder, trying to breathe. "If she's not sick, then what's wrong with her?"

He gave me a wide grin. "She's in labor."

"What?"

"She's gonna have puppies. And it's going to be pretty soon."

"She's pregnant? That's impossible!" I said. "She hasn't been around any other dogs. She's been with me every second since..." I stopped and looked at him. "How long are dogs pregnant?"

He nodded, "Only a few months. Usually about 60 or 70 days."

"Oh my God!" My knees buckled and I dropped to the floor,

leaning against the wall. Wiping the tears from my face, I looked up at him. "Do you think they are Charley's?"

He raised his shoulders and lifted his brow. "I don't know, but we'll find out pretty soon."

An hour later, I was petting Charley in the other room when Jake walked in, grinning, "It's over," he said. "Come see."

When I walked back into the room to see Donna, she was sound asleep, lying in a large dog bed. In between her legs, she was cuddling four tiny puppies. Their eyes were still closed tightly. Three of them were female, almost white in color, but the other one, the male...was a redhead.

When I looked back at Jake, he raised his brow and tilted his head. "I have an idea." He picked up two of the puppies and handed them to me. Then he picked up the other two and said, "Follow me."

We walked down the hall to where he was keeping Charley. Jake kicked open the door with his foot and walked in the room. Charley was lying on the bed motionless, but his tail began to move slightly when we walked in.

Jake laid the two puppies down in between Charley's legs and motioned for me to do the same. The puppies instinctively began searching for something Charley didn't have – nipples full of milk. When they couldn't find them, they began to whine loudly.

Charley's tail started to move rapidly, wagging further and further with each swing and his eyelids began to twitch.

I dropped to my knees beside him and petted his head. "Open your eyes, Charley," I said, fighting back my emotions, "Come on, you can do it. Open those eyes, buddy and see what you have done!" After a few moments...he slowly opened his eyes, blinking rapidly, trying to focus.

Jake's jaw dropped and I burst out crying. "I knew you could do it!" I screamed. "It's me, buddy! Can you see me?"

He slowly lifted his head and looked me in the eyes. When he did, I laid down and pulled him and the puppies into my arms. "Thank you, God! Thank you," I whispered over and over as I wept, squeezing them hard.

After I calmed down, I sat up. "Charley, look down. Can you see them?"

He slowly raised his head and looked at the puppies between his legs. "They're yours, Charley, yours and Donna's. Three girls and a boy."

He looked up at me, opened his mouth and tried to speak, but only made a slight sound. He looked back at the puppies squirming between his legs, then back at me. He tried to speak again, then dropped his head back on the bed, exhausted. But his eyes remained open.

Jake ran out of the room and came back a few minutes later dragging Donna's bed, with her still sound asleep, into Charley's room. When I saw what he was doing, I helped him slide her next to Charley.

Only moving his eyes, Charley watched the puppies feeding in between Donna's legs. When I squatted down to pet him, he lifted his head up and looked at me. "Woof," he barked softly.

I'm pretty sure he gave me that silly smile, but I couldn't see his face from all the tears flooding my eyes.

~

OVER THE NEXT SIX MONTHS, Molly and I grew accustomed to having round the clock nurses coming and going on their shifts, and had accepted them as part of our daily lives. I insisted that Melissa be bathed every day and that she received her physical therapy every afternoon. Marshall had found a nutritionist and because of it, Melissa had actually gained some weight.

I had converted my home office to a makeshift hospital room, with an adjustable bed and a hydraulic lift to help move her when needed. I even installed medical machines with video displays to monitor her vitals. I had equipped the room with everything, but Brenda went absolutely ballistic when she saw the monitors.

She hated the entire idea, and was totally against me having Melissa there in my house anyway. "It's not a normal thing for a little girl to have to deal with," she ranted. "Why can't you understand that? Having her comatose mother lying in a bed in a room next to hers, listening to her heartbeat echoing off the walls, waiting for it to stop? Don't you see how something like that could damage her? Melissa needs to be in a long-term care facility, not in your damn house, but if you have to have her here, at least take out those friggin' machines!"

Before I agreed, Brenda had unplugged them, pulled them out of the room and spent almost two hours rearranging and decorating her room. When she had finished, it resembled a suite in an upscale bed and breakfast. Only the side rails on the bed gave it away.

Each day after school, Molly would go sit in her mother's room and talk to her, telling her all about her day, and would often read to her from one of her favorite books. I wasn't sure it was healthy for her to do it, but she seemed to love it, so I let it go on.

I usually spent *my* evenings sitting next to Melissa's bed, sipping my wine and talking to her as well. I had no idea if she could hear me and was listening, but every night when I left her, I prayed that she would either wake up and let me know that she had heard every word…or would pass quietly and peacefully in the night.

At that point of my life, I would have been happy either way, but there was no way in hell I was going to make the decision to take her off the feeding tube and let her starve to death. I was tired of making God's decisions.

# 33

# THE VISION

O ne year later...

WITH THE WAVES crashing at our feet, holding Molly's hands between us, Annabelle and I lifted her up and swung her back and forth over the water as she giggled and laughed.

When the three of us were walking back, holding hands on the beach toward the wooden walkway Annabelle suddenly stopped and looked at me. "Oh my God!" She gasped. "This was her vision!"

"Whose vision?" I asked. "What are you talking about?"

Her eyes were wide open. "Melissa's vision!" she said. "I told you about it, remember? It was right before Jerry took her. Melissa told me that she was having nightmares about her liver failing, and seeing you and me walking on the beach with Molly between us. We were all laughing and holding hands." She locked eyes with me. "Grant, this is exactly what she saw. All of her premonitions have come true."

I stood there looking at her for a moment, thinking about what she had said. "Her liver did fail, she was right about that, but I'm pretty sure this isn't exactly the vision she saw in her dreams."

"Of course it was!" she retorted. "It's exactly was she told me she had seen. That's why she was so insistent that we were supposed to be together."

"That's sort of my point," I said aiming my finger at her belly. "If this was her exact vision, do you think she would have missed seeing that? She would have told you about it, wouldn't she?"

Annabelle looked down and rubbed her baby bump with her hands. "I see what you mean," she said, laughing. "It's kind of hard to miss this."

With Annabelle on one side and me on the other, we lifted Molly up the steps. As we all walked on the sandy, wooden walkway over the dunes toward my house, I heard Marshall's voice.

I looked up to see him and Brenda standing on my back-deck waving. "Our plane was delayed, but we finally made it," He called down to us. "But I guess that was a good thing, because look who we found at the airport." Drake stepped out onto the deck and waved.

Annabelle shrieked. "DRAKE! YOU'RE FINALLY HOME!" She took off running.

Drake ran down the stairs and met her halfway. When he reached her, he lifted her off the ground and spun her around as they kissed.

Then he gently sat her down, dropped to his knees and kissed her belly. "How's my baby boy doing?" he said, grinning up at her.

Molly ran up and wrapped her arms around him. "Welcome home, Uncle Drake!"

Drake lifted Molly up and put her on his shoulders. With her giggling, holding on to his head, he took Annabelle's hand and they slowly climbed the stairs back up to my deck.

When I made it up the stairs and joined them, I opened the refrigerator and grabbed three beers and two Cokes. I handed a beer to Drake and Marshall and sat the Cokes down in front of Annabelle and Molly. I looked at Brenda. "Red or white?"

She smiled wide and said, "I think I'll have a Coke, too."

I tilted my head, surprised. "Seriously? You don't want wine?"

She glanced over at Marshall and smiled. "No, I can't drink any wine for a few more months."

"You taking medication or something?"

Still smiling wide, she said, "No, nothing like that. It's just that I'm not supposed to drink in my condition."

"No!" Annabelle screamed.

"Yes!" Brenda said, nodding her head.

Totally confused, I looked across the table at Marshall. He was grinning from ear to ear. "What's so funny? What's she talking about?"

Marshall raised his eyebrows and leaned forward. "Are you really this dense? Think about it, dumbass!"

It was so obvious, but it was the last thing I was expecting to hear, so I just stared back at him like an idiot.

"Daddy," Molly said, rolling her eyes at me, "she's gonna have a baby."

"Who's gonna have a baby?" I yelled.

Brenda reached across the table and grabbed Annabelle's hand and held it up. "We are!"

~

AFTER ANNABELLE and Drake had left, Marshall, Brenda and I remained on the back deck, listening to the crashing waves and watching the sun go down. I lifted my beer. "I'm not sure I said this earlier, but congratulations, you two. And I pray if it's a girl, she looks like Brenda."

Marshall laughed and lifted his beer. "As long as she gets my brains."

She whacked him on his arm. "Ignore him. I'm not even sure it's his. It could be the mailman or that cute UPS guy."

Marshall rolled his eyes. "What about the pool guy?"

She shrugged her shoulders. "Oh yeah, I forgot about him. You never know."

"I used to kid Melissa about her lawn boy," I said laughing, "but she always said that he was too young for her, but maybe in a few years." My voice cracked. I could feel my emotions building up inside me, so I turned my head, looked at the ocean and fought them off.

You haven't called and talked to us in a while," Brenda said. "How are you doing?"

"I don't know," I sighed. "Better, I guess. I'm finally sleeping again without those pills."

"That's good," Marshall said. "I saw the article in *Architectural Digest* about your project. It was great. I bet that article got your phone ringing. Are you staying busy?"

"The Beverly Beach Project is almost sold out because of that article," Grant said with a smile. "I've already taken on a new project. So yeah, I'm staying busy."

Brenda frowned. "You're not still working around the clock, are you?"

"Believe it or not, I'm keeping regular hours. I get home around five. I want to spend as much time as possible with Molly."

"You're doing a great job with her," Brenda said. "She seems so happy."

"I'm trying, but I think most of the credit should go to her child psychologist. She really loves her and she tells me that Molly is doing great."

I lifted my beer and took a sip. "Wilson and Connie have been a Godsend. They've become her adopted grandparents and are always there when I need someone to watch her. I think she's gonna be just fine."

"What about you?" Brenda asked. "Have you even considering dating again?"

I looked at her and frowned. "No, not yet."

Marshall glared at me. "Why not? You know that's what Melissa would want you to do."

"Yeah, I know, but I can't do it, not yet. Besides, I seem to be bad luck to the women I get involved with."

"That has to be the dumbest thing I've ever heard you say," Marshall snapped.

Brenda reached across the table and took my hand. "I can see how you may feel that way, but honestly, you don't really believe any of this was your fault, do you?"

I let go of her hand and looked away. "That's not really why I'm not dating. I just keep praying that someday…"

"Grant, look at me," Brenda whispered. "I know what is in your heart for Melissa. We all want her to wake up, but you know in your heart that's not going to happen. Not after all this time. Grant, you can't wait forever. You know she wouldn't want you to…for your sake and for Molly's."

"I know, I know," I said, looking away.

The glass patio door slid open. "Dad, he's done it again," Molly said, reaching out and handing me a puppy.

I held him up and looked him in the eyes. "What did you do this time?"

He lifted his lips, exposing his tiny front teeth. "Woof," he said in a high-pitched squeak.

"He messed up your bedroom again," Molly said.

Holding the redheaded little jerk in my arms, I walked to my bedroom and looked around the room. The floor was covered in confetti. Tiny pieces of paper that used to be a rolled-up blueprint.

"You little bastard!" I yelled, sitting him down on the floor. "Did you do this?"

He raised his head and lifted his lip again. "Woof."

I heard a noise behind me. It was Donna with the three other puppies, standing in the door way. The three puppies' colors had changed as they had gotten older, from white to a light golden brown, the exact same color as their mother. But the little devil standing in the middle of the confetti was a dark mahogany red, just like his father.

I looked down at him. "Sir Charles Radcliffe the third, what have you got to say for yourself?"

He growled. "You don't like that name, do you?" He growled again. "Well that's too bad, cause that's what I'm calling you from now on. Sir Charles!"

Defiantly, he raised his head, lifted his lip and growled again. "Arrrr, arrrr, arrr, woof woof."

"Molly walked in the room and put her arms around my legs. "What are we going to do with him, Daddy?"

I looked down at her and smiled, "We're not gonna do anything, someone else is."

Holding the puppy by the loose skin behind his head, I walked to the living room and set him down next to Charley's bed. "You've laid around long enough. It's time you get out of that bed and do something about this monster you sired. He's destroying the house!"

Charley raised his head and looked at the puppy. It took him a few tries, but finally he slowly pulled himself up to his feet, standing over the puppy. He lifted his lip. "Woof."

The puppy looked up at him, lifted his tiny lip and squeaked, "Woof," back at him.

Then they turned, looked up at me, and both of them, at the same time...gave me those stupid smiles.

# 34

## IT'S TIME

Over the months, Little Charley and the rest of the puppies had grown like weeds. *Little* Charley wasn't so little anymore. Because they were Charley's puppies, I wanted to keep them all, but it soon became obvious, that six large dogs, two nurses, Molly and me, all living in a small beach house was never going to work. No matter how hard we all tried to keep the place neat and picked up, the house always looked like a tornado had just gone through it. And carrying fifty-pound sacks of dog food up those steps every couple of days was not only breaking me, it was taking its toll on my poor back. After several long tearful discussions about it with Molly, who was now nine going on twenty-one, she finally agreed to let me find three of the dogs a new home.

I'm not sure Donna and Charley knew what was going on when I left them with Molly in the house and loaded their babies in my truck and drove away, but I'm pretty sure Little Charley did. On the way, he snuggled close to them and licked their faces constantly. When I pulled up to Jake's house, it took me a few minutes to get all the leashes attached to the dogs and get them headed in the right direction toward the front door. When I rang the doorbell, Detective Reynolds answered it. When the dogs saw her, they all started barking excitedly and began running in circles, wrapping their leashes around my legs, tripping me.

When I fell on my ass, tangled in the leashes, she burst out laughing. "Grant? Is that you?"

I looked up at her and smiled. "Yep, it's me."

Jake stepped out of the door, ran over and began rounding up the dogs. "What the hell happened? Why are you sitting on the ground?"

I stood up and brushed the dirt off my butt and smiled. "I was doing pretty good until she came out and got them all riled up."

She laughed. "I had nothing to do with this. Is this Charley?" she said, dropping to her knees, petting him. "Wow, he looks great!"

I nodded. "Charley *IS* doing much better. He's finally walking again," I said, "but that's not him. That's his son, Sir Charles the third. And he is just as much of a pain in the ass as his father!"

"I bet he is. He does look like trouble," she said, laughing as she scratched his belly.

"So, what are you doing here?" I asked. "Dropping off another dog from one of your crime scenes?"

She was dressed in her usual dark drab pantsuit and gun, with her hair pulled up into a bun. She lifted her eyebrows and smiled. "No," she said, "I was on my way to work when Jake called to tell me you were bringing the puppies over. I hope it's okay, but I want one of the puppies."

"Really? You're going to take one of them? That's fantastic. I really didn't want to give them away. I love these little girls, but six large dogs in a small house isn't gonna work. But knowing that you have one, well...that's just great!"

"Detective Johnson is on his way over as well," she said with a grin, "he wants one, too."

"Even better!" I said. "Now if we can find the last one a good home..."

She started laughing. "I guess Jake hasn't told you."

"Told me what?"

She lifted her eyebrows and grinned. There was another reason I came here this morning. Jake wanted me to come by to meet..." she paused, shrugged her shoulders, looked up at me and smiled, "his new boyfriend. I think they want a puppy, too."

My jaw flew open. "Boyfriend?" I whispered.

She nodded her head. "Jake's a great guy and thank you for trying, but you were right, he's gay," she sighed. "I guess I'll just have to keep looking."

~

WHILE DRAKE FINISHED SERVING his last year in the Marines, Annabelle moved back to Boone with her parents to have her baby. It was a healthy 8-pound, 10-ounce boy they named Albert, after her father.

Two months later, at three in the morning, Marshall called to tell me that I was an uncle. Thirty minutes earlier, after five hard hours of labor, Brenda had given birth to a 7-pound, 4-ounce girl.

"She wants to talk to you," he said, putting the phone up to Brenda's ear.

"Grant," I heard her whisper, "She's so beautiful. You have to come see her soon."

"We're on our way," I said. "Molly has been counting the days."

"We wanted to ask you something," she said.

"Sure, what's up?"

"We'd like to name her Audrey…would that be okay with you?"

My heart jumped and my eyes filled with tears. "I would love that."

~

MOLLY FELL INSTANTLY in love with Audrey and didn't want to leave, but I had booked a flight to Boone to visit Annabelle to see her little boy, and once we got there, she fell instantly in love with him, too. When we finally arrived home from our two-week trip, Molly ran into Melissa's room and began telling her every detail about it.

Leaning against the wall in the hallway just outside the door, I listened carefully to her talking to her mother as if she was listening. My heart ached with every word she said.

During our week-long visit with Marshall and Brenda, I had gotten quite an earful. Brenda, being who she was, just couldn't help herself and had spent hours talking with Molly, evaluating her psychological health.

The night before we left, Marshall had called to let us know that he had to attend to an emergency and would be late. When Molly started yawning, I told her to go to bed, opened a bottle of wine and poured two glasses.

"I had no idea how much I would miss this," Brenda said, leaning back in the chair and taking a long sip of her wine.

I took a swallow, set my glass down on the coffee table and looked at her. "So, how is she doing?"

She lifted her brow and nodded her head. "Overall, pretty good."

"But," I said with a smile, "she could be doing better, right?"

She leaned forward and set her glass down. "Marshall is a brilliant man. He has the quickest and most logical mind of anyone I've ever known. That's one side of him. But he has another side. The non-logical, loving side. If you want to know the truth, I think he may love you just a little bit more than he loves me. But the problem is, because he loves you so much, he allows that love to block his brilliance and logic. I hope that after all this time and everything we've gone through, you know that I love you, too, but maybe not as much as Marshall."

She lifted her glass and took another sip. "It's time, Grant, "Melissa is not going to wake up and I think you know that. I wish she would, I miss her, too, but that's not going to happen. You are being selfish and it's time to stop this! Remember what she wrote in her DNR? 'Under no circumstances do I want to be kept alive in a vegetative state.'" She repeated it again, slowly, "*Under no circumstances.*"

I nodded and leaned back, but didn't respond.

"It's time. Let her go and do what you know in your heart she would want you to do. You can't possibly believe that this is the life she wanted for Molly...for you...for herself." She took another sip and locked eyes with me. "At the very least, move her to a home. Please,

Grant, for Molly's sake. Let her go or at least move her out of your house. It's not healthy for either one of you. It's time, Grant."

~

AFTER LISTENING to Molly talking to her mother the night we got back for our trip, I knew Brenda was right. It wasn't healthy for Molly or me, and I was doing exactly what Melissa had feared. She *was* being kept alive in a vegetative state and no matter how hard it was going to be to let her go, I had to do it…she deserved better. The next morning, I contacted the hospital and talked to her doctor, letting her know of my decision.

"Mr. Nash," she said, "This will not be a pleasant thing to watch. For you and your daughter's sake, I think it would be best to bring her here to the hospital, so I can monitor the process. This is something you don't need to do at home."

"How long will it take?" I asked.

"There's no way of knowing for sure, but usually anywhere from three to seven days."

I didn't tell Molly why her mother had to go back to the hospital and vowed to myself that I would never, ever tell her. I was sure she would never forgive me if she knew the truth.

~

I WAS asleep when my cell phone rang at 3:15 a.m., four days later. I didn't have to look at the caller ID; I knew it was the hospital.

"Mr. Nash, I am the attending nurse at The Flagler Hospital. The instructions I have for Mrs. Hollingsworth are to call this number if her vital signs show she is entering her final stages. Unfortunately, I am seeing those signs now. Her oxygen levels are dropping quickly, and I suspect she will pass soon."

I jumped up, threw on some clothes and rushed to the hospital. When I walked into her room, she was surrounded by nurses holding her hands, stroking her hair and talking to her softly.

It was a sight I'll never forget - a beautiful and graphic image of how wonderful nurses truly are. Looking at them reminded me of a flock of angels. An image of the stained glass in the chapel flashed in my head. It was the picture of several angels surrounding Christ's body in the tomb, taking him back to heaven. Seeing the nurses around her calmed me down and gave me a feeling of strength and peace. When the nurses saw me, they quickly left the room, leaving me alone with Melissa.

Her eyes were closed, but her mouth was open and she was breathing rapidly, gasping for air. Her heart was barely beating, but the sound of the slowing beeps from her heart monitor still filled the room, echoing off the walls.

The second I took her hand in mine, she appeared to calm down, closed her mouth and stopped gasping for breath. Her heart rate actually sped up a little, but the beep from the monitor seemed softer somehow.

I bent over her bed and kissed her. "I'm here," I whispered, stroking her hair with my fingers." "You can relax now, don't worry, everything's going to be all right." I wiped my eyes with my sleeve.

I stood there silently, watching her breathe for a few moments. "Do you remember that first night we spent together walking along the beach? When I asked you what you thought heaven would be like, and you went on and on about the beautiful mansions and the streets lined with gold. You said that everyone there would be so happy, because they would be finally free of all the burdens of human life. Do you remember that?"

I lowered the side rail of her bed, climbed in beside her and pulled her into my arms. "I hope you're right about that, because you deserve to be happy for a change." Holding her tight, I could hear her breathing softly, as her heart rate gradually began to slow down again.

"You once told me that there was more to the miracle of Rita's transplant, that you were actually praying for something else. You promised to tell me what you were praying for someday, but you never did. I've been thinking about that a lot lately and I think I know what you were going to say. It was me, right? You were praying for me to come make things right for you and Molly. I believe you've known for a long time you would not live to see her grow up. And I believe you also knew that Jerry wouldn't be here, either."

A single tear appeared in her eye and rolled down her cheek. Gently, I wiped her face with my hand. "Maybe I'm wrong about this, but I honestly believe that when Rita and Audrey died, it was your time, too. But because of your prayers, God stepped in and brought me to you, so I could fall in love with Molly and take care of her. I honestly think Molly is the *special* one in all of this. She must be meant to do great things in her life and that's what this has been all about. It's the only thing that makes any sense.

I'm sure Marshall was right. It *was* an august harvest, arranged by God himself to give us a little more time. Time to make sure Molly grew up the right way, so she could give the world her gift, whatever that may be.

And I know now that being here for her is that *'much more to do'* part Rita was trying to tell me about."

I cupped her face with my hands and kissed her for a long time. Another tear slowly appeared and rolled down her cheek. I wiped it from her chin and stared down at her pale, thin face. "Melissa, I hope you can hear me, because I want you to know that I've got her, I swear I do. You don't have to worry about Molly any longer."

I'm not sure, but I think she heard me, because when I said that, her lips curled into a slight smile. At least that's what it looked like to me.

My entire body started trembling and tears soaked my face, as it became obvious that her breathing was getting slower and slower.

"Goodbye...I love you".

A few moments later, holding her tightly in my arms, staring down at her beautiful face, Melissa opened her mouth, took one last breath...and drifted away.

# EPILOGUE

W e buried Melissa on a rainy, cold Tuesday. It was a small, private, invitation only funeral. The small, private part was not my idea; I was just following her specific instructions. She had given those instructions to Rob on the same day she had changed her will and signed her DNR, two weeks before Jerry kidnapped her. There was no question in any of our minds that sad morning, that Melissa had somehow known what was about to happen to her and her ultimate fate. It was a short, closed casket service, again at her request.

After the service, Brenda, Molly, Marshall and I rode in the limousine, following the black Cadillac hearse that carried her body to the gravesite.

I had followed her instructions exactly for the actual funeral at the church and had only invited her good friends Connie and Wilson, her lawyer Rob, and Brenda and Marshall. But since she had not been specific about the graveside burial, I allowed Connie to spread the word around town. When we pulled up, there were over a hundred people surrounding the gravesite, all waiting patiently to pay their respects, standing there under their umbrellas in the pouring rain.

I was a little shocked but happy to see some of the faces. All of her neighbors were there and Annabelle, Drake and her parents had driven all the way from Boone, North Carolina to attend. Les Patterson and many of the architects that I had met working on the Beverly Beach project from his firm were there with their families. The president of Flagler College, who had been a close friend of her father's, was there with his son, and several of the Saint Augustine city council members were there as well.

Jake, Charley's veterinarian, and his partner were there, as well as Detective Johnson, his wife and Anastasia.

When I stepped out of the limousine and started walking toward the gravesite holding Molly's hand, Anastasia walked up to me and gave me a gentle smile. Then she slipped her arm around mine, walked with me and Molly the rest of the way to the gravesite and held on to me tightly throughout the burial service.

We laid Melissa to rest next to her beloved father and her mother, a mother she never knew. I smiled at the thought of them finally meeting for the first time in heaven.

After the funeral, my house was standing room only for the rest of the day with mostly strangers arriving, bringing food and gathering in small groups swapping stories about the times they had spent with Melissa. Without me having to ask, Annabelle, Anastasia and Molly worked together as a team, greeting the guest as they arrived, serving them food and drinks.

I am not good at these sorts of gatherings, so after a few hours, I slipped out quietly and took Charley, Little Charley and Donna for a slow walk on the beach. When we made it back to the wooden walkway, Anastasia was sitting there on the bottom steps.

"All clear," she said with a smile. "Your house is a mess, but it's safe to go home, they're finally gone."

I sat down beside her and grinned. "How did you know how to find me?"

She laughed. "I saw you when you made your escape with the dogs. I knew you guys would make it back here eventually."

Charley walked up to her, lifted his paw and smiled. I started laughing. "I think he wants to apologize for barking at you that day in my house."

She took his paw and shook it. "Apology accepted," she said, laughing, "Charley, it's nice to finally meet you on good terms."

"Woof," he said, licking her hand as she petted his head.

"That's a good sign," I said, grinning.

She tilted her head and lowered her eyebrows. "What's a good sign?"

I reached over and petted his head. "Charley is the best judge of character I've ever known. And he only lets the people he trusts and likes pet him."

She looked at him and asked. "I passed the test?"

"Woof, woof, woof," he said, giving her his best smile.

Her laugh filled the air like a beautiful song. I had forgotten how much I liked her laugh. "So, how's the search going? Have you found someone who's not afraid to date a beautiful woman who carries a gun?"

She grinned. "Not yet, but I haven't given up. I'm still looking."

"That's the spirit," I said with a chuckle. "Just be patient. One day out of the clear blue, you'll find him when you least expect it."

With the dogs lying in the sand at our feet, we sat there silently for a few minutes, watching the waves crashing on the beach. "Well, I guess I better go," she said, "I have to work tomorrow."

We stood and started walking on the sandy wooden pathway over the dunes toward my house. "I wanted to thank you for helping with the guests earlier and especially at the gravesite."

"I was hoping you didn't mind, but when I saw you get out of that limousine, you looked like you needed someone to lean on."

"And you were right, I definitely needed it. This has all been pretty hard."

I walked her to her car and opened her door. "You never told me what you named your puppy."

Her face lit up. "Susie Q, like in the song."

I raised my eyebrows. "Are you a Creedence Clearwater Revival fan?"

"Yes! I love them! I have all their albums." she said, followed by that great laugh.

I smiled and said, "That's one."

"One what?"

"Never mind," I said, closing her door, "It's a private joke. Who knows, I may get to tell you some day."

She frowned. "Ok then, someday I'll remind you to tell me."

"Give me a little time to get through this and back on my feet and maybe I'll tell you," I said grinning. "Why don't you bring Susie Q over sometime? I know Donna and Charley would love to see her."

She smiled up at me. "That sounds like a great idea. Call me.

∼

IT TOOK a few months to get Melissa's money transferred out of the offshore accounts that Jerry had forced her to put them in. Rob, working with the FBI, had overseen everything and had also made arrangements for Melissa's aunt to have a proper funeral. I took Molly and it was beautiful, but very sad. Melissa had inherited her house, so while we were in Savannah for the funeral, I met with a realtor and had it listed for sale.

I wasn't sure what to do with Melissa's house, but I knew that it couldn't be good for Molly seeing it every day, sitting there empty with all of her mother's memories inside. So after I did a few minor repairs and had it painted, I called Wilson and had him put it up for sale. I assumed it would take several months to sell it, but it sold for the asking price in less than twenty-four hours and the new owners wanted to take possession immediately.

When I arrived at the title company, they told me that the new owners were running late, so I settled around the large meeting table and waited for them. When they finally showed up and walked in the room, my mouth flew open and I almost spilled my coffee. It was Brenda and Marshall.

"You guys bought it?" I yelled.

Marshall gave me a wide grin. "Yep," he said, "I sold my house in Houston and needed a new house anyway, so I figured why not buy Melissa's?"

I tilted my head, confused. "Why did you sell your house in Houston?"

Brenda looked at Marshall and laughed. "You're right, he really is kind of dense."

"Are you moving here?" I asked with wide eyes. "Permanently?"

Brenda ran around the table and hugged me. "Yes, we are."

I looked up at Marshall. "But what about your practice? And the hospital?"

Marshall pulled out a chair and sat down across from me. "What about it?" he said with a smile. "I love what I do and as long as I'm affiliated with a hospital and close to an airport, I can keep doing it, and I will.

"And so will I," Brenda added.

"But my job isn't as important to me as it once was. I don't know about you, but all of this, what we've all lived through in the last few years, has had a profound effect on me. It changed me and made me realize what is truly important in my life. In the end, what we do for a living, what we do with all the time we spend working, doesn't really matter. What *does* matter is what we do with the rest of our time and *whom* we spend that time with. Brenda, Audrey and I have decided that we want to spend it with the people we love...with you and Molly."

∼

BEFORE CHARLEY WAS SHOT, he had a favorite spot. If I couldn't find him, I always knew where to look. With his head high, and his long shiny mahogany red hair blowing in the breeze on top of the tall berm behind my house, he would sit there for hours, staring out over the ocean. He wasn't supposed to get up there, because the berm along with the lush sea oats and grasses were protected land. I tried to tell him, but he ignored me and climbed to the top of that berm almost every day. He especially loved being there when the sun was rising or setting. He absolutely loved that spot on top of that berm.

Because he wasn't strong enough to climb up there anymore, almost every morning, I would pick him up in my arms and carry him up to the top and leave him there until he barked for me to come get him. It was a pain to do, but I didn't care. I was just so thankful to have him back in my life.

~

A FEW MONTHS LATER, Anastasia brought Susie Q over one Sunday afternoon for a visit. Charlie, Donna and little Charley went absolutely nuts. It was quite the reunion. They had so much fun I decided to invite Jake, his partner, and Detective Johnson and his wife over a few weeks later to bring the other two sisters for a full dog family reunion.

We set up on the beach and ate hamburgers and hotdogs while watching the dogs play in the surf and run up and down the beach. They had an absolute blast.

It was a little sad to me to see Charley, always trailing behind the other dogs twenty or thirty feet, trying his best to keep up. But he never gave up and was always smiling.

During that day, I couldn't keep my eyes off of Anastasia. I think she and Molly were having just as much fun as the dogs were — playing in the surf together and rolling around in the sand wrestling with the dogs.

Over the past several months, she and Molly had bonded and had become very close. She had surprised me one Saturday morning when she and Brenda rang my doorbell to pick Molly up to go shopping. I was lost as usual, in deep thoughts about my newest project I was designing and hadn't realized that it was back to school time and Molly needed new clothes. Rather than bothering me, Molly had called Anastasia and Brenda.

"Card please," was all Anastasia had said to me that morning and it wound up costing me a small fortune when they returned, but Molly was over the top excited about her new wardrobe and put on an hour-long fashion show for me when they left.

After our dog reunion beach day and everyone had gone home, I asked Anastasia to stay and have a glass of wine with me on the back deck.

Molly and the dogs were worn out and were sound asleep when Anastasia and I finally settled around the table on the deck with our wine.

Although it was a full moon and the reflection from its bright glow on the dark ocean was especially breathtaking that night, I hadn't noticed. My eyes were focused on her.

"How do you live here and get anything done?" she said. "I would never leave this spot. I can't get over how beautiful this is. And this cool ocean breeze is spectacular."

"I've been here almost three years," I said, "and it still takes my breath away."

She lifted her glass and motioned toward the beach. "It looks like Charley loves it, too."

I turned and saw Charley, who had somehow made it up to his favorite spot by himself. He was sitting erect with his head held high and his long mahogany red hair was flowing in the breeze. It was a beautiful sight.

Anastasia took a small sip of her wine and smiled. "Are you ever going to tell me?"

I turned my head and looked at her. "Tell you what?"

"Tell me what *'That's one'* means. You said you 'might' tell me someday."

I shook my head and smiled. "I did say that, didn't I? Well, actually I was going to tell you after we had a few dates."

"So you don't think all these times I've been over here in the past few months qualify as 'dates?"

I nodded. "No, ma'am. I wouldn't call them dates."

"And why not?"

"Well, ma'am, in Texas we don't call it a date unless it ends with a little smooching. And I'm pretty sure we haven't even held hands before."

She stood, walked around the table and sat in my lap. "To be real honest with you, cowboy...I didn't think you were interested."

I took her face in my hands and gently kissed her for the first time. When our lips touched, I felt a jolt of electricity run through my body.

She jerked her head back. Her eyes were wide open. "What was that? I felt a shock. Was that static electricity?"

I smiled and shook my head. "I'm not sure. Let's try that again and see."

This time, my heart skipped a beat and the tingles ran all the way down my spine. "Did you feel that?" I whispered in her ear.

"Yes," she whispered back. "What on earth is causing that?"

I pulled my head away and stared into her eyes. "To answer your first question... *That's one* means...that's one more thing that I love about you."

Her red hair was blowing in the ocean breeze almost covering her face, but in the bright moonlight, I could see her eyes glistening as they filled with tears. I gently cupped her face again with my hands and softly ran my thumb over her wet, pouty lips.

"Anastasia...I'm not exactly sure what causes those shocks and tingles we are feeling, it's only happened to me once before. But I think...and I'm praying...they're caused by something called...love."

**The End**

# A NOTE FROM BEN

Thanks for reading *An August Harvest*. I hope you enjoyed it. I was inspired to write this novel after hearing a story about someone I admired greatly. The things she had lived through in her life were unimaginable, but somehow she survived... and through it all she never lost her faith in God or herself.

Hearing her incredible, tragic story made me realize how lucky and blessed my life has been, but it opened my eyes to the harsh reality that life to some...can be difficult and very unfair.

Terrible and tragic things happen to good people every day. Some are destroyed by it, but some are not. It all comes down to how they answer the question of...what now?

The ones who don't let it destroy them, the ones who somehow live through it and build new and positive lives, are the ones who deserve our admiration and are the true hero's in this world.

*An August Harvest* is also available in print and audiobook formats along with my other three novels, *Sing Roses For Me, Serpentine Roses and Children Of The Band* exclusively on Amazon. Just search for Ben Marney Books to find them.

One more thing... Writing is a lonely job, so meeting and getting to know my readers is a thrill for me and one of the best perks of being an author. I would like to invite you to join my "Private Readers' Group" and in return, I'll give you a free copy of *Lyrics Of My Life*. This is a collection of autobiographical short stories about my amazing life so far. I really would like to meet you! Go to my website.

www.benmarneybooks.com

Made in the USA
Monee, IL
10 February 2021